Alive Again

Alive Again

John Class

Aventine Press

Published by Aventine Press
1023 4th Ave #204
San Diego CA, 92101
www.aventinepress.com

ISBN: 1-59330-281-9

Library of Congress Control Number: 2005927497
Library of Congress Cataloging-in-Publication Data
Alive again

Printed in the United States of America

Introduction to Alive

In the last battle at Megiddo, Lev Aron's final memory was of an explosion that severed his left hand and shrapnel that punctured his body.

But now he felt more alive and vibrant than ever before.

He could not find any sign of his wounds.

He found himself in a strange and different world, a world that seemed to embody the desire of the collective dreams of humanity, and yet a world that was surprising.

Scriptures began to fit together before his eyes in unexpected reality.

He would be given a mission. He would face the adventure and drama of human history as his life touched the lives of many others from previous generations.

He would experience love and passion in a dimension he never imagined possible.

He would meet with pockets of resistance and intrigue.

Was his new life real? Would the power of the Anointed withstand the power of evil?

Just how far back in time would the love of Christ reach?

And what depths of depravity could the love of Christ heal?

Prologue

I was always the one that knew all the answers. Even when I didn't know, I would try something—anything. Act first…think later. If I did what I thought was right, everything would work out. It usually did. Sitting and praying was usually my last resort.

What was it that my brother Jake used to say? That we should depend on the arm of the LORD? That was not for me! We should fight! There was courage in fighting whether we win or lose!

Only this time, I didn't know what to do and I couldn't even think. We were trapped. There was no place to go. No counter move to make. We would all die and I knew it. What glory was there in dying?

We had met the enemy on the plains of Megiddo, hoping to slow their advance toward Jerusalem. The invading army would overwhelm our small companies that had been ordered to many different villages in Judea. We had lost contact with the other Israeli forces. As far as I knew, we were the last hope for Jerusalem and for Israel. But, we were surrounded and getting shelled continually. Almost all of the men around me were either dead or wounded.

A rocket exploded near me. I had my left hand up to protect my head. My lungs burned and I was having trouble breathing. I looked at what remained of my left hand only to see a grotesque bloody stub.

A brave medic reached me only to find I was mortally wounded and tried to stop the bleeding arm and chest wound. I asked him to tell my wife Rebekah, "I love …." The noise from the gunfire became quiet to my ears as this world faded away.

Preface

The Christian religion teaches that there will be a resurrection of the dead. The resurrection was central to early Christianity. Jesus taught,

- *"Marvel not at this: for the hour is coming, in the which all that are in the graves shall hear his voice, and shall come forth" (John 5:28, 29).*

Jesus told Martha,

- *"I am the resurrection, and the life" (John 11:25).*

Even though Jesus uttered these words, death has continued unabated. Billions have died and are waiting for Jesus to call them back from the tomb. Does anyone doubt that Jesus will keep his promise?

The apostles spoke of the resurrection with equal vigor. When Paul was in chains before King Agrippa, he said,

- *"Why should it be thought a thing incredible with you, that God should raise the dead?" (Acts 26:8)*

When the church at Corinth began to fail in their fidelity, one of the difficulties confusing them was the resurrection. Paul addressed them saying,

- *"Now if Christ be preached that he rose from the dead, how say some among you that there is no resurrection of the dead? But if there be no resurrection of the dead, then is Christ not risen: and if Christ be not raised, then is our preaching vain, and your faith is also vain. Yea, and we are found false witnesses of God; because we have testified of God that he raised up Christ: whom he raised not up, if so be that the dead rise not. For if the dead rise not, then is Christ not raised: and if Christ be not raised, your faith is vain; ye are yet in your sins. Then*

*they also which are fallen asleep in Christ are perished. If in
this life only we have hope in Christ, we are of all men most
miserable. But now is Christ risen from the dead, and become
the first-fruits of them that slept" (1 Cor. 15:12-20).*

Paul's message corrected any misunderstanding the church at
Corinth may have had about the resurrection. If Christ was raised as
the **"first**-fruit," there must logically follow **"after**-fruits." The time
would be *"when the Son of man shall sit in the throne of his glory"*
(Matthew 19:28).

The resurrection is a foundation doctrine of Christianity—there will
"be a resurrection of the dead." This great Christian teaching awakens
us to an exciting drama to be played on earth. The resurrection of "all
that are in the graves" presents gripping scenes of love, tenderness,
and happiness to our mind's eye.

But the guilt, shame, fear and humiliation that **have** slept with
the dead will also be addressed in the "regeneration." Shakespeare
said, "The evil that men do lives after them; the good is oft interred
with their bones." However, because of the resurrection, the good that
men do will return with those who live again—and so will the evil!
The resurrection will give "evil" an even longer life. When men are
called forth from the grave their entire past will be a vivid reality. God
has said, "Is not my way equal?" (Ezekiel 18:25) Shakespeare also
said that, "All the world's a stage, and all the men and women merely
players." That being true all the "players" will return for the second
act to be played out in the regeneration.

During the resurrection, truth will be everywhere all the time.
Authors of lies, deceptions, half-truths, insincerity and dishonesty
will have an unwanted copyright to their deeds. The full account of
their activities will be revealed. Truth will be the only information
permitted. There will be no "hiding place" during the whole period of
"regeneration" (Isaiah 28:17).

Christ "shall not judge after the sight of his eyes, neither reprove
after the hearing of his ears: but with righteousness shall he judge the
poor, and reprove with equity for the meek of the earth" (Isaiah 11:3-
4). All things will be open and naked. Christ will not need witnesses
or testimonies to know the truth of every situation. He will read the
heart.

The first requirement for human recovery will be the recognition
of the need for rehabilitation—the need to be reconciled to his fellow
man and to God.

Some have thought that the time of reconciliation between God and man was taking place today. However, the period of time from Jesus' day to the present has been specifically designated for the call and development of the "bride of Christ."

After the Bride has been selected, the stage will be set for the "times of restitution of all things, which God hath spoken by the mouth of all his holy prophets since the world began" (Acts 3:21). This will be the time of the resurrection, when mankind will be reconciled to each other and to God.

The resurrection will not take place in a literal twenty-four hour day, but in the "**times** [years] of restitution."

Restoring mankind to perfection will be an educational process. This restoration process will be the most exciting and rewarding experience in human history. It is this resurrection and "times of restitution" of earth's millions that we endeavor to give meaning to in ALIVE AGAIN.

Of course, any work of this nature requires projection of thought. We know enough of the real past to understand what living again might entail. Each individual's past will be the platform for a new starting place.

Most Christian writers have climaxed their stories with the saints being taken to heaven or a fictitious "seven years' tribulation" taken out of Biblical context. No one has yet successfully described heaven. Books pour forth on the "rapture" and "Armageddon"—and that is where their vision has stopped, consigning the majority of mankind to an eternity of flames.

ALIVE AGAIN will light up the screen to cover the most thrilling and meaningful period of human experience. It is one thing to live and die. It is quite another to come alive again with the full knowledge of the past, with complete recall of every thought and word—to meet the challenges of a new world which will demand "righteousness."

We often hear the expression, "if I had this life to live over again." The resurrection will not give anyone "this life to live over again"— but it will provide something even better. None of the growth and maturing of past human experience will be lost.

In our present life we start out a total blank. By the time we have learned the many lessons of life, we have also accumulated a multitude of mistakes in the process. In the "regeneration" people will have the advantage of having learned many things by personal experience. They will be greatly benefited by these experiences of life as they start out on the long journey of reconciliation to their fellow man and to God.

Every life has a story to tell. The past will meet the future in the resurrection process. The grave interrupted every virtue and ended the burning love of countless billions. The grave also closed the door on every vice and evil. The door of love and the door of evil will open again, flooding human hearts with love and light, but also bringing shadows of evil into full view before all eyes.

Ebenezer Scrooge was reminded of the past, brought to see the present from a new perspective, and was shown where his path would lead if unaltered. This provided an extraordinary impetus for changing his life. Scrooge was given another chance while he still lived. Mankind will have that belated opportunity when they are called forth from the grave.

ALIVE AGAIN addresses the hidden Gospel. While the entire Bible speaks of the Gospel of "restitution," most religious leaders have felt this knowledge would interfere with their present mission of saving the world. Not that anyone has had much success in converting the world, but it sounds altruistic as a present goal. However, the time for the world's conversion is future. The world will be converted when Christ raises the dead with the view to their reconciliation to their fellow man and to God.

Yes, "there shall be a resurrection of the dead, both of the just and unjust" (Acts 24:15). How will the resurrection drama unfold when "death and hell delivered up the dead which were in them"? (Revelation 20:13) What will the regeneration be like? The best way to learn of the resurrection power is to live it with those having returned.

"You who lie in the dust, wake up and shout for joy…"
(Isaiah 26:19).

Chapter One

The searing pain was gone. Instead of roaring guns and exploding shells, I heard the lively sounds of chirping birds. I lay quietly—afraid to open my eyes—afraid to see my badly torn body. But my body felt relaxed. I wanted to move, but I laid still, listening to my breathing.

I slowly opened my eyes. This wasn't the hell I had been trapped in. A bouquet of flowers decorated the table next to my bed. This was no hospital room.

My mind told me my left hand had been blown off—that only a stump remained. Yet, I was looking at my left hand all in one piece. When I tried to move my left arm it responded without pain—I was able to move my fingers easily. Did I dream up that terrible battle, or were these peaceful surroundings a dream? I was totally confused.

I felt my chest. Where was the wadded shirt I had stuffed into my wounds to try to keep my lungs from collapsing? It was gone and no scars remained. Sunlight streamed through the open window. My lungs breathed the fresh air without effort. I continued to examine my body—there was no evidence of wounds.

I vividly recalled the situation engulfing our soldiers. We had moved out as an advance guard to delay the overwhelming invasion forces. We met the enemy on the plain of Megiddo, hoping to slow their advance toward Jerusalem.

We knew they wouldn't use heavy artillery on Jerusalem for fear of destroying the holy sites sacred to Muslims and Christians. Small companies of Israeli forces were spread throughout the villages of Samaria and Judea to make it impossible to annihilate us in one sweep. Our generals were brilliant in their strategies, but the invading army was overwhelming. It looked futile.

I heard the thunder of heavy artillery at a distance, and our guns were quickly silenced. My unit was the last to fall. A helicopter strafed my position and I felt hot metal penetrating my body. I heard an explosion not far from me, felt a jolt, then piercing pain. With shock and panic I saw that my left hand was gone and there was a gaping wound on my chest. I struggled to breathe. Grabbing a shirt from my gear with my right hand, I pushed it into my chest wound.

"It's over," I mumbled. I felt far removed from the battlefield, and the jarring sounds around me seemed muted. My blood was everywhere. It was all over for me. I remember a medic reaching me, but I was beyond his help. I whispered, "Tell Rebekah, my wife, 'I love ...'" is all I remembered.

The brightness of the day faded out of focus into swirling darkness. I began to lose consciousness. Gunfire faded into absolute silence.

Questions Racing Through My Brain

Questions were racing through my mind as I got out of bed. Where was I? Had surgeons repaired my arm? Why was it so quiet? How long had I been unconscious? A strange uneasiness gripped my stomach as I suddenly became aware of memories that had been forgotten and buried. I had the sensation of my whole life passing before my eyes in slow motion, yet so vividly. Images of childhood trucks dissolved into those of Hebrew-school pranks; memories arose of adolescent insecurities and the struggles to be my own person, and then to Rebekah, the woman I was destined to marry. A flood of memories was fresh in my mind as though they had just happened. This was not the moment for me to be basking in memories. I needed a lot of information to explain my present situation. Standing between two worlds and understanding neither of them fully, but certainly understanding least of all my present situation, I was in a daze.

Clothing had been neatly placed on a chair next to the bed. I quickly dressed, startled at the realization that I was putting on what looked like my favorite khaki shirt and brown pants, except that they were not well worn as mine had been. These looked new. I shivered when I realized that everything fit perfectly, even down to my favorite style of shoe.

As I opened the door, I heard faint voices. I tiptoed quietly down the corridor to a large, beautifully furnished room. Voices came from another room. They suddenly stopped. Perhaps they heard me. I froze. Should I remain or make a break toward the door? Too late. In walked a young man smiling with obvious delight. We stared at each other.

How strange—he looked a little like Rebekah. On second thought, he looked like my son, Allon. But it couldn't be—Allon was just a ten-year-old boy. The person standing before me was a grown man.

Reunion

"Dad, it's you!" Allon shouted.

"Lev!" A woman with long dark hair entered the room. She ran toward the tall man who stood with his mouth hanging open, his eyes wide with astonishment. He recovered from the shock of the moment and opened his arms wide to receive her embrace. Allon threw his arms around the both of them.

"Thank God," he said, "You're with us again, Dad!"

Lev laughed for sheer joy and disbelief. "How did I get here? Where am I? Where are my wounds?"

Rebekah placed her hand on his mouth.

"One question at a time, Lev, darling. A lot has happened since that horrible day at Megiddo when you left us. Why don't we go into the kitchen and talk over a cup of tea?" She put her arm around her husband and led him into the kitchen area.

They sat around a table laden with an assortment of fruit. Rebekah poured the tea and a delicate aroma, more pronounced than coffee but also more savory, filled the room. Lev was so full of emotion he could barely speak. He just sat there, his eyes first on Rebekah, then on Allon and then back to Rebekah. He shook his head slowly in joy and disbelief.

Rebekah looked younger and more beautiful than he remembered last seeing her. Her olive skin was smooth and her long black hair was thick and lustrous. The mole on her right cheek was gone. She was the most beautiful woman he had ever seen.

Allon was a young man and it was almost like looking back at himself in his younger years, only with Rebekah's eyes. Lev felt pure satisfaction, sitting there in the presence of the two most important people in his life.

Before they ate Rebekah offered a prayer of thanks to God, just as she always had.

"Thank you, Lord for Lev—for bringing him back to us—from death to life, for you, O Lord, provide life to all those returning."

Her simple prayer was spoken with such heartfelt gratitude that Lev was startled.

His mind flashed back to the battlefield. Had he really died? Nothing made sense—but why should it matter anyway? He was alive; he was whole and well. His wife and son were with him.

Lev sipped the hot tea, more to hide his confused state of mind than to satisfy his thirst. The tea was strangely refreshing and seemed to calm his emotions.

He looked Rebekah straight in the eye. "You're going to tell me I died, aren't you? Wasn't it Mark Twain who said, 'Reports of my death have been greatly exaggerated'? Isn't this getting a little carried away?"

"Dad, your whole company was wiped out in the siege against Jerusalem."

Lev nodded slowly, as he remembered how the whole unit had been savagely pounded with heavy shells and strafed with heavy machine gun fire. He knew his battery of guns must have been the last silenced. He vividly remembered an explosion that ripped off his left hand. He remembered the pain that melted into numbness and the thought that this wasn't supposed to be happening to him. He remembered the medic whom he told to tell his wife, "Good-bye, Rebekah, I love …," and then quietness, darkness, and nothing more.

"Lev, darling, I don't know how to tell you this, but you were killed in battle. We sadly buried your remains in our family plot when at last we found you."

"How can I possibly be alive? How can I be sitting here talking to you? What is going on? Why am I here if I'm supposed to be dead?"

"Because you're not supposed to be dead. You've been raised from death. Allon, your brother Jake, Rachel and I have been making preparations for your return. We built this house for you, and planted your orchard and garden."

Lev furrowed his brow in confusion. "You mean this house is for *us*, don't you?" He emphasized the word "us."

Rebekah paused. He read in her face a look of uncertainty. She looked almost frightened. Lev had a strong desire to be alone with her.

"Excuse us for just a minute, Allon. We need to talk privately."

He took hold of Rebekah's hand and led her out of the kitchen to another room down the hallway. He faced his wife and held both of her hands in his.

"Rebekah," he whispered as a torrent of memories flooded his mind—her scent, the feel of her lips, and the feel of her strong and supple body against his own. "I need to be alone with you. I want to hold you."

He felt her pull away from him.

"No, Lev, it's different now."

"'*Different*'? What do you mean different?" His memories of passion began to melt into confusion and an anger born of fear. He could never bear their relationship to change. Rebekah was his lover and his wife. How could anything possibly change all the times they had shared? Anger came through his voice, and he repeated his question with a more demanding and deliberate tone.

"What do you mean '*different*'?"

Rebekah stared at him with wide eyes. "We are living in a very different world now," she said. But her voice was weak, and her eyes had locked their gaze into his. She seemed suddenly unsure of herself.

"Our marriage—all marriage relationships—ended when we died." She looked away from his face.

Lev felt his knees grow weak. He stared at the woman before him for what seemed an eternity without saying a word.

Finally Lev spoke. "You can't mean that, Rebekah, look at me." He cradled her face in his hands and gently lifted her head so that their eyes met.

"Don't you remember the times we've had together? Our honeymoon—remember the rainstorm and the cave we found on our first night together?"

Rebekah's mouth trembled and he saw her dormant memories of passion come to life in the depths of her brown eyes. He pulled her closer.

"Yes, I remember, Lev. I remember," she mumbled softly. "And I want it back, too. But it is different now. Couples only live together to raise young children. After the children are grown, everyone lives in their own homes. We find it ideal to live alone and sometimes with guests." Her voice trailed off.

"The husband-wife relationship is no longer needed now that the world is filled with people," she added very quietly.

"What do you mean the world is full of people? How do you know that?" Lev was plainly agitated.

"Men of God have explained all of this to us. I know it seems crazy, but we've been on this New Earth for many years now, and things are not the same as they used to be."

"Men of God—right! And you believe everything they tell you? What if they're imposters?"

"Lev, I have seen their miracles with my own eyes. And what they say about relationships is true."

"How can you say that? Doesn't our marriage mean anything to you? Don't you love me anymore? I don't get it. What's happening to us?"

His own unsettling questions made him feel suddenly lightheaded.

"Lev, I do love you." Tears streamed down Rebekah's face and her hand touched his cheek to his jaw-line. Her touch was tender.

Lev felt a measure of reassurance, and slowly pulled her face closer to kiss her. She did not resist. As their lips lightly brushed together he felt a strange depth of affection and tenderness sweep over him and something made him divert the kiss into an embrace. The love that he felt for her was stronger than he had remembered before, but somehow it was— *"different."*

He felt startled. He thought the same word Rebekah had used. "We are living in a very different world," she had said. "Different." Somehow a kiss of passion seemed out of place, but this comfortable embrace fulfilled him. His love and affection for this woman filled every fiber of his consciousness and he felt a deep sense of joy and exhilaration.

"I don't understand this new world, Rebekah."

"Neither do I, entirely. I understand in my head the way things are—but I have wondered what it would be like when you were finally raised. It confuses me."

"And me." He relaxed his embrace and then stepped back. He felt extraordinarily happy, and extraordinarily confused.

Eden Fruit

Rebekah took Lev's hand and slowly started back toward the kitchen.

"If it's a shock to you, it is for me also, especially now that I am with you. We need to give ourselves time. I love you more than I ever have, Lev."

The light in her eyes calmed his confusion. He had to trust Rebekah. Suddenly it felt enough to just be in her presence. He believed in her love for him, and he knew she would not lie to him. From the moment he first laid eyes on her, she held his heart and his every thought. That was in their teen years in high school. He was shy where girls were concerned back then, and unable to talk with her beyond the awkward surface conversation of acquaintance. But a few years later they really got to know each other at the Hebrew University and had become inseparable. They married at twenty-three. Allon was born the next year. They had been married twelve years when he had died. He had implicit faith in Rebekah, but he did not like some of the wild ideas she spoke of. He couldn't imagine not living with his wife.

*"And on either side of the river was there the tree of life,
Which bare twelve manner of fruits,
and yielded her fruit every month:
And the leaves of the tree were for the healing of the nations"
(Revelation 22:2).*

Chapter Two

Rebekah took her place at the table where Allon waited and Lev did the same. She continued speaking as if the two had never left the room.

"The Men of God I was telling you about—actually there's more in their office than just men, it included all the faithful men and women of the *Torah*—they have all been raised. They are called the Ancients—Abraham, Isaac, Jacob, Sarah, Deborah and others—and they are very much alive. They are now in charge of Israel, and many nations have already asked to be under their authority. Soon the whole world will be under their righteous control."

Rebekah reached out to place her hand over Lev's.

"The men of God said that if we wanted to have you returned to life, we could make provisions for your return. The former King David told us you could be raised once the necessary arrangements were made. So you are here with us today because of God's loving provisions. I know it's hard to believe, but it's true. You are here! You were raised this morning, just as they promised us. Allon and I were waiting for you to come out of your bedroom. And many others are being raised."

Lev stared at the table and felt comforted by the warmth of Rebekah's hand, a familiar feeling in a very unfamiliar and unbelievable circumstance. He could believe he died, but could not fathom how he could be alive again. He was afraid that at any moment everything would disappear and he would wake up on the battlefield.

He switched his gaze to the bowl of fruit that centered the table. Allon took something that looked like a mango and bit into it. Lev did the same. The skin was orange and as delicate as a nectarine. The taste was unique—a most refreshing combination of orange and mango. Lev tried to bring the conversation to something more concrete and logical.

"You're probably going to tell me this fruit is a genetically altered laboratory special," he joked.

"No, Dad. You probably won't believe this either, but the Ancients brought back these fruit seeds from the Garden of Eden," Allon spoke with assurance. "The seeds were stored in pottery, kept perfectly for over 6,000 years. The first thing the Ancients did when they returned to Israel was to grow these seeds into seedlings and then into trees. The very same trees that God had planted eastward in Eden are growing again in Israel. Soon they'll be growing all over the earth."

"There's special vitality in the fruit of these trees. Remember how God drove Adam and Eve out of Eden, 'Lest he take also of the tree of life, and eat, and live forever'?" Rebekah asked.

Lev looked doubtful. He had not heard scripture quoted since his young days in school. "So you're saying that this fruit we're eating is from the trees of life from Eden, and if we eat it we'll live forever?"

Rebekah nodded. "Yes, Lev, but don't try to figure it all out; you'll experience the effects of this fruit soon enough. Since we started eating it our energy, strength and brainpower have improved. The aging process is gradually reversed. No more glasses, dentists or doctors. When perfectly fed, the human body begins to return to perfection."

"I have to admit that I was disappointed not to see lox and bagels for breakfast. But this Eden fruit is better than any fruit I've ever eaten." Lev sat up a little straighter. "But I do reserve the right to doubt your 'live-forever' story."

Allon pursued the subject. "Dad, did you ever wonder why God didn't just destroy the tree of life? Instead he protected it by the angels who guarded it."

Rebekah finished the thought. "When God planted the Garden in Eden, he didn't intend to plant it all over again. He had a purpose in keeping 'the way of the tree of life.'"

Lev's response was skeptical. "So you're saying that the Cherubim that guarded Eden were also engaged for centuries in harvesting the seeds of those Eden trees. And now these Ancients, as you call them, are raised and have access to the Eden seeds and they plant them everywhere, and if we eat this fruit we'll live forever?"

Lev's mind was strangely alert. His intellect was easily able to put together and understand the concepts they presented to him, but he was not at all sure that these new ideas made sense. He diverted the subject to give himself time to think.

"Well, my mind feels like it's been 'raised,' but where's my old mangled body? This one isn't quite like I remember it at the last."

"It's where we buried it, Dad," Allon responded. "We'll show you your tombstone and the place where we buried you. Scripture says that God will give each person a new body. That's why you have a whole new healthy body. Your genetic makeup is identical. The identity of Lev Aron has been replayed into the new body that God has given you."

"Wow, I have a lot of catching up to do." Lev felt frustrated and inadequate. There were too many things he didn't understand. Rebekah and Allon knew so much—and he, nothing. He knew his past, but the present was still an overwhelming mystery. How would he earn a living? Would there be enough fruit? So many questions made him feel insecure.

The biggest shock was his private encounter with Rebekah. He could not fathom the idea that marriage was no longer a reality, yet he himself felt that something was different about their relationship. He still bristled at the word *'different'* and all its implications. Even his son Allon had grown into a man who no longer needed him. Lev realized that he was more dependent on his son than Allon was on him. Allon was at home in a world where he was a stranger. Their roles had totally reversed in this new world. Lev didn't like it one bit.

They talked through the morning. Lev learned how both Rebekah and Allon had managed after his death, and how suddenly the world had changed for them after the battle against Jerusalem.

"The Lord intervened and fought for Israel as He did in the battles in the days of the Prophets. The enemy was miraculously destroyed, but I'll let your brother fill you in on the details." Rebekah suggested this gently. She knew that Jacob and Lev had had a sharp contention over what to do in the face of the forces invading Israel, and she knew it would be best for them to talk it out.

"Jake, Rachel and their daughter Annie will be here soon," she added.

At the mention of his brother's name Lev felt uneasy. They had argued hard, as was their habit. Lev had believed that win or lose they should fight courageously to the bitter end. Jake had not been concerned about displaying courage in battle, but rather about finding the courage to depend on the arm of the Lord. Lev remembered the feeling of exasperation as Jake referred again and again to the prophecy of Ezekiel 38 and how God would destroy "Gog," the armies that were mobilizing to attack them.

Lev didn't believe that Jake was right then, and he didn't want to believe it now. But after the fact, it seemed that what Jake had expected actually happened. And this world seemed to be a better place, a beautiful place. Lev felt uncomfortable. He realized that before he had left God totally out of his thought process, and that his experiences were challenging his old way of thinking. He was in a new world with an old world mind set and he was not ready to accept the new way. He decided to keep his thoughts to himself.

Rebekah stood up and began to walk toward the door. "Let's take a walk. We'll show you your estate." Lev and Allon followed her outside. "The house is only temporary—you may want to change it down the road. The land is yours—you might as well get acquainted with a part of your eternity."

Lev looked around, unable to recognize any distinguishing landmarks. "Can't figure out where we are...."

Allon smiled. "We're in southern Israel, near Beersheba. This used to be the Negev desert. Rains fall here regularly now. As you see, everything grows abundantly."

This was certainly true. They walked in a verdant garden filled with shrubbery and flowers. Patches of green grass formed a thick carpet beneath their feet. Lev couldn't help noticing there were no weeds anywhere.

"How did you manage to keep this weed free?"

"Dad, you'll have to get used to the fact that we're living in a different world. The curse God placed on the earth has been lifted."

Words from the *Torah* came unexpectedly to Lev's mind, and his memory surprised him. He repeated them slowly to himself, with curiosity. "Cursed is the ground because of you; through painful toil you will eat of it all the days of your life."

"We don't need to use herbicides like in the old days—they added poisons to our food chain. When the Lord lifted the curse from the earth, weeds gradually disappeared," Allon said.

Lev liked this new development since he despised the chore of weeding. "You mean no one has to weed anymore?" he asked with a hint of excitement.

"You got it, Dad! As nations come under the authority of the Ancients, the curse is lifted. Rains become abundant—'for in the wilderness shall waters break out, and streams in the desert.' Like King David told us, 'Then shall the earth yield her increase.' Our harvests are phenomenal."

Lev knew instinctively that Allon referred to a prophecy from the book of Isaiah the thirty-fifth chapter as well as a prophecy from the book of Psalms. He again wondered at this newfound memory for the Scriptures he had not heard since he was a child.

As they walked around the estate Lev noticed the grove of trees planted uniformly apart, some laden with Eden fruit, others with blossoms and still others with small green fruit.

Allon pointed to the grove of trees.

"These trees are unique—most of them bear fruit in different months, so that every month there's a new harvest for our nutritional needs and it gives us what we call '*Rapha*' fruit, because '*Rapha*' means to heal. But the 'tree of life,'" Allon placed his hand on a the silver-smooth bark of a beautiful tree with willow-like sweeping branches filled with delicate leaves and luscious fruit, "bears Eden fruit all year round—we call that fruit '*Olam*' because that Hebrew word means 'forever,' and its fruit provides a constant source of vitality. And there's always more than we need. While we eat other fruits and vegetables for variety but we partake of '*Olam*' fruit everyday and the '*Rapha*' fruit everyday It is in season and the leaves of the twelve trees are used for making our popular tea. 'The leaves of the trees were for the healing of the nations' (Revelation 22:2). When we prune the trees we save the leaves of branches we cut off; it provides abundantly for us."

Rebekah smiled. "The sweat and toil are gone. We don't spend near the time cooking and preparing food as we did before. Your appetite for meat and fish will disappear in a few weeks. Sometimes we eat Eden bread and occasionally Eden cake and pastries."

Lev remembered Rebekah's sweet tooth and her craving for meat. He found it amusing to think that she had adjusted so happily to this new diet.

"Life is exciting, Dad! There's nothing to hurt or destroy anyone anymore. All our resources are spent in building and planting to prepare for the return of the ones we love. There's so much to learn so that we can take care of the life that's all around us. And no resources are wasted on war or weapons."

Rebekah had led them in a large circle that now headed them back to the house. "We'd better get back—Jake, Rachel and Annie will be here soon."

As Lev followed his wife and son to the house, he took a deep breath. He felt vibrant and alive, confused and apprehensive. Childhood teachings, that were formerly meaningless, were beginning to fit together like the pieces of a puzzle. Scriptures were working in his mind and he could begin to see the fulfillment of the words of the Prophets. But something in his thinking was still resisting against this new arrangement.

Jake

Lev had been looking forward to seeing Jake and Rachel since the moment Rebekah had mentioned their visit, and yet he felt an uneasy knot in the pit of his stomach. He sat at the kitchen table, absorbed in his thoughts as Rebekah and Allon continued a conversation outside. He looked forward to meeting his niece, Annie, who was only a child when he departed. He thought about his relationship with his brother, who had been close, some of the time, intense most of the time, and strained all of the time. Jake sought God and Lev sought independence and freedom. He was embarrassed to think of their last meeting.

"It's easy for you to pray and seek God when we are facing such an attack. You pray and I die. Is that how you want it?"

Lev's words had tumbled out in anger, and he could not take them back. The look of pain in his brother's face made him feel sick. He knew in his heart that Jake would have joined the military in a moment even when conscription had been eliminated in a period of peace Israel had enjoyed. However, it was not in God's purpose. But in the heat of argument, Lev had implied that Jake was a coward. He also recalled that he belittled Jake on several occasions for his spiritual discipline. His scathing words had caused a distance between them that went beyond the undercurrent of competition that had always defined his relationship with his brother. Soon he would be facing his brother again.

Lev reminisced about Jake and Rachel. They had been childhood sweethearts from the first grade. Jake—the serious, studious, pensive, skinny, the almost emaciated *Torah* scholar. Rachel—the vivacious, outgoing blond, verbal, people person, humorist, excelling in arts and crafts. They were living proof that opposites attract.

None would have guessed from her cheery mannerisms the difficulty she had endured. Rachel was the sunshine of Jake's life. Jake was the stability and inspiration in Rachel's world.

Rachel's home life had been full of friction. Rachel's mother, Sylvia, an aggressive, contentious woman, nagged her husband Irving to death with her aspirations for wealth and status. Jake had lifted Rachel into another world with his visionary *Torah* ideals, as unrealistic as Lev thought they were. Rachel was the perfect homemaker with a flare for art and drama, adding sparkle and smiles to Jake's life.

Though he felt a pang of apprehension when he thought of seeing his brother again, Lev still looked forward to being with them all, to be reunited with part of the family he thought he had lost forever.

*"The people of Jerusalem are strong,
Because the LORD Almighty is their God"
(Zechariah 12:4-5).*

Chapter Three

"They're here!" Allon announced. Lev sprang up, running to meet them. He embraced Jake tightly, then vivacious Rachel, and then Annie.

Jake patted Lev on the back. "We've been waiting and working for your return for months! Lev, it's great to have my big brother back!"

Jake, animated and excited, continued his rapid-fire dialogue. "Hey, why are we standing here? Rachel made you a 'resurrection cake'. Let's celebrate!"

Lev was speechless. They headed for the kitchen, settling around a large table. The sweet aroma of flowers and pungent tea filled the room. Lev wondered why he was not given a choice of coffee or tea, because he was an avid coffee drinker, but he dismissed this as an oversight. Anyway, this was different tea than any he had ever tasted, and it was just as stimulating to the senses as coffee, kind of bringing the vital organs to attention. He drank the delicious tea gratefully. After a few moments he regained his composure.

"What a beautiful cake!" Lev said appreciatively. "It looks like a rainbow!"

Each layer of the cake was from a different fruit having a vibrant color. Lev watched as Rebekah cut the cake into large portions.

"Pretty big pieces, eh, Rebekah?" Lev teased, surprised at his ability to joke amid a backdrop of fluctuating emotions. "Reviving the sweet tooth from the old world, are we?"

"You only get raised from the dead once, Uncle Lev," Rachel smiled in a light-hearted defense of Rebekah. Everyone laughed.

Lev suddenly became aware of the young lady who had eyed him intently since they had entered the room. When their eyes met, Annie spoke.

"You do look a lot like my dad, Uncle Lev. I can tell you're brothers. Dad told me all about you—it's like a dream, seeing you here today."

"I'm *still* not sure it's real."

Annie nodded and tried to imagine what it would be like for someone to suddenly find himself in another world after being killed on a battlefield. She felt a pang of sympathy for her uncle, whom she already felt quite fond of. She leaned over from her chair to give him another hug.

"I'm sure glad you're here with us, Uncle Lev." She straightened up in her own chair. "How do you like your new house? We all worked on building it for you. We've looked forward to this moment for months!"

Lev sensed Annie's genuine concern and found he was fighting back tears.

"How can I thank you all enough? Everything is great. I keep thinking if I blink, you'll all disappear on me and I'll wake up in my battle position."

The Battle for Jerusalem

Lev fixed his gaze on a knot on the tabletop as he regained his composure.

"I was in shock when I left this world, and I'm still in shock. Last thing I knew my hand got blown away, and then as if nothing had happened in between, I find myself sitting here with the people I love. I can't express my feelings."

There was a brief silence and Lev was overwhelmed. He stared at his cup of tea and finally drank the last of it. Again, the tea helped him feel a sense of emotional balance and he was able to speak. The tea acted as a stimulant because it awakened all of his senses.

"So tell me what happened after that day in the battle field when we were defeated. I thought all of you would share a similar fate."

Lev remembered being outnumbered. A sinking feeling had gripped him when he heard the proposed plan of the enemy, the words that Jake was just now repeating.

"Rumor was that the enemy would use neutron bombs on our beloved city Jerusalem. They would spare the sacred sites and sacrifice the people. The enemy planned to enter a lifeless Jerusalem with all its inhabitants dead from radiation."

Again there was a brief silence. Lev felt pressured to smooth over this serious turn of conversation that interfered with a family celebration.

"Sorry to be so negative. Let's enjoy my rainbow cake!"

Jake asked a blessing on the food. Lev realized for the first time that Jake knew God in a deep and personal way. He always sensed his brother's religious devotion, but now he could sense the relationship behind the religion. It made Lev feel empty and a little ashamed that he had only experienced an outwardly religious life. He didn't really know God, and he wasn't sure he wanted to change that. The Jewish faith had been no more than a venerable tradition to him and the events of this day left his old priorities shaken. He had lived a shallow religious life, but God was certainly showering kindness on him. He felt unworthy.

The conversation continued in a light vein while they dined. Lev kept picking up bits of information about life under the Ancients. Their rulership role made sense to him. Certainly people of such high moral stature would manage things better than the squabbling politicians had done.

"This cake is incredible," Lev remarked with his mouth partially full, which made his words slightly muffled—"Never tasted anything like it!"

His face reddened when he realized that he had spoken about the exceptional cake so spontaneously that he had forgotten his manners.

Rachel smiled. She found Lev's awkwardness endearing and her heart went out to him because of the inner turmoil she sensed from his behavior.

"We have different ingredients than we had before. The flour in this cake is made from dried Eden fruit—combination of the *Rapha* fruit and the *Olam*. Who says healthy food can't be delicious? Life is healthier and simpler now. We manufacture only what we need, and commercial enterprise for profit is nonexistent. Love replaces profit and the major challenge facing each of us is how to prepare for the billions yet to be raised. Our nation has made provisions for Jews to return to their homeland. But to make provisions for every human being that ever lived is definitely a large scale project—beyond *my* imagination!"

Again the conversation paused. Lev felt it was a good time to ask his questions about the final battle.

"What happened after our first outpost was destroyed?"

Jake's expression turned solemn. "It is really quite a story, Lev. Word of your defeat reached us almost immediately. Your unit was one of many small pockets spread throughout Israel. The enemy hoped to destroy the advanced guard and then give Israel the ultimatum to surrender Jerusalem. When your outpost fell, a number of Israelis decided to mount a resistance in the Western part of the city. The enemy countered with an attack on that half of the city."

Rachel spoke the words of the Prophet Zechariah with great emotion. "For I will gather all nations against Jerusalem to battle; and the city shall be taken, and the houses rifled, and the women ravished; and half of the city shall go forth into captivity, but the residue of the people will not be cut off from the city."

Lev shuddered as he imagined the scene these words portrayed. He saw the invaders mow down the people, pilfer their homes and rape the women. He heard cries of anguish and despair, and in his heart he himself wondered, "Where was God?"

"They took the opposing forces of the Western half of the city that wasn't slaughtered back to their headquarters at Megiddo. Those of us holding out in the Eastern half of Jerusalem knew we would have to either surrender or face the neutron bombs when they returned."

Jake's level voice continued, a backdrop to the vivid pictures forming in Lev's mind.

"The enemy could claim they'd given everyone a fair chance to surrender. Some of us decided to stay within the walls of the Old City. We placed our lives in God's hands. Whatever he willed, we were prepared to accept."

Lev closed his eyes and pictured the group of men and women ready to accept death on the strength of their faith. He acknowledged the conflict in his heart to admire these people on the one hand, and to belittle their helplessness on the other.

Lev interrupted, half in irritation at himself for almost caving in to sentimentality when brute strength had always been his approach and solution.

"Jake, wouldn't it have been better to die fighting than to let them kill you with radiation?"

Jake smiled sadly. He understood the stubborn independence of his brother.

"You haven't changed, Lev. Hear me out. The enemy paused another day to regroup. Never had a mightier army been assembled against Israel. But despite their victories, the invading forces were nervous and worried.

A Small Group of Christians Support Israel

"A small group of Christians had warned them repeatedly against invading the Holy Land. They were labeled as religious fanatics, and no one could keep them quiet. They pointed out the prophecy of Ezekiel 38 and warned the civil and religious leaders that complete annihilation awaited the forces coming against Jerusalem. That morning the enemy started moving against the defenders of Judea...."

Lev sank back in his chair as his mind continued to translate the words of his brother into pictures. Lev saw the day as it had dawned, with thick clouds and traces of fog, with no breath of a breeze anywhere. He felt the eerie forebodings of the enemy troops as they started out at the first traces of light. He felt the air when it became heavy and hot. And then he felt the enemy's panic as their communication systems broke down.

"Clouds gathered and visibility became nearly impossible. The enemy forces could not be recalled because their communications had completely failed. Field commanders didn't know why communications had ceased. They assumed it was some secret weapon of the Israelis to sabotage their communications."

Lev imagined the masses of the invading army—some marched while others drove tanks and trucks as they headed through the shrouding fog at the Megiddo pass. He saw the mounting fear as the enemy soldiers felt electrical energy that made their hair stand on end. He saw some men waver, and some turn back. But the great mass of the enemy force moved forward, intent on their purpose to wipe out the Israeli defending forces and then leave Jerusalem, the prize, until the end.

"A sudden firestorm broke out. A mighty and deadly firestorm broke out upon the enemy armies," Jake continued.

Lev pictured the ensuing confusion as the equipment in motion collided. Tanks and trucks crashed and overturned. Helicopters and aircraft hurled full speed to the earth. He saw the enemy naval ships fire at nothing because their instruments failed, and then suddenly fall quiet with a lifeless crew. He smelled the acrid smell of burning rubber and felt the heat.

"'The Lord also shall save the tents of Judah first, that the glory of the house of David and the glory of the inhabitants of Jerusalem do not magnify themselves against Judah.'"

Lev was surprised that he recognized these words from the prophet Zechariah. He noticed his brother's face had been radiant as he recited those holy words, and it both fascinated and frightened him.

"God saved the tents of Judea first, but He waited until that dismal morning, after the military strike against the Western part of the City had taken half the city. He waited until the enemy approached the Israeli forces spread out throughout the holy land to destroy them. The enemy planned to reserve Jerusalem as the last trophy but was defeated in the hills of Judea."

Everyone in the room was silent. Lev could not keep himself from asking another question.

"Jake, what effect did this devastating turn of events have on all the nations who sponsored this invasion?"

Jake explained that the leaders suspected something had gone terribly wrong when all communication with their forces was lost.

"What made things worse was that the churches had convinced the national leaders that unless they controlled Jerusalem, Armageddon would break out. When news of the utter defeat of the invading armies reached the nations, the people were outraged with organized religion for helping to initiate the catastrophe. It became very similar to the days of the French Revolution, but this time on a worldwide scale. Church tradition and belief was questioned and labeled as useless. Churches were burned, priests and ministers were hunted down and there was no place to hide. Now all could see clearly that the very army the religious leaders had blessed and sent down to save the world from Armageddon had, in fact, precipitated God's judgments."

"What happened to those Christians who stood in support of Israel?" Lev asked, admiring, in spite of himself, the strength of those individuals who spoke out when they were so entirely outnumbered.

"That small group of Christians refused to be silenced, as you remember, they stood before the world renouncing the plan to invade Israel. The government of Israel actually interceded on their behalf before the invading armies ever entered Israel. Israel made it clear that these Christians were not connected with them in any political way, nor was there any collusion between them."

Lev felt tightness in the pit of his stomach. He repeated his question.

"So what happened to those Christians who stood in support of Israel?"

"They were harassed and threatened by government leaders. And when the mobs turned violent, they made no effort to differentiate between faithful Christians and those who had used religion for their own agenda. Panic spread throughout the world, and religion was seen as the enemy because it was apparent to all that the churches that had blessed this invasion were most certainly misguided. The band of believers never recanted their belief in a God who would deliver Israel and then bless the entire world. They died at the hands of the mobs."

Again Lev was haunted by a vision of a group of men and women ready to accept death on the strength of their faith. But this time the men and women were from a "rival" religion that had persecuted his own people, and yet *this* band of believers had put their lives on the line in defense of his people. Lev shook his head in confusion, but he could not deny the respect he felt for them.

He weighed the conflict in his mind; this business about laying life on the line for faith was a battle of sorts. The enemy was Fear, and the weapon of defense was Faith. People of Faith were fiercely independent, and they were ready to wage their warfare to the death, outnumbered—just as he had been in literal battle.

Lev leaned over, his elbows on his knees and his arms supporting his head, and he stared at the floor. He heard his brother describe the carnage of that day, when the majority of the invading armies died on Israeli soil without any effort at all on the part of Israeli resistance.

Jake continued, "The nations are in the process of being healed of their hostility toward our nation and our people. They are beginning to see that God had a purpose in mind for Israel—a place to begin the healing of a very sick world. They are seeing that we are willing to share the blessings God has given us, and that we wish to accept all who love God as our brothers and sisters."

Lev still stared at the floor, his mind grappling with the devastation of war, the faith of believers, and the possibility that the pain and chaos was meant to make a final blessing possible for all people.

Return of the Ancients

"There were other dramatic events soon after the final battle. It was reported that the men and women who pleased God in ancient times were again present in Israel. They appeared on NEB—New Earth Broadcasting, and this really startled people. These Ancients were the first to be raised," said Jake.

Everyone in the room was aware that a battle raged in Lev's mind. They quietly continued the conversation, with the desire that Lev would see the full picture and breadth of God's purposes.

Rachel added to her husband's account.

"Some tried to dismiss the Ancients as frauds, but their intelligent presentations and the wisdom of their leadership in Israel awakened the world. When they made known that they had Eden seeds and Eden fruit, the world laughed. But when the nations saw the documented proof of the effects of the 'trees of life' on the people, soon many nations began to clamor for it. No amount of money nor any honor could bribe the Ancients. The only way to secure the fruit was for each nation to come under their leadership."

Allon spoke up. "People in power didn't want to come under Israel's leadership at first. But the healing and the abundance in Israel became a living example to the world. The prophecy of Zechariah 8:23 became a reality. 'In those days ten men from all languages and nations will take firm hold of one Jew by the hem of his robe and say, 'Let us go with you, because we have heard that God is with you.'"

Annie also spoke. "Not all the nations seek help from Israel now, but those who don't are experiencing drought. It seems strange, but some of the most educated people are finding it the most difficult to welcome the Ancients and the Messiah they represent."

At the mention of "Messiah" Lev sat up and cocked his head quizzically to one side. "Messiah?" he repeated the word as a question.

"Yes, Uncle Lev. Jesus, the Messiah." She said the words easily, in a gentle tone, and with love.

Lev sighed. As a Jew he had been taught to avoid the name of Jesus. No one in the room seemed to share this tradition.

Rachel continued, "When the invading forces were destroyed, we knew that it could only be our Messiah who had intervened on our behalf. Jesus revealed himself to us, even as Joseph revealed himself, when he said, 'I am Joseph your brother.' The understanding of those who had trusted God was suddenly broadened—'They shall mourn for him, as one mourneth for his only son, and shall be in bitterness for him, as one that is in bitterness for his firstborn.'"

Lev was startled by such intelligence and love. And he was startled by the concept of grieving for the one he had been taught to despise.

"Today, all inhabitants of Israel are under the authority of Christ." Jake's voice carried on. "His power is everywhere as we see millions raised to life. Lev, your very life is firsthand evidence. It is the power of Christ that brought you back to us. And healing and forgiveness follow his power. He is not the Christ taught by the burning hell-fire and brimstone preachers, but he is Jesus the Messiah, who comes to reconcile and bless our people and all nations. He did not deliver us to bring recriminations against us, but to free us."

Lev leaned back in his chair and closed his tired eyes. He had never been comfortable with the treatment Jesus received. Jesus certainly had done nothing worthy of death much less death by crucifixion. This thought awakened in him a sense of the unfairness of it. He realized Jesus with almost an empire over his passions submitting to this cruel and ignominious death. He could not grasp why this man died or how it made him the deliverer of Israel, but he felt a sadness make its way into his heart. He sensed that this grief was not meant to make him feel guilty, but to make him feel a gratitude that could free him. He had always felt uncomfortable at hearing of Jesus' death, but he began to sense that in some way that Jesus' death and resurrection had made it possible to live again. He felt the warm touch of Rebekah's hand on his. She must have felt the struggle within Lev's heart for she had been silent all this time. Lev was vaguely aware of Jake, Rachel, Annie and Allon, as they each stood up and quietly asked to be excused.

"See you a little later, Uncle Lev," Annie promised.

Lev felt too exhausted to respond. Rebekah helped him to a reclining sofa chair in the corner of the room and, sensing his need for time and for rest, she left him alone.

"O taste and see that the LORD is good:
Blessed is the man that trusteth in Him"
(Psalm 34:8).

Chapter Four

Once again Lev was seated at the table with his family. He felt rested, but not yet ready to face the questions over the New Earth concepts of Messiah, believers and the billions yet to be raised. It was too much for him to deal with right now and it made him feel uneasy. But he was still curious about many things. Hoping to keep the conversation on the lighter side, he launched into another question.

"So what has it been like for you with all these changes?" he asked.

"Well, it's been quite a contrast. We lived through the darkest days on earth and now we live on a New Earth. Living through the dark times has really made us appreciate what it's like now," Rachel said.

Jake interjected, "But even in the most desperate times when it looked like our nation would be wiped off the map, we both believed the prophecies. One of my richest memories is when Rachel and I went into Old Jerusalem to pray at the Western Wall."

Lev realized their faith was real, and here again was the true-to-life evidence. He felt a wave of embarrassment as he remembered his angry and insulting comments regarding his brother's faith. Apologies were foreign to him, but he forced himself to speak. His face felt flushed.

"I...had no right to speak to you the way I did about your faith, Jake. It seems like I've always been trying to prove to myself that I am better than you. I'm..." Lev took a deep breath, and then he sighed. "I'm really sorry."

Jake smiled. "Apology accepted. I've had my share of trying to prove to myself that I was better than you too, and I regret my own attitude of superiority and its effect on you. As far as faith goes, it can be hard to grasp, and it takes time and experience. But now there is living evidence all around us of the things that weren't visible to the human eye before—the promises of God are being fulfilled before our eyes."

Lev appreciated his brother's quick response to his apology. He felt as if a burden had been lifted from his heart, but he still couldn't relate to the kind of faith their lives portrayed. He sighed again.

Rachel changed the direction of the conversation.

Lev's New Home

"Lev, it's time to show you your new home. We'll take you on a tour of the house so you can find everything you need."

They started at Lev's bedroom where he had awakened. The room was bright and airy with a large bed, a chest of drawers, a desk and a computer area. From there, sliding patio doors with windows led to the garden. Lev loved the openness—from nearly every window he could see the garden.

"You'll find all the clothes you need in the chest of drawers and in the closet," Rebekah added.

Lev opened a drawer and rummaged through the shirts. "What is going on?" Lev questioned as he pulled a checkered shirt out of the drawer. "These are like my old shirts, except they're new—like the shirt I'm wearing, and these pants, and these tennis shoes. Explain *that*."

Rebekah smiled. "It's one of our ways to help people feel at home in their new surroundings. We try to supply people with some things that are familiar to them. So I chose to have some of your favorite clothing made for you. I even requested tennis shoes like your old ones."

Lev bent down to examine his shoes. He stood up and smiled as he returned the shirt to its place in the drawer. He found the attention to detail humorous and was impressed with the forethought and effort that had been put into the preparation for his return. His attention turned back to the tour of his new home.

The closet was large and lit with a translucent ceiling. All the ceilings radiated light similar to sunlight, and the light switches had dimmers. The bathroom was large. Lev saw himself in the mirror and stared.

He looked more closely at his reflection and smiled. His features were similar to how he remembered them, but his teeth were straighter and he felt no space where a wisdom tooth had been missing. He had become so totally engrossed in this discovery that he was oblivious to his audience as he opened his mouth widely before the mirror and tilted his head back and forth. No fillings and sure enough the space between his teeth was gone.

"Surprised to find yourself looking so good, aren't you, Lev?" Rachel said with a hint of humor.

Lev, startled, nodded and looked a bit embarrassed.

"No more scar on my forehead." Lev felt a familiar uneasiness creep over him as he spoke these words, and immediately distracted him. "And I have the movie star smile I always wanted," he said half joking.

Allon spoke up. "Dad, your smile really does look better than before."

Lev checked out the mirror again and saw everyone smiling. "You all have movie star smiles!" he teased.

Annie jumped in. "Uncle Lev, you won't find anyone in Israel with bad teeth or with any kind of deformity. Imagine being a teenager with no skin problems! It's great!"

Lev directed his attention to Annie. "Tell me, Annie, where do you go to school?"

"School isn't like it used to be. All the courses are on television. You can tune into any subject you want to learn about. The Ancients teach most of the classes. They are really good teachers. History has been rewritten to relay the truth about every event. Every subject is exciting."

A New Dictionary

Jake spoke. "Even the dictionary is changing. There is a large group of words that are now considered 'archaic' because they're no longer a part of our world. Words like doctors, nurses, dentists, psychiatrists, lawyers, ministers, courts, judges, jurors, police, prisons, locks, hospitals, nursing homes, wheelchairs, braces—not a word, hearing aids, canes, glasses—not a word, pain drugs and medication."

"Words like armies, guns, bombs, tanks, warplanes, warships, rocket launchers, navies, torpedoes, atomic bombs, hydrogen bombs and neutron bombs, nerve gas, germ warfare—the list could go on... About one-quarter to one-third of the world's wealth went into tools to destroy life. Not any more! The old grow younger, and there are no politicians. People live by love instead of by greed," Rachel added.

"I'll have to see it to believe it. I can't even imagine these changes," Lev said, as the small group entered the guest room that had twin beds and French doors that opened onto a patio.

The little company walked toward the rear of the house to a large orchard filled with flowers and plants of all kinds, as well as vegetables in small quantities. The lush growths made Lev think of a jungle, and the deep greens and splashes of color dazzled his eyes. He sat on one of several wooden benches overcome by the beauty that surrounded him. The others joined him.

"This is quite a little paradise, isn't it?" he spoke softly.

"Just imagine, Lev, this little paradise will be for every man, woman and child who has ever lived," Jake assured.

"Yea, right," Lev thought to himself. He could barely grasp the reality that *he* was here. To think of others—many others joining them on this New Earth—it was too much to imagine.

"So where's the electric meter?" he found himself asking in order to distract his mind from issues that seemed too overwhelming to consider.

"Isn't any," Allon explained. "Batteries can now store energy at almost 100% efficiency. Electricity for light and heat is provided by solar cells."

"Guess that makes things easy!"

"Sure does," Allon confirmed. "Life is simpler, and easier than it used to be. People choose the work that suits them best, but it's more like a part-time hobby. There are so many places to see and so many people to meet. But the most challenging task of all is to build and plant in preparation for the billions who are yet to be raised."

Lev felt uneasy again. "Billions," he thought. "How can this be real?" Then he spoke aloud. "So exactly how this being 'raised' thing work?"

Jake was unfazed by Lev's obvious mistrust. "The object is to gain a sense of connection with our human family. Christ has all of us playing a part in the regeneration. You've heard the expression 'the last shall be first.' Those who died last are generally the first to be returned to life. First, all of your generation is raised—then the second generation, then the third. The further back we go, it snowballs. There will be more and more people making preparations for less and less people. When we come to Adam and Eve, the whole world will have the privilege of preparation for their first parents. Now *that* will be a celebration!"

Celebration was not quite the word that Lev would have chosen. It sounded to him more like chaos. Lev didn't hide the edge of disbelief in his voice.

God's Ways Are Equal

"So what about people who had no descendants to receive them back to life? What about Sodom and Gomorrah? What about whole towns that were wiped out by the Bubonic Plague? Who's going to prepare for them?" he challenged.

Rebekah explained. "Those who really love their fellow man will join together to bring back the lost generations. It will be a kind of test. It's easy to prepare for those you love, but it's quite another matter to prepare for people you don't even know, or the likes of Hitler and Nero."

"Count me out on having anything to do with Hitler," Lev responded with intensity. He shivered at the thought of that man being raised and felt a wave of revulsion at the thought of anyone who would want to help the process. "People like him don't deserve to be raised," he added.

"Remember, Lev, God's ways are equal." Rachel's voice was patient and even. "No one is beyond recovery if they accept responsibility for the past and make a genuine effort to change. Messiah will help them, and anyone who accepts his help will have an opportunity to gain human perfection. For some it is very difficult. Some have such hatred and anger in their hearts that they have a hard time adjusting and may still wish to hurt people. Some may choose to never respond to the opportunity in front of them."

Lev could only shake his head in disapproval. He again avoided the subject of Messiah and continued to comment on the outlandish idea of raising people like Hitler. "This doesn't sound like a very safe or promising world to me! What's to keep an angry man from harming his enemy?"

"Violence isn't permitted. Powerful spiritual forces are present everywhere to enforce righteousness. Consequences are immediate and effective. You'll see soon enough how it works," Rebekah assured him.

Lev was not at all satisfied with this aspect of the New Earth. In his puzzlement he would have asked other questions about consequences and how this world could be as safe as they said it was, but it was obvious that the small group had decided to end this phase of the conversation. Everyone but Lev stood up.

New Earth Broadcasting [NEB]

"Let's go back to the parlor to see what the Ancients have to say tonight," Rachel announced.

Lev was the last to enter the room where everyone was seated. Allon pressed a button and a life-size screen lit up the wall. Several men and women of amazing beauty and vitality were in a round table discussion. Their speech was authoritative, but also gentle and wise. Lev felt captivated by their conversation. He found a chair, sat down and watched with rapt attention.

"So, *these* are the Ancients," Lev murmured to himself.

Isaac, obviously a great organizer, spoke of the accelerating work of regeneration. David had a charismatic personality. He announced that two additional countries—Ghana and Ethiopia—had officially asked to be under their authority so that God's blessings might begin to come to them. Lev could see that he would be a powerful influence on new nations learning to seek God.

Samson announced that Eden trees and plants would be shipped to the two nations. Lev chuckled to himself when he noticed this man's muscles. "He probably loads the half ton crates of Eden trees by hand," Lev thought out loud.

Barak, who had been a general in the days of the Judges, was in charge of organizing the land allotments. He explained that surveyors would lay out land grants and provisions for the people of Ghana and Ethiopia. Rahab warmly discussed that the first priority in this new project was to plant Eden trees as soon as the surveyors designated individual sites.

Abraham and Sarah reviewed the architectural plans for each nation. Sarah showed pictures of parks and forest preserves, explaining that most cities would be leveled with only minor centers remaining to sustain certain industries that were needed. There would be no more concentrations of people in congested cities.

Abraham reminded his viewers that volunteers were needed to work with the animal kingdom.

The lessons, program and methods for training animals according to the New Earth's gentle methods would be offered at eight in the morning, one in the afternoon, and eight in the evening. Those who wished to volunteer should contact 1-800-ANIMALS.

Abraham impressed Lev as being the most capable executive officer that had ever existed. Lev was disappointed when the program neared its end and Abraham made his closing announcement: a list of people scheduled to awaken tomorrow in this area would be provided in the evening news. Those who wished to prepare for the raising of a relative were to contact Abraham and his assistants at 1-800-RESURRE. Lev felt a strange curiosity sweep over him. He did not trust the ways of this New Earth, yet he felt drawn to something about this "raising" work, as if there was some purpose for him to fulfill. He consciously made note of the number.

"Confessions"

"The next program," Rebekah explained, "is called 'Confessions.' It's on every night between 8:00 and 9:00. One of the Ancients moderates the interaction of the discussions between people who have been raised. We watch as they face those they have wronged, and their subsequent confessions and repentance. It's quite a program, good for those who are willing to be honest before the nation and good for us to see their examples for our own life situations."

The next hour flew by as they watched Jacob mediate discussions between Sammy and the various people in his life. Sammy had married four times and had fathered twelve sons, all in various degrees of conflict and jealousy. His first two wives, Linda and Nanette, with whom he had eight sons, both had demanded a divorce. His third wife Eva died of colon cancer and left him with two young boys. Shoshonna, Eva's younger sister, became his fourth wife and they had two boys.

Sammy faced a nightmare of tangled conflicts. Jacob was able to give wise advice to guide the family through their admissions, apologies, and plans for reconciliation because of his own past experience with four wives and twelve sons, and the rebellion, rivalry and healing of his own family's resentments.

Lev found the program fascinating. It gave him a ray of hope that tangled emotions and conflicts that he foresaw would be settled. They discussed the program, and soon it was time for everyone to leave.

"Don't worry, Uncle Lev, we all live within a mile from here," Annie said as she hugged her uncle. Jake, Rachel, and Allon hugged Lev in turn, and then went out the door to ride their bicycles to their homes.

Last of all to leave was Rebekah. She smiled and gave Lev a quick hug, but Lev would not let her go.

"Stay with me, Rebekah," he pleaded. "There's so much I want to talk to you about. So much I don't understand. If you would just stay here I would be able to sort out my thinking, and...."

Rebekah pulled herself away, and put her finger over Lev's lips.

"Shhhh, Lev," she whispered. "I'd like to stay with you, but I can't. Tomorrow, though, I can hardly wait until we can spend time together. I love you...."

Before he knew what happened, she kissed him lightly on his cheek and went quickly out the door, leaving him with the incongruous feelings of playfulness and rejection. Lev felt an aching need to have Rebekah near him. He wandered around his quiet house, talking to himself.

"This New Earth gave her back to me, and this New Earth keeps her away. This New Earth gave me back my son, and my brother and Rachel. This New Earth gave me back my hand." Lev passed by the bathroom and he looked at his reflection in the mirror. "This New Earth gave me straight teeth, and a mind that can remember in more detail." Lev had reached his bedroom. "And yet this New Earth gives me memories that I still can't bear to dwell on and questions that I still don't have the courage to ask."

He flopped face down on his bed and continued talking softly to himself.

"I hate some of the things that happened in my old life. But, You've given me a new life, God. You gave me life. I don't know what to say or what to think. I never gave You anything, and You have given me everything!"

Lev's mind returned to the day's discussions and to the sheer joy of being with the family he loved. The holy words he had spontaneously remembered came again to his mind, and he felt comforted.

"Maybe You were there all along, giving me hints of what was to come, but I just wouldn't listen...."

He remembered the startling references to Messiah and felt the resistance—the traditions of his people rise—in his heart. Yet the very word 'Messiah' now brought to his mind a vivid picture of a man called Jesus hanging on a cross. He felt the same strange cleansing sorrow that had clutched at his heart earlier. Resistance and grief warred within him.

Lev knew that the Messiah had been central to the Jewish hopes, and he began to realize that they rejected their Messiah when they should have received him. He was not going to be stubborn this second time. He was ready to accept him and to obey him. The evidences of the Messiah's power were manifest everywhere. Then he fell into a deep sleep.

"The law will go out from Zion,
The word of the Lord from Jerusalem"
(Isaiah 2:3).

Chapter Five

He surprised himself when he naturally awoke soon after the day had dawned. Lev Aron, the proverbial snooze-button-king, jumped out of bed, showered, and took a walk outside in his garden. It made him smile to think that he had accomplished more before 7 a.m. on this day than on any of the early morning hours in his former life. He enjoyed gathering fruit and vegetables from his own garden, and he savored the taste of his simple breakfast.

Lev left his house and headed down the same road that Rebekah and Allon had taken the previous evening. There were many others walking in the same direction. He walked briskly; glad to be alive and strangely excited about a new day. Lev was surprised when he had a sudden impulse to catch up with the group of people in front of him. He usually kept to himself. But today he felt like talking. He jogged for a few yards and placed himself in their midst.

"Shalom—may I join you?" he asked with a hint of breathlessness.

"Shalom—of course—but we haven't met yet."

"Oh, right—my name is Lev—Lev Aron." Lev put out his hand to shake the hands of his new friends.

"Lev Aron…You came just when they said you would," a woman said.

"Yes, right on time," a young man added.

"You live down the road from here, don't you?"

"We watched your family build your house." Lev was barraged by varied comments.

"Rebekah was your wife, and Allon your son…nice family…."

Lev felt suddenly a little suspicious, of everyone's interest.

"I suppose you know my shoe size, too," he said with hostility.

The people that surrounded him seemed amused. A young man responded. "No, actually I don't know your shoe size. Good news just travels fast around here." He paused. "So, you're going to join us for our Morning Worship?" he said as both a question and an invitation.

"Guess so…" Lev said, not really knowing what that meant. He felt a mixture of curiosity, excitement and resistance, a composite of feelings that was beginning to become familiar.

John, the Former Paraplegic

"Hello, Lev. Name's John." A young man with wide cheekbones and fine blonde hair offered his hand to Lev. He sensed Lev's feeling of discomfort and could not keep himself from sharing his exuberant voice in hopes of warming the chilled waters. "Sure is a good feeling to walk. I just can't get over it. You and I—we are actually strangers walking together!"

Lev raised his eyebrows and glanced sideways at the man who had caught up to him to match his stride.

"You might want to give Lev a little background so he can appreciate your excitement," a young woman suggested with a smile.

"Good idea, Marsha. Thanks." John looked at Lev. "I guess I sounded rather off the wall. But I meant every word of what I said. I was wounded in a Palestinian uprising with a bullet in my spine. I became paralyzed from the neck down."

Lev slowed his pace as he listened to John, and he felt embarrassed in view of this man's experience that he had been so snappy over some friendly-neighborly interest.

John described how he had become bitter and angry in the old world. He saw his total dependence on others as degrading, humiliating and a huge burden.

"Those were the darkest days of my life. I felt absolutely useless and was a constant burden. I couldn't even scratch my own nose. I wanted to end my life."

"How did you manage to keep your sanity?" Lev asked.

"One day I had this flash of insight. I realized that my character was just as paralyzed as my body. There was nothing I could do to regain my mobility and coordination, but I realized that I *could* do something about the anger and negativity that crippled my spirit. So I started doing character calisthenics."

"Character calisthenics..." Lev repeated.

"I worked on my eyesight by looking for something good or beautiful in everything around me. I stretched my spiritual arms by finding ways to reach out to people by making them tapes of humorous stories. I practiced spiritual aerobics by building up my ability to persevere and to be patient—especially with those who cared for me. You get the picture. And it worked over time by changing my outlook. Oh, occasionally I would still get down in the dumps, but gradually my attitude changed. And very gradually my life seemed worth living again."

"Wow!" That was all that Lev could think of to say, until he thought of four more words. "That is really amazing!"

"I died from leukemia a few years later, and the next thing I knew I was in bed, wondering why my toes were moving. You should have seen me in my first day of new life."

Lev pictured the young man skipping and shouting and running around his garden barefoot.

"Watch this," John whispered. He ran a few steps ahead, did three cartwheels and a flip, and then landed in final pose on one knee with his arms extended to both sides and a look of triumph in his eyes. "The power of Christ is beyond what we could ever imagine, Lev, don't you think?"

Lev chuckled and shook his head in amazement. He couldn't help but appreciate the child-like gratitude and excitement in John, though he could not yet relate to this 'power of Christ.'

John relinquished his end-of-performance pose and continued to walk with Lev. "We're just about there," he announced.

Lev's First Worship Service

The first thing Lev noticed as they approached the place of worship was the hauntingly beautiful music that filled the air, played by a stringed quartet. They entered a large courtyard where about forty people sat on benches and chairs. Lev was happy and relieved to spot Rebekah and Allon and sat down directly behind them.

He clearly heard the words of Psalm 145, sung from the heart by these worshipers.

"The LORD is good to all, and His mercies are over all His works.

All Thy works shall praise thee, O LORD;
And thy saints shall bless thee.

They shall speak of the glory of thy kingdom, and talk of thy power;

To make known to the sons of men his mighty acts,

And the glorious majesty of his kingdom..."

The words and music made him shiver. They reminded him of Jake, Rebekah, and each of his family members in their eagerness to share their new world with him.

A man stood up and read another few verses from the Psalm.

"The LORD upholdeth all that fall, and raiseth up all those that be bowed down.

The eyes of all wait upon thee; and thou givest them their meat in due season.

Thou openest thine hand, and satisfiest the desires of every living thing."

Lev thought of the Eden fruit that his family claimed would awaken the mind, revitalize the body and reverse the aging process, and how it was available only to the nations that looked to God and the Ancients. It was from God, a God who opens His hand to satisfy the longings of His people.

The man continued reading verses that were unfamiliar to Lev.

"The hour is coming and now is, when the dead shall hear the voice of the Son of God, and those who hear shall live."

Lev felt himself stiffen at the words "Son of God" and he stared at the tiles at his feet while the congregation joined again in song.

Lev scanned the worshipers. This room was filled with Jewish brothers and sisters who sang of Christ as their Messiah. It puzzled him. They associated Christ with God's love and the fulfillment of what all nations desired. Lev remembered Jake's words from the previous day's discussion in regard to Messiah. "He did not deliver us to bring recriminations against us, but to free us."

Lev felt the familiar triad of feelings—curiosity, excitement, acceptance but also an inner resistance. These feelings oscillated within him to begin with. Lev was pensive, and his antagonism to the Messiah was melting. Increasingly he found acceptance and thanksgiving in his heart. He thought of John who had eased his dispair without any help from the Messiah. He used positive thinking but it did not remedy his problem. Surely only the Messiah could have brought such happiness to him from the depths of despair and anguish to uninhibited joy he saw today. Only a loving and omnipotent being could do such wonderful things. Then he couldn't help but breathe a prayer—"Help me to understand my new life—and this Messiah...."

When the service was over Lev stood up and slowly walked towards the door in a daze.

"Hey, Lev, you're here! What did you think?" Rebekah's voice snapped him back into the present.

"It was—memorable," Lev stumbled over his words, "uh—it was—different—I liked it—and it confuses me."

He looked into Rebekah's eyes and saw understanding there and felt comforted. "Why didn't you tell me about the services?"

"I knew too well, darling, that if I had told you to be here, you would've resisted going. I was pretty sure you'd hear about it from your neighbors on the road." Lev smiled at how well his wife knew him.

"Maybe I need more of that tea," Lev said as he remembered its calming effect on his roller-coaster emotions.

Rebekah smiled. "Oh, so you noticed the tea. We call it 'resurrection tea'—it's especially for those who are raised, to help in their adjustment time, though it's good for everybody. It's made of ground up leaves 'which bare twelve manner of fruits, and yieldeth her fruit every month: and the leaves of the tree were for the healing of the nations.' A combination of resurrection tea and Eden fruit are great for balancing emotional energy."

"Hi, Dad!" Allon interrupted. He gave his father a hug. "Good service, don't you think?"

Lev smiled to see his son so enthused about a worship service.

"Why don't we stop at your house for a mid-morning snack, and then when Jake and Rachel arrive we can head over to some of your old stomping grounds so you can see how things have changed," Rebekah suggested.

Visit to Jerusalem

Lev, Rebekah and Allon ate Eden fruit as they sat on the garden bench at Lev's house. Lev felt his mind sharpen and his body became energized—he felt more like his talkative self again. "You were right, Rebekah, there *is* something to this Eden fruit and balancing the system. Who'd have guessed that I would be eating the same food as Adam and Eve ate, *from my own garden?*" Lev laughed. "You said I'd forget my former diet—and you were right. It's happening already! So where's the tree of the knowledge of good and evil?"

"That tree isn't in your garden, Dad."

"But why not? I already know plenty about evil, and I'm starting to learn a lot more about 'good.' So wouldn't that tree help me? Why isn't it in my garden?"

"There's a reason why things are the way they are," Rebekah said. "The trouble with you is you want to know all the answers to everything right now. That tree is unavailable at this time. You'll learn about it soon enough."

Another mystery, Lev thought to himself. People today had a way of telling you everything and keeping you guessing all at the same time.

Before long the doorbell rang. Lev walked quickly to the door and invited Jake and Rachel in with hugs. It seemed like he would never tire of greeting his family. He looked at his younger brother with new respect. Jake had always been wise for his years, but now he seemed even more seasoned, mellowed and knowledgeable. Jake had once depended on him, but now he needed Jake. "Relationships are subject to change in this new life," Lev thought to himself.

"So, what's the plan, little brother?" Lev asked, playfully punching him gently in the abdomen.

"We have time to make it to Jerusalem, and we might even have the good fortune to meet one of the Ancients. If there aren't too many visitors, they'll usually grant a short interview," Jake answered.

"We'll see, though—they've been especially busy these last few days because two new nations have asked to come under the authority of Christ and the New Covenant," Rachel added.

Lev ignored the comment about Messiah, as he so often did, and continued along the subject of the Ancients.

"I hope someone has time...they certainly seem to be exceptional people," Lev said as the group headed out the door. "By the way, what's the secret to locking up this house? Can't find the lock, and I don't have a set of keys."

"Dad, no one has locks or keys anymore," Allon explained. "They went the way of the fly swatter and the mosquito spray—you'll notice there aren't flies and mosquitos and no screens on the windows either. Crime doesn't happen here."

Lev shrugged, "Whatever," he mumbled, still unable to believe that this world was immune to thieves.

The four climbed into Jake's mini-van and buckled up. It was compact, yet comfortable.

"Quiet motor," Lev observed. "Bet this van can fly. There's probably no restriction on speed or speed limits."

"Not really, Lev. We operate our vehicles at lower speeds. There's no reason to be in a hurry and it creates less risk for accidents. Each car has sensors, so if something gets in the way, we automatically stop." Jake patted the dashboard of his van as if it were an old friend."

Lev shook his head with a smile. "Someone in this new world thinks of everything."

Conversation continued non-stop as they drove, and after a time they reached a hilltop from which they could glimpse the Beloved City. The entire landscape was covered with orchards and small homes. Occasionally they passed larger buildings.

"What are these buildings?" Lev wondered out loud.

"Those are factories. We have been taught to make the materials we need using the simplest and most efficient methods. We make clothing, building materials and other items that are needed in large quantities. The materials are made to last and are totally recyclable. Nothing is wasted," Jake answered.

Rachel continued. "As each nation joins Israel, the same procedures are followed. Everything is decentralized. Cities are turned into parks and forests. But people can visit small cities for specialized needs, like exhibits and cultural centers for the arts, museum and community needs."

What Entertainment Is There?

"So what do people do for entertainment?" Lev asked.

Rachel spoke up. "Did you know that in the old world the average housewife spent one-quarter of her waking hours watching television, and younger people watched from twenty to thirty-five hours a week? Unfortunately a lot of the programs and movies weren't a very positive influence."

Lev felt a twinge of embarrassment when he remembered the programs and movies he used to watch, and how completely out of place they would be in this new world. "I guess I was one of those couch potatoes—and I can tell you that I don't think I'd want to describe the content of what I watched to one of the Ancients."

"Well, now people work for about three hours a day—the rest of our time is free. There are lots of volunteer projects that people can join, and there are lots of skills and information to learn in order to help people return to their new life. Houses, furnishings, clothing, and equipment must be prepared to welcome people back," Allon responded enthusiastically. "There's no chance of getting bored!"

Rebekah continued. "And with Eden fruit our minds have amazing retention—in a matter of a few years we can actually develop a photographic memory. Every one of us can become a 'genius.'"

As the vehicle gradually ascended toward Jerusalem, the holy city came into view. "Around her heart my city carries a lonely ancient wall." Lev recited the words to *Jerusalem of Gold.* "This City of Peace is still ours," Lev said softly in a tone of wonder.

"All the combined forces of the world were not able to wrest it from us. The Lord secured it for us for his own glory, as a place to begin the worldwide blessing," Jake commented. He pointed out the buildings where the Ancients were housed. Lev expected some spectacular high-rise buildings, but instead he saw simple well kept, but very plain houses. Traffic was light and the sidewalks were not crowded with people.

Familiar with Old Jerusalem and its vulnerability in Israel of the old world, Lev posed a question. "Isn't there any police protection here? Aren't the Ancients vulnerable to terrorist attacks?"

"Dad, what makes you think they are unprotected? I would feel sorry for anyone who tried to lift a finger against any of them! You obviously don't understand yet—there are powerful spiritual forces that prevent anyone from hurting or destroying."

Lev made no comment.

They drove toward an information center, parked, and entered the building. Jake told the woman at the desk of their desire to have a few minutes with one of the Ancients. The woman spoke on the phone and smiled. "You are very fortunate. Isaac has time, and he will meet with you. He'll be here in just a few minutes."

"That's pretty amazing, that someone of such importance would be willing to take time from his busy schedule to meet unknown people." Lev spoke softly to the others.

"What do you wish to see me about?" a voice spoke to them from behind. Isaac walked up to the group of five and graciously extended his right hand to each of them. "Shalom," he said. "Whom am I addressing?" Isaac was a dark haired man with a wide infectious smile and a princely charm.

Jake had the presence of mind to speak. "My name is Jacob Aron, and this is my brother, Lev, who has just been raised. This is my former wife Rachel and Lev's former wife, Rebekah. May I also introduce Allon, Lev and Rebekah's son? We are showing Lev our new country and trying to help him believe that everything that has happened is more than a dream."

Isaac smiled, and Lev felt instantly comfortable. "Welcome back to Israel now and forever, Lev. I heard you were one of the last ones killed when all nations came against us. You fought bravely. I was raised from death, as were the other Ancients, just as you have been.

"I know how you feel, Lev," Isaac continued, as he looked intently into Lev's eyes, "because I felt the same way. The next day the Lord intervened and brought us deliverance. When I died I was a weak, old man. When I awakened, I was vibrant and full of energy with a perfect mind and body.

"The world we had come back to was in total chaos. We could not imagine how to bring order and peace to such a condition. We did not accomplish it on our own. I want you all to know that we were not the ones in charge.

"Christ and his Anointed were in power and in total control. We were in daily contact with them, as we are now, to receive information on how to proceed. Christ is the one who brought back peace to our Beloved City. It is more of a miracle than when God provided the lamb in my place in Mount Moriah. Though Christ has all power in heaven and earth, his communications with us are gentle, which reminds us that he *is* 'the Lamb of God.'"

Lev was spellbound in the presence of this man of God. He finally found his voice. "Thank you for allowing me to return again to the land of the living."

"All we did was schedule your return. Only Christ has the power to give life. He is the one to thank."

A New Volunteer

He felt strangely inspired and he found himself offering his services. "When may I volunteer for work? When may we begin preparing for our father's and mother's return?"

"On the 25th of May the senior Arons are scheduled to return. You will have ample time to build their homes and cultivate their gardens. If you wish to donate spare time to other projects, feel free to do so. All you have to do is watch for the information on television so that you may know how to proceed."

Then Isaac smiled and with a twinkle in his eye he said, "We do not allow any sick days here."

The small group laughed. Isaac shook their hands. "May God bless you and keep you. Shalom, my friends."

"Thank you," each one of them called out as Isaac turned and disappeared through the door he had entered.

Lev felt a sudden excitement in being part of this new world, in being part of this great restitution project that would begin for him with making preparations for his father and mother.

"Wow! That was incredible!"

As they walked to the van they continued to talk. Rebekah's voice was filled with excitement. "Isaac is amazing! It's just as exciting as the other times I have met with the Ancients! He talked to us like we were his equals. I could have listened to him talk all day."

"Did you notice his total recall? He told us the exact date of mother's and father's rising."

"And he knew about my experience on the battlefield," Lev added.

Jake joined in the excited conversation. "We just saw a perfect human mind at work. The Ancients received a 'better resurrection' than we—rose to perfection immediately because they had demonstrated their faithfulness in their previous life. It's no wonder that God has chosen them to be our leaders under Christ."

They took the scenic route home, as they discussed the lives of the Ancients and all they had been through. After a while Lev sank back in the van seat, lost in thought as he stared at the scenery as it changed from the regenerated Dead Sea now teeming with life, to the grandeur of the rocks and cliffs of Masada, to the miles of orchards, gardens and the occasional home cottages which replaced the dry, rocky terrain he remembered.

Lev looked forward to his visit to the factories and to his part in preparing for the return of his parents; though the more he thought of it, the more he wondered if he would get along with them once they were raised. His misgivings, however, were overpowered with the elation he felt to have met Isaac. He felt a greater measure of comfort in realizing how qualified the Ancients were to handle the authority they had been given, in view of their testing and experiences in the Old World.

Maybe with men of such caliber in charge, there was hope for the resolution of the many conflicts that would inevitably accompany this 'raising of billions' that he kept hearing about. But people like Hitler awakened? Who could imagine the reasoning of such a thing? And what kind of restraints could keep such people from committing violence in this new world? And when and under what circumstances would the tree of knowledge of good and evil be available?

"A bruised reed shall he not break"
(Isaiah 42:3).

Chapter Six

On the strength of a simple breakfast of freshly squeezed orange juice, carefully selected figs, dates and Eden fruit, and with the inspiration of the early morning Worship Service, Lev, Rebekah, Allon, Jake and Rachel left Lev's home for the factory the next morning.

"The factory is only a twenty minute walk from here, so we may as well use our legs," Jake said as he popped one last fig into his mouth. He led the procession, walking briskly. "By the way, I must compliment you on your selections for our breakfast." Jake directed his comment to Lev and smiled. "You have a knack for choosing *Olam* as it comes in season. The other fruits were at their peak of ripeness. I'm impressed, Lev."

"I can't take all the credit," Lev grinned as he quickened his step to keep up. "The fruit was God's idea, and I can't get over how much I like it. I don't have any craving for meat at all. But I guess I'm not in quite as good of shape as all of you are," he added breathlessly, as again he quickened his step. He had started out beside Jake, and now found himself struggling to keep up with Allon and Rachel in the back row of the little group.

Jake took the hint and slowed his pace. "We used to eat until we were full. Now we eat until we are *fulfilled*."

"God made this food to satisfy every fiber of our human appetite," Allon joined the conversation with no hint of shortness of breath. "Our biochemistry needs to be balanced to provide electrical energy. What we call being alive is when our electrical sensory impulses are alert and functioning."

"So when I died…" Lev spoke softly, thinking out loud.

"Your electrical sensory impulses ceased," Allon interrupted, excited to complete his explanation. "Only what God stored in His memory was retained. When you were raised, all those electrical impulses were restored to your newly created brain cells and God gave you a body that matched the blueprint of your genetic code."

Lev was fascinated. "So when I died, the electrical impulses ceased, and I know first hand what that was like—I was as 'dead as a doornail,' as they used to say—I knew nothing until three days ago," Lev mused, as another verse from Scripture came to his mind, "the dead know not anything" (Ecclesiastes 9:5). "And my mind actually feels more alive than ever before. I keep remembering verses that I only heard once or twice in my earlier years...."

"You'll feel a big difference in your body, too, as time goes on," Rebekah teased as she purposely picked up her pace from a walk—to a brisk walk—to a very brisk walk—to a run. She continued to talk effortlessly while in the lead, with Jake, Rachel and Allon who ran three abreast at her side. "You'll find that it is a pleasure to be physically active," she projected her voice loudly so that Lev who trailed behind could hear, "and to be involved in factory work, and other projects. But it's all up to you. You can sit around all day if you want to," she said as she looked back at him, her face flushed and her eyes bright.

Again Lev struggled to keep up with the seasoned sprinters of this new world. "I'm—not—one—to want—to sit—around," he said between heaving breaths. "I like—to keep busy—and I like—to be in shape—but do you think we can—slow down—and smell the Eden flowers?" Lev suddenly slowed his labored sprint, and the others immediately followed suit.

"Good try, Dad," Allon said as he patted his father on the back. "It's only a matter of time and Eden fruit until you will outrun us all."

"Yeah, right!" Lev said, still catching his breath. The slower pace gave Lev the opportunity to notice the groves of trees planted on marked plots. Some houses were completed and others were in the process. "So where's the lot for Mom and Dad?"

"We'll show you their estates soon. Look, Lev, there's a cottage being built by people who don't even know the people who will be living in it. I know the woman who's in charge of the project. I've worked with her at the factory," Rachel mentioned as she waved to a young woman who was inspecting a newly laid foundation.

"So what's up with the living family? Why aren't they helping out?" Lev asked.

"In the last generations divorce rates were high," Rebekah answered, "and trying to get children from broken homes to build for parents who had left them doesn't happen as easily as we would like. There are a lot of feelings to work through understandably. Parents who deserted or abused their children may not have children eager to receive them back. It's sad, but true. Volunteers must be found to prepare for those people."

"You would think that the regeneration process would be filled with joy…and it is, in part, but it's also filled with challenge—the challenge of facing ourselves and others, of being completely honest and making amends. The hurtful things people did live long after them. It takes determination, and the help of Messiah, to get them through it all so that they can become a better person," Rachel added.

Lev looked down at the ground as they walked on. He now believed in the Messiah, but he needed to know him more intimately. His family really believed in this Christ and his ability to reconcile, but he could not fathom it.

Factory Visit

"There's the factory, Dad." Allon pointed to a large building surrounded with an orchard grove of trees that provided a picnic area for the workers.

Lev noticed there was no security guard or receptionist. They walked right into the factory. Lev was immediately fascinated with the process he observed. Sand was brought on conveyors to a giant hydro-oxy furnace. When the temperature created molten glass, another conveyor brought ingredients that added color and necessary strength. The molten mixture was then poured into molds that created a hollow block and were sent by conveyer down the line for cooling. Then insulation was pumped into each block. Lev watched as the hardened product was placed on skids by eager workers and packaged for shipping.

"They sure seem to enjoy their work…but there's not that many of them." Lev looked around. "Where is everybody?"

"Actually, this plant only needs fifteen people to keep it running. Rebekah and I work in the office, and sometimes on the line, and sometimes we help pack the blocks for shipping."

"*You* load the blocks?" Lev asked as he looked from Rebekah to Rachel. "Isn't that a *man's* work?"

Rebekah flexed her arm to reveal a well-developed bicep. "Eden fruit is the answer! No, really we use equipment to load everything," she smiled.

"You two really are in good shape," Lev chuckled. "I think you could beat me in arm wrestling at this point," he added, not totally comfortable with this new insight. "So is this how things are done?" Lev questioned, to redirect the conversation in order to avoid his vague feeling of being threatened, as he saw another sign of the role changes in this different world.

Allon answered his father, aware of his discomfort. "In our area we have plenty of sand, so we make bricks of glass. The factory does the primary heating of sand overnight and in the morning we do the final touches and start production. We usually only work two to three hours a day, and then another shift takes over. Trucks carry the materials to the building sites. There are other factories that make the plumbing, heating and electrical components. Engineers visit the plant every month to teach us how to do the maintenance and help us keep things running smoothly."

As they continued their tour Lev wandered away from the four to watch the blocks in the molding process more closely.

"Fancy meeting you here, Lev," a voice said sarcastically. Lev's stomach tightened before he had time to place a name to the familiar voice that addressed him. His eyes narrowed as he turned and saw Reuben Meyer, a rival from his high school days. A flood of memories came back in an instant.

Lev remembered himself clearly in those old days. He was wiry and slightly clumsy, having not yet grown out of his adolescent awkwardness. He would often fly to his younger brother's defense out of fierce loyalty and as another way of proving himself and easing his sense of inferiority. He was shy and lacking in confidence where girls were concerned and his face reddened even now at the memory of his struggle to find himself. He adored Rebekah Obadiah at first sight, but could not bring himself to approach her in a serious way.

Reuben Meyer did not make it any easier on him. He had some vendetta against Lev that he had never understood.

When Reuben learned of his classmate's feelings for Rebekah, he played the charmer with her and he played the part well. He taunted Lev with his success. "So, Lev, how are *you* gonna spend your Saturday evening…want to come along with me and Becky?" And then he humiliated Lev before the whole school by setting it up to look like Lev had broken into the office and changed everyones grades on the computer register. Even Lev's parents believed Reuben's story.

In his last year of high school, Lev became more aggressive and sure of himself. He avoided Reuben and Rebekah. That summer he joined the military even when conscription was no longer automatic because of the deceptive peace Israel seemed to enjoy. He and Rebekah became serious about each other at the Hebrew University four years later, but the anger and humiliation he felt over what Reuben Meyer had done to him still burned in his heart.

"I heard you were killed in that first battle against the invaders." Lev was sure he detected a hint of sarcasm in his voice.

"Yes, that's right." Lev felt annoyed and it showed in his face and tone.

"Still mad at me, huh?" Reuben stood there and grinned. He took a step toward Lev and spoke in a quiet voice.

"So, how's Rebekah? Guess neither of us gets her in *this* world…"

Lev's jaw twitched and he tightened his fist.

"So is it a win-win or a lose-lose?" Reuben questioned Lev. "Still having trouble standing up for yourself, hey, Lev?"

Lev's First Consequence

Lev's arm swung with all the strength of his anger behind it, and he was startled when it made no satisfying connection. His arm had suddenly gone limp. He stared at his lifeless right hand, and turned quickly away.

"See ya, Lev." Reuben called out as Lev quickly exited the room.

"He got me in trouble again," Lev thought. "He knew this would happen, and he did it just to get me." Lev was so consumed with anger over his arm that dangled helplessly by his side when he bumped headlong into Rebekah.

"Lev, what happened?" Rebekah questioned.

"Reuben Meyer." Lev replied.

"I should have warned you, Lev. Look at your arm."

Lev looked embarrassed. "I lost my temper and tried to flatten him. Guess this is one of the New Earth consequences you wouldn't tell me about."

"I knew you'd experience it for yourself, just like we all have. Grudges don't die easy."

"I don't get it. Nothing happened to Reuben," Lev said with a feeling of injustice. "He knew very well this would happen and I'm the one being punished."

"Your consequence is for *your* reaction. Don't worry about Reuben," Rebekah tried to sooth Lev. "No one will get away with anything in the end. He obviously has not repented of his past deeds. Give him time. He was raised just recently, and there are a lot of issues he needs to face. But he has a lot of time to own up to his misdeeds—at least one hundred years."

"Now what do I do?" Lev looked down at his arm and felt embarrassment. "I thought I was starting to make a little New Earth progress, and now look at me," he said more to himself than to Rebekah.

"Lev," Rebekah gently lifted his head to bring his eyes from his arm to her face. "You need to call the office of the Ancients. You need to tell them the truth. They will know exactly what happened when they confer with Christ. They will probably talk with Reuben also." Rebekah pressed the "A" for the pre-programmed number and handed the cell phone over to Lev.

Lev held the phone to his ear with his good hand and stepped out of the building and sat at one of the picnic tables. When a voice answered, "Office of the Ancients, how can I help you?" Lev took a deep breath.

"Uh … my hand is … unusable and … I need to talk to one of the Ancients."

He was told to hold on for a minute.

"Shalom, this is Sarah, how may I help you?"

Lev took another deep breath and felt even more embarrassed as he pictured the beautiful stately Sarah, former wife of Abraham whom he had seen on TV. "My name is Lev Aron, and I am ashamed to say that on my third day of life, I tried to deck an old enemy."

"Tell me about it," Sarah's voice had no note of condemnation in it. "I want the whole truth. Be brief. Be honest. Tell me what happened today, and give me a summarized history of the past, so that I may know whether you were reacting to an old injustice that was done to you. Of course, you realize that we do not determine the truth ourselves. It is Christ or one of his Anointed that will inform us of this matter."

Lev repeated to Sarah Reuben's provoking comments and the memories that came flooding back to his mind. He tried to be honest in his account, and he felt nervous to think that these Ancients had access to a Messiah he only began to know, as well as a complete history of his past.

"I'm sorry for what I did—well, actually, I still kind of wish that my punch had connected—and I'm sorry that I'm not totally sorry—and that's the truth."

"Thank you, Lev Aron. If everything you have told me is true, your arm will be restored within the hour. You will appreciate the process of healing as it happens. You do sound troubled, and I want to assure you, 'a bruised reed shall he not break,' words from my dear friend Isaiah. This is all part of the process of growing up into this new world. May God bless you."

Lev sat at the picnic table lost in his thoughts. Soon his family joined him.

"So, Dad, I hear you tried to spar with the enemy. I remember my first consequence quite well, and it wasn't my last." Allon gave his father a playful shove on the shoulder, as he sat down by him.

"We've all been through it, Lev, and we'll all have other corrections in the future. It's just a matter of learning a new way of thinking, and a matter of the building up of character. You're either building character or destroying it. Reputation is what people think we are. Character is what we really are. God and Christ know the difference." Jake gave his brother an understanding look, and each of them in turn shared a consequence and how it had affected their lives.

"It's embarrassing and it's awkward," Lev said as he stared at his hand. The first time he lost his hand was in battle and the second time...he smiled to himself. "Guess I lost this hand in a different kind of battle."

After a refreshing lunch the rest of the afternoon was spent in the factory so that Lev could become thoroughly familiar with the whole procedure. He noticed a tingling in his right arm shortly after the discussion on consequences, and very soon much of his ability to move his arm and his wrist had returned. By the time they left his fingers were fully restored to their agility.

Lev was quiet on the walk home. For the first time since he was raised, he was grateful to return to his empty, quiet house. He wanted time to think.

He sat on a bench in the garden he loved, puzzling over the resentment that he still clung to. He ate some Eden fruit for his evening meal, aware that he needed both its healing and life-giving support.

He stared at the luxuriant greenness that surrounded him and found he was talking aloud.

"I don't know why I have this burning anger. I've tried to let go of it, but it comes back to haunt me. I don't really want anger in my heart; for I know it is very destructive." The ring of the phone interrupted his thoughts.

Reuben's Apology

Lev walked quickly to the kitchen phone. "Hello?"

"Shalom…" There was a long pause and Lev uncomfortable as he recognized the voice.

"I'm calling because Sarah of the Ancients warned me that my behavior today was not acceptable, especially since I had done harm to you some years ago. She told me that I must apologize for my past and present behavior. So I apologize." Then he hung up.

Lev shook his head slowly, stunned as he placed the receiver on the phone base. "Well, that was an interesting apology," he said with a hint of humor in his tone. "I wonder if that was a sincere apology, because it seemed so artificial to me." He went to pick up a pen with his right hand, and realized that his hand was actually all restored.

"Healed hand, unhealed heart," Lev realized, and he felt a deep pang of regret. He walked to his bedroom feeling thankful for the complete healing of his hand, but felt that his anger had not been dealt with yet. If he didn't gain a victory over his anger it would cause him more trouble to be sure. He knelt down by the bed. "God, my right hand is restored, but not my character. I think I've really failed under the test."

Sarah's voice came to his mind. "A bruised reed he will not break," she had quoted from her 'dear friend, Isaiah.'

A Bruised Reed

Lev felt tears well up in his eyes. He felt like a bruised reed, weak and vulnerable to his own anger and hurt. He resolved to exercise a greater discipline in his life hereafter. "I have got to take charge of my emotions. While anger will always rise in given circumstances, I don't have to allow it free reign."

Then Jake's words spoken on the first evening of Lev's new life came vividly to mind. "He is not the Christ taught by the burning hell-fire and brimstone preachers, but he is Jesus the Messiah who comes to reconcile and bless our people and all nations. He did not reveal himself to us to bring recriminations against us, but to free us."

Lev sensed the length and depth and height and breadth of the love of God to provide his Son, and of the love of the Son to willingly give his life; and he could find no words.

Lev remembered his own thoughts on the first day of his new life. This business about laying life on the line for faith was a battle of sorts…Christ the Messiah had faced the battle. His followers had.

And now he also, was engaged in a battle...and he had to choose his allegiance.

Grasping the light quilt and sheet firmly in both hands, Lev pulled them down and still fully clothed, crept into bed. A quiet peace came over him as he thought of the events of the day. He was learning slowly to mend his ways. He decided he was going to learn from this and all of his experiences, since only a fool refuses to learn.

"I will instruct thee and teach thee
in the way which thou shalt go..."
(Psalm 32:8).

Chapter Seven

Rebekah awakened from sleep not fully refreshed. She had spent the evening in meditation and prayer thinking about the need to confess her first indiscretion to Lev. He had such a good heart but this would be hard for him to deal with. The confrontation with Reuben had been difficult enough for him but now to deal with her past indiscretion would be adding another burden. In her former life together she had purposely avoided telling him of her abortion because she didn't have the courage to do so. She kept putting it off hoping it would go away. She hesitated to tell him now, for she still did not have the courage to confess the sin of her past.

Rebekah stood in the middle of her garden refuge, garden basket in hand, and took a deep breath. She loved the feel of the cool grass beneath her bare feet. She let her eyes trace the silver branches and felt a sense of awe as she gathered the Eden fruit that had become ripe. Gathering fruit for the day had become a religious experience for her. The food taken from the trees of her Creator reminded her of her indebtedness to Him and of His constant provision and wisdom. The Eden trees were a testimony of the love of God and Christ. They provided vitalizing nourishment that satisfied human hunger completely. They gradually, yet powerfully balanced the energy systems of the body, so that health and balanced thinking became available to all. She never tired of the time spent in her garden orchard.

Her love for green and growing things was part of the heritage handed down to her by her parents Benjamin and Deborah Obadiah. They had developed their natural talent for horticulture in the New

Earth, and their services were known and appreciated by all who ate Eden fruit. These trees were part of their expression of love to her and to the human family, as they were in charge of the largest groves and shipments of Eden trees in the world.

"This is a day that you have made," she spoke softly, and then took a bite of the sweet fruit from the small harvest in her garden basket. "I am afraid, but I must do the right thing."

This Is the Day

Rebekah watched Lev closely during the worship service that morning. He seemed different. She watched his expression as the leader read from the Psalms.

"Blessed is he whose transgressions are forgiven,

Whose sins are covered.

Blessed is the man whose sin the LORD does not count against him

And in whose spirit there is no deceit."

His eyes, so full of adventure and life, closed, and he tilted his face toward heaven, and smiled. Rebekah's heartbeat quickened and she smiled also. She knew immediately that he was at peace with the Messiah.

"Great service, don't you think?" The service had ended, and Lev playfully tousled Allon's hair.

Allon looked at his father in confusion. These were not the same stumbling comments he had heard from his father before. "Yeah, Dad, it was."

"You know, I'm enjoying my seven day orientation to this New Earth agenda, but I'm starting to feel a little guilty. I'm on my fourth day and I haven't really gotten my hands dirty, as they used to say. There's so much to do, and I want to do my part. We've got to start building for my parents, and then who knows what. There are courses to be learned, and animals that need training, and there's—"

Rebekah placed her hand over Lev's mouth. "Slow down, Lev. The Eden fruit must be working. Take one thing at a time. Let's catch up with Jake and Rachel and plan the day." Rebekah pointed outside the worship ground to Jake and Rachel who waved as Rebekah, Lev and Allon made their way toward them.

As they walked together toward the house, Allon cleared his throat. "I have an announcement to make. I have been asked by one of the Ancients—Enoch, to be exact—to go to Ghana, Africa. They need some volunteers to help build factories, survey land, plant trees and organize housing. Since I've done all these things already, he said I would be well qualified for this assignment."

Lev looked at his son and gave him a pat on the back. "I'll miss you, Allon. I just got to see you, and now you're traipsing off to a far away place.... If I work hard at my studies and learn modern technologies, maybe I'll be able to join you. But I have so much to learn. You're a lucky young man."

Worry About Snakes

"I feel excited about the assignment, except for the deadly snakes. I heard that the mamba snake couldn't be out-run. I'm just trusting that when Christ says 'nothing will hurt or destroy' that it includes the animal world."

"I bet Annie would like to go with you, Allon, as soon as she finishes her classes. She was always rather fascinated with snakes," Jake said.

"All she needs is a little more building and surveying experience and she'll be ready to join our overseas services," Allon observed. "And I'll take her natural ability to deal with animals anytime."

After breakfast they decided to walk to the institute of technology where Jake volunteered. Jake took the small group to his department first.

Lev was amazed to see how far advanced computer science had come. Computers were even smaller, faster and very stable. They no longer crashed.

"I suppose these computers are immune to old world disease," Lev said with a smile. "You put Eden fruit somehow into the motherboard, right?"

"Well, not exactly, but you're getting the idea, Dad. There are no computer viruses and no hackers."

"You won't believe the improvements, Lev. I helped design the chip that is coming off the line." Jake pointed to the window that housed a room that was dust free and climate controlled. "Many of these computers are being sent to Ghana with Allon."

"Ghana will be turning out their own computers in a year or so." Allon saw his father raise his eyebrows in disbelief. "Really, Dad, progress comes quickly when a nation comes under the authority of the Ancients. The poverty that still exists around the world will be easily reversed once they receive Eden fruit and are taught basic building skills. The main obstacle is that nations do not choose to come under the authority of the Ancients."

"So what's the problem? Isn't Eden fruit enough reason for nations to cooperate?"

"Some nations are really hesitant to seek help from Israel. Old world prejudice and pride are in the way," Rachel offered.

Lev shook his head. The scripture said that Messiah would not falter or become discouraged, but it sounded like a discouraging and demanding task to him.

Jake informed the small group that the plant's efficiency made it possible to easily provide the area with all the computer and electrical housing components needed. "This allows us to send equipment to other countries just coming on line. Hopefully, in three years the whole world will be equipped."

Jake continued to explain that the automated equipment for this factory was produced in a plant up north and that Ghana would have all the materials needed to set up several factories shipped next week. "It'll take a year to have a factory like this running at full capacity in Ghana. Allon will help set them up, and the people will be trained to operate and maintain them."

"That's pretty amazing," Lev commented.

"The mechanical and temporal things needed for those who are raised are the easy part. Getting people to change their thinking—the heart of stone for a heart of flesh—that's the real challenge."

The Hebrew Language

Lev thought of his own loss of temper on the previous day and turned red. "Have to agree with that one. So, Allon," he spoke quickly to divert attention away from his embarrassment, "How will you manage the language problem?"

Allon explained that at first they would need interpreters. Thanks to his photographic memory due to Eden fruit, he would easily learn their language, and the Ghanans would learn a modernized version of Hebrew that used a modern alphabet to make it more readable and Arabic numerals and the decimal system.

"Hebrew? All the nations are learning Hebrew? I can't imagine someone like Hitler coming back goose stepping around and clicking his heels together while trying to speak Hebrew!" Lev found his attempt at humor to be rather awkward. "Isn't it about time to eat something?" he said faintly. He was once again in the position of wanting to avoid something that made him uncomfortable.

Ms. Millie

Lev and the family joined a picnic table of friendly people in the midst of lively conversation.

"I had a nervous breakdown and committed suicide." A woman spoke freely. "I was so depressed that I was not able to have children, and my husband and his family despised me for it. My husband left me for a younger woman. Nothing could reach me in my despair and feeling of failure, not even my second husband. It was all I could take."

Lev looked at the vibrancy and happiness that emanated from this woman. "But you look so happy—Miss—or Mrs. —," Lev fumbled for words.

"Millie is my name," the young woman laughed. "That's because I am truly happy, Mr. —Mr. —," she teased.

"Mr. Aron. Mr. Lev Aron." Lev smiled in return.

"Some people I didn't even know helped me through it once I was raised, and I was introduced to one of the Ancients, Hannah, who also bore the grief of barrenness and a second wife who gloated over the fact that she had had children. I made peace with Messiah in my heart, and I found strength and joy that I had never known before. And he blessed me as Hannah was blessed. Frank and I are raising a child who was given up for adoption by her teenage mother in a nation that was reticent to come under the Ancients." Millie smiled again. "I love this child with all my heart. I could not have experienced this depth of joy if I had not experienced such bitter disappointments. My first husband and his wife are to be raised in about a month, and Frank and I are preparing for them."

Lev stared at Millie in disbelief. "A heart of stone to a heart of flesh," he whispered to himself. It was his first real insight into a miraculous process he could not have imagined—the joy of gladness exchanged for the sackcloth of mourning. This was the power of Messiah before his very eyes, and he felt overwhelmed.

"Thank you, 'Ms. Millie,'" Lev said as he extended his hand.

"Mr. Lev Aron," Millie said as she clasped his hands in both of her hands, "You are so welcome."

Rebekah's Secret

Lev stared at Rebekah from across the table of her kitchen. A candle cast a flickering glow about her face. They had just finished a simple dinner, and Lev had hardly paused for breath in his excitement over the events of the day. Their own son Allon was going to Ghana. Computers had been revolutionized, and in three years the newest technology in computers would be available throughout the world. He could not stop talking about 'Ms. Millie' and the transformation that had happened in her life. "Ms. Millie is amazing to me. She destroyed her life out of despair, and look at her now. She is a radiant woman raising that baby and there is no trace of bitterness in her. I just can't believe it. She and Frank are actually preparing for the return of her selfish husband and his second wife...."

Rebekah burst into tears. Lev was silent. He suddenly realized that he had been doing all the talking. He reached for her hand. "Rebekah, what's wrong?"

Rebekah stared at Lev's hand, placed over her own. "I have something to tell you, Lev, something about my past."

"You can tell me, Rebekah. I promise I'll stop talking long enough for you to say whatever you need to say..." Rebekah smiled slightly through her tears.

"I know this is the time to tell you this, especially after hearing Millie's experiences this afternoon." Rebekah sniffled and removed her hands from Lev's. "You never knew that I had an affair as a teenager. And I became pregnant. And then I aborted the baby." Rebekah tried to speak through her sobs, "And—the baby will not be—raised, because it was—aborted before the quickening of the embryo."

Rebekah hid her face in her hands, and continued to weep. "That child—could have life—if I had not destroyed it. Millie is caring for a baby that was deserted at birth. But the embryo I—aborted—will never know life."

Lev felt barraged by emotion. He watched his beloved Rebekah in silence and tried to think of something to say that would be comforting. He finally spoke.

"It must have been hard for you, Rebekah, to keep this in your heart for all those years. I knew you were a 'free spirit' back then. I'm sorry that this is so hard for you now, especially knowing the child will not live."

Rebekah wiped her eyes with her hands and looked across the table at Lev. "I thought I was exercising freedom when I was being actually immoral. Hormones drove me and I fell into temptation. My immoral conduct led to an even greater sin. And none of it had anything to do with freedom. I used freedom as an excuse to get what I wanted, and in the end it caused great pain, and prevented a fetus from coming to birth."

Lev stood up, walked over to Rebekah, reached for her hand and pulled her to her feet. He led her to the sofa and sat by her, his arm around her, in the quiet of the evening.

"You know, Rebekah, I have accepted the Messiah and at last have been reconciled to him. Godly sorrow results in repentance and repentance that result in carefulness and an endeavor to cleanse one. And that's what I see in your life. Worldly sorrow doesn't work that way but brings discouragement and pain."

After a long while, Rebekah spoke again. She sounded tired and drained. "Thank you, Lev, for listening. But there's one more thing I need to tell you." She hesitated, "The father of my child was Reuben Meyer."

Lev could not speak. He touched the smooth skin of his forehead where a scar could no longer be found and felt the pressure of his own secrets he did not yet wish to openly express. He was in turmoil of jealousy and humiliation as the memories of Reuben's vindictiveness returned to his mind. And then a great sadness swept over him. He did not know how to reconcile his sorrow for Rebekah with his outrage over this new instance of Reuben's intrusion into his life. He sat quietly by Rebekah's side for a long while, and then he stood up. "I better go home, Rebekah. I'm too tired to think." He made his way to the door and disappeared into the night.

"Make me to hear joy and gladness;
That the bones which thou hast broken may rejoice"
(Psalm 51:8).

Chapter Eight

Lev tossed and turned all night—wrestling with the secret Rebekah had confided in him—and with the secret he had never confessed to her. The thought of Reuben and Rebekah made his stomach churn. But he knew deep inside that one confession deserved another. He had not told Rebekah of his first marriage that ended in tragedy. Lev had never told Rebekah about Anya.

In frustration Lev turned on his computer and started aimlessly surfing the web. He tried to review the latest developments in the new nations that had accepted Messiah's rule. But he couldn't concentrate on anything. Then Lev opened the Resurrection site that listed names of individuals and the scheduled dates for their raising. He searched the long list for a familiar name.

Lev's eyes froze. "Anya Stein Aron." He stared at the letters of the name with a blank look, and then read on. Anya Stein would be resurrected in six months. The brief biographical note said: "Russian Jew, civilian, killed in military ambush in Jericho by Hamas terrorists on June 15."

"Anya," Lev whispered with a look of anguish on his face as he nervously rubbed his forehead. He had not spoken that name since her tragic death had occured. In an emotional awakening, Lev recalled the beautiful dark eyes that came with the name "Anya."

Lev had consciously determined to set aside her memory. He had refused to dwell on her death or to speak of it to anyone. He leaned over the computer table, his hands holding his head.

A Night of Darkness

In the summer of his eighteenth year after joining the military, Lev had fallen in love with her by a chance meeting. Anya was a fledgling journalist for the *Jerusalem Times,* and he was a private in the military. They had married after a short courtship.

Lev had placed his light olive green military jacket on her shoulders just as she was leaving for Jerusalem. She was on her way to pick up the final draft of an article she had been working on with another journalist and to visit her sick sister.

"Don't drive back tonight, Anya, it's too dangerous at night." Lev stopped her as she was about to leave the house, held her shoulders and looked solemnly into her eyes.

"Don't worry, love, I won't drive alone. I'll be careful. I just don't want to be away from you a minute more than I have to."

"Anya—please—"

Anya interrupted his plea with a quick kiss and left the house.

Several hours had passed, and Lev remembered the feeling of anxiety that came over him. He phoned her journalist friend.

Maya's voice was concerned.

"She left an hour and a quarter ago," Lev said, "just before dark. She should have been in Jericho by now."

Lev ran out and rushed into his car, and his tires threw gravel as he sped out of his driveway. He drove fast through East Jerusalem toward Jericho. He watched closely along the winding road for signs of anything that might lead him to Anya. The Jericho-Jerusalem road seemed even more steep and winding at night. Cliffs towering on either side seemed like ominous sentinels. He drove faster than he should have around the curves, narrowly missing an oncoming car. And then he saw something that made his heart pound hard.

On the side of the road, in a canyon-like area, Lev saw the vague outline of three twisted vehicles. He stomped on the brakes and spun to a stop. He grabbed a flashlight from the glove compartment and ran to the wreckage. The small light revealed torn bodies, some burned by firebombs and some riddled with bullets. As he reached the third vehicle he saw a fourth.

His heart sank when he saw Anya's blue Blazer. It was riddled with bullet holes. The windshield was shattered. It had been stopped from further descent down the canyon slope by a huge boulder. Lev frantically pointed his light to the interior of the car. Blood, scattered papers and shards of glass were everywhere. He searched the ground on the other side of the car and fell to his knees. Anya's clothes lay at his feet, torn and bloody, and his coat was sliced through with a clean cut. "Nooooo!" he moaned, as he drew the bloodied clothing into his hands and buried his head in them. He imagined the beautiful dark eyes of his Anya, filled with fear. His eyes desperately searched the area for her body, but to no avail.

"Noooooo," he cried out again, his voice hoarse from sobbing. Lev knelt there for what seemed like a long time. And then suddenly he stood up and rushed back to his car, quickly calling the army and was assured they were on the way. On an impulse he decided to go farther down the road to find the one who did such a thing to his beloved. He drove faster than he should have on the curvy road, but he was a good driver. As he rounded the next curve Lev struck a sharp object in the road that blew his right front tire and caused him to lose control of his vehicle. Nothing he could do would remedy his situation as the car careened off the road. He saw boulders, trees, heard a deafening crash, and then there was nothing but blackness.

A Silent Memory

Lev's whole body ached when he awakened. He was in a hospital with a head injury. While in the hospital he was tormented by his last memories of Anya. He could not bear to think of what happened to her. Once at home and still in shock, he packed away Anya's things mechanically. His gruff responses to friends and family in regard to anything related to that night warded off any mention of her.

Lev recovered very slowy from the trauma of his accident, too slowly to return to duty in his remaining time of service. He therefore plunged himself into engineering studies at Hebrew University, taking the most difficult classes he could find. He disciplined himself physically by exercise trying to regain former strength.

Later Lev met Rebekah again while at the University.

He worked at leaving his painful thoughts in the shadows, and never spoke Anya's name outloud until just moments ago. The only outward sign of the trauma he bore was the scar that had branded his forehead. Now there remained only a scar in his heart from the memory that he had chosen to push aside.

Lev walked to the kitchen and made himself a cup of resurrection tea. He slumped into a kitchen chair and drank it gratefully, as he stared into space at nothing in particular. He felt his body relax and his heartbeat returned to normal.

He was exhausted, but could not sleep. What would it be like for Anya to be raised after experiencing such a brutal end to her life? What would it be like for Rebekah? Finally, he reached for the phone and called her.

"Rebekah—sorry to wake you up, I have something to tell you."

Facing the Pain

Rebekah waited for Lev in the predawn light of morning. She felt the cool morning breezes as she stood by the open front door of her house. Rebekah watched Lev slowly walk toward her home. His expression told her that he was troubled.

"Lev, what's wrong?" Rebekah spoke as soon as Lev reached the doorway. Lev placed his hands on both her shoulders and drew her close to him.

"I need to talk to you."

Rebekah took him by the hand and led him to the sofa.

"How about some resurrection tea?" he asked weakly.

"Done!" she stated, pouring the already brewed into two cups on an end table by the sofa.

Lev drank the tea, leaned back and closed his eyes. He took a deep breath and sighed. "Rebekah," he began, "I have one regret about this new life I've been given. When we're raised, our mind has the ability to remember every memory we've ever experienced. I guess we also have the ability to avoid the pain of a memory. That's what I've been doing since the day of my return."

Rebekah's eyes were fastened on Lev as she listened carefully to his every word. She knew that he was sharing something deeply important.

He repeated the name on the resurrection list that gripped his mind the moment he saw it. "Anya Aron." He repeated the brief description that followed, "Russian Jew, killed in an ambush in Jericho by Hamas terrorists on June 15." And then slowly, Lev described his first wife Anya and her visit to Jericho. He recounted his anxiety over the lateness to arrive and his panicked drive over the winding Jerusalem-Jericho road. How he had found three cars, all bombed and shot up and the bloodied and mangled bodies, the only witnesses to what had happened dead.

Lev rubbed his forehead then squeezed his temples with the same hand, trying to continue, barely able to speak.

"I found her car—her blue Blazer—just a short way down the slope—full of bullet holes—glass everywhere, and blood—and I looked for her—and all I could find—" he paused, and Rebekah placed her hand over his shoulder. "All I could find were—her clothes—ripped, blood—" Lev broke down into uncontrollable sobs.

"I'm listening, Lev." Rebekah's voice was soft and understanding.

"And there was a—long straight rip across the jacket I gave her to wear—and I knew—that it was my fault—"

"I gave her my coat—" Lev continued with a strained voice that sounded higher than normal. "The terrorist saw the coat—the military insignia on it—and he took out his rage on the Israeli military—on her—."

"Oh, Lev, how horrible," Rebekah said as tears spilled over her eyes.

"I couldn't bring myself to talk about it. I was angry—I don't know at whom—Hamas, the world, maybe even a hidden anger with God. And I felt so guilty. I insulated myself from the pain, by running away from my memories and by my own stubbornness. Maybe I didn't want to face the pain because I couldn't."

Rebekah finally spoke again. "I think I may know a part of this story," she offered quietly. "You must have driven back in search of the terrorists and gotten into a car accident yourself. Your family gave me the scarcest of explanations after you and I started dating. I knew you had a scar on your forehead and scars on your heart. I knew you lost your first wife in some tragedy, but I never asked you. They warned me not to bring up anything about it to you. I am so sorry," she said.

"But, Lev, please listen to me," Rebekah pleaded amid her own tears. "It was not your fault. You are not responsible for the rage that poisoned that man's heart. You loved her, and you gave her your coat so she would be warm. That's all."

Lev said nothing in response. Rebekah could see he was exhausted, and she continued to hold him, as he lay slumped over the arm of the sofa. Rebekah tried to picture the dark-eyed Anya that Lev had loved so deeply. She cried for his anguish of memory and for his inability to face his pain. She cried for Anya's last brutal moments—Anya, who was to be resurrected in six months.

"Oh Lord," she silently cried, "I pray not only for Lev, but for myself. Make me ready to welcome Anya, the first woman that Lev ever loved. Make me willing to comfort her."

Darkness Comes Over Me, My Rest A Stone

Rebekah stole away quietly so as not to awaken Lev, showered and dressed and gathered Eden fruit from her garden orchard. She slowly walked to the worship service, lost in thought and prayer while she munched on the remaining piece of fruit. She sat on the bench, present and yet far away, seeking for a way to comfort Lev, a way to comfort herself, and a way to face Anya. Rebekah returned home with a renewed sense that this life would have many new and "beginning again" experiences that would be beautiful and that would enlarge her heart.

Lev awakened to the sweet aroma of freshly made tea. He felt as if he had forgotten something important. He walked to the kitchen, irresistibly drawn by the promise of Eden food and in anticipation of a conversation with Rebekah.

She was seated at the table, waiting for him. He took his place at the table. "I missed worship service," he announced with a voice that sounded still half asleep. He felt his stomach tighten, startled by the realization of what he had said earlier. "And I told you about Anya, didn't I?"

Rebekah smiled. "Yes, on both accounts. I let you sleep," she said as she poured out servings of resurrection tea.

"Yes, Lev, and some thoughts occurred to me as I was wrestling with your revelations and with mine. The Lord knows how to bring hope to every extreme experience, and he knows how to still the turmoil for you, for me and for Anya. This is nothing new that has happened to you and to me, and all these experiences will bring us to a larger place."

Lev simply nodded. They prayed silently and remained silent until they finished their late breakfast.

"I'll hang in there, Rebekah. I feel better. Not quite so overwhelmed. And it's got to be hard for you. But you'll hang in there, too."

Rebekah and Lev moved to the sofa. He looked at his former wife, barely able to contain his feelings, and smiled. "I really love you, Rebekah." Her radiant smile echoed the same words back to him. She leaned on his arm and closed her eyes and smiled in a long and comfortable silence.

Lev finally spoke. "I am amazed at our relationship now, and how deeply I feel for you. I am more deeply in love with you than I was even in the former days, but it's..."

"Different," Rebekah added. "And it feels so right and so good to have you as my friend." Rebekah continued. "It has to do with the resurrection change and Eden fruit. Our sexuality becomes dormant when we eat it. It wasn't until Adam and Eve ate of the forbidden fruit that their sexuality became awakened."

"Hmmm, never thought about it—the tree of knowledge of good and evil.... makes sense. After they ate it they realized they were naked."

Rebekah went on. "That tree was put there to control human sexuality. If Adam and Eve hadn't sinned, people would have lived forever and they wouldn't want to have children indefinitely, because eventually the earth would have been filled. Procreation would have been controlled by abstaining from the fruit of the tree of knowledge of good and evil and just eating Eden fruit."

"Maybe young men and women were meant to awaken their sexuality only when they were emotionally and spiritually ready for such a commitment." Lev sighed. "That sure would have avoided a lot of heartache and problems in the world we used to live in..."

"I'm just happy to be on this New Earth with you, Lev, with a new sense of why I'm here."

"Me too. And I don't feel like I'm missing out on anything. I'm satisfied, and I'm grateful." Lev and Rebekah were silent, content to listen to the birds that had begun to chirp, and content to lean on one another, barely aware when sleep stole upon them.

Later that morning the ring of the phone awakened them. Rebekah was the first to find it wedged between the sofa pillows.

"Hello?"

"Rebekah, this is Dad. When are you bringing Lev to visit our Eden tree farm?"

"I will allure her, and bring her into the wilderness,
And speak comfortingly unto her.
And I will give her her vineyards from thence,
And the valley of Achor [trouble] for a door of hope"
(Hosea 2:14, 15).

Chapter Nine

Benjamin Obadiah awakened just as the sun began to transform the early morning darkness into pre-dawn hints of color and light. He surveyed the acres of land that surrounded his humble cottage, land that had been entrusted to his care by His Creator. His attachment to Eretz Israel seemed to run in his blood. His Obadiah forebearer had been one of the earliest settlers of *Petah Tikvah* in 1878. With sheer will and determination and the sweat of his hands, this wiry young man had cultivated and built up a land when there was no precedent of modern agricultural success. With a shovel in one hand and gun in the other, he was ready to defend the land that he believed the God of Abraham had given him. He endured the rigors of pioneer life and built the first kibbutz in Israel. It had remained intact even through the final trouble. This land had become a *'Door of Hope,'* true to its Hebrew name.

Five generations later, Benjamin had been born and raised in Petah Tikvah, where he grew to love the land and thrived on his Great Great Grandfather's passion. In his early twenties he married Deborah, a strong woman who studied horticulture with him at the University and who wanted to live her life at his side helping green life grow in Israel.

Now the moment he had been waiting for arrived. Deborah had walked over to his estate at this early morning hour to join him, as she so often did, so that they could watch together in awe as the early morning purples and pinks heralded the rise of the golden sun over the land. They watched the sun begin to gradually pour out its golden light, row-by-row, and line-by-line upon the distant acres of fruit trees that grew uniformly and rather closely together. This moment of morning light shining on the life giving Eden trees made Benjamin's heart soar.

Benjamin and his wife Deborah were one of the first to be directly contacted by the Ancients soon after the final battle. From the moment he tasted the *Olam* and *Rapha* fruits of Eden, he felt he had tasted the God-ordained destiny for his life. His love for the earth, for the water and for the sun, and for the miracle of life had been the passion of his former life. He was known for his ability to grow fruit trees and flowers. He made them flourish by the love in his voice and the intuitive wisdom of his pruning hand. "Ah, little one, I see you are struggling to grow. Here, I will help you." He talked to his trees as naturally as he talked to his God.

The Mission of Eden Trees

The scope of his mission took his breath away; just as witnessing the sun's healing ascent on the acres of Eden trees took his breath away. The original invitation came from Abraham himself. It was to be his honor and privilege to cultivate the Eden trees and to share this perfect nourishment with the nations. Each sunrise reminded him of the work of the Christ—filling the darkness of the world with light and life. And he, Benjamin Obadiah, was chosen to play a small part in the sharing of the blessings that the Lord had bestowed on the land of Israel, the joy to be shared throughout all the earth.

He would never forget his first meeting with the Ancients. They were kind and gentle, and yet they spoke with complete authority. He had expected men with long white beards and women with gray hair and faces that were weathered and mature. But they were young, poised and brilliant, and they greeted him and his wife with warm handshakes and a hearty "Shalom."

"Two years…in two years the trees will be ready to be shipped and planted in the whole world. They will bear fruit quickly." Abraham's voice was strong. He described a way to accelerate the growth of the hearty seeds, with the use of growing tanks and a controlled atmosphere of heat and New Earth soil nutrients.

"This project is a top priority for it holds the key to the reviving and healing for countless millions. Your project will be one of many. Hundreds of millions of trees will be started each year." Abraham had pointed to clay pots that lay at his feet. "Each kind of seed has been preserved for over six thousand years. They are each specially marked. The most important seeds are the *Olam* trees of life.

The next moment was indelibly impressed upon Benjamin's mind. Abraham looked at him straight in the eye, and his voice had become almost stern. "No one is permitted to take any of these seeds home or to plant them or to send them to anyone anywhere without our instruction. Violation of any of these instructions will result in immediate consequences. Your assignment is vital to the work of regeneration. Benjamin, do you understand the responsibility we are entrusting you with?"

"Yes," Benjamin had answered. "I understand. We shall do our utmost to fulfill your trust in us." Deborah had solemnly nodded her assent.

The sun had started to pour its golden rays across his ten thousand acres of orchards as far as his eye could see. Deborah reached for his hand, and he looked into her eyes with adoration. Her hand was strong, tempered by tireless hours of cultivation. They had grown old together in the former world. And now they grew younger together on this New Earth. His thick glasses were no longer necessary, for his failing sight had become keen and clear. Her arthritic pain had faded, her slightly bent over posture had straightened, and she was vibrant and beautiful. His love for her and for her steadfast devotion to the God of Israel was only rivaled by his love for the Father, the Son, and their life-giving trees. His greatest longing was to share the world of blessings he had been given with the people of the nations. His heart was full.

Benjamin walked down a row of seedlings that had been recently planted, and Deborah followed. He knelt by a seedling that looked smaller than its other leafy companions. "Ah, little one, I see you are struggling to grow. Here, I will help you," he said, as he pulled a small shovel from his back pocket and gently cultivated the dark earth around the small tree.

The Obadiahs

Rebekah was the first to leave the car and run up the flat-stoned pathway that led to her Dad's home. "Dad?" she called out. "Mom?"

Lev had the same feeling upon entering Benjamin Obadiah's home as he had when he first saw Rebekah's place. It was a home filled with warmth and character. There was life everywhere. Vines grew from pots and climbed around the large living room window, little clay cups on the windowsill held a variety of tender plants, and delicate ferns decorated the table and almost every available flat space in the small room. Seven small *Olam* trees were placed on a shelf on a wall that was otherwise bare. The words that hung above this place of honor read: "You open your hand and satisfy the desire of every living thing."

Lev noticed Jake and Rachel sitting with Deborah and Benjamin at the table. Benjamin looked robust and healthy—the wrinkles in his face had faded into youth.

"Father!" Lev cried out, "You look great!" Benjamin's face lit up as Lev rushed over.

Lev walked over to his mother-in-law and gave her a hug. "Mom, you look so young."

They stood by the large front window of the living room, in full view of the acres of Eden trees.

"Wow! This is awesome. So many Eden trees—so much potential for blessing the people of the nations—right in your own backyard." Lev placed his hand as a visor over his eyes so that he could better take in the panorama against the strong morning sun.

The hours flew by as the Obadiah family huddled around the kitchen table catching up on one another's lives while snacking on Eden tea and cakes. By late afternoon Benjamin took the group on a tour of their Eden project.

"This is where God does his silent work, preparing the lifeline for the entire human race," Benjamin stated with a sense of awe. "And before our eyes, a great reversal is taking place."

Benjamin explained that in the old world, as the people depended less and less on the land for their livelihood, the concentration of people grew in the cities. The goals people once sought in building the Tower of Babel were partially realized as industrialization took over and cities grew even more in power and influence of commerce than politics.

"But now people are being brought back to the land." Benjamin bent down and patted the earth around a small family of Eden trees. "Each person is becoming self sufficient in regard to food and energy. Soon the world will become decentralized, and the means to control and dominate others will no longer exist."

"Decentralization. Every man dwells under his own vine and fig tree, right?" Lev added in excitement. The verse had come to his mind with no effort, and he repeated it as spontaneously as it had entered his brain. "That's from the Prophet Micah, chapter four. Now how did I know *that*?" he asked.

Everyone laughed at his childlike excitement and sincerity. Benjamin placed his hand on Lev's shoulder.

"Eden fruit, my man," Benjamin said with a smile. "The power of God-given nutrition. It awakens the memory and enlarges the capacity of the brain gradually. As the memories are brought out into the open and into harmony with Christ, nutrients eliminate energy blockages that caused trauma and distress to be locked into a person's thinking. It is truly the lifeline of the entire human family."

"Right in your own backyard," Lev added.

"To be used to bless all the people of the nations in Christ's time and way," Deborah said as she looked up to the heavens, and then into the eyes of her companion in the service of the King.

"Let's get to work. You tell us how we can help, Benjamin. We're at your service." Jake offered.

"Lots to do, and our time here is limited. We will have to leave tomorrow afternoon, so we're home in time for Sabbath." Rebekah said as the group continued their walk down the long rows of Eden trees, under a clear blue sky and a golden sun that warmed them all.

"Whoso will not come up of all the families
of the earth unto Jerusalem
To worship the King, the LORD of hosts,
Even upon them shall be no rain"
(Zechariah 14:17).

Chapter Ten

Lev awakened to a beautiful day. Benjamin, returning indoors with a harvest of fruit, greeted everyone with a hearty "Shalom." After breakfast, they strolled to the chapel and arrived just minutes before the service.

The Obadiahs were greatly appreciated for their contributions to horticulture. Even before the earth started to yield its increase, they had made the area a flourishing garden.

Benjamin began the morning service.

"The process of destroying the earth has come to an end. Anyone who caused two blades of grass to grow where only one had grown left the earth a little richer. Those who trampled that one blade of grass, leaving none to grow, made the earth poorer. For some, being told that they would go to heaven; it mattered little in what condition they left the earth. If everyone was going to heaven, why should they care about the earth? The more miserable the conditions on earth, so much better would heaven be.

"Intervention by Christ has changed this. The Ancients returned with a mission to restore the earth back to Edenic conditions. They not only saw this vision in the prophetic past, but today are providing the resources, wisdom and commitment to attain this goal.

"They closed the imagined escape hatch to heaven and opened the door to a beautiful earth that men have dreamed about as 'Utopia.' We are happily engaged in this great endeavor to restore the earth to God's original purpose—man's home forever. God be praised, Amen."

When the service ended Lev met many who were working with Benjamin on his important assignment. A few who had recently returned from the dead were the center of attention. Some had died in battle in defending Jerusalem as Lev had—others died from illness and disease. In the old world the birth of a baby was quite exciting, even though his or her personality was somewhat of a blank, but when one returned from the dead he was the same person with a genetically duplicated body that God had been pleased to give him.

Lev talked at length of the power manifested in returning the dead in such an orderly manner. It had been alleged by many that the resurrection would be limited to one twenty-four hour day with billions coming back in their recomposed bodies—arms, legs and body parts flying through the air to be reassembled into the original body. The reality was quite different, dignified and orderly. Christ gave each person a new body, one that pleased him, and this was taking place in the Lord's one thousand-year day.

As Lev returned to Benjamin's home, he was aglow with the prospects of a restored and healed world. As each person labored and sacrificed, they would benefit from following a Savior who came to "save that which was lost." Having purchased them with his blood, Christ now was engaged in the process of restoring mankind to an earthly Paradise.

Benjamin and Deborah demonstrated purity their life and work. It was easy to see why the Ancients had singled them out for a pivotal role in the great horticultural project to provide life to all. Lev felt it was an honor and inspiration to have the Obadiah's as part of his family.

Ghana

While they ate lunch, Deborah announced, "Two more nations have asked to come under the authority of Christ and the Ancients. We are always happy for this news—it means that blessings will start flowing to them. These recent nations have had no rain because of their refusal to accept the leadership of Jerusalem. Just as the prophet said, 'And it shall be, that whoso will not come up of all the families of the earth unto Jerusalem to worship the King, the Lord of hosts, even upon them shall be no rain.'"

Benjamin added, "Some nations are on the verge of starvation, but pride and prejudice won't permit them to yield. However, when they see others being blessed, they will finally decide to accept God's blessings instead of resisting them. When that happens we'll need to expand our shipment of trees as well as set up additional tree nurseries.

The amazing thing is that we have been ready as nations requested assistance. We would never have been able to plan so perfectly ourselves. As soon as these nations accept our leadership, the rains come to them. We'll have shipments of Eden trees going to these two nations as soon as surveyors lay out the land for planting and building houses. Already we have most of the major nations on the road to Eden."

Allon then said, "Gramma and grandpa, I want to tell you that I'll be leaving for Ghana, Africa. Ghana asked for Israel's assistance, and work is underway. Enoch contacted me and told me the Ancients agreed to send me to Ghana. I'll help build a factory like Uncle Jake works in. I have all the blueprints at home—he's been showing me a lot of pointers."

Benjamin beamed brightly and said, "Allon, that's great news! We know you can do it with the Lord's blessing. We've already shipped small Eden trees to Ghana. We also shipped trees that will bear Eden fruit rather quickly. These trees will be harvested for the benefit of the sick and aged. Most people will share health and vitality and join in with the great work of restoration. By the way, Ghana is close to the equator. It's always had plenty of rainfall—the soil is very fertile. Under such favorable climate the trees should flourish abundantly. Maybe I'll get to visit you there. I'll speak to Abraham. Our operation here is working flawlessly. There are plenty of people to carry on."

"That would be great, Gramp! Perhaps Gram will come, too. You two are the most qualified people to manage such an operation. Your names have become a legend," Allon exclaimed.

"Thanks for the compliment, but the praise belongs to Christ. Without his blessings our work wouldn't succeed. We've received steady rains so that all our seeds flourish. I was told it would be so, and it has been. If we had to make arrangements to water these seedlings, it would certainly complicate our work. The earth is yielding its increase in phenomenal ways. Plants grow more quickly and robustly—there are no diseases or bugs. We simply plant the seeds and step out of the way!"

"Gramp, you make it sound so easy. Everybody knows that you two didn't miss any detail in planning this project. You can look at a plant and tell what it needs. Solomon may have been wise in lecturing on plants, but you know how to make them flourish."

Benjamin added, "Well, Abraham did say that when Deborah and I have things working smoothly here, we'd be called upon to visit other countries to supervise similar projects. Our work is easier because the Lord is blessing the earth—it no longer withholds rich harvests. Everything grows twice as fast and yields a four-fold return. I can't believe the yields we get today. We can't take any credit ourselves— it's the Lord."

Homeward Bound

Soon it was time to prepare for the journey home. Benjamin and Deborah, glowing with love, were happy to see Allon taking on the Ghana assignment. "With the Lord, all things are possible," Deborah told Allon.

The family traveled homeward along the Mediterranean to show Lev other parts of Israel. Arid stony land had been transformed into a fruitful paradise. Biblical history taught what crops grew best in which areas. Nightly rains and dew watered the ground. Weeds and diseases had disappeared. The earth generously yielded its treasures without sweat and toil.

The majestic view of the beautiful Mediterranean left Lev in awe. But he was reminded that this same sea had been cruel as well. How many ships lay on its bottom? Storms had risen, sometimes lasting for days, and many ships had not endured the battering wind and waves. How glad Lev was to know that none had been eternally lost at sea. Christ's voice would call them from their watery grave in their appointed time. They would not be returned in the sea itself, but just as he had been, in homes built for each one with abundant provisions for life.

Jake interrupted Lev's thoughts. "The Ancients have told us of progress being made in controlling terrible hurricanes and earthquakes. Man was supposed to 'replenish the earth, and subdue it.' Through the years men had no idea how to 'subdue' the elements of earth. They knew how to destroy the earth, but not how to tame it. There are courses on how to accomplish this. Already, there's been a significant drop in the violence and destructiveness of natural disasters. Christ is responsible for changes in weather patterns, but he will not do for man what man can do with self-effort when properly instructed. We still have a long way to go."

Rachel continued, "Many thought Utopia would be boring. They imagined there would be nothing to do but eat, sleep and stroll around. Never, in our wildest dreams, did we imagine a time so challenging mentally, morally and scientifically. We had no concept of the great work involved in bringing thirty billion people back from the dead!"

Rebekah added, "Fortunately for everyone, God made the plans and provisions for what is taking place. Nothing has been left to chance or human error. If 'God so loved the world, that he gave his only begotten Son,' it's reasonable He'd give everyone a full opportunity to benefit from it. The hardest question to understand is why God permitted such things as the Holocaust or the so-called 'Holy' Inquisition. It is difficult to understand such actions that bordered on total depravity. Savages were known to be notoriously cruel, but they were ignorant and superstitious. I'm referring to educated people and men of the cloth."

Allon agreed, "We won't have to wait very long for answers, Mom. In three or four years some prominent people from the Third Reich will be returning. Men of the cloth who were in league with Hitler will be back. I'm sure everyone will have some rationalization to explain his or her deeds. However, their excuses will sound hollow. The devil can't provide a smokescreen now. He's bound in his storage pit. People will have to own up to their crimes against humanity. A devil-may-care attitude once pervaded society. No one expected to be called into account."

Gustav Johnson, Sweden

It was good to stretch their legs, walking along the shore. They rested at a small oasis where several others were sitting. As Lev looked for a lunch table, he saw a middle-aged man with a foreign accent who invited them to sit down. He introduced himself as Gustav Johnson from Sweden. Gustav was in Israel by invitation of the Ancients.

While Sweden had accepted the conditions laid down for their entrance into a league with Israel, the nation was having trouble complying with all of the conditions. They thought they could function as they once had, making only modest changes. Consequently, Sweden had not yet received the full support and expected help. Gustav explained that he had landed in Tel Aviv and had been given a car to journey to Jerusalem. Samuel, the Ancient who had made the arrangements, wanted Gustav to see the land of Israel firsthand.

Lev offered the blessing on their basket of luscious Eden fruit, and then offered some to Gustav.

He took some, and his face lit up with delight. "I must tell you, this is the most delicious fruit I have ever tasted," Gustav said.

Lev said, "I had my first taste of Eden fruit six days ago, when I was restored to life. I've been walking on air ever since. I died in the last battle defending Jerusalem. When I returned to life, I tasted Eden fruit for the first time—little did I know how quickly it would restore vitality and clarity of mind. After you live on this diet for a few days, Gustav, you'll immediately feel the difference."

Gustav said, "After tasting Eden fruit and hearing your testimony, I'm becoming a believer. Strange that you said you died and that you are now restored back to life. We've heard of this happening in Israel, but no one in Sweden has experienced it. My son also died in that battle. He was a part of a small contingent that went from our country. Civil and religious leaders brought about that siege against Jerusalem, and the common people were coerced into the ordeal. That's why, when it was apparent that the Lord apparently destroyed our invading forces, people were outraged with those who had precipitated this fiasco. The leaders had claimed that this mission to take Jerusalem had been blessed by God. They had promised great rewards to those who helped them fulfill their ambitions. This time it blew up in their faces and they paid with their lives."

Jake said, "I hope you'll persuade your people back home to quickly accept the conditions of the Ancients. They'll have to learn to answer to Christ, and nothing they do will be outside of his directions. As you pass through Israel you'll see how peaceful, efficient and orderly everything is. No effort is wasted or duplicated. Because of the Eden fruit, we don't have sick or incapacitated people. Consequently, all but small children are active in the great regeneration project. The biggest problem is the baggage people bring with them from their former lives. Bad habits, sinful ways, and plain old selfishness still live in their hearts. No human weakness will go away without personal effort. Everyone will either overcome their sins or be overcome by them. Help is provided for all equally, but not all are eager to change."

"I'm most happy to have shared my table with you," Gustav responded. "I not only needed to hear your experiences, but also to taste your food. I confess I was a little glum because when I landed at the airport there were no officials greeting me personally—only this car was provided. I expected as ambassador from Sweden the red carpet would be rolled out for me."

Jake said, "Gustav, Christ doesn't roll out the red carpet for anyone. You must roll out the red carpet for Christ. You have nothing to give him except obedience and appreciation. The sooner you and your people bow to him, the sooner you will be in line for blessings you cannot begin to imagine. Sweden was a professed Christian people— why is it so hard to bow before Christ? We Jews have a long history of rejecting our Messiah, but we've come under his authority."

Rebekah added, "Remember the story of Naaman, the Syrian captain who wanted Elisha to cure his leprosy? When Naaman was told to wash in the muddy Jordan seven times, he was angry. He almost returned home without doing it. Finally, better counsel prevailed, and he grudgingly complied. To Naaman's amazement, he was cured. We hope Sweden will comply with every requirement laid upon them. Sooner or later, they'll have to. The sooner they bow before earth's new ruler, the sooner blessings, honor and life will come to them."

Gustav smiled, "You've made your points perfectly clear. Sweden's pride has almost closed the door to a quick and productive turnaround. I admit I had a little chip on my shoulder coming here. When no official greeted me, I felt pretty much like Naaman. Thanks for clearing my head—I needed this. I feel better prepared to meet those Ancients in Jerusalem."

Lev said, "We only helped you to see matters a little more clearly sooner. When you meet Samuel and some of the other Ancients, you'll be impressed. You've never met anyone perfect yet—but, when you do, you'll be overwhelmed. They're handsome and bright. They speak with authority, yet are kind and gracious. We were privileged to meet Isaac a few days ago. They're extremely busy and won't spend unnecessary time with you. Remember, they're only servants of Christ. All the requirements come from him—they are only his mouthpieces. I never bowed my knee to Christ before, but now that I've come back to life through him, I realize my indebtedness to him. The best place to meet Christ is on your knees. Just listen to Samuel and those with him. Do everything they tell you. It's that simple. You either comply or you don't receive the benefits. From the day that you comply with their terms, you'll be swept off your feet with their grand restoration process."

Gustav thanked them profusely. "It must be providential that I met you today. I needed an attitude adjustment and you've helped me. I think I'm ready to meet Samuel. Thank you so much! That delicious Eden fruit is already clearing the cobwebs from my brain!"

The small family sat in silence together, awed by the love and power of the God of Israel, happy to have served as ambassadors of Christ. The trip had been thrilling for Lev.

"Tomorrow is our last day of vacation—what's the schedule? Allon will be departing soon after. Maybe, we could check where my folks are having their houses built."

Rebekah answered, "Tomorrow is Sabbath—we'll spend more time at the chapel than usual. But the sites for their homes aren't far. After lunch we can check the sites and make a to-do list for construction. Once the foundation is prepared, material will be delivered for building."

Reuben's Family

Lev, Jake, Rachel and Annie returned to their own homes in the early evening, sensing that it was a good time to catch up on personal responsibilities. As Lev walked to his cottage he thought of the week ahead and looked forward to the work he would soon begin on the home for his father and the home for his mother. He decided he would carefully divide his quiet time to include a study of God's word, as well as a study of the educational programs on building and technology provided by the Ancients.

His quiet meditations were abruptly ended when he heard the sound of a woman weeping. She sat by the side of the road, her head in her hands.

"What can I do to help you?" Lev asked, surprised at his own directness.

The woman continued to weep as if she had not heard his offer to help her.

Lev knelt down besides her, placing his hand on her shoulder. "If there is something I can do, I'd be happy to. I'm in no hurry."

"Hey!" a man's gruff voice called out. "What do you think you're doing?" Lev stiffened. It was Reuben Meyer. Lev looked up into his face. Reuben was flushed with anger. "Good job, Lev, making my wife cry. Now that's what I call great New Earth PR."

Lev shook his head in disbelief. "I heard her crying and I stopped to see if there was anything I could do to help."

"Well, there isn't. You're welcome to leave."

Just then Lev noticed a little girl had approached Reuben. She tugged at his pants to get his attention. "Daddy—"

"Get back in the house right now!" Reuben snapped. The little girl ran for the house, and Reuben collected his wife and walked slowly in the same direction.

Shadows of the Evening

Later that evening Lev turned on his computer to search for courses he could choose to study. Out of the great variety of subjects he chose the house-building course since this was to be his first privilege of service. Two hours flew by as Isaiah presented clear instructions, with humor and enthusiasm that totally absorbed his attention.

Lev got up and sat on his garden bench munching on Eden fruit. He had experienced the joy of being returned to his family with a whole, healthy body. He had met vibrant people who had overcome overwhelming obstacles, like John the former paraplegic. He experienced his first humbling consequence. He had resisted this new way, had felt overwhelmed, and found that conforming to the new arrangements made life more pleasant and that yielding brought more happiness than resisting. Strangely, there was no reward for stubbornness in keeping the old ways. By bringing their secrets out in the open he had begun a far deeper relationship with his former wife than he could have imagined possible. He had faced some of the pain and insecurity in his past and had begun to heal, though this second encounter with Reuben made him feel sick all over again. He had witnessed the transformation power at work in the life of the radiant 'Ms. Millie.' He had visited with the Obadiahs. He had met Gustav Johnson by a strange turn of events overruled by Christ and his Anointed.

Lev came inside, changed his clothes, and prepared for the night. He lay on his bed staring at the circular sunroof above him into the vast expanse of stars in the night sky. He reached for his Bible on the nightstand and turned to the passage.

"Like a shepherd; he shall gather the lambs with his arm, and carry them in his bosom, and shall gently lead those that are with young" (Isaiah 40:11).

He nodded his head in agreement. The Shepherd's care was tender and gentle, beyond his expectation. Then his thoughts returned to Reuben.

"Why would Reuben be so hateful? Part of this new life is being able to eat of the Eden fruit that tempers emotions and vitalizes the body. Why does my anger and irritation at Reuben keep returning?"

Lev closed his eyes with a sense of uneasiness and curiosity. And then he drifted off into sleep.

*"And it shall come to pass in that day,
That I will seek to destroy all the nations
That come against Jerusalem"
(Zechariah 12:9).*

Chapter Eleven

On Lev's first Sabbath day he decided to take his Bible to the services, as they would be longer and more informative. He was invited to join others walking to the chapel, some of whom he recognized. But there was one person Lev had never seen. Joseph Goldstein had returned only yesterday. He had been slain in the attack on Jerusalem.

Joseph recalled, "Remember, Israel, because of the peace process had given up much of their military strength. We were like an 'unwalled village.' We were poorly prepared as a nation for war and much less for the lightning siege against Jerusalem. They brought troops in choppers, landed them outside the city and continued to bring in back up forces by trucks and tanks. Meanwhile after landing and releasing their troops safely out of range of fire, the choppers and aircraft with heavy gun power strafed those resisting in the city—they had awesome firepower. It didn't take long to quiet our resistance. They were pleased to take part of the city, and now felt after they cleaned out the pockets of resistance in the rest of Israel would then meekly surrender.

"Neither they nor we thought they would attack Jerusalem until the scattered army of Israel was subdued. But because they had rolled over our initial resistance so quickly and easily the enemy decided on a lightning strike against the Western city when they saw how vulnerable we were. Our surrender was painful—we were treated savagely. Men were shot even though they had surrendered. Women were treated shamefully. The enemy decided to load captives into trucks, tanks and helicopters, but they didn't have room for all. The rest of us were shot. When the machine guns opened fire, death came to most of us. All I remember was the hot slug in my body—then I blacked out. I woke up yesterday."

Everyone had a story to tell of the last days. At the time it seemed as though a dark force was making its last effort to destroy the Jews and take the Holy City.

They arrived at the chapel in time to sit and collect their thoughts before the services began. As Lev sat with Joseph Goldstein, he could almost feel his excitement at being alive again.

The day's text was taken from Matthew 11:28, "Come unto me, all ye that labour and are heavy laden, and I will give you rest." A volunteer from the audience explained that this verse primarily referred to the Christian era when Jesus was gathering his elect; however, Jesus had not changed in character since then, and he still had the same role of a burden bearer. He encouraged them to share that same spirit, and to uphold others who bore burdens and heartaches. He reminded them that all of them existed in the covert of Christ's mercy and they needed to develop some of the same Christian character graces as those in the past.

When the services ended, they had gladness in their hearts. No one was eager to leave. They shared experiences about death and life and were enthralled with descriptions of God's great power in the work of regenerating the human race. Each bore scars from their previous life. Their struggle was in replacing the heart of stone with a heart of flesh. None were capable of doing it alone. Only through Christ could it be accomplished—and then, only by those who were honest enough to seek a new heart and mind.

Allon's Farewell

The Aron family walked to Lev's home with happy hearts. The plan for the day was to tour the two sites that the Ancients had assigned to their parents. No one seemed to mind the short walk. A grove of Eden trees was already beginning to bear fruit. The excavation for the foundation was done for both homes and the footings were laid.

"I think we can finish this job in two months," Jake announced.

"Wow, things really happen quickly these days," Lev commented.

Rebekah tapped Annie on the shoulder and ran the other way around the circle of her family, and stopped by Lev and rested her chin on his shoulder. "Its easier when there are no divorces in the family."

"I really envy you," Rachel interposed, "because everything just falls into place for your parents. My parents live rather far apart—and it will make helping each of them more difficult, but the Ancients have a way of helping things to work out."

Lev changed the subject. "How do the sewage systems work?"

Jake replied, "Each unit is a complete sustainable ecosystem. The household waste is recycled into fertilizer. Every six months the finished compost is ready to be used for fertilizer on the trees or plants in the garden. The system separating solid waste from the liquid waste is very efficient. Wastewater is purified and absorbed in an evaporative plant bed. The waste is dried, compacted and heated before being removed so no harmful bacteria survive. It is completely odorless. We have no central water pumping stations and no waste sewage systems. There are no waste removal trucks hauling garbage to pollute the earth. Thoreau would find what he longed for when he said, 'Simplify, simplify, simplify.'"

They soon headed back for a late Sabbath lunch. It would be the last time they would be together for a while. Rebekah sighed at the thought of her son leaving. She felt both pride and sadness, and found she was staring at the young man who was once a little boy building tree houses and roads for little toy trucks in their backyard. At this moment most of her living families were together in one place, and she felt supremely happy.

Annie, asked the blessing on the noon meal—a very sincere and heartfelt prayer of thanks. "Thank you, Lord, for the earth is full of your unfailing love. Please bless Allon, Lord. We will miss him. Help him in his work in Ghana. Bless the nations and lead them to the true Messiah, in whose name we pray, Amen."

Allon finished eating and said, "Well, I really should begin to pack."

Rebekah was holding back tears. "Can we see you off tomorrow morning?" Her voice was hopeful.

"Thanks, Mom, but the Ancients have arranged for a car. I'll miss you," he said as he stood and walked over to embrace his mother. "And remember, the Ancients said I could come and visit in order to spend some time with Grandma and Grandpa when they are raised. It won't be long and you'll be stuck with me again." Everyone stood and exchanged goodbyes and embraces.

"Still afraid of those mamba snakes, Allon?" Annie hugged Allon and her eyes shone with the light of teasing and affection.

"Yeah, I thought maybe I'd pack you along with my things so you could teach me about them. Maybe you could be my snake-protector." Allon's eyes reflected back the same humor and love.

In a matter of moments Allon had walked out the door on his way to another world.

The Battle Reviewed

In the family room Jake was reflecting on the last battle for Jerusalem, contrasting his position with Lev's.

"Lev, I almost knew what was going to happen to you that day. I knew you were angry with me because you felt I should be willing to die in defense of our nation and city. In my heart, I knew I would gladly die for such a cause. I had been studying Zechariah 14:2 at that time—'For I will gather all nations against Jerusalem to battle; and the city shall be taken, and the houses rifled, and the woman ravished; and half of the city shall go forth in captivity, and the residue of the people shall not be cut off from the city.'

"I knew our people had been successful in battle ever since the rebirth of our nation in 1948. But, I began to realize we were divided as to whether we should wait on the Lord or go out to fight the enemy. You and I, Lev, represented both sides. I knew Rebekah was disappointed with me that I didn't go. Even Rachel was disappointed with the path I had chosen."

Jake continued, "I had read all of Zechariah 14 and knew we were standing on the threshold of a great divide. The nations and the religious world of that time were going to learn the hard way that they were wrong about Jerusalem. Only a small group of Christians stood up and said that the invasion would result in a catastrophic disaster.

"These Christians recognized the truth of the same scripture verses that I and some other Jews did. To us it was as clear as day what was going to happen. But religious bigotry had made Jerusalem the Holy Grail that must be taken from the God-forsaken Jews. Once the churches had placed God's banner over their mission, they couldn't back down. They had made their position clear—that by saving Jerusalem for the Christian world, they would be saving the world from Armageddon. They had been wrong about many things before, but no one could prove their wrongness about a burning hell, or immortal soul by observation.

"This was a bad time to be wrong. The whole world would witness that they were not representing God, but the vested interests of a Satan-led debacle.

"I remember those Bible-believing Christians quoting Zechariah 14:3 on the newscasts, saying, 'Then shall the LORD go forth, and fight against those nations, as when he fought in the day of battle.'

"The Christians that opposed them delivered a message that was received with scorn and anger. Those poor witnesses of Christ were publicly ridiculed and denounced. Some were violently assaulted and a few were killed. Our nation tried to intercede on their behalf. Our ambassadors made it clear that these good Christian people had no political affiliation with our nation and that they were only stating their own beliefs—but no avail. The forces were already on their way to assault our land. This was going to be their final solution to the so-called Jewish problem.

"Because the peace process caused us to disarm and because the vast numbers coming against Israel made it impossible to prevent their landing and deployment. You know the facts about the day you met the enemy better than I, Lev. You were there dug in trying to hold back the overwhelming forces with something like a flyswatter. You were outnumbered in every way. They had not only come with a vengeance, but never were forces more prepared for victory. This whole operation was to be nothing more than a clean up, lasting no more than a week. If our resistance proved difficult, they were threatening to use neutron bombs to defeat us. How long could Israel hold out against such odds and deadly techniques?"

Rachel interjected, "I never was gloomier than on that day when Lev's outpost was overrun. My heart was with those fighting for Jerusalem. I thought that if God would intervene at all it would be by allowing our forces to beat the hundred to one odds against us. When the first day ended and our forces had gone down in defeat, I had really given up all hope that Israel would survive. I knew Jake still clung to the hope that God would defeat the enemy apart from our efforts. I know what happened the next day was not a reward for my faith. I had no faith whatever that God would intervene to save us. Zechariah belonged to another time and place. I had no faith in that prophecy or any other. We Jews had unjustly suffered so much, for so long, that I had lost my faith. I felt God had forsaken us and we were left to have our bones picked clean by the enemy."

Rebekah added, "Rachel's viewpoint was mine. I knew Jake was being true to his belief, but I thought clinging to scriptures wouldn't work this time. I knew he was no coward, but to me Lev was doing the honorable thing. Men had to stand up for what they believed. I had little hope that Lev would survive that awful onslaught. I knew that Lev would not be the first man in the world to die fighting for his belief. When I received Lev's message that fateful day, I was waiting thinking some word might come. When the news came that our initial forces had been destroyed, I knew what had happened to Lev. It was over for him and all our advanced forces. It was the worst day of my life. I had lost Lev and we were about to lose our nation. There was nothing but darkness before us. I wished that I had Jake's faith. He was heartbroken to hear of Lev's death, but he assured me not to despair. Surely, God would look down from heaven and fight for us as he did at the Red Sea or at Jericho. But I didn't have such faith. While I appreciated Jake's condolences, it sounded like he was whistling in the dark."

Lev said, "Jake, I was angry when I left you before the battle began. However, I was sorry that I had been so hostile to your position right after. When we dug in to defend ourselves against the enemy, it seemed so hopeless. I wondered if God really cared about us. He was secure in his high and holy place. Why should he be involved in this messy and cruel war? Why should he care? Even as I thought these things, I could not help thinking of how often God had involved himself with Israel throughout history. We were not worthy of his care and attention, but maybe we were beloved for our father's sake. He was still the God of Abraham, Isaac and Jacob.

"Could God allow us to fail and fall as a nation after so many centuries of dealing with us? I felt that this was the moment of truth. Either God would save our nation or we were lost. So, Jake, while I was angry when I left, there on the battlefield, my mind was coming to the same conclusion that you had already reached."

Rebekah said, "My tears flowed all night long. I still had lost you, Lev, and despite my personal loss, I didn't want to see our people falling helplessly before these invaders. I prayed fervently that God would remember us. Why had he regathered us from all the nations? Why had he permitted us to possess the land of our fathers? Why couldn't the nations stop hating us? What made us so terrible in their eyes? I cried and questioned God throughout the night.

Death Was in the Air That Morning

"When the morning came, I saw dark clouds such as I had never seen before—it was eerie. The enemy felt a sense of doom. Their radios and electronic equipment had failed. Men were panicking in their tanks and vehicles. Pilots found that their navigational equipment was malfunctioning. The enemy's top brass wanted to call off the attack, but they couldn't communicate to their troops."

Rachel agreed, "Yes, I couldn't sleep either. In the morning when I saw the darkness, I knew some catastrophic event was pending. I remembered that God fought for Israel in days of old, and for the first time I believed he was about to break loose upon this massive enemy. I thought of all those young people in the invading army who were really just victims. Their crazed leaders had promised them victory and a final resolution of "the Jerusalem problem." This was a similar drumbeat that Hitler had used, only with him it was the extermination of the Jews—with them it was to take control of the Beloved City."

Jake interjected, "Jerusalem was in the hands of the people God had intended it for. The church tried repeatedly to take it and promised heaven to any who died in the attempt to take Jerusalem. Muslims, using the same motivational tactics even made a more generous offer—heaven, plus seventy-two virgins. Both religions were aware of Isaiah 2:3, 'Come ye, and let us go up to the mountain of the LORD, to the house of the God of Jacob; and he will teach us of his ways, and we will walk in his paths: for out of Zion shall go forth the law, and the word of the LORD from Jerusalem.' With Jerusalem in the hands of Jacob's descendants, all other claims to represent God were in jeopardy. God's Word never mentioned Rome as the source from which the Lord's Word would emanate. Neither was the Word to go forth from Mecca. Obviously, they had to try to seize this Holy City to make valid their claims as God's agencies of blessing. Wresting it from Israel they would lay claim to this city."

"I see," Lev said. "They felt by having Jerusalem they would prevent Israel from fulfilling Isaiah's prophecy—no wonder they failed! When God destroyed this invading host he accomplished two things in one blow. He exposed their false claim to be the real representatives of God and Christ, and He prevented them from capturing Jerusalem so they couldn't send forth the 'word of the Lord from Jerusalem.'"

Rebekah added, "If this war had gone on for a year or two, maybe no one would have seen that it was God that had placed Jerusalem squarely in the hands of the descendants of Jacob. When the world witnessed Divine intervention on such a gigantic scale, immediately the truth was clear on this subject, once and for all time. The perpetrators had no where to hide, and no way to explain the total annihilation of their forces."

Jake suggested, "Let's watch some scenes taken after this very sad war."

They found vivid scenes of the carnage of that battle on the Internet. As far as the eye could see corpses lay strewn about. Tanks, trucks, and all kinds of military equipment littered the roadways. Most had been in motion when their occupants died and some had smashed into the others, some had overturned, and others went over ravines. Planes could be seen falling from the sky. The airplanes that were still on the ground waiting for their turn to take off remained there. Landing craft came, laden with dead men. Ships in the Mediterranean, which were preparing to shell Judah, lay still in the waters with dead crews.

God had saved Israel, but at what price for the enemy. At first, the nations couldn't believe what had happened. They simply felt the Israelis, who were clever people, had found a way to jam the communication with their troops. When Israel contacted the various nations perpetrating this disaster, they thought it was a trick. They were invited to send commercial jets and dignitaries to view what happened. Within a few hours their planes could be seen flying slowly over the battlefields. The home nations were angry even before the commercial jets surveyed the carnage, but when they reported that the whole invading force was dead and showed their film footage of the sad remains of their once invincible armies and navies, the nations revolted in anarchy.

First and foremost, the religious leaders were turned upon. When the mask of being God's agents for peace in the world was removed, they were seen as the hate mongers they really had been. Next, the angry masses went after the financial and political rulers. There was nowhere to hide. In their last effort to take Jerusalem, they had lost everything.

Lev's First Week Ends

The afternoon was over. They had been so engrossed in discussion that they had lost track of time. They then enjoyed an evening meal.

"Now that our week's vacation is ended, what are you planning to do, Lev?" asked Rachel.

"Well, I intend to take some courses to bone up on projects I hope I can contribute to. I was thinking of calling the Ancient Worthies and asking their advice. I am perfectly willing to go wherever or do whatever they say. My preference will not stand in the way of serving where needed. I am a debtor to all who have made my return possible. Divine power brought me back from the dead, and I also have my health, strength and well being back, with more vitality than ever before. I owe Christ a debt of gratitude. The fact is that there is nothing that I can do for Christ. I hope that he will accept what I do for others as done unto him."

"I think that's wise on your part to check with them for openings they may need to have filled. If the assignment you get has technical aspects, they'll give you time to learn what you need," Rebekah responded.

Soon the time came for all to return to their homes and commitments. This had definitely been the best week of Lev's life.

"For then will I turn to the people a pure language,
That they may all call upon the name of the LORD,
To serve him with one consent"
(Zephaniah 3:9).

Chapter Twelve

On the morning of his eighth day of life, Lev found himself reading a map in order to find the site assigned to the Schultz family. His week of orientation was over, and eager to find his niche in this new world, he had phoned the Ancients to ask if any project was available in his area that had a particular priority.

"Yes, in fact, there is." Huldah the prophetess spoke clearly and with enthusiasm. "There is a couple and one child who was killed in the Palestinian uprising. They have no surviving relatives. You may help with their house if you wish. They will be living in one house because the child will need both parents." She gave him directions. "You may start today, because other volunteers are working there now. You are under no obligation to accept this assignment, you know."

"Put me down, Huldah, I'd like to start today. Just add me to your volunteer list. I'll do anything. I've been given so much it's the least I can do."

A new voice interrupted Lev's recounting of his early morning conversation. "It's great to have you with us, Lev. I'm Joel and this is Joseph." Joel motioned to the young man who was helping him set cement blocks for the foundation. "And this is Mary, and that's Marta."

"Hi," said one. "Hello," said the other. Both young women took time to give a quick wave and then went back to their job of mixing the mortar. Both women had smears of cement on their faces, and it made Lev smile.

"They really get into their work, don't they?" he said playfully.

Joel looked over at the women and smiled. "Yeah, they do. Wait till we switch jobs, when they carry the cement blocks and lay them. They really keep us jumping to keep up with the mortar. They're pretty amazing workers."

Lev looked over at the two women and felt the familiar feeling of intimidation in facing this New Earth change of roles. "So what do you want me to do?" he asked quickly.

"You can carry the blocks over to us. That way we'll keep them busy." Joseph suggested.

They developed a rhythm to their work. Lev felt a part of their team and enjoyed the physical activity in the morning sun.

"So how old are you?" Mary asked.

"In old world years or in New Earth time?"

Mary laughed. "In New Earth time."

"Eight days old, today," Lev said as he carried a block and set it down.

"Still wet behind the ears…" Marta smiled. "Joseph and I are the oldest ones here. We're over twelve years old."

"I'm four months old and so is Joseph," Mary offered.

"We were the 'babies' until you came along." Joel gave Lev a pat on the back. "So how does it feel to be eight days old?"

"Great! I'm overwhelmed with all that has happened. I came face to face with myself and with Messiah all in the first week, and the whole thing's been an adventure."

They continued to talk while they worked through the morning. There were two more rings of cement blocks to set, and the foundation would be completed. Before he knew it Joel announced it was time for lunch break.

Each of the four sat in the orchard as they munched on their fruit.

"Sure is handy having all these Eden trees around. Fast food!" Lev laughed.

Mary rolled her eyes and threw Lev some Eden fruit. "Fast food without all the additives and side effects!"

"Old World Caution: this food contains ingredients and chemicals that could cause depression, fits of anger, arthritis, bronchial congestion and death," Joel said in his most official voice. They all laughed.

"I used to love French fries. I can hardly imagine it now." Joseph nodded his head in disbelief. There are a lot of things I can hardly imagine now that I'm here.

Last Memories

"So tell me about yourselves. What was your last memory of the old world?" Lev asked.

Joseph spoke first. "Marta and I both lived through the last battle. Mary and Joel have a harder story to tell."

Mary continued. "Nothing too pretty. We knew the enemy troops were under orders to not destroy the holy sites in East Jerusalem and didn't think they would attack us in the Western part of the city until after the surrounding territories were subdued. However, those who assembled in the Western city were the ones who were going to fight the invaders. We thought we would be the last resistance. As it turned out, the invaders were so pleased with their early victory that they sent a lightning force to take the Western part of the city. When they arrived with tanks and trucks and infantry who were attended with an array of choppers and gun aircraft they had such amazing firepower that they thinned the ranks of our resistance. They wouldn't have had it so easy if we had remained in our houses prepared for house-to-house combat."

"We fought bravely for awhile," Joel added, "but most of us were in the open and couldn't withstand the fire from the sky. We had little choice but to surrender. Some were taken prisoner, and I was one of the ones who was shot."

"My last memory," Mary looked into the sun with her hand as a visor above her squinting eyes, "was of being raped and then shot in the head by the man who assaulted me."

Lev clenched his fist, imagining the scene. He could not bear the thought of this vibrant young woman having been treated so brutally. Lev felt a familiar wave of uneasiness sweep over him and nervously rubbed his forehead. There was silence among the five.

Finally, Lev spoke. "I'm sorry."

"It was hard for me at first, being in this new earth with my old memories. But I'm okay now. In fact, I'm happy. I'm about to request to help prepare for the return of the man who assaulted me."

"I'll go with you, Mary," Joseph offered.

"Mary, you are so brave. I'm not sure *I'd* be ready to do that." Marta reached out and gave Mary a quick embrace from the side.

"Not so much brave, as blessed." She smiled and stood up. "Time to get back to work!" She eagerly took Joel's place and motioned for Marta to join her.

"It's our turn to set the blocks. Lev, you can prepare the mortar with Joel, and Joseph—how about carrying the blocks?"

"How about the three of us guys working on the mortar?" Joseph suggested in fun. "That way they won't show us up," he said in a softer voice, which everyone heard. Everyone laughed and took on their new jobs with enthusiasm.

"We usually only work for three hours on a project like this. But we have only a month until our loved ones are scheduled to be raised, so we wanted to finish this house so we can continue building for our own families," Joseph explained.

Lev felt as if he had known them for a long time, and he worked with all the strength and vigor of his eight day old resurrection body. He thought of their stories as he hustled to do his part in the work. He was impressed with the love and courage he saw in Mary, and he longed for such memories to be forgotten. No, not forgotten. He wished with all his heart that such things had never happened. If only people had understood the truth, that everything they did would have to be exposed and faced when they were raised, perhaps it would have been a deterrent to evil.

"Time to call it a day," Joseph announced at mid afternoon.

Lev embraced each of his new friends and headed toward his home. As he passed by Reuben's house, he half expected to see a little girl and a weeping woman, but saw no one.

"He's got lots of things to deal with. If there's a way I could help him, I would be glad to do so." Lev thought as he walked on.

Ezra

Lev awakened early the next morning and decided to jog to the place of worship after a quick breakfast. He was pleased to notice that his ability to run had improved since the day he trailed his family in their New World sprint.

Lev sat on a bench by the grove of Eden trees that bordered the chapel area and took off his shoes to feel the cool grass beneath his feet. Two sheep were grazing on the lawn below the trees. Lev watched them closely as they neatly consumed an area of excess grass. "They don't need to weed, and they don't need to mow," he said to himself, amused. Lev noticed the sheep had also eaten the Eden fruit that had fallen to the ground. Healthiest sheep alive, he thought, and they provide a wonderful service free of charge. Lev walked over to the animals, knelt down and patted them on the head gently.

"Hello, you hungry woolly ones," he said, amazed that they responded to his touch with a curiosity which made them draw closer to him. One of the sheep nuzzled up to his face, which tickled his nose and made him sneeze. He laughed at himself and realized what a joy it was to be close to these animals and to see signs of the whole land gradually turning into a peaceable kingdom. He enjoyed the cool morning breeze for a long while in the company of the friendly sheep.

Then Lev saw a man with thick brown hair and a strong build walk into the chapel courtyard with a confused look on his face.

Lev walked toward the man and held out his hand. "Hello, I'm Lev Aron. Are you looking for someone?"

The man took hold of Lev's hand and shook it. "Shalom. I'm Ezra, and I'm new here. I was just raised yesterday, and I didn't want to miss the worship service."

"Well, you're in the right place, just a bit early. So you're anxious to attend the worship service. I was raised eight days ago, and I admit that I was rather confused and hesitant at first." Lev led the man to the bench and motioned for him to sit beside him.

Ezra smiled. "I'm just grateful to have life again. I was sent to Europe to gather intelligence on the forces that were coming together against Israel. I was undercover as an industrialist there on normal business. I was to contact the Israeli intelligence and bring back the information."

Lev noticed that Ezra's right hand had begun to shake. He placed his hand on Ezra's shoulder as a reassurance. "They arrested me and then interrogated me for days and then let me go. Their forces were ready to move into Israel. So they decided to dispose of me and make it look like suicide." Ezra paused. "I was in my hotel room. The last thing I remember was a blindfold around my eyes and a rope around my neck. They stood me up on a chair—" Ezra clenched both of his hands, "and the next thing I knew my feet were dangling and I was fighting hard to breathe. It seemed like I struggled a long time, and then there was nothing."

Lev sat in awkward silence as he thought of something to say. "I'm sorry, Ezra." He wished he had some resurrection tea for him and then got an idea. He walked over to the grove of trees and picked some of the Eden fruit, walked back to the bench, and handed the fruit to Ezra.

"Thank you, Lev," Ezra said, as he munched on the fruit. Lev could see the tension slowly drain from the man's hands.

"That was a hard way to die, Ezra."

"Yes, it was. I had been given to fits of depression in the old world and had thought at times of taking my life, but when my life was being taken from me, I fought hard for it. I never realized how strong the will to survive is wired into us."

"Well, we weren't meant to die in God's original plan. If Adam and Eve hadn't sinned, the kingship of man would have been realized much earlier in time. And none of these terrible things would have happened. But we would have missed the lessons from tasting the bitter fruit of disobedience."

"I much prefer the taste of this fruit."

"Amen to that," Lev said as he stood. People were beginning to make their way to be seated in the chapel. Lev walked over to the chapel benches down toward the inner aisle to make room for others. Ezra followed.

"I want to understand why these things happened to me. And I want to know who this Messiah is. And I want to feel at home. I don't want to shake when I think about my death."

A soothing melody began that made Lev feel at peace. "It all takes time. Keep talking about what happened to you, and keep eating Eden fruit and drinking resurrection tea, and your feelings will naturally surface and be calmed. Let Messiah's sweet influence through the words of the Prophets see you through your experiences. Try volunteering on projects to prepare for the awakening of others. It will all fit together sooner than you think."

After the service Lev heard Ezra whisper the words of the theme text for the day word for word, just as if the worship leader spoke it.

"'He will rescue them from oppression and violence, for precious is their blood in his sight... All nations will be blessed through him, and they will call him blessed.' Thanks, Lev." Ezra extended his hand to Lev. "I have a lot to think about."

"You're welcome, Ezra," said Lev as he embraced his new friend. "Shalom."

Lev met Rebekah among the numbers of talkative people in the courtyard and embraced her. They greeted other worshippers, engaged in lively conversation, then walked and talked quietly together until they reached Rebekah's home. There they parted ways. Rebekah got ready for her shift at the factory, and Lev continued to walk toward his home to prepare for his afternoon's work, amazed at the intensity of emotion that people had to face in dealing with their old world experiences.

Aaron, Eva and Ami to Return

Lev reported for work at the Shultz's site, and he worked hard and quietly, thankful for the temporary distraction of good physical labor.

Mary commented during their afternoon break. "Did you know that because we have helped prepare this home, we would have the honor to be here when Aaron, Eva and Ami are raised?"

Lev's determined expression was replaced with a broad smile. "You're kidding. That's great! That is so great!" Lev emphasized each word in his last exclamation and everyone laughed at the eagerness and joy in his voice.

"We should be able to finish the project in less than a month, in plenty of time for the scheduled date for their awakening," Aaron said.

Lev reviewed the work that still needed to be completed. The actual house frame and blocking would be easily finished, as would the electrical work and plumbing. Flowers and vegetables had to be planted in the atrium. Furniture had to be delivered.

"This family died in the Palestinian uprisings," Marta informed the group. "A tragic time for our people and the Palestinians, as well."

"I'm willing to put a little bit more time into this project, to make sure we're done on time," Joel offered.

"Me too," Mary added.

"I can't wait for their day to come." Marta said.

"Count me in," Lev said as he helped prepare the site for the next day's work. As he walked home he thought of the privilege of helping this family.

E-mail from Ghana

The moment Lev found the e-mail from Allon, he raced to the phone and called Rebekah. "Rebekah, check your e-mail right away. We've heard from Allon."

"Hello, Lev," Rebekah said with slight irritation in her voice, as she emphasized the formal greeting that Lev had forgotten in his excitement.

"Hello, Rebekah, sorry, I was so excited to get word from Allon… How did it go for you today?"

"It went okay. I stopped to see Millie and her children after my shift at the factory, and it did my heart good. How was it for you today?"

"It was great...we'll have the honor of welcoming the Schultz family when they return."

"That's wonderful, Lev! I think it will be a treasured experience because of all the hard work you've put into their home," Rebekah said. "I've got to go now. Thanks for telling me about the e-mail."

"Goodbye, Rebekah, I love you!"

"Goodbye, Lev. *I* love *you*, too!"

Rebekah placed the phone on its base, logged on to her computer and downloaded the e-mail from Allon. She read its brief message with tears in her eyes.

Dear Mom and Dad, Uncle Jake, Aunt Rachel and Annie:

Shalom from Ghana. Africa is beautiful. The people here have a strong sense of family and they are devout in their religious worship. Poverty is everywhere, but already that condition is being reversed. They received us with warm hospitality and genuine affection. They are eager to help and many building projects are underway. I caught on to the native language quickly. They are excited to learn building techniques and they will have no trouble becoming skilled in electronic and computer technology.

Eden trees are being planted as fast as the land is surveyed and laid out. The sick and physically injured are the first to receive the fruit; since the supply is still limited some has to be imported. The Eden fruit works quickly. What a joy to see the little blind boy they call 'Moses-Russell' regain his sight. He ran into my arms last night with tears in his eyes. "Allon-Aron, Allon-Aron, you brought this fruit and now I see! I see you! But your face—are you sick? I will share my fruit with you, Allon-Aron." He thought I looked sick because he had only seen his dark skinned family, and here I was, light skinned!!! What a joy to see the lame walking, lepers cleansed and the scourge of AIDS quickly healed.

Morning worship services are crowded. They sing wonderfully, from the heart. They love to talk about the scriptures and they have many questions. They can't wait till Grandma and Grandpa Obadiah come. They want to meet the man who grows the 'miracle fruit from God.'

We're making good progress establishing factories so that soon they will be manufacturing all they need to prepare for the generations past to be raised. It is so exciting to be here, and so far, no mamba snakes.

  Miss you all, and love you,
  Allon

Rebekah smiled as she shut down her computer. She got up and went outside. She sat on her bench in the garden orchard and looked up through the lattice of silver branches and leaves at the sunset sky.

She felt the need to seek out Millie that afternoon. As she held in her arms the infant daughter that had been assigned to Millie's charge close to her heart, she felt a bitter pang of loss, and she cried freely. Millie sat with her and they talked. Rebekah was able to share the experience of her decision to abort her first child. Millie wept with her and shared with her the anguish of her longing for a child and her inability to conceive. And then they laughed as the infant smiled and marveled at the baby's perfectly round face. Then it was time for Rebekah to leave. "Thank you, Millie; this has been so wonderful for me." Rebekah left Millie's house feeling a little taller and a little stronger.

Rebekah remembered the reflection of the baby's face as she stared at the evening sky. And as the red glow dimmed to purple, she imagined little Moses-Russell running after Allon in her mind's eye.

"And I will make them and the places round
about my hill a blessing;
And I will cause the shower to come down in his season;
There shall be showers of blessing"
(Ezekiel 34:26).

Chapter Thirteen

Lev sat on the sofa in the living room of the small Schultz cottage that he and his four friends had worked so hard to complete. His heart beat faster than usual in anticipation of the miracle he was about to witness. It was like a birth and he felt like the father.

"I gathered the Eden fruit, and I brewed the resurrection tea," he informed Marta. "Did you bring the Eden pastries?"

Marta smiled, "Yes, Lev, for the third time. Why don't you sit down? There's not much more we can do." They had chosen to skip the chapel service so that they could make the preparations, and now there was nothing more to do but wait.

Lev closed his eyes and pictured from the briefing he had received from the Ancients the last events this small family would remember. They had been on a family drive and happened to make a wrong turn. Aaron must have realized it immediately. They were in hostile territory. Lev imagined the lump in Aaron's throat and the sweat that suddenly appeared on his forehead. Aaron and his wife Eva were pulled out of the car and beaten by the mob. Aaron's last thought had been for his small daughter, Ami. "Please," he had pleaded, "have mercy on the child." But a Hamas terrrist shot the little girl who was cowering in the back seat of the car.

"*Allah Akhbar!*" [Allah be praised], he had shouted, with a tone of triumph. Some in the crowd shook their heads and left immediately to show their disapproval. All three died and the crowd quickly dispersed as an Israeli patrol appeared.

Lev knew the time was close at hand. He rose and began to pace the floor. Soon a man and a woman he had never met would find themselves in a room they had never seen. Lev and his friends would have the privilege of comforting them. Then their daughter Ami would be raised.

Lev strained his ears for signs of life. He thought he heard a door open and turned to face the bedroom entrance. Aaron stood there in the doorway, frightened and ready to run. Lev spoke softly, "Shalom, Aaron. It's safe here. You, Eva and Ami are safe now."

Aaron's brow was furrowed. "Safe," he repeated to himself as he looked around the room to reassure himself that it was a truly safe place. He spoke to himself again, "Maybe I was having a nightmare." Aware again of Lev's presence, Aaron sighed in relief. "Thank God. Look, I don't know who you are and I don't know what I am doing in your house. Forgive me if I have intruded upon you. My last memories were horrible and I can't quite figure out..."

At that moment Eva's door opened. She had heard Aaron's voice and had quickly dressed. When she opened the door and saw her husband, she rushed into his arms. "Oh, Aaron, I thought I had lost you."

Lev watched at a respectful distance for a moment and became aware that from the kitchen archway his four friends were also watching from a distance. Tears came to his eyes as he watched the two hold each other.

They talked in quiet sentences with tears and joy.

"I must have had the same dream as you, Aaron." Eva said. And then she stiffened. "Where's Ami," she inquired with sudden concern. She looked around the room and saw Lev.

"It's safe here, Eva. We'll explain everything to you both soon. Ami is in the room down the hall. You should both go to her now. She will need you to comfort her so that she knows that she's safe here, too." The questions the couple wanted to ask were forgotten as they immediately headed for the door to Ami's room.

Ami

Aaron and Eva entered Ami's room and found her wrapped in blankets on the bed. She appeared to be sleeping, and her small chest rose and fell slowly and evenly. Eva squeezed Aaron's hand with tears streaming down her face as they quietly walked closer and saw that Ami looked healthy and happy in her sleep. Then Ami began to stir, and her little voice screamed out, "No!" She began to thrash around and then to sob. Both parents rushed to her side. Eva sat on the bed and scooped her up, blankets and all, then rocked her gently with Aaron close beside. Lev closed the door when he saw that Eva and Aaron were prepared to give Ami the comfort she needed.

Lev and his four friends stood in a circle in the living room. They heard Ami's sobs and the soothing voices of her parents.

After a time the sobs of the child were quieted and suddenly they heard a giggle, and then another and another. The five friends looked at one another with wide smiles, inspired by the infectious giggles of the little girl. A laugh escaped Marta's lips first, and then Mary's, and soon each of the five were laughing and crying at the same time. Joel gave a last squeeze of his hand, looked toward Ami's door as if he expected the family to emerge at any moment. He headed toward the kitchen to continue preparations. The others followed, except for Lev. He sat on the sofa for a few more minutes and wiped his eyes, then rose when he saw Ami's door open.

The small family emerged, Eva and Aaron arm in arm and little Ami hiding behind her mother while holding her hand.

"Shalom, Eva. Shalom, Aaron." Lev extended his hand in the gesture of a friend. "And Shalom to you, Ami," he said as he slowly and playfully tilted his head and leaned around Eva to catch a glimpse of the little girl who only hid her face deeper into her mother's skirts. "Breakfast is served," he announced as he motioned toward the kitchen.

Lev joined the kitchen crew and Marta helped the three to be seated, and then joined them. In a scene that resembled a well-run restaurant, they served Eden pastries, Eden fruit, and Mary poured resurrection tea. Joseph prayed and then seated himself at the table.

"First a toast," Lev suggested. He remembered clearly the confusion he had felt when his last memories of trauma melted into a feeling of well-being. He remembered the disorientation accentuated by being in a strange new place, and he wanted to encourage each of the three to drink the special tea of Eden tree leaves. "To your new lives." Eva and Aaron sipped the tea carefully, and then gratefully drank of it until their cups were empty. Lev saw the calming effects of the tea as the lines of uneasiness in Eva's face smoothed into a more relaxed expression of curiosity and peace.

Ami tugged at her mother's sleeve and pointed to the glass just out of her reach. "I'm sorry, Ami, I forgot all about you," Eva said as she lifted the cup, tested the tea for temperature and then handed it to her daughter. All eyes were on Ami as she took a careful sip and then guzzled down the cup of tea. Her dark round eyes were all of her face that could be seen as she drank. When she finished she placed her cup on the table and tugged at her mother's shirtsleeve again.

"I want more, please," she whispered rather loudly, which set the whole group to laughing. Ami did not seem to mind for she was intent on watching Mary pour the warm beverage into her cup. She smiled and again put the glass to her lips.

"Wait till you try this," Lev said playfully more to Ami than to her parents. "Its Eden fruit and it's better than candy." He took a bite of the fruit that had been placed on his plate.

"Eden fruit...you mean like the Garden of Eden?" Aaron asked, as he bit off a piece of fruit. "Wow, this is good," he said, "Did you try this, Eva—best fruit I've ever tasted."

These comments broke the ice and a lively conversation ensued. The five friends introduced themselves and took turns responding to questions. They explained that they were living in a new era, that a battle involving many nations had taken place at Megiddo and had been won by God and that after that the raising of the Ancients, the People of God, had come to pass. They explained how the seeds from the Garden of Eden had been preserved and planted in Israel, and the miraculous effects of the fruit on both the mind and body.

"It's amazing, the stamina this fruit brings," said Joel.

"And the clear thinking," Marta added.

Ami climbed off her chair as the discussion continued and disappeared into her room. In a moment Ami returned with one hand behind her back as Aaron asked the question, "Where will we live?" When Ami approached the table and again pulled on her mothers sleeve the discussion stopped. She mutely stretched out her hand to show her mother the surprise she was hiding. A very soft brown stuffed puppy looked at Eva with very large sad eyes.

Barakel

"Ami! That's just like the favorite toy you lost," Eva said in amazement.

Ami nodded her head quickly in excitement. "Yup. Just like Barakel."

"We thought that it would help her to feel at home," Mary explained.

"Barakel—that means 'Blessed of God,' doesn't it. A *great* name for your puppy—from now on your life will be full of 'Barakel,'" Lev added.

Eva shook her head from side to side in disbelief as she lifted her daughter into her lap. "It's beyond my imagination how all this could be happening. You are all so kind," she said as tears welled up in her eyes.

"You will live here," Joseph said in answer to the original question that was asked before the flow of conversation had been interrupted. "*This* is *your* home."

"You had no relatives who survived you, so we volunteered to build this house for you," Joel continued. "You will live here without fear. No one will ever harm you again. You have everything to sustain you forever right here."

"Who is the great benefactor that has provided us with this home? How will we pay for it?" asked Aaron.

"Messiah. All these blessings are from Jesus, the Messiah," Mary said gently.

Aaron and Eva looked at each other in confusion. The conversation continued briefly on prophecies of the *Torah* which were fulfilled by the life, death and resurrection of Jesus, and then the work of blessing that they were now experiencing.

"Soon you will be privileged to receive your parents and your sister back to life again. You will be able to build houses and plant orchards for them. This process will go on until all the dead are raised to life, finally including Adam and Eve."

"Whoa," Aaron, said, as he pushed his chair a few inches from the table. "That's a lot to think about."

"Why don't we show you your new home?" Lev suggested, realizing that Aaron and Eva had reached the point of overload that he remembered so well. "You'll have plenty of time to sort things out. I felt totally confused and overwhelmed, but it didn't take long for things to make sense," Lev reassured them as he rose from his place at the table.

Lev and Mary led them through the house and the orchard while Joel, Joseph and Marta cleaned up after breakfast. After the tour Lev and Mary led them to the orchard where they sat on benches and continued to talk. Ami played in the grass by the 'Trees of Life,' munching on the fruit that had fallen on the ground and trying to feed it to her puppy.

"So what was your last memory, Lev?" Aaron asked.

Lev shared his experience, as did Mary. When Mary finished describing her brutal experience and how Messiah had healed her heart of all hatred, Eva took Mary's hand in hers.

"You understand, don't you?" she asked quietly.

"Yes, I do. Tell us about your experience, Eva. It will help to talk about it."

"Our experience was brutal also, and I remember the panic I felt when I thought of what they might do to Ami." She looked over at her daughter and smiled.

We Made a Wrong Turn

Aaron filled in some of the background details. "Most Palestinians were made to believe that we had stolen their land and nation. The Arabs were historically nomads in this region, and Jews and Christians lived here also, but the Arabs claimed it as their own—even though there never had been a Palestinian nation. When the peace process turned sour, the Palestinians were encouraged to retaliate against the Jews. We made a wrong turn into an Arab community and our car was spotted."

Eva took a deep breath and continued. "Soon we were surrounded. They smashed the windows of our small car and dragged both Aaron and I out into the street. They were kicking us and beating us with their gun butts. Ami was hiding in the back seat of the car. I remember hearing Aaron make a last plea for her life, I heard Ami scream and I heard a gunshot. Then I remember nothing, absolutely nothing, until this morning." Eva had tears in her eyes and she tightly held Aaron's hand in hers. "It's like awakening after a terrible storm and watching a beautiful sunrise," she said as she again looked over at her daughter.

Eva added, "They were taught hatred in their homes, in their schools, and their news reports. A lifetime of learned hatred can't go away in a moment."

Aaron rubbed Eva's hand and looked directly at Lev. "You said we would be safe." His tone was serious. "But these people will be raised with the same memories that I have. Some of those who killed us were full of rage. How will the heart of stone be replaced with a heart of flesh?" His eyes locked their penetrating gaze into Lev's.

"They had to be brainwashed into that kind of conduct." Lev spoke softly, with confidence. "The power of Messiah is greater than anyone's hatred or desire to destroy. Nothing is allowed to happen that will impede the voluntary progress and growth of any of our human family. 'They will neither harm nor destroy on all my holy mountain.'" Lev quoted the Prophet Isaiah.

"'For the earth shall be full of the knowledge of the LORD, as the waters cover the sea.'" Aaron finished the verse and looked puzzled.

"You're probably remembering a verse that you haven't heard in years, right?" Aaron nodded his head in agreement. "It's the effect of being raised with a new brain and it's the effect Eden fruit has on it." Lev smiled to remember his own confusion and pleasure at his newfound memory for scripture. "There's another kind of brainwashing on this New Earth. The knowledge and experience of God and Messiah cleanses the heart, and the experience of being blessed, of being healed in body and mind, erases the need to hurt and destroy ourselves and others."

Lev continued, "And for those who resist this natural process of healing, there are immediate consequences so that they cannot carry out any action that would destroy another's spiritual progress."

"It seems impossible," Eva whispered, "but so does the fact that we've been raised with no wounds, and that you," Eva looked over at Mary, "have been healed of your own hatred and the trauma of your memories." Eva looked over in concern at her daughter who was now on all fours pretending to be the mama dog.

Joseph said, "And it will be a healing that happens more quickly than you would guess. She will forget the horror she experienced for periods of time, like she is now. But there will be times when her memory returns to that terrible scene, and she will feel fear. Talk to her about it. Give her plenty of resurrection tea and Eden fruit. Love, in time, will remove the terror of that event and leave only a memory that has odium but no trauma."

Uncle Lev

The afternoon and evening were spent answering questions, pausing for meals, and times of play with Ami. Each of the five visitors found themselves on the floor with Ami at one time or another, chasing her around. Lev hadn't played with a child in a long time.

Later in the day Eva and Aaron requested to see the footage of the war against Jerusalem. They believed the prophecies that spoke of the victory of God on behalf of Israel over the enemy forces that would come against her. But it was another thing to watch the Scriptures unfold before their eyes.

Goodbyes were said early in the evening. Ami gave each of the visitors a hug until she came to Lev. She pulled on his pant leg, and he knelt down beside her. "Uncle Lev, will you come to my house tomorrow?" she asked.

"Yes, Ami, I will. First we'll go to a special meeting where people sing songs to God. And then we'll go on a special trip to Jerusalem.

You'll get to see the People of God. Remember Daniel in the lions den?"

"Yup." Ami nodded her head in agreement. "Thank you, Uncle Lev," she said as she gave him the biggest hug her little arms could muster.

"You are so welcome, Ami." Lev got on all fours and panted like a dog, and chased Ami straight into the arms of her mother.

"Goodnight, Eva." Lev embraced her and then her husband. "Goodnight, Aaron."

"Shalom, kind friends." Aaron responded.

As the five visitors left, Lev turned to give the new family one last wave. Ami was playing touch noses with her puppy, while in the arms of her mother. Eva was resting her head on Aaron's shoulder and Aaron's big arms were wrapped around her delicate shoulders, his fingers gently stroking Ami's dark hair. "Barakel," Ami giggled. He knew he would always remember that image of hope and joy.

"Blessing," said Lev quietly as he walked away. "Blessing in place of tragedy and fear, for all my human family."

*"For as the heavens are higher than the earth,
So are my ways higher than your ways,
And my thoughts than your thoughts"
(Isaiah 55:9).*

Chapter Fourteen

Lev had enjoyed watching the Schultz family during the worship service that morning. Ami had introduced her puppy to everyone she saw and gave her new friends Barakel's paw to everyone to shake.

Aaron and Eva met another family who had lost a loved one by mob attack, and they were able to share their experiences and weep together. Lev had watched Aaron's expression of concern turn to joy as he heard the various testimonies on how the leadings and spirit of Messiah had brought about healing of heart to ones trapped by fear, hate, and prejudice.

Lev had introduced Aaron, Eva and Ami to his own family when the service ended. He looked as if he was the proud father of the three newly raised. "Isn't she wonderful?" He had asked Rebekah and Annie in reference to Ami. "They went through a terrible ordeal, but I think they'll heal quickly.

Rebekah had noticed his animated pride immediately and playfully had put her hand over his lips. "You're like a new-father chatter-box, Lev. It's pretty special to be part of someone's raising, isn't it?"

Lev had been quiet for the first time after the service ended. "I guess I am a little bit wound up. So was it this exciting for you when I was raised?" he asked.

Rebekah had nodded her head and smiled. "Yes, Lev, I wouldn't trade the experience for anything."

Aaron, Eva and Ami Meet John the Baptist

Lev and the small family had eaten a simple lunch of Eden fruit at Lev's home and had taken the journey to Jerusalem in a car borrowed from Jake. They now were waiting in the reception room to meet one of the Ancients.

"Uncle Lev, where is Daniel? I want to meet Daniel!" Ami sat on the floor by her mother and father on the wooden bench of the reception room of the main office of the Ancients. She played with her puppy and was filled with excitement to think of meeting the People of God she had heard about from her parents.

"We'll have to wait and see which one of the Ancients is able to meet us. It will be a surprise." Lev leaned over, patted the puppy on the head and smiled. Ami was a joy to be with, as were her parents, he thought.

"Shalom," a deep male voice called to them. A tall man with a dark beard approached the small group. "I am here to meet Lev, Aaron, Eva and Ami." He shook each hand warmly, and when he came to Ami he knelt down so as to see her eye to eye. "And you must be Ami," he said and his smile was radiant. He extended his hand to her and she put her puppy's paw in his. "Shalom," the tall man spoke directly to the puppy, "you must be a special friend of Ami's. And your name is—?"

"Barakel. Her name is Barakel. And she is happy to meet you. And she wants to know if you are the one who slept all night with the lions."

The man chuckled. "Ami, I'm afraid you have me confused with one of my good friends, Daniel. *My* name is John."

"I don't think my Mommy told me any stories about John. Are you from the Bible?"

"I certainly am. I was the very last prophet. And I was a special friend and cousin to Jesus the Messiah."

Ami looked up at her mother in confusion, who said, "I never knew about John, honey, we're learning about this together."

John proceeded to paint a simple portrait with his words of who Jesus was, how he was the Lamb of God, and how the prophecies pointed to his unexpected ministry of humiliation and death. "And now," John continued, "he is using his resurrection power to bless you and your Mom and Dad, and all the families of the earth."

Ami pulled on her father's pant leg and whispered, "Will you please pick me up so I can see Mr. John better?"

"In fact," John went on, there is good news today. We have a few more nations who wish to come under Messiah's rule." And then he looked directly at Lev. "One of those nations is Germany. They held out a little longer than some of the other nations, but they have had no rain. They finally decided to accept the authority of the King. I'll be making a visit there next month."

Aaron and Eva were fascinated. "Germany! And they are willing to put aside their reticence to accept the Messiah of the Jewish people?" Aaron asked incredulously.

"There are still some who aren't happy about the transition. It will take patience and love to help them overcome their feelings. But the love and healing of Messiah are hard to resist in the long run."

Lev spoke before he had time to think. "I'd like to help in any way I can."

Aaron raised his eyebrows. "I admire your courage, Lev. I'm not sure I'm ready to venture into a nation with such a history. But, then, I'm only a day old…"

"Actually I'm not that much older than you, and I know I'm not highly qualified for much yet." Lev began to feel nervous realizing he had just offered his services without fully thinking it out, and then continued his run-on sentences to John the Baptist. "I'm really not that old at all, I want to help and I'm studying diligently. I hope I'll be prepared soon, but I know I'm not ready for much yet…"

John chuckled again, and looked into Lev's eyes as if he could see right through to his heart. "I'll make a mental note of this. The name is Lev Aron, right? I appreciate what I sense are love and a sincere desire to help pass on blessings to others, and I also sense the hesitation and fear in your heart. You will only be asked to do what you are able to do through Christ, and only when you are ready. The healing is the work of Christ and his Anointed—we are merely the instruments."

John then talked directly to Aaron and Eva. "You both have experienced the brutality of hatred and prejudice." The prophet's eyes filled with tears as he looked into the faces of Aaron, Eva and little Ami. "I also have experienced this brutality, as have so many of our human family. Be assured that our dealings with all nations are in absolute truth and sincerity. We are not ambassadors that go forth to make deals with anyone. Christ has set the terms. These terms are fixed and unmovable. People must comply fully and, as time goes on, wholeheartedly. This will be true for Germany as well as all the other nations. There is no need to fear, for the power and protection of Christ is all around us."

"God will bless you, Ami," John said as he tousled her dark hair and then patted the puppy's head. "Shalom to each of you. God's blessing will surely follow you." He left as suddenly as he had appeared.

The four stood there in silence, watching John walk across the large reception room to another office door. Ami was the first to speak. "He's as nice as you are Daddy," she said with eyes as wide as saucers as she blew a kiss toward the door that the Prophet John had just entered.

Germany on the Horizon

Lev drove the Shultz family home and then went to Jake's home. Lev, Jake, Rachel and Annie had a brief discussion over dinner. Lev told them more about the Schultz family, their encounter with the Prophet John, and the news of Germany's desire to come under the New Covenant arrangement.

"I even offered my services in Germany."

Jake looked surprised. "Lev, you've always been very troubled about the role of the Germans in the Holocaust. You've either lost your mental faculties or you've developed more character than I thought you had. I hope you realize that all the prejudice and hatred shown the Jews won't go away overnight."

"Yes, I know that," Lev said, suddenly very serious. "And that scares me, and perhaps I spoke too quickly. But John reassured me that the healing work belongs to Christ, and that we are only asked to do what we are able to with his power. If the Ancients are willing to go there, why can't I go to assist them? And I was thinking I died once trying to live my life in my own headstrong way. I don't mind some sweat and toil and even resentment until the world learns to bow their knees to Christ."

"Maybe you were speaking straight from your heart when you offered your services, Uncle Lev," Annie spoke up, "and if they ask you to serve in Germany, it will be because they know what's in your heart, and because you have been prepared in a special way. I want to volunteer for whatever they want me to do. If they chose me to go to Germany, I hope I would say yes."

"Well, big brother, if you are willing to go, and if John the Baptist ever calls you, tell him you have a brother who is willing to go also."

"Include me, too." Rachel added.

Anya's Date

Lev walked home in the early evening twilight and decided to go a little out of his way to see if Rebekah was home. As he came to her house he noticed the lights were on, so he knocked on her door. She invited him in.

"Lev, you're beaming. You had a great day with your new family, didn't you?" she said as they embraced.

"I did, Rebekah, and not only that, we were able to talk to John the Baptist." Rebekah was interested and excited as Lev reported the events of the day and the conversation with John.

"They couldn't have a better person going to Germany. He dealt with corruption of power in government and he faced the fear and prejudice that led to his beheading. God was working through the long centuries of history to select leadership for this very time. I guess he prepares us also for the ability to carry his blessing to others."

Rebekah motioned for Lev to sit at the kitchen table across from her. "Lev, I've been doing a lot of thinking about Anya. I'm looking forward to meeting her."

Lev leaned back in his chair and stared at Rebekah as she continued to speak. "She will be raised in five months. I want to help. Lev, let's phone the Ancients and find out if there's anyway I can help."

"Rebekah, you are amazing. I can't tell you how much this means to me," Lev said as he reached for the phone that Rebekah had already placed on the table. He dialed the number for the Ancients and waited.

The receptionist listened to Lev's inquiry regarding meeting someone who was to be raised soon and his desire, to be of some help. She took down Lev's name and Anya's name and asked him to hold the line.

"This is David, Lev. How may I help you?"

Lev explained Anya's relationship to him, and that he knew that she had a sister named Angela, and how he and his second wife Rebekah wanted to be of help to her. David gave Lev Angela's phone number and address and suggested that when the time came he should meet with Anya first, to bring her up to date, before Rebekah was introduced to her. He added, "As the time draws closer you can make definite arrangements with Angela to be there when Anya is raised."

Lev hung up the phone and dialed Angela's number. "I'm calling Anya's sister, Angela now," he informed Rebekah as he waited for someone to answer. Lev was delighted when a young woman answered and remembered his name.

"And the spirit of the LORD shall rest upon him —
The spirit of wisdom and understanding,
The spirit of counsel and might…"
(Isaiah 11:2).

Chapter Fifteen

The minute that Ariel Aron opened the door and entered the living room that he did not yet know was his, Rebekah and Lev simultaneously called out "Dad" and rushed forward to embrace him. Allon watched close at hand, unable as yet to break through for a hug.

"Lev!" the tall, well-built man exclaimed with a smile. "Rebekah!" he added, as he held both her hands in his. "You look so well, the both of you. I must have a screw loose, because nothing is making any sense. You have some explaining…" Ariel stopped in mid sentence as he saw another young man stand before him who looked vaguely familiar.

"And who might this young man be?"

"Grandpa, it's me, Allon." Lev and Rebekah stepped aside so that Allon could embrace him.

Ariel broke the embrace and held Allon by the shoulders and looked deeply into his eyes. "You were a child when I last saw you. How can this be? Where am I? Where is Hannah? I remember clearly she was at my side…" Ariel shook his head and his brow was furrowed as he looked at his three very dear family members. "All I remember was an explosion of some kind. But here I am without a scratch on me. I just don't understand…"

Lev placed his hand on his father's shoulder. "Dad, come and sit down with us. We have some catching up to do." Lev led his father to the kitchen table. Rebekah sat with him while Allon poured resurrection tea.

"Here, Dad, drink this," Rebekah encouraged. After Ariel had taken a few sips of tea, Rebekah made her announcement in a gentle voice. "You died in that explosion, Dad, you and Mom both. But now you are raised from death by the power of Messiah. "

Ariel placed his cup quickly on the saucer and the hot tea sloshed high from side to side. "Do I look like I was mangled in that explosion? I have never felt better in my life."

"It was the same for me, Dad," Lev offered. "I was killed in the final invasion against Israel. The last thing I remembered was losing my left hand, and I had the same questions. Did you look in the mirror after you were awakened?"

"Now that you mention it, I did. And I was surprised that my partial plate was gone and all my teeth were straight. I looked for my glasses and couldn't find them, but I don't seem to need them anymore...I must admit I am puzzled, but hey, I'm not complaining. I like all the changes!"

"Did you notice you had a full head of hair, Dad?" Lev continued to probe.

Ariel nodded in affirmation as he ran his fingers through his salt and pepper thick, wavy hair. "Hmmm." He acknowledged the question with only a sound and instinctively reached for the cup of tea and drained its remaining contents quickly.

Rebekah gently rubbed Ariel's hand. "You died in that awful explosion, and so did Mom." Rebekah recalled the evening she had gotten the news. Ariel and his wife Hannah were courageous people, true to their convictions. Neither of them was afraid when they had moved from the safer Tel Aviv area to a new complex in Hebron. They remained confident, as the Palestinians grew more and more militant. It was at the market place in Kiryat Arba that one of the Hamas set off the explosives in his suicide belt. They were close to the blast and the flying nails and pieces of metal ripped through them.

Tears welled up in his eyes at the mention of his wife. He gripped Rebekah's hand tightly. "Hannah—where is she now? Is she all right? Where is she?" he asked in an urgent tone.

"She'll be with us soon, Grandpa," said Allon. "In fact, she's probably asking the same questions about you right about now. She's with Jake and Rachel. They're within walking distance and will arrive here soon. We'll have our first breakfast together."

Rebekah remembered the report of her mother-in-law's last words. "Ariel, where is my Ariel?" she had pleaded.

"She's alright, then? Thank God. I'm here, she's there, you three are here, Jake and Rachel are there, we are healthy and whole, and Messiah has come." Ariel lifted his hands toward the heavens to emphasize his last words. He smiled, and then laughed, and then he began to weep.

Lev and Allon drew closer to Ariel by moving their chairs, and Rebekah knelt at his side with her arm around his neck. Rebekah saw the sparkle return to his eyes as his emotions calmed and the startling reality of the New Earth began to dawn on his consciousness. He ate Eden fruit with gusto and amazement. He marveled at the origins of Eden fruit and its powers. Their conversation continued until there was a knock at the door.

Hannah

"Ariel—where is my Ariel?" a sweet voice called from the doorway as Hannah, Rachel, Jake and Annie entered.

Rebekah smiled. The crowning moment for which they had worked had finally come. The five of them, often accompanied by other volunteers, had worked on building the two homes for Ariel and Hannah with untiring enthusiasm. The work had progressed smoothly for the past two and a half months with no mistakes and with no need of a boss, for each of them knew exactly what needed to be done at every stage of building. The clothing and household necessities were secured, and the garden was in full bloom. They had sent word to Ghana to make arrangements for Allon to be present for the raising of his Grandparents. And now was the climactic, miraculous moment when they would see Ariel and Hannah together they would be a family again after so long.

Hannah and Ariel found their way to one another in the center of the living room, as they embraced and wept. And then they broke their embrace and stared at one another. "Not a scratch on your dear face, Ariel, not one."

"Hannah, you are alive and well, and more beautiful than I can remember," Ariel said in awe and wonder as he cupped her face in his hands.

Aron Family Reunion

The morning passed quickly as the Aron family took the time to catch up on what had happened in the old world and the changes that had taken place on the New Earth. They marveled at Eden fruit, they marveled at the fruit that Allon brought from Ghana, and they marveled at their circle of family and the love that had been poured upon them.

Slowly, their uneasy confusion and uncertainty melted into a state of peaceful questioning. They had toured Ariel's home, and then Hannah insisted that they tour her home also, though she was still perplexed as to why they were to live in separate houses. That gave the small family an opportunity for exercise and gave the senior Arons a chance to get acquainted with their community.

After they returned to Ariel's home they sorted out their last memories of the explosion. They watched footage from the final battle. Ariel and Hannah wept at the scenes of destruction, and then they wept at the scenes of healing and joy recorded as many nations came under the authority of the Ancients.

Ariel spoke with emotion as they gathered around the dining room table for a late lunch.

"This is the day we had all prayed for, when God would again visit his people. Never did we realize how God would rise so mightily on our behalf. And yet the mercy of Messiah does not end in Israel. It only begins here, to be shared with all the people of the nations."

"At last we have a chance to rectify our mistakes." Hannah's voice sounded perplexed. "That was the tragedy of the past. By the time we learned certain lessons, it was too late to undo the consequences of our choices." And then her gentle voice trailed off. "There are things I would have done differently…"

Rachel spoke up. "We were victims of dark spiritual forces that made wrong appear right and right appear wrong. Not just from the inside in our own thinking, but from the media and from schools. We were conditioned to lay aside the absolute laws of God and replace them with popular misconceptions."

Allon continued. "We all had our misconceptions. The terrorist that took your lives took his, also. He died thinking that his actions would be rewarded in paradise. He died thinking that his hatred and violence were the answer to the problems of his people. He was born and bred on a diet of hatred. Thank the Lord, his violence was not the last chapter, but the beginning of another chapter in his life. He will have all the healing and support he will need to learn to love."

Rebekah had watched both Ariel and Hannah as they had stared at Annie and then at Allon. They had seen Allon as a young boy, but only remembered Annie as a small child. They were delighted with them both. Rebekah could see how these two young people were strong and tangible evidence to an older, newly risen generation of the New Earth changes. Seeing Allon and Annie made them realize that a time lapse had occurred. The preservation of identity in the resurrection was uncanny. Both these young people bore unmistakable and endearing resemblance to the sons and daughters-in-law they loved dearly. To have loving family members around when one was raised was a tremendous blessing, which eased adjustments and brought such joy. Rebekah marveled at the loving provisions of Christ.

"Annie, you're such a mature young lady, so poised and charming." Hannah broke her silence as fruit was passed across the table. "You must be advanced in your schooling."

Annie explained the changes in the New Earth education and how the Ancients taught classes which were available on the computer and on television. "And it's so easy to learn now. Eden fruit does wonders for the mind! Our ability to concentrate on complex subjects has increased tenfold. We take courses to prepare us for tasks and assignments, so that we can volunteer our services where we are needed."

"We are building, planting and creating for the generations yet to come. Knowledge is pouring in and everyone is mentally qualified to absorb it and to contribute and enhance it, not to destroy, but to pass on the blessings. Jesus, the Christ, is a wise user of knowledge. He doesn't judge by the sight of the eyes, but he will judge with righteousness," Allon added with an allusion to the Prophet Isaiah.

"Christ in the book of Isaiah...and to think I never saw it before," Ariel spoke softly.

The conversation continued on through lunch. Like a sponge, both Hannah and Ariel seemed to absorb with no apparent struggle the truth that the Messiah was Jesus.

"He knows how to deal with my heart, and he knows how to deal with the poor soul that destroyed himself and us as well." Hannah said, as Ariel nodded in agreement.

"It's starting to make sense," Ariel murmured. "All the prophecies I used to ponder—I just didn't see that the Messiah was the sacrifice our law was pointing to and that his kingship over Israel and the world would be after he had gathered his 'Anointed' as you call them."

Rebekah wasn't surprised at their quick acceptance that Jesus Christ was their Messiah. Ariel and Hannah were good people by any standard of judgment. They loved God, and they loved the *Law* and the *Prophets*. The old world synagogue meetings were the highlights of their week. Ariel had taken special pride in his younger son Jake's rapt attention during services, but Lev's lack of interest was a source of constant irritation. Rebekah tried to prepare herself for the time when the conflicts from the past would come up again.

"Your heart is much more open than mine was, Dad. It took me a week to come to the point of recognizing Christ as Messiah," Lev chimed in.

"You were always too busy to listen." Ariel said with a hint of irritation in his voice. "But you, Jacob, you were the one that was always ready to learn." Ariel patted Jake on the back.

"That was years ago, dear, let's not bring up old baggage," Hannah advised Ariel in a gentle chiding voice as she shook her head in disapproval.

Rebekah saw Lev wince at the memories his father's comment awakened in his mind. She suppressed a desire to change the subject because she knew it was important that issues be exposed and dealt with.

"It's like you were afraid to measure up, afraid to be the young man you were destined to be," Ariel said.

"Ariel, look at your son *now*, look at him *now*." Hannah's voice grew more insistent.

An Embarrassment

Ariel seemed to be lost in a daydream of his own from the past, and he continued on as if Hannah had not spoken.

"And then you changed those grades when you were in high school. You brought embarrassment to my family."

Lev's face darkened in color. Jake sat straight up in his chair, ready to come to his brother's rescue, waiting for the proper moment.

"Dad, you never gave me a chance to explain that," Lev said with deliberate calm.

"An embarrassment…"

"Ariel, Lev is trying to talk to you." Hannah added in an urgent tone.

"Its okay, Mom, I can speak for myself," Lev said as he gave his mother a quick smile. "Dad, you are right that I was fidgety and that I didn't care to learn about the Scriptures. I was independent and I didn't think I needed God. I missed out on a lot because of that attitude, but that doesn't mean that I needed your attention or your praise any less than Jake. I spent my whole life trying to prove that I was worth your attention. You didn't mean to, but your favoritism for Jake pitted us against each other."

Jake sat back in his chair with a look of admiration in his eye as he saw Lev speak some hard truths to his father that his brother would never have dared speak in his former life.

Ariel looked uncomfortable as he nervously moved his cup from one position to another on the table before him.

"Dad, I want you to have another cup of tea, and then I want you to really listen to what I have to say."

Rebekah sat up and reached for the pot of tea, and poured it into Ariel's cup quickly. Ariel drank the cup of tea obediently and then stared at his cup.

"Dad, please, I want you to look at me."

Ariel raised his eyes to look into his son's face. "Dad, its true the grades were changed but it was set up to look like I had done it, but I didn't. Dad, I want you to hear what I am saying. *I didn't change the grades.*"

Ariel looked down at his empty cup, and again repeated his mantra as tears filled his eyes. "It was so embarrassing." He rose, excused himself and walked to his room and shut the door behind him.

"He's sorting it all out, Lev, dear. Give him some time." Hannah said with a faltering voice as she patted Lev on the hand.

"I needed time myself, Mom, on my first day. I also became overwhelmed. For me it was acceptance of Messiah. For Dad, it's…"

"Accepting the past, his and yours. Accepting that his two sons were very different, but their differences made them no less special. I can see now, one of the things I would have done differently, Lev. I would have tried to give you a chance to speak for yourself instead of always trying to smooth things over. We never got to the bottom of anything. I see now that I would not let you or Jake grow up, as you needed to. I hurt you both by coming to the rescue all the time and it interfered with your relationship with each other, as well as with your Father. But you have grown up so much, Lev, being able to speak your mind the way you did, with respect and directness. I'm just sorry that Ariel has so much to sort out on his first day of life."

Ariel's Apology

The conversation continued around the table for another hour until the door to Ariel's room slowly opened.

Ariel cleared his throat as he approached the table. "Excuse me, please, for my outburst. I especially ask your pardon, Lev." Ariel walked to Lev's chair and put his arms on his oldest son's shoulders. He bent over his son and whispered in his ear. "We'll talk sometime soon, son. It's long overdue," and then he took his place beside Hannah.

"You've got to give an old man a little time to realize he's not too old to learn," Ariel added in good humor and lightheartedness again filled the room.

"And forgive us our debts, as we forgive our debtors"
(Matthew 6:12).

Chapter Sixteen

The following morning the Aron family went to the factory. Ariel and Hannah were thoroughly fascinated by the New World factory. They were amazed at the processes that made the materials for construction of homes so simply and efficiently. Lev had to smile as he watched them. They seemed delighted with every phase of the New Earth.

Ariel could not get over their first worship service of that morning. "A perfect way to start each day—and with such good participation—and with such beautiful hymns," he exclaimed.

"And women speak and share their hearts as the men do. There is such inspiration shared at these meetings." Hannah's face beamed as she joined in Ariel's accolade of the worship service.

They had met other newly raised individuals and their families and had heard the stories of the prayers and preparations that each generation was making for the next. They were beginning to sense the breadth of the restitution work and realized that they were witnessing a great reversal of the death process. A carefully designed return to life was in progress, bringing joy and gladness to those who learned to love. The same process brought anxiety and concern to those who had not learned to love. But the anxiety and concern were vital to the learning process, and people were given opportunity and support to face their mistakes.

The apprehension of facing his father that Lev had initially ignored had subsided as he realized he had the strength and maturity to be his own man. He had all the confidence in the world that, given a little time, the conflicts between them would be resolved. And he was willing to wait if need be. Lev already sensed that his father watched him through less critical eyes.

As Rachel and Rebekah continued to show the senior Arons around the factory, Lev excused himself to find Reuben.

Reuben's Confession

"Shalom!" Lev called out when he spotted Reuben.

Reuben's eyes dropped and he remained silent, looking at the ground, until Lev stood directly before him. "Just leave me alone, Lev. Leave me to my misery. That's what I deserve."

"Why would you say that, Reuben?" Lev asked.

"I've made too many mistakes. They are like weights pulling me under. I don't have the energy to bear these burdens anymore. I deserve to be miserable," Reuben added, still staring at the floor.

"We've all made mistakes. We've all hurt others and ourselves. But regardless of our mistakes we've been given a great gift. Nothing we do could lift the sentence of death from us. But Christ showed such love—the willingness to die so we could live. It's a gift Reuben—that no one deserves—it's a gift—and our part is to accept it."

"You don't know, Lev, you don't know what I've done."

"Christ knows, and he chose to raise you to life."

Reuben looked up quickly as if those words had struck a chord within him. Tears filled his eyes.

"I never told anyone before, but I am responsible for my son's death. My wife, my son, my daughter and I were on a camping trip. It was reported that he fell and died. The truth is I struck him in a fit of anger, and he fell backward with his head striking a rock and then slid down a rocky ravine. Even my wife doesn't know the truth. I hate myself for not owning up to it—but I can't."

"Christ already knows what you've done, Reuben, and he has raised you to a new life. He has given you a new beginning..."

Reuben interrupted. "I've delayed asking for my son, Joseph, to be raised. How can I face him? How can I face his mother? How can I face all the people who consoled me, thinking his death was accidental? I am a murderer and a hypocrite. I was sorry when I returned to life because the pain was still there."

"And there is one way to dispel the pain. Be honest about what you have done. There is forgiveness with Christ." As Lev spoke these words, he felt his stomach tighten as his mind riveted on the phrase 'a murderer and a hypocrite.' He was suddenly struck with a realization of the life he had taken in warfare. That did not count as murder, but it was still a burden on his heart because the life that he took was precious to someone. Such are the fortunes of war. He lost his life while taking the life of another. Reuben's son's death was not premeditated murder, but was accidental manslaughter.

Lev's Confession

"Reuben, something you said has made me aware of something about myself. Just before I died in combat, I shot an enemy soldier. I waited; carefully aiming my gun so that when the enemy lifted his head I fired. I saw the soldier fall as my bullet struck him, and then I received no more gunfire from him. That was grim business, the killing business. I didn't have any pleasure in his death. I never forgot the feeling of knowingly taking a human life. I didn't like it, even though that was my job—my duty. War pitted man against man. For a moment I was the victor. The next minute I was hit and died.

"True, I killed a soldier in a time of war, but I realized he didn't want to die. I hope to meet the man I killed and ask his forgiveness.

"Taking life seemed such a final act, but since Christ is raising the dead to life, it is only a temporary sleep until he lives again. Your son knew you didn't want to kill him. True you were angry, but he will be glad to awaken in your arms. He loves you."

Lev felt Reuben's arms around him in an embrace, and he returned the gesture. The two men wept. "We both have our sad memories, hey, Lev?" Reuben said. "If you can be reconciled with the man you killed, then maybe there's some hope for me."

"I know in war we were taught not to feel pity for the enemy, but how often I wish now that I had not been involved in that grim killing business."

"So what's the next step for me, Lev?"

Lev wiped his eyes with his arm and stepped back. "You need to own up to your past and to tell the truth, Reuben. You will need to confess your mistakes and let the healing begin."

"For the first time I feel like there's hope, Lev. And the guy that helps me see it is the guy I set up in high school to look like a fool. Plus I rubbed my relationship with Rebekah in your face…Go figure…"

"What about going to the worship service with your family tomorrow morning? I'll save you a place, Reuben."

"I have avoided those meetings all this time. I thought I would be darkening that holy place with my presence. I knew the truth would be known one day, Lev, but I couldn't face the pain it would bring my family and friends."

"What about the pains of staying as you are now?"

Reuben thought about how short tempered and miserable he had been and the effect on his daughter and wife. He nodded his head slowly. "Yea—I need to fess up. It's destroying me from the inside—and my family, too."

"I'll be there tomorrow for moral support, Reuben," Lev said as he extended his hand and the two shook warmly.

Countenance of Friendship

The next morning Reuben arrived at the worship service with his family and quickly found the places that had been saved for them beside Lev.

Lev put his hand on Reuben's shoulder and smiled. "You can do this, Reuben, I know you can," Lev said.

Reuben was the first to testify. Tears spilled from his eyes as he told the truth about his son's death on the camping trip, his attempts to cover his abusive behavior toward his son and his misery of heart.

"When I was raised from the dead, the weight I carried formerly was right back on my shoulders. I was sorry to be alive and I'm sorry that I have made others miserable because of my own misery. But now I am seeking God's forgiveness and the help of Christ and his Anointed. I have sinned against God, and I have sinned against myself and I have sinned against my son and my family and friends."

Reuben's wife stood up and walked quickly toward him, tears in her eyes as she embraced him. Then his little daughter ran up to the two of them, calling out, "Daddy, Daddy, come sit by me." Reuben scooped her thin frame into his arms and held her there. He spoke in a gentle voice as he and his wife walked back to their seats. "Daddy has been mean, but I will be different now. You'll see, Pumpkin."

Lev stood up immediately and did not leave his position beside Reuben. "I have my friend Reuben to thank for the testimony I am about to give." Lev placed his hand on Reuben's shoulder in a gesture of respect.

"I am very good at avoiding guilt, and his confession to me yesterday made me realize that there is something that I have not dealt with openly in all my new days of life up to this point." Lev described the battle scene in which he took a human life. His voice broke with emotion as he shared the truth of his rage at the enemy soldier.

"He had no name, and he had no face to me. He was no one's son, no one's father, and no one's husband. He was a—'nobody.' And I killed him. Maybe it was my suppressed anger with those who murdered my wife Anya or maybe it was just in the heat of battle, doing what a professional killer should do as I had been taught. I don't honestly know."

Lev went on to share the mercies of having the Lord in his life, and having received his family back. "So here I am. I stand before you and before God, admitting what I was afraid to admit, and wanting love to replace the hostility that once possessed my own heart."

The service ended with a number of testimonies and a short study on the challenges of scriptural values led by the study leader. At the end of the service Reuben and Lev embraced and then found themselves surrounded by fellow worshippers, each sharing a word of comfort or an experience. Lev noticed his father take Reuben aside. They talked together for a short time, and then they embraced. But Ariel did not speak to Lev until they had arrived at Hannah's cottage. The rest of the Aron family continued into the house while Ariel approached Lev and stood before him. He bit his lip.

"Lev, I owe you a hundred apologies, probably more, for all the times I spoke critically of you, for comparing you to your brother and for not accepting you for who you were. Reuben confirmed everything you said. He set you up and I refused to believe you." Ariel put his arm around his son's shoulder.

"Lev, I see now that I was an embarrassment to myself. In my earlier years I was a lot like you—a bit fidgety, not all that interested in services. I actually stole my Rabbi's prayer shawl. I never did own up to it. And all the time I felt like everyone knew that I had taken it, and that I was an embarrassment to my family. So when I used to call you an embarrassment I really was embarrassed at myself. I didn't have the trust I should have had in you, and this is especially wrong since you were indeed worthy of my trust and confidence. I failed you son, I failed you."

Ariel began to walk toward the house, his arm still around Lev. "But what I see in you now, son, is a man who seeks God, who reaches out to others, who is not afraid to say what he thinks. A man who is not afraid to face what is in his heart. I love you, son."

Ariel stopped and embraced Lev. Then the two men walked side by side, talking quietly together, eager to make a fresh start. This time mutual love and respect would produce a loving relationship.

"There is a generation that are pure in their own eyes"
(Proverbs 30:12).

Chapter Seventeen

Lev was eager to find another assignment. He had inquired at several factories, but most were adequately staffed. He didn't want to spend all his time studying, though it wouldn't have been time wasted. He was learning at an accelerated rate.

He had majored in electrical engineering in college, however, information had far surpassed that day. Computer technology fascinated Lev. Not only was knowledge advancing at a rapid pace, but also methods of teaching were superior. In a month he learned more than he had formerly in a year.

Jeremiah Cohen

Early in the morning Lev received a call from an old college friend, Jeremiah Cohen. He said that he would be in the neighborhood for several days and asked Lev if he might stay with him. Lev hospitably invited him.

Jeremiah had gone on to become a rabbi, and Lev had lost contact with him over time. Lev clearly remembered Jeremiah's arrogance, though most people had patiently ignored it. Jeremiah mentioned that while visiting in the area, he would be available to serve in the chapel services and had asked Lev to make the arrangements. Lev didn't know what to say. No rabbis or ministers officiated in any of the chapel services he was attending. In fact, most rabbis and ministers had become discredited due to their lack of understanding of the Bible and their previous affiliations with various political parties.

Lev didn't know how to answer Jeremiah in a polite manner. He had tried to explain that the services were different than those the synagogues used to provide. But Jeremiah had been insistent that he would speak at the chapel. So Lev had given him directions to his home and had told him the time of the meeting.

Jeremiah arrived soon after Lev hung up the phone. After the usual greetings, Jeremiah told Lev that he, too, had died and recently returned to life again. His death was not due to the war, but to an auto accident shortly before the siege against Jerusalem. Lev brought Jeremiah to the chapel early enough to introduce him to Rebekah, Jake, Rachel and Annie.

Lev inquired of those in charge if they might use Jeremiah Cohen, a former orthodox rabbi, in the morning service. They seemed reticent to do so, and questioned Lev if Jeremiah was intending to take over the meeting. However, they decided that if Jeremiah wished to say a few words of testimony on the Lord's leadings in his life, he would be welcome to do so.

After the hymns and a prayer the leader announced that they had a visitor, Jeremiah Cohen, who had recently returned from the dead and wished to say a few words.

Jeremiah, instead of sharing a testimony from his seat in the audience, bounded up to the podium, introduced himself, shook the hand of the study leader and proceeded to give a sermon.

"I am Rabbi Jeremiah Cohen," he introduced himself to the audience. "And I hope to testify to a truth that is not yet recognized. I am here to speak to you regarding the importance of holy leadership."

Lev sensed a wave of uneasiness wash across the room. He closed his eyes, bit his lip and continued to listen.

"We have sinned as a nation by fighting for our land. And our blessing has been, and still is, held back as a result. When Messiah wills it, he will give us our land without any violence, and an immediate blessing of all Jews will be the full measure of his blessing."

Jeremiah went on describing the ravages of war and violence and how not one life would have been lost had Israel surrendered the land that the nations had demanded.

Lev detected obvious signs of impatience from the audience as people squirmed and whispered to one another. He spoke for nearly twenty-five minutes philosophizing on the fortunes of the war. Jeremiah finally closed with a lengthy prayer and then the words, "May we realize the true peace of Jerusalem in our hearts and in our teachings, and may we repent of our old vain traditions of violence and greed."

After the service many people surrounded Jeremiah. He looked satisfied at first, and then he looked perturbed as people questioned and challenged his position. The Lord had moved so decisively in defending His land and people, the audience wondered how anyone dared to be so bold as to suggest other possibilities, but Jeremiah was impervious to any criticism.

They walked back to Lev's home in silence. After sharing tea, Lev decided it was time to bring up Jeremiah's sermon.

"I cannot support what you said in your morning sermon, Jeremiah. God moved mightily against the enemies of Israel. Any suggestion that an alternative approach would have been more pleasing to the Lord is a serious presumption. The nations tried to take what God had given to His people. God punished the nations for their aggression. Bible prophecies clearly show that God would defend Israel by destroying the invading enemies, and history has proven the accuracy of His word. I'm sorry, Jeremiah, I just cannot agree with your perspective."

A lively argument ensued. Lev watched Jeremiah become more and more agitated. The veins in his forehead protruded and he spoke so rapidly that Lev found it hard to get a word in. When Jeremiah took a deep breath and wiped the perspiration from his forehead, Lev took the opportunity to speak.

"You are dangerously close to being silenced by spiritual forces that do not allow preaching anything that is untrue." Lev then shared his own experience in regard to Reuben Meyer.

Jeremiah was plainly annoyed at Lev's criticism. "Well, your punishment was deserved and understandable. I've heard of these consequences when people have resorted to aggression of some kind. But I said nothing that had any violence associated with it. My whole idea was that violence would have been avoided had Israel agreed to the terms the enemy had placed upon them."

"Yes," Lev said, "but you were implying that if your superior wisdom had been used, the results might have been much better. That seems dangerously akin to suggesting to the Lord a better way. There's another kind of violence, Jeremiah, violence against God's Word and how He has chosen to fulfill His purposes."

Lev poured two cups of tea as the two men seated themselves at Lev's kitchen table.

Jeremiah Stays On

Jeremiah suddenly became calm. "I have an appointment during the day, but may I spend the night with you? I should like to stay over for your chapel service tomorrow. Perhaps I might clarify my position."

"You are welcome to stay in my home, Jeremiah."

After a quick lunch Lev felt relieved as Jeremiah walked out the front door. He spent part of the day doing a little pruning of the trees, which he had recently learned how to do. The day passed swiftly. Much of the afternoon he spent in studies both of the Bible and secular works.

Jeremiah returned in time for their evening meal together. He offered a lovely blessing on the food and closed his prayer in the name of Christ.

That was good to hear from a once orthodox rabbi Lev thought. Jeremiah was a talented speaker, but no matter what subject came up, he managed to express strong opinions. Some Lev could agree with, but most left him at a loss for words.

Lev tried to direct the subject into pleasanter channels and asked Jeremiah if he had ever contacted the Ancient Worthies.

"No, they are very busy and I do not wish to place any burdens on them," he said. "I know they are great men and women of God and I rejoice that such capable people are managing our affairs and will shortly be doing so for the whole world."

Lev told of his two contacts with them and how impressed he was with their wisdom and graciousness. Lev related how his right arm had become paralyzed and how he had phoned Sarah.

"She was the kindest person, but she firmly told me I was to tell her everything as truthfully as possible. She said that Christ would reveal the whole truth, and if I tried to color the event it would only prolong my punishment. She soon returned my call, after finding that I had told the truth and that there was provocation involved in the incident. She promised that within the hour I would be healed."

Jeremiah seemed interested, but made it clear that Lev's violent behavior was inexcusable. It only seemed to strengthen his position that the attempts the Israeli soldiers undertook to defend the city were unnecessary. Had they surrendered, the carnage of that fateful time would have been avoided. He argued that the Messiah would have peacefully brought them victory. Everything Lev said seemed to only strengthen Jeremiah's position and resolve as to his correctness.

Lev mentioned Ezekiel 38:16, 21, "And thou shalt come up against my people of Israel, as a cloud to cover the land; it shall be in the latter days, and I will bring thee against my land, that the heathen may know me, when I shall be sanctified in thee, O Gog, before their eyes…And I will call for a sword against him throughout all my mountains, saith the Lord God."

Jeremiah could hardly wait until Lev finished the quotation so that he could again revert to his idea that this only confirmed what had happened and not what needed to happen. Lev found himself very uncomfortable with Jeremiah's constant assertions of a theory that seemed so presumptuous and wrong. The evening was spent in a rather strained discussion. Jeremiah's sense of authority and rightness made any healthy exchange impossible. He was quick to challenge everything that did not suit his theory.

Before retiring for the night, Lev again felt the need to warn Jeremiah that Christ might settle the truthfulness or falsity of his theory. Lev could tell Jeremiah was confident that Christ would vindicate him.

In the morning they walked to the chapel. They arrived in time to greet many of the assembled worshipers including Jake, Rachel and Rebekah. As the singing started, Lev could tell that Jeremiah had more on his mind than worship. He was seeking to have the podium. The fact that his message was rejected yesterday didn't seem to matter. He was obsessed with expressing his viewpoint and would not be dissuaded.

After the prayer Lev waited to see how he would seek to present his viewpoint again. Without hesitating, Jeremiah boldly asked the study leader for the floor in order to apologize for his presentation yesterday. This surprised Lev who thought that perhaps it meant he was beginning to see the error of his position. His request was granted.

"I do apologize for my presentation yesterday."

I must reiterate—and hopefully clarify the position I tried to explain yesterday. I—I—I—." Jeremiah's eyes widened with fear and his face flushed with embarrassment, He motioned with his hand, and still no intelligible words came out of his mouth. As hard as he tried, the only word sound he could make was "I." The study leader led him back to his seat next to Lev.

Each worshipper knew that Christ's power had ended Jeremiah's ability to speak. The theme of the meeting suddenly shifted, as one after another stood to share a consequence they had experienced and the lesson learned.

Lev saw tears spill from Jeremiah's eyes as he stared at the floor.

The moment the service was over Jeremiah Cohen stood and made a quick exit to the street. His pace was deliberate and Lev followed behind him, wishing to give Jeremiah space. Lev reflected again on the time he had lost the use of his right hand. Jeremiah's consequence was more severe in that it was public, but it was just attached to the public nature of his attempt to teach. He had been headstrong and arrogant, and he had pushed his views with no willingness to consider anyone else's testimony.

Jeremiah's Confession

Jeremiah pointed to the phone on Lev's counter. Aware that Jeremiah wished to communicate with the Ancients, Lev dialed. He spoke with a receptionist who referred him to Deborah.

"Shalom, Lev, what seems to be the problem?"

"Hello, Deborah. I am calling on behalf of Jeremiah Cohen, a former Rabbi. His voice was taken away at our chapel service this morning while he attempted to teach that the Jews should have surrendered without resistance to the invading forces against Jerusalem and have avoided the massive destruction that took place."

"Put him on your second phone, Lev," Deborah responded.

Lev and Jeremiah walked to Lev's bedroom and Lev handed the second phone to Jeremiah. Jeremiah sat on the bed, pressed the talk button and slowly raised the receiver to his ear. Lev sat in the chair across from him, the other phone pressed to his ear.

"Are you listening, Jeremiah?" Deborah asked when she heard the click on the phone Jeremiah held. Jeremiah's hand trembled. He grunted, and motioned to Lev to say 'yes'.

"Jeremiah is on the phone, and he is listening," Lev reported. "I will continue listening only if you wish me to."

"Stay on, Lev," Deborah said. "Listen carefully, Jeremiah. We have been aware of your viewpoints and of your eagerness to express them. We allowed you some leeway because we thought you might profit from the responses you received from others. Today we reached the end of our patience. You have chosen to ignore the fact that God dealt with the nations as was required to make them yield to His sovereignty. A violent world sent armies to invade Israel, and the fact that Israel defended herself was foreseen and used by God as a tool for teaching that war no longer will be acceptable and the necessity of dependence on His spirit rather than on the physical might of military power.

"Your type of sin is very serious. Much of the trouble in the old world was because people felt capable of establshing truth by a system of rationalizing. You are not free to teach anything you believe to be true. Preaching one's treasured opinions is not allowed any more. Only preaching the truth is allowed. You need time, Jeremiah—time to sort out your thoughts and time to come to grips with your arrogance. You will be speechless for two weeks. When your period of silence is ended it will be your challenge to retrace your steps and to share what you have learned with those you attempted to teach. You will be given the help and support that you need. Do you understand, Jeremiah?"

Jeremiah sat on the bed with his arm supporting his forehead. He looked almost white and the phone shook in his hand as he glanced at Lev and nodded his head in agreement.

"He is nodding 'yes,' and I believe he understands."

"Good. Are you still listening, Jeremiah?"

He nodded 'yes,' and Lev conveyed his message.

"I am sorry to have to be so stern with you, but you have been headstrong in teaching erroneous concepts. You never listened to anyone because you held others in contempt. You must face your stubbornness, Jeremiah. I hope you understand you are being thoroughly chastised at this time. You may call me after you have confessed that your viewpoints were erroneous. I want to hear your acknowledgement of sin in your own words when your voice is returned. Shalom to both of you."

Jeremiah absentmindedly put the receiver on the bed beside him. Jeremiah looked pathetically weak and shaken. He reminded Lev of a lost child. Lev placed his arm on Jeremiah's shoulder and led him to the guest room he had used the previous night. Jeremiah refused the offer of food and let Lev lead him to his room.

"If there's anything I can do for you, Jeremiah, knock on the desk," Lev suggested.

As he entered his room, Lev saw him fall on his knees in prayer. That was the best medicine for anyone smarting under his chastisement. Lev felt sorry for him, even though he had been so headstrong. He had been able to receive rebuke and criticism from Deborah because he knew she was in absolute authority and not subject to any errors in judgment. The medicine she had given him was good for his heart. It may have been bitter to taste, but afterward it would yield the peaceable fruit of righteousness.

Jeremiah spent the remainder of the day in seclusion. Lev could see him kneeling in prayer and motioning with his hands from time to time. It was obvious to him that Jeremiah had taken his lumps like a man and would undoubtedly arise from his knees a better person.

Jeremiah finally came out of his room in time for the evening meal. He gave Lev a hug, which took him by surprise, because Jeremiah had always been intellectual and never emotional. He didn't seem to mind that Lev had witnessed his chastisement. His arrogant demeanor was gone. Lev offered the blessing on the food.

Deborah had taken more time with Jeremiah then anyone Lev knew, but not a second of that time had been wasted. Jeremiah, though speechless, indicated his change of heart. He smiled, and for the first time listened, as he had never listened before. His lack of speech enabled him to listen to the Lord. He now knew that he had refused to listen to anyone, even God's Word.

Jeremiah spent the evening in his room praying and reading the Scriptures. When Lev turned in for the night his light was still on.

In the morning Jeremiah wished to go with Lev to the garden. He wrote on a pad that he would leave after breakfast for he had a long drive home. He gave Lev a farewell hug and wrote that he'd be back when his speech returned. 'Pray for me,' he urged in writing.

Lev invited him to return and said, "Shalom."

"If I say, 'Surely the darkness shall cover me;
Even the night shall be light unto me.
Yea, the darkness hideth not from thee;
But the night shineth as the day: the darkness
And the light are both alike to thee.
(Psalm 139:11-12).

Chapter Eighteen

What else do I need? Lev wondered aloud, as he paced the kitchen floor of Anya's home and rehearsed the list of things that had been done. "Resurrection tea in her bedroom, Eden fruit and Eden bread at the table—gotta find extra blankets," he mumbled absentmindedly as he bumped into Angela.

The stack of blankets that Angela carried fell to the floor and she laughed.

"Lev, calm yourself. She'll be here soon. No need to panic as she will not disappear if you don't do or say the right thing."

"Calm yourself, Lev," he repeated as he made his way to the sofa of the living room. "Calm yourself." For the second time in his new life Lev felt like an expectant father, full of excitement, anticipation and a bit of apprehension. He leaned back and closed his eyes and reviewed what he had learned in the past six months since his raising. Facing the truth was actually a relief compared to the stress of avoiding it. Once he let himself face the pain of the memory he had repressed, he was able to be open to its truth. He was not responsible for Anya's brutal death.

Lev's mind returned to the present moment. Very soon Anya would be raised to face her own painful memories, and she would thrive.

Anya's Return to Life

Sounds came from Anya's bedroom. "Go, Lev, go to her." Angela patted her brother-in-law on the arm and embraced him when he stood. "Life will begin all over again and you must help her write the first chapter in her life," she whispered.

When Lev entered Anya's room he gasped as he saw her delicate body beneath a light quilt and her beautiful face in peaceful repose. Her breathing was even and she rested quietly with an occasional stir. He knelt by the bed, in awe of the miracle that he was witness to. She had died many years ago, and here she was, more beautiful than he remembered, and whole, with not a trace of any kind of wound anywhere. He watched her closely as her breathing quickened and her moans became louder. Her head began to turn restlessly from side to side. Her face contorted as if in pain and beads of sweat formed on her forehead.

"No!" she breathed. Her hands reached out beyond the blanket and Lev instinctively grabbed them. As if caught in a nightmare, she spoke between labored gasps, her eyes still tightly closed.

Lev spoke gently, but with a firm tone. "Anya, it's okay now. It's over." He gently stroked her forehead. "You're safe. No one can hurt you now."

Anya's body relaxed. Fearful dark eyes suddenly opened and looked into his. She sat up, the quilt still around her, and burst into torrents of weeping in Lev's arms.

"Oh, Lev, I thought we would be separated forever."

"You're fine, my love."

"Lev, it was terrifying—what he did to me..." She clutched onto Lev so tightly he felt it difficult to breathe for a moment.

"I know, Anya, I know. It's only a memory now—only a memory. Where are your wounds?"

Anya relaxed her grip. Lev watched intently as Anya looked at her hands, her arms, and then felt her face and her stomach with her hands. Then she stared at Lev in disbelief, a look of amazement on her face. For the first time since her rising, she consciously realized that she felt no pain. "Where are my wounds?" she repeated Lev's question slowly to herself in wonderment. She looked Lev in the eye and stared at him briefly and then looked again at her arms. "I'm okay—Lev—this is impossible—how could it be—he butchered me—but now I am whole."

Lev reached for the pot of resurrection tea and poured two servings into the two mugs on the nightstand beside the bed.

"Here, Anya, drink this," he offered. He watched her with great affection as she drank. When she finished her serving he poured another, and then drank his own tea.

"It must have been a dream," she whispered, "but it was so real, Lev, and so awful."

"Anya, dear Anya," Lev spoke to her in a soothing tone as he stroked her long dark hair. "It was no dream, but it *is* over. You have been raised to life on a New Earth, and no one will ever hurt you again. Messiah has come to us, and by his power you have life once again."

Anya and Angela Reunited

Anya found the clothes that were tailor-made to her size. She dressed and joined Lev in the kitchen. "Angela!" Anya exclaimed, as she saw her sister for the first time. They embraced amid tears of joy. "It's been so long," Anya said between her tears.

"Longer than you know," her sister responded. "I've been waiting for you for a very long time, and praying for your resurrection."

"Are you really saying I died and now I'm alive again?" Anya questioned as she sank back into the kitchen chair.

"Here, Anya, have some more tea, and some fruit. We all have a lot of catching up to do," Lev said as he placed their two cups on the table and seated himself across from her. Angela filled the teapot with more tea and joined the two at the table. They sat there, smiling and staring at one another.

"You look so mature—and so healthy. Your teeth are straight, Lev." Anya laughed and looked from Lev to Angela and back to Lev with love in her eyes. "My husband and my sister—it's just so unbelievably wonderful," she said as tears spilled over her eyes.

Lev shifted his weight with a feeling of uneasiness, as he wondered how they would explain the different realities of this new life to one who had such memories of her own to deal with.

"I died and now I'm alive, by Messiah's power, you say. It's unbelievable, superbly unbelievable," Anya said shaking her head in smiling disbelief.

"That's how I felt when I was raised—supremely happy and supremely confused."

"I'm happy, Lev, but I still feel afraid. How do you know I'm safe?" Anya furtively glanced around the room, looked at Lev and then at the plate of Eden fruit in front of her.

Lev and Angela described the process of consequences, and of the spiritual power of Messiah, his Anointed and the Ancients.

"The memory is horrid," Anya blurted out. "I don't know what to do with it."

"Drink more tea, eat some fruit, and talk to us about it," Lev suggested as he placed his hand on hers. Anya began to eat a bit of the fruit of Eden, savoring the taste and texture in each bite, as Angela explained the powers of life and healing in Eden fruit. When Anya finished her fruit and Angela her explanation, the three were silent.

Horrid Memories

Finally Anya spoke in a shaky voice. "I thought I was safe, Lev, because I was driving in a caravan with some of your friends from your battalion headquarters. I just wanted to come home to be with you. All of a sudden I heard commotion and firebombs exploding and to avoid hitting the cars in front of me I ended up down an embankment." I heard the harsh sound of bullets and breaking glass, and then the voice of a man. He motioned me to get out.

"Before he forced me out of the car I..." her voice faltered. Tears ran down Anya's face as she continued her story, and tears ran down Lev and Angela's face as they listened. Lev felt as if he were there, in some surreal dream, watching the events unfold before him.

"I fought hard to get away. I clenched my teeth and fought until I was thrown down to the ground and held there. The man sneered at me in Arabic, and I understood his words clearly, spoken in guttural tones as he proceeded to pin me down and to beat me with the butt of his gun.

"'Allah the merciful! Allah the great! Allah be praised! Death—to the infidel People of the Book!' he said.

"It was common for terrorists to mutilate their enemies by cutting off private parts and legs. I fought like a fierce lioness. But I could not escape his rage. He slashed at me until I was bloody and naked. I was raped in a pool of my own blood. I stared into the starry sky and then I closed my swollen eyes.

"Suddenly the man stood. There were lights, and voices. I faded back and forth in and out of consciousness.

"The next thing I knew someone was bandaging my arms and legs. They wrapped me up in a sheet and dragged me to a vehicle.... There were two of them—women—strong women. I remember a jostling, uncomfortable ride, and then I remember being on a bed. I was delirious." Anya's voice broke and she could barely speak.

Lev pulled his chair close to Anya's and leaned into her, his arms around her shoulders. "I am so sorry," he whispered, "for all you have gone through, and so grateful to have you with us again." Lev was silent for a short time, and then he explained how he had found her car, her clothing that was ripped and bloody, and how he sped off to find the perpetrator, lost control of his car and found himself in a hospital with massive head injuries.

"I could never bear to speak your name until a few weeks ago," he confessed.

"I am sorry for you also, Lev." Anya's voice was weak. "Finding my car and clothes must have been so difficult," she said as she sat up and then crumpled back into her chair, with her eyes closed. "And now, I am here, I am healed, and I am reunited with two of the people I love most in the world." Anya said slowly with a tired voice.

Angela poured Anya another cup of tea. Lev and Angela continued in light conversation until Anya had finished her tea.

"You need rest, Anya. Come." Lev and Angela simultaneously stood and positioned themselves on either side of Anya to support her as they lead her to her room.

"Please don't leave me, Lev," Anya requested in a small voice.

"I'll be right here," Lev assured her.

When Anya awoke she smiled up at Lev. Lev and Angela spent the next few hours talking with Anya. She loved her house and garden, and liked the short program that featured the Ancients on NER. When Lev explained that he had been raised six months ago, over twenty-five years after their marriage, Anya looked surprised.

"I have no sense of time," she commented to herself.

When Lev explained that this was her home, and that his home was not far from her, Anya again looked surprised.

"You remarried before you died, Lev, and you are living with your second wife." She spoke with no particular emotion. Lev looked uncomfortable. "I'm glad you remarried, love. It makes sense." Anya tried to reassure him.

"I did remarry, but I do not live with her on the New Earth. Relationships are different in the new world." Anya listened without comment to his explanation of the family and how marriage had been replaced by deep and satisfying friendships. Lev continued. "I married Rebekah about four years after your death and she and Angela have worked very hard to fix your home."

The three were silent until Anya spoke.

"I guess I have some adjusting to do. But I am grateful—and confused and overwhelmed all at the same time."

Lev nodded. "I remember the feeling," he mumbled.

"Come, Angela, sit with me. Lev and I have caught up, now it's time for us."

Lev watched the two sisters talking animatedly and it brought a smile to his face and relief to his heart to hear their laughter. He sensed that Anya was giving him a chance to leave so that she could have space in order to absorb the differentness of the New World arrangement in his absence.

He embraced Angela and then he stood before Anya. She held his face in her hands, and then drew him close to her. Lev saw the spark of passion in her eyes and the hunger to press her lips to his, and then he saw a flicker of confusion as she chose to embrace him instead. He remembered a similar moment from his own first day's experience.

They embraced for a long moment, and then Anya whispered, "I love you, Lev. I am so grateful for all you and Angela have done. I'm grateful to Rebekah, also. She eased your pain in the old world, and she is helping me in the new. I want to meet her, Lev. Is that possible?"

"She wants very much to meet you also. She wasn't sure when it would be a good time for you."

"Tonight, Lev. Can you come by with her tonight?"

Lev nodded in agreement.

Anya and Angela sat on the living room sofa and easily resumed their discussion. Lev, with awe and gratitude looked a final time toward the two sisters who were teasing one another and giggling. "I'll be back," he announced as he walked out the door.

Anya Meets Rebekah

Later that evening Lev and Rebekah stood at the doorway of Anya's new home. Lev rang the doorbell.

Angela invited them in and embraced Lev and then Rebekah.

"How is she doing?" Rebekah asked Angela in a low tone.

"Very well. She really wants to meet you. Come," Angela said with her arm still around Rebekah's shoulder as she led the two to the kitchen. Anya stood as they entered the room. Rebekah stopped a few feet away from Anya. Her radiant smile and dark dancing eyes welcomed Rebekah and absorbed the details of her appearance with love and approval.

"Rebekah," she said softly.

"Anya?" Rebekah responded with tears in her eyes. The two embraced and wept in one another's arms. "I've prayed for you—all you've been through—I am honored to meet you."

"And you have been working so hard with Angela. She told me all about it. I am so grateful."

Rebekah broke their embrace and held her at arms length as they looked deeply into one another's eyes.

Lev and Angela stood at a distance to watch the introduction they had wondered about. They hung in the background, engaged in their own discussion, in order to give Anya and Rebekah some time to get to know each other.

The next hours passed quickly, as the four shared laughter and tears over past and present experiences. They discussed the work of preparing for the raising of the next generations.

The evening ended with a torrent of laughter as Rebekah and Anya shared memories of Lev's idiosyncrasies, which helped them work through their old world feelings toward one another and toward Lev.

"It's getting late. Before we leave—I brought something for you, Anya," Rebekah announced. "Lev, do you have that package?"

Lev handed Rebekah a package wrapped in paper covered with wild flowers. "I wanted you to have this," Rebekah said as she took the package from Lev and offered it to Anya.

Anya opened the package and whispered, "Oh it's beautiful!" as she examined a journal with hand-painted vines on the cover. "It's very similar to the last journal I had—in the old world."

"Yes, I know. I arranged it especially for you. Lev told me how much you loved to write."

Anya was overcome with emotion. The room was suddenly silent as the four thought of the precious reunion that had come to pass.

"Here am I; send me..." (Isaiah 6:8).

Chapter Nineteen

The Arons had barely entered the reception room of the Ancients' headquarters and sat down when Allon's name was called. The whole family rose and walked toward the room they were directed to. Others who were waiting looked on in surprise to see such a large family have an audience with one of the Ancients. Enoch was concluding a phone conversation when the Aron family was ushered in and seated.

"Ah," he said, "you must be Allon, with whom we are all pleased." Allon rose from his chair and felt the vigorous handshake of the authoritative, yet friendly man before him. "And you must be Ariel."

Ariel stood bolt upright.

"Yes, yes, I am Ariel, raised just two months ago, and this is my lovely wife—former wife—Hannah, and we are pleased and honored to meet you."

Hannah stood beside her husband and nodded her head in mute agreement until she found her voice. "An honor, Mr. Enoch, a great honor." She patted Enoch's hand, which Ariel had not yet released from their initial handshake.

Still shaking Enoch's hand, Ariel continued in a soft voice, as if he spoke to himself. "You stood above the others. You lived in a world that was plunging headlong down a road of destruction. And yet you walked with God. I cannot express to you the greatness of this honor."

Enoch's smile lit up his face with life and his white teeth were a stark contrast to the sun darkened skin of his face. He chuckled heartily, and then looked Ariel straight in the eye. "An honor for me, also, to meet others who seek Christ and who are willing to face what is in their heart."

Ariel, taken aback, released his grip. He instinctively knew that Enoch was fully aware of the struggle he had experienced. Enoch continued down the line with a personal comment for each member of the Aron family.

"Your son has been doing a remarkable job in Ghana." He directed his gaze to Lev and Rebekah. "The people there love him very much and they try hard to do everything he shows them."

Then he spoke directly to Allon about the operation he was overseeing and about the people he was working with. He mentioned his joy at hearing of Moses-Russell and the healing of the little boy's blindness and his eagerness to learn more of Christ. The only complaint that had been raised by the people of Ghana was that Allon had encouraged them to take some time off from work. Enoch requested an update on the timeframe for when the electrical components and computers would start coming off the line. Allon projected it would be at least several months.

"That's excellent," Enoch asserted. "Will you then be ready to take on another assignment? Are you on board for further service?"

"I've enjoyed my stay with my family, yet I am anxious to get back to the people of Ghana. I can hardly imagine leaving them for another assignment, but I'm at your service. Put me on the top of your list of volunteers."

Lev and Rebekah, Assigned to Germany

Enoch then turned to Lev much to his surprise. "And what about you, Lev? You have been studying hard. You have been dealing with the issues in your own heart and you seem to have a talent for reaching out to others. We need some volunteers to help our operations start in Germany, to make sure they understand our blueprints for society, our instructions and the latest computer technology. Many of them speak Hebrew, but if you choose to go on our behalf you'll have a few months to learn German."

Enoch sensed Lev's hesitation and reassured him immediately, reminding him of the effects of Eden fruit on the mind. He assured him that he would be able to learn a language in three or four months without even an accent, and that he would have no trouble learning about the leading computer technology from Jake.

"Will you consider this assignment, Lev?"

Enoch paused, but did not give Lev a chance to answer.

"In a year all people of the twenty-first century will have been restored to life, and those of the twentieth century will be returning. Germany is unique in its contemporary history. There has never been a generation that sustained such indoctrination of hatred towards the Jews as that generation with the exception of the Islam. These are the influences you will be dealing with as you instruct them on the technology they will need. Don't be surprised if you meet some resistance and prejudice. You are equipped to deal with these challenges."

"Yes," Lev's voice sounded weak.

"You sound frightened. But I assure you, you can do this job, otherwise we wouldn't have asked you. Actually, Christ selected you, not me. He wouldn't select anyone who wasn't qualified for the task."

Lev sank down in his chair in disbelief.

Enoch addressed Rebekah. "Are you willing to go abroad for the King?" he asked her with a look of excitement in his eye. "You will also need to learn German."

Rebekah nodded her head.

Enoch continued to explain that should she accept the assignment, she would also act as liaison officer for the various gardening operations in Germany. He stressed the importance of her part in the mission, as Eden trees and orchards must be available as generations are raised.

"If a technical problem arises that cannot be resolved, or if you need support in any of your encounters, you may call me personally any hour of the day, and if it is an emergency, that will include the night. This is my personal telephone number. Give it to no one. Memorize it and destroy this card. This goes for you also, Lev."

Enoch pulled out two very small phones that looked like regular cell phones and gave them to Lev and Rebekah. He explained that these provided secure phones that could only be deciphered in the offices of the Ancients.

The rest of the day passed in a blur of excitement. The whole Aron family had the honor of having lunch with some of the Ancients. Enoch introduced them to Huldah, Barak, Deborah, Samson and Samuel. When Enoch called on Ariel to pray, Ariel's words were simple and brief. "Dear Lord, We cannot fully express our gratitude for this temporal provision and all you have done for each of us here, and for all of our human family. In Messiah's name we thank you, Amen."

Each of the Aron family ate quietly while trying to take in the startling reality of the honor that was theirs. They shared the same simple diet of Eden fruit and grape juice, and listened intently to the lively conversation. They joined in the contagious laughter as they listened to stories that ensued as the Ancients shared stories of the transformations due to Eden fruit of resurrection joy.

The mood sombered a bit when Samuel spoke of the urgency of their mission.

"Our task is to help reduce the number of people who will sympathize with evil and falsehood during the time when Satan is loosed. The present time is the opportunity for the people of the nations to learn to love and recognize the voice of the Shepherd. All of our work here is for that one purpose."

Annie's Challenge—Uncivilized Tribes

The Ancients then invited Annie to serve among some of the isolated tribes either in Africa, South America or Indonesia after the short time it would take her to finish her studies. These people were interested in the blessing of resurrection, but were reticent to deal with 'civilized' people who had a history of exploiting them. Her youth and her love for animals and nature would make it easier for them to accept her help. Rachel was also questioned as to her willingness to serve according to the needs that arose.

"Jake, we need you where you are heading the cutting edge of technology. We cannot release you because the sooner we upgrade our sciences the more efficient the entire world becomes. You are doing a magnificent job and you are a great team player."

Annie cleared her throat and mustered the courage to ask a question. "Excuse me, Enoch, but why would every day people like me be chosen to visit the nations?"

Enoch delivered a final announcement. "You have been first blessed and so you and others like yourself are the first equipped and chosen to be bearers of the blessing to others. Your greatest asset is that you are every day people who live in the power of the New Earth. When the regeneration process is well underway, we Ancients will have more freedom to visit nations personally. But until then we are kept busy organizing the redistribution of the land, coordinating Eden tree shipments and creating advanced programs to school people in the information and technology they will need. Your willingness is not only helpful, but crucial, and we will contact you as assignments arise."

Enoch rose and opened the lunchroom door, with a hand motion that suggested that the lunch meeting had come to an end. The Aron family arose. "Shalom, and God Bless you," he said, as each family member shook hands with each of the Ancients and left the room.

Lev stared at the stars through the skylight above his bed, in awe of the handiwork of God in the heavens and in the earth. It had been a day of blessing. Enoch's description of the previous generation under Hitler made him uneasy. Would he be able to handle his upcoming mission? He thought about Enoch's words.

"Don't be surprised if you meet resistance and prejudice," Enoch had said. "You are equipped to deal with these challenges. You will be representing Christ and he will give you wisdom."

"I will take the stony heart out of their flesh,
And will give them an heart of flesh…"
(Ezekiel 11:19).

Chapter Twenty

Four months had passed by quickly since Lev's invitation to go to Germany. He had studied computer technology under the tutelage of Jake. He and Rebekah had practiced German together. She learned faster than he—her accent was almost perfect. They were both amazed at how quickly they had learned and how fluent they had become in so short a time.

Lev had to smile as he remembered their first halting conversations together. After a few weeks of studying they had made a rule that they would only speak German when they were together. At first it was laborious. "I need—to secure—warmer—clothes—no—clothing—for our trip," and then they would laugh at one another's fumbling words.

Berlin

Their plane departed from Tel Aviv at 6 AM on December 21st according to plan.

"You will fly to Berlin where the government of Germany will provide apartments for you during your stay. You will be provided with Eden fruit." Enoch had explained to Lev in their last phone conversation.

Eden trees had not yet begun to produce fruit in Germany. They imported the fruit and most of it was distributed to the old and those who were ill. Both he and Rebekah would be added to that list of Eden fruit receivers.

Lev sighed as he recalled Enoch's solemn words. "Remember, Lev, your mission is two-fold. You will help them to accept our superior technology, but more importantly you must show them the qualities of heart and mind that will help them to overcome their latent prejudices. There are years of anti-Semitic indoctrination to be unlearned. Please call me weekly at the minimum. Speak whichever language you like— I know them all. Shalom and God bless you."

Two German officials, Herman Steubel and Hans Goebel, met them at the airport. They were taken to a restaurant. "Order whatever you like. Money is no consideration," Hans instructed.

Rebekah gave Lev an amused grin and spoke tactfully.

"Actually, we are accustomed to vegetarian meals. I'd love this spinach salad, and then the fruit in season for dessert."

"Can't I tempt you with prime rib?" Herman Steubel asked in a pleasant tone.

Rebekah laughed and responded with a twinkle in her eye. "Once you start eating Eden fruit, you will turn down prime rib hands down."

"Now *that* is hard to fathom, my dear. Turn down *prime rib* for *fruit*? Over my dead body…"

"That's what it may come to, Mr. Steubel," Lev said in a teasing tone.

They all laughed, the ice was broken, and they continued to discuss the powers of Eden fruit and how by eating the fruit of Eden the aged and ill showed rapid improvements and vitality.

They ordered immediately and their food was brought to their table in record time.

"Germans like efficiency." Herman smiled as he saw Lev and Rebekah's startled expression at the prompt service they were given. "And that seems to be the point of Eden fruit," he added quickly, as a tie-in to the previous conversation. "We should get along very well," he announced confidently as he sat back in his chair.

"You know we have observed very carefully what has taken place in Israel." Hans leaned forward, eager to enter the conversation. "There is no doubt that the dead are being returned to life and a great work is underway. We are eager to receive these blessings and we are eager to comply with the terms that are laid-down by the Ancients."

Hans Goebel suddenly looked away from Lev and Rebekah to study the mountain of potatoes on his plate and began to toy with them with his fork. "We have been chastened for our mistakes," he said in a quieter tone. "Those in charge of the invasion suffered a worse fate than our soldiers did in Israel."

Herman Steubel coughed nervously. "I'm anxious to see your New Earth computer, Lev, and anxious to be on this New Earth cutting edge of technology."

Hans Goebel changed the subject to the weather. "It is mild for this time of year."

Lev reverted back to the former subject. "The Ancients move with amazing efficiency in everything they undertake. When you meet them you will see the incredible intelligence that permeates their every expression. They know how to deal with conflict, and mistakes with a perfect mix of mercy and accountability. It is important that everyone knows that they are totally under the authority of Christ and his Anointed."

"And Christ and his Anointed can be trusted to heal the human heart," Rebekah added.

"Well, then I'd say their work is cut out for them," Herman said under his breath. Dinner continued with conversation that covered the safer subjects of the Eden fruit that would be provided the two visitors and the travel arrangements that would be made upon their request, and the more difficult subjects of the resurrection of past generations and how pockets of resistance would be handled.

After dinner they transported Rebekah to her rooms, and then drove a few blocks down the street to the stone apartment. Arrangements were make to pick him up at 8:00 the following morning.

Lev was relieved to find his computer and luggage had arrived undamaged. As he unpacked he munched on the Eden fruit he found in the refrigerator, and felt invigorated, wondering what the next day would bring. These two government officials had good intentions, but had much to learn about the New Earth arrangements. At this point they had one foot in the old world and one toe in the new.

Ghana's Computer Challenge

Lev felt nervous as Hans and Herman drove him into the heart of Berlin to a large marble building with the old world inscription "*Größe ist Intelligenz.*" (Greatness is Intelligence). The high ceilings and sculptured columns echoed as they walked to the consultation room each carrying a black suitcase.

The morning session began with an assembly of leading scientists in the computer and electronic fields. Hans introduced Lev with a warm and friendly preamble that overstated his qualifications. "A graduate of the University of the Ancients, with years of experience on the cutting edge of computer technology, I present to you Mr. Lev Aron."

Lev motioned for the applause to end. "I was raised from death within this year after having been dead for twelve years," he announced simply. The room grew absolutely silent. "I died in the final invasion. My greatest surprise when I was awakened was that my wounds were gone. My left hand, which I had lost in my last minutes of life, was whole and healed. I am, in fact, quite ambidextrous." There was a ripple of laughter from the audience and another round of applause.

"The blessing that has begun in Israel is spreading throughout the world. For example in Ghana the most advanced factories are being built there. Within a few months they will be creating state-of-the-art homes, computers, electronics and one of the most extensive projects for restoring the trees of life."

"How could Ghana be among the front-runners in modern technology?" someone questioned from the back of the room.

"Sir, are you sure of your facts?" A loud voice came from a man in the front row that held a thick file folder in his arms. His thinning hair was still quite blonde and his dark blue eyes flashed in defiance, though his voice was patronizingly friendly. "These people have only recently advanced. While they might have a few bright minds, they certainly cannot be in advance of the Western World, now, can they?" He smiled after his question, and many nodded in agreement.

Lev smiled in return, grateful to move the focus of progress from Germany and Israel to Germany and Ghana. He shared the incredible learning curve of one of the young men Allon had worked with and how, with the help of Eden fruit and the advanced teachings of the Ancients, he had become a computer specialist in a matter of months. "And this is an example of the types of computers they are beginning to manufacture in Ghana." Lev began to unpack the black cases.

"I should be surprised to find technology to equal this anywhere. But that is my challenge to you." Lev continued to set up the computer. He described its stability, its ability to perform multifunctions, and how easily it was manufactured. "I will leave this with your people to test and to compare it with your computers. You will then be able to measure its capabilities and report its weaknesses to me. We know of your great advances in computer technology, and we welcome your frank evaluation of this machine. The schematics are available. You can reproduce this New Earth computer if you so choose, but it must be your decision."

There was a moment of silence as the scientists digested the challenge before them. Another round of applause followed, and Lev noticed that many heads nodded with an air of confidence. Lev read their intentions easily: they would take this challenge seriously, and they hoped to prove this new technology inferior.

After a short break Lev invited the men to try the New Earth computer and test it however they wished. Lev watched with interest to see the various approaches and he studied the men to find insight into their thinking.

Lev directed a side-by-side testing between their computer and the new one. After a series of brief comparative tests, the Germans decided this was of no use since the New Earth computer was obviously superior to their own. The testing then turned solely to this new computer.

As the day wore on Lev had many opportunities to speak with various people, and many were fascinated with the educational benefits and programs that were available with the use of New Earth technology. He explained that educational programs would take over television programming with the exception of world news from Jerusalem.

"What if someone did not agree with the New Earth version of the news? What if someone attacked the Ancients?" someone asked.

"All of the Ancients are protected by the strong spiritual forces of Christ and His Anointed. There are instantaneous consequences for wrong doing that would result in harm to anyone." Lev briefly described his own consequence when he tried to physically assault Reuben. He felt overwhelmed at the undercurrent of resistance he sensed in the room and he wondered if any of these men might challenge this warning and try to damage the computer.

The testing continued throughout the day. Lev made some final comments before he left them. "I will leave the computer here for anyone who wishes to make a more detailed study. You have a week to make your evaluations. If you should decide to go with this new technology, I will instruct you as to the manufacturing procedures. Good day, friends."

Herr Mueller's Incident

When Lev arrived the following morning, he found a room full of agitated men, some in heated argument. Hans Goebel approached him immediately.

"Excuse me, Mr. Aron, but something terrible has happened. Mr. Mueller has been rushed to the hospital. Something has happened to his hands. He is unable to use them."

Lev sensed what had transpired and inspected his computer. The panels had been removed, and the small electrical surge protector had been disconnected.

"Please take me to the hospital. I must see Mr. Mueller. I know how to help him, but I must speak with him personally."

The room grew suddenly silent, and all eyes watched Hans lead Lev out of the room.

Hans and Lev drove quickly to the hospital.

"Please, I need to see Mr. Mueller." Lev spoke in fluent German to the nurse who stood behind the desk of the nurse's station.

"He is being x-rayed and you will have to wait." The nurse looked down and returned to her task of making notes in the patient charts.

Lev hesitated, but then persisted. "I have a very urgent message for him from the leaders in Israel. I would like to see him as soon as possible."

The nurse's eyes shot up and Lev could feel her cold stare bore through him when he mentioned the phrase "leaders in Israel."

"I will check to see when the x-rays will be done. This man has suffered paralysis of both arms. Don't you think you could wait and allow him to be treated?"

Lev sensed that his persistence was an irritation to her.

"I understand, nurse. At the earliest convenience I would like to speak with him—thank you." He left the desk and sat down in the hospital waiting room beside the tall bearded man who had driven him to this place.

"I did not know you were a medical doctor," Hans asked, with an edge of sarcasm in his voice.

"No, I am not a doctor, Hans. But I think I know how he became paralyzed. And I think I know how to help him."

Hans sighed loudly and shrugged his shoulders. Both men sat in silence as they continued to wait.

Lev closed his eyes and his mind quickly reviewed the stream of events that brought him to this hospital in the heart of Berlin. Here he was, his third day in Germany, sitting in a hospital waiting to see Mr. Mueller. He thought of Rebekah's comment during their phone conversation the night before. He had mentioned the resistance he felt from some of the men, displayed in their comments and in their body language.

"Of course there are obstacles, Lev. Enoch warned us, and so did the Prophet Isaiah. He wrote, 'Prepare ye the way of the people; cast up, cast up the highway; gather out the stones; lift up a standard for the people.' He told us there would be stones and obstacles in the way of those who would seek Him by an alliance with Israel. Our mission is to help remove the stones, so that the people of the nations will be free to journey closer to their Sovereign Ruler and their ultimate blessing. We are stone-removers, and that's exactly what we are doing and it's exactly according to His plan."

Lev's train of thought was interrupted when Hans finally spoke up. "We trusted you, Lev. I hope there were no harmful chemicals or gasses in that computer that precipitated this paralysis. We normally look into the frame to examine construction and layout, and we did proceed as normal. Perhaps we were wrong."

"You would have found nothing, Hans. Christ and His Anointed don't need chemicals and gasses. They have spiritual powers. We have no secrets. It is just as I explained. Mr. Mueller is experiencing a consequence."

"Excuse me," the nurse's voice interrupted their conversation. "Mr. Mueller is able to see you now, in room 242."

A Heart of Flesh

Lev recognized Mr. Mueller immediately, as the man with defiance in his blue eyes. He lay in bed, and his eyes stared at the ceiling with a blank, sullen expression.

"Good morning, Mr. Mueller," Lev greeted him. Mr. Mueller continued to stare at the ceiling and said nothing.

"Mr. Mueller!" Hans exclaimed. "We were so concerned when we heard about your—incident. Have the doctors found anything?"

Mr. Mueller shook his head. "Thank you, Hans, very kind of you to be concerned."

"I am sorry for what happened to you. I have come to inform you that your condition may be easily corrected," Lev added even though Herr Mueller refused to look him in the eye.

"Your condition may be remedied very quickly, but you must call the office of the Ancients and tell them exactly what happened. You were paralyzed for the same reason I was—for doing something that Christ and his Anointed deemed worthy of intervention because if unchecked, the action would have brought about harm. They can read the thoughts of our minds and they know what is in our hearts and how our actions will affect others. You must tell the Ancients the whole truth, and if you do, your paralysis will be lifted. I started to feel life return to my arm within an hour after I talked with them. May I phone Jerusalem for you?"

Mr. Mueller's face grew red and it was evident from his anguished expression that this decision was brutally difficult for him. He was silent for a time, his eyes shut tightly.

A young doctor knocked on the door and entered the room.

"Mr. Mueller, we have found no diagnosis on the basis of our tests. Feeling any discomfort at all?" The doctor talked briefly with his patient and then left.

Mr. Mueller turned his head to the wall opposite Lev. "Please make the call, Mr. Aron," he said in a shaky voice.

Lev pressed the speed dial for the Ancients and held the phone so that Mr. Mueller could speak with Elizabeth. Hans left the room as soon as Mr. Mueller began. He explained that he disconnected the surge protector had moved the jumpers and his arms became unusable. He confessed that he did not want the new computer to be accepted because his life's work had been the development of computers. "Yes, yes, yes," he spoke in response to Elizabeth's counsel.

"I know this new computer is far superior to ours. It is just difficult for me to admit this…. What must I do to regain the use of my arms? Yes…yes…yes… Thank you, Fräulein Elizabeth. You have been very kind."

Mr. Mueller looked at Lev for the first time since Lev had entered the room. "Please take the phone. And—thank you, Mr. Aron."

Lev called to Hans from the doorway of the hospital room and asked him to prepare for Mr. Mueller's release. Hans looked from Lev to Mr. Mueller with a puzzled expression and saw the afflicted man's head nod in agreement. He shrugged his shoulders and then proceeded to the nurses' station.

In the next hour Mr. Mueller spoke quietly, with an occasional look at Lev. He spoke of how difficult this experience was for him and of his hard work and persistence that had finally created a thriving business and a new line of computers.

"But Elizabeth pierced my stony heart—I have stones in my heart, Lev, stones—and for the first time I see that my wish to protect my technological empire is blocking the way for my own daughter and wife being raised to life. I worked myself to death when they were alive and I continued after they had died. And my empire would prevent many others from receiving their loved ones. And it would keep me from my own healing—of hand and of heart."

Tears welled up in his eyes as he continued. "I do not wish to live this way any longer."

When the three men walked to the nurses' station, the doctor expressed his displeasure. "Your case is still being studied and we have no diagnosis at this point in time. It will be dangerous to release you before we know the cause of your trouble."

"Ah, but Doctor, I am feeling better," Mr. Mueller responded. "I believe I can sign this paper myself."

He was able to raise his right arm to the desk, hold the pen and write his name, though the letters did not resemble the flowing, flamboyant style of his normal signature.

The Doctor raised his eyebrows, and shook his head. "Very well, then."

"You will never believe what helped me," he said leaning his head toward the Doctor and speaking with a quiet voice. "It was a call to the Ancients in Jerusalem."

He smiled and turned to Lev and Hans. "Shall we go, gentlemen?"

"Thy kingdom come.
Thy will be done in earth, as it is in heaven"
(Matthew 6:10).

Chapter Twenty-One

Something was wrong. Lev could sense it, but he was unable to figure out what. One of the computers was not performing optimally. So he compared the configuration of the second NE computer to the first one. All the settings seemed to match. But the uneasy feeling that he was missing something would not go away.

There were no more detectable pockets of resistance to the new technology since Mr. Mueller had shared his experience with any who wanted to know what had happened to him. His honesty dispelled the general suspicion that his paralysis was due to some cruel use of sophisticated poison or nerve gas that would leave a permanent injury as a testimony of the superiority of the Jewish race. When the men at the Science Institute saw the change in Mr. Mueller's attitude and life, they gained greater respect for Lev and for his cause.

With a new spring in his step Mr. Mueller would approach a scientist on his staff, put his arm around his shoulder, and talk in confiding manner. "Imagine the joy of receiving your son Jerold back to life, Peter. I cannot wait to see my wife and daughter again, and our efforts to produce computers and New Earth technology only make these hopes more of a reality, for the resurrection will not take place until homes are prepared and Eden fruit is available."

Anticipation and excitement continued to grow as the men viewed the training sessions recorded by the Ancients. They were eager to start production as soon as possible. Fires of passion for life were being fanned, but Lev sensed that somewhere amongst these men there was a wet blanket. He also had the feeling he was being watched and followed. He knew he was a curiosity and that people studied and speculated about him amongst themselves, but he sensed a more intense scrutiny. When he jogged or took a walk on break, he noticed furtive movements out of the corner of his eye.

He finally found the inconsistency in the configurations late that evening, and he felt both relief and anxiety. He took a walk in the silver shadows of the half moon and phoned Enoch on his secure phone to discuss the present situation and then did some serious thinking as he jogged around the block.

Suddenly he stopped and looked behind him. There was an unmistakable sound of footsteps not far behind. He walked more quickly and chose a circuitous route toward his apartment and still he sensed that someone was there. He stopped again suddenly, and squinted as he surveyed the area in the surreal light of a partial moon.

"Whoever you are, show yourself," he called out calmly. "There is no need to be afraid." When no one responded he continued his walk at a brisk pace until he reached his apartment.

Worship Service Attendance Multiplies

The next morning Lev went to morning worship and was surprised it was so crowded. Lev stood in the back with Rebekah and a number of others. Lev was grateful for Rebekah's presence, which was actually an unusual occurrence since they tried to be at different services so as to be in contact with more people. The churches had been entirely abandoned after the final invasion of Israel due to the general disillusionment that people had experienced when the promises of the church leaders bore the fruitage of utter chaos. But through the years small numbers met together in secret places, trying to make sense of the turn of events and the strange reports they had heard regarding the nation of Israel.

The numbers grew quickly each day as word spread throughout the area of Mr. Mueller's consequence and change of heart, and of Lev and Rebekah's testimonies regarding New Earth blessings from the land of Israel. Today's audience was overwhelmingly large and there was an unmistakable air of excitement.

Lev stood up during the Testimonies, saying, "My name is Lev Aron and I'm from Israel. I thank the Lord Jesus, whom my people once rejected, for all he has done. I was raised almost a year ago. I had died in defense of our land on the first day of battle during the final invasion. I am overwhelmed by what has been given to me. My first wife was raped and killed by a terrorist. My parents died in a suicide bombing. When I died my second wife and son thought they had lost me forever. We are all alive again and together, and I can't describe the joy of seeing them for the first time, and of growing closer to them than I ever imagined." Lev wiped a tear from his eye.

"I received the help and direction I needed to work out my fears and conflicts. I contacted the Ancients to find out how I could help in the work of preparing for others to be raised. I helped build a home for a family that had died in the Palestinian uprising, and being there when they were raised was amazing—it was like being a new father again. That's why I am here to help organize your technology so that your country can build homes, grow Eden trees and prepare for the return of your loved ones. It is an honor to be here with you. And I thank Christ for this new beginning."

A hushed silence stole over those assembled, and then the rustle of excited whispers filled the room as people caught the vision of the joy of resurrection and the joy of preparation.

Lev stepped aside as a large plain woman with gray hair tucked in a bun on the back of her head approached the front of the church.

"I lost my son, my only son, in the siege against Jerusalem. I miss him. He was the last of my family left on this earth. I want him back. I thought I would meet him in heaven but I see I'm on the earth. But it's not a bad thing. God's will is now being done on earth like in heaven. For the first time I understand something I never understood before—'all that are in the graves shall hear his voice.' Now I know that I will see my son again on earth, this New Earth."

The woman wept with her face in her hands, and Lev put his arm around her. At that moment he sensed a conviction rising in his heart. Since the day he had spoken with Reuben and helped him own up to his son's death, he was eager to find the last soldier he may have killed before he was taken out in battle. He wanted to help build a home for his return.

As Lev led the woman to an empty place on the wooden bench, he felt the sensation of being scrutinized, and he became determined to identify the person pursuing him. He looked up and his eyes fell upon on a very thin young man in the back of the church. The man's eyes were red and swollen and he stared at Lev intensely for a long moment and then cast his eyes down to the floor. Lev immediately recognized him as one of the apprentices employed by the Science Institute under Mr. Mueller.

Other grieving mothers testified of their experiences and desire to be united with their families once again and to understand the plan of God in view of the times of darkness they had seen. One man testified to the power of Eden fruit and his gradual return to health and youth.

"I used to be stone deaf, but now I can hear the whispers in this room, thanks to the Eden fruit."

When the service ended people full of questions and excitement surrounded Lev and Rebekah. They discussed the powers of Christ and his Anointed, the Ancients, the powers of Eden fruit and the process of making it available to the general public, and what could be done in preparation for the raising of their own families.

As the crowd began to thin, Rebekah noticed Lev's attention was drawn to the back of the meeting room.

"Lev, what's wrong?"

"He's gone," Lev replied.

"Who is gone?" inquired Rebekah.

She could see that Lev still remained perplexed because he had received no direction from the Ancients regarding the change of configuration he had noticed.

They walked from the worship services to Rebekah's apartment. They lingered on the cobblestone sidewalk bordering Rebekah's new place of residence.

"I just don't get it, Rebekah, why hasn't Enoch contacted me?"

"Watch and wait, Lev. God's will *is* starting to be done on earth... even here in Germany."

Fritz Rammel

For the past two days Lev had come to the same park an hour before his usual shift ended at the Institute. He came with a Bible, desiring to read and meditate. Today his mind kept thinking about the Sabbath service. He now realized that the man he had seen at the chapel was Fritz Rammel, who had not shown up for his usual shift since the worship service.

Lev sat on the wrought iron park bench with his Bible open before him for a long time. He watched a woman place chunks of bread on the grass, a silent magnet that drew gray birds to the sustenance they sought. When she moved, the birds scattered. She stooped, offered more bread and stayed very still. Soon the pigeons came to her again, pecking away at their late afternoon meal. She let the bread be the magnet, Lev mused. He thought of Fritz Rammel and sighed, wishing that he could break through the anxiety that was troubling him. He seemed frightened and on the horns of a dilemma.

Lev thought over the last days' events. All was going well at the Science Institute. Enthusiasm ran high and the men were eager to start production. The team of engineers was quick to understand the schematics and absorb the teachings of the Ancients regarding the manufacturing processes necessary to produce components for New Earth computers. Everyone seemed to understand and accept that the components were not only vastly superior to anything they had worked with before, but they were easier to create and more durable.

Tomorrow Lev would be ready to release all the technical information needed to begin the process of mass-production of computers and electronic technology. Mr. Mueller continued to be a beacon of light, radiating new direction and guidance for his staff because of the great peace he had found in a renewed attitude in facing the inevitable changes that must take place in order to prepare Germany for the great work of regeneration.

Rebekah had informed Lev that a change had been made in the design for the gardens that would bring a continual harvest of Eden fruit and other fruits and vegetables to the German people even in the cooler climate of the country. Instead of gardens and orchards in each home, there would be specially designed energy efficient hot houses warmed with fuel cell energy. Lev and Rebekah were both excited about this new development and looked forward to their first opportunity to assemble the hot houses.

Lev had finally found and corrected the errors in the computer's settings. He was sure it had been tampered, but the only word he had received from Enoch was the brief message: "Continue in your work and do not lose heart. Shalom and God bless."

He still had no idea how to deal with the computer vandal, and for some reason no one had been stricken with any impairment of speech or motor skills. And where was Fritz Rammel? He finally slumped down in the bench, closed his eyes, and gave up trying to figure everything out.

Lev opened his eyes at the flat sound of the flapping of wings and the cry of disturbed pigeons. He saw pigeons scattering quickly, their heads bobbing with each step. The woman had gone and in her place he saw Fritz Rammel in the center of the grass mutely trying to coax the birds back.

"They're kind of skittish," Lev called out. Then he continued to read the open Bible that rested on his lap.

Fritz Rammel stared at Lev and took a step away from the bench, stopped, saw Lev's half smile, took a step toward the bench and stopped again. Lev chuckled quietly to himself, his eyes still glued to the page of his Bible. Fritz Rammel's curiosity finally got the best of him, and he quietly approached the park bench and sat down on the other end of it.

"I've been watching you," he announced.

Lev continued to read.

"And I've been watching Mr. Mueller. Things are not right. In fact things are *wrong. Everything's* wrong." Fritz spoke quickly in a hoarse tone that betrayed his nervousness. "And I don't know what to do with myself. I've been watching you—and I think you know a lot of things—and I just don't know what to do."

"I'm all ears if you have something you want to talk about." Lev did not look up from his Bible.

A Web of Wickedness

"I'm tearing myself up inside, Mr. Aron. I heard the testimonies in that worship service and I know how much those women want their families back. I would too if I were them, but I'm not them and—"

Lev could see from his peripheral vision that Fritz was wringing his hands. Fritz took a deep breath in order to continue. "I am the fifth generation of a family with staunch Nazi affiliations."

Lev took a deep breath and continued listening.

"I'm not a neo-Nazi myself, but for years I lived in denial of many things that happened because I didn't want to believe they really happened. The outcome of the siege on Jerusalem really made me think—I don't understand, but it seems to me that God has protected the little nation of Israel throughout the centuries, and when we saw the miraculous turn of events, I was convinced." Fritz continued to wring his hands.

"I believe the reports that come from Israel about Eden fruit and the raising of the dead. I believe your and Rebekah's testimonies, and I know the resurrection will bring happiness to millions. But not for my family." He paused and looked briefly over at Lev, and then stared at his restless hands.

"My family—some of them—would prefer to remain dead than to live again and to face those they sent to the gas chambers. A 'new beginning' as you put it, would be a burden for them, and a burden for the rest of my family. It would be a burden to *me*." Fritz Rammel buried his face in his hands. His body shook as he wept silently.

Lev turned to face Fritz and placed his hand on the young man's shoulder. "I appreciate your honesty, Fritz. You have a lot on your mind."

"And then I think, maybe my apprehension is justified in thinking of their return to life if I was them. Maybe I would not want to return to face the shame and guilt of my past deeds. My great great Grandfather and many of my other relatives were part of the 'Final Solution' to destroy innocent men, women and children for not being part of the Aryan race. Among others they targeted the Jewish people. And here you are, a Jew, coming to help our country. This bright future you talk about doesn't seem at all bright to me."

"Serious sins have been committed by many people in the past, Fritz, not just your family. We were told not to follow a multitude to evil. The mob psychology made people capable of evil they would never have done so on their own. It is not 'in our blood' to be so wicked. To those courageous enough to admit their sins and seek forgiveness, sin can be and will be forgiven. Christ can forgive sin. That doesn't mean that sins committed will go unpunished. It will not be easy but even the heinous sins of the Holocaust can be forgiven."

For the first time in their conversation Fritz looked into Lev's eyes and did not look away.

"Fritz, I killed people on the battlefield. They were nameless and faceless people who happened to be the enemy I was trained to kill. We were pitted in battle against each other for reasons that were not clear. Men have been doing this for centuries. Thank God, that is ended now. War was the result of not being able to find any other solution. However, soldiers who died on the battlefield won't share the same burden as those who deliberately murdered helpless people. Yes, those responsible for the Holocaust are going to face a lot of people that they murdered and it is not going to be easy. However, they can be forgiven and reconciled to those they murdered if they have the character to show godly sorrow for their sin. It won't be easy, but it is certainly possible. This is what the regeneration is for, to help people who have lost their way, to bring about change and healing from the inside when the Spirit of God 'is poured out upon all flesh.'"

"My parents and grandparents were indoctrinated with hate. I don't believe they enjoyed their nefarious task, but once they were caught in the 'web' they did not have the strength to free themselves. Their part in the inhumane crimes insured their survival, and so they survived with blood on their hands and their reward was a hollow life filled with guilt. They had nightmares about the gas chambers..."

"It was a strong web, Fritz; they were pulled into it by hatred and mass psychology. Christ knows the face of hatred firsthand. He died facing hatred more intense toward him than the two criminals at his side. And he knows how to give each of us every opportunity to regain innocence and love. It will take great effort and courage, but this opportunity is available for all those willing to change their lives."

A Magnet That Draws

"If I could only believe this to be true."

"Seek righteousness in your own life, and then you will understand."

The pigeons had begun to return to the center of the grass and Fritz rose to try to feed them again.

"You'll have better luck if you leave the pieces of bread all around you, and stay very still. Let the bread be the magnet.

Fritz returned to seat himself on the bench beside Lev. As he threw bread pieces about two and three feet away, he spoke.

"I have two confessions to make, Lev. First, I was the one who tampered with the computer. I changed some settings in the configuration. It was my lame way to interfere—a silly way to interfere with the regeneration process. I was trying to slow down the imminent pain my parents and grandparents would feel when people would be made alive again. I'm sorry. But at the same time, I was drawn to you—you were like a magnet to me."

Fritz surveyed the bread he had scattered in the grass and saw the pigeons begin to gather and peck. "I wanted to hear your experiences and your opinions, and I wanted to see how you lived—so I followed you around for a few days."

Lev smiled. "I knew someone was following me—but I didn't know it was you."

"I have one more question, Lev. What about people who actually created the web of evil we were talking about. Are they to be regenerated also?"

"The same sacrifice that frees any one of us from the sentence of death frees all of us, and the same power is theirs to grasp hold of— but it will, again, take great courage and effort. There is so much to be faced."

"Even people like Hitler?" Fritz asked.

Lev felt a shiver crawl up his spine.

"Even people like Hitler?" Fritz asked again.

"Yes, even people like Hitler."

"Come to me, all ye that labor and are heavy laden,
And I will give you rest"
(Matthew 11:28).

Chapter Twenty-Two

Lev thought back to his morning phone call with Enoch.

"Enoch, I have a strong desire to find the name of the soldier I killed. I've been praying about it, and now I'm asking you, how do I go about finding out? Is there anything I can do to prepare for his resurrection?" Lev spoke into his secure phone on his way to work. "If I can be of help, I request to stay here longer."

"We already know of your desire, and we are pleased to grant it. The soldier you killed was Fred Gruber. Both parents had abandoned him when he was a baby and he was raised as an orphan.

"Meantime, continue to oversee and troubleshoot the computer manufacturing in your territory. Others from Israel are doing the same and we are right on schedule. We are pleased with the production of homes, computers, and with the production and distribution of Eden fruit in Germany. The Lord has blessed you and Rebekah in your work and the others who have volunteered in that country."

Lev was pleased with the praise from Enoch. He had been pleasantly surprised at the rate of progress in building and in planting. Land had been divided and allocated by the Ancients. The old ways were being torn down and the new ways were being created. Many joined in the efforts, caught up in the vision of regeneration joy. Because of Eden fruit the elderly were growing younger, the sick were getting well and they heartily joined in the restitution work. It was most fascinating to watch the changes.

People would come up to him on the street and announce their latest health report. "Mr. Aron, I got up this morning and I wasn't even stiff. Know anyone that needs a walker?" "Don't need my glasses any more, Mr. Aron. Now what do you think of that?"

Lev had made many friends and knew many by name as he walked or jogged along the streets of Berlin.

Preparing to Meet Fred Gruber

Four months passed by quickly as Lev helped to build Fred Gruber's home and as he kept up with challenges at the Science Institute. Lev did not know how he would face the soldier he had killed in heat of battle, especially a soldier with the antisemetic sentiments that Fred Gruber carried in his heart. He did not know what process would bring about reconciliation to this broken family. The name of the neo-Nazi hate-group made Lev freeze inside.

Yet the restitution work continued all around him and in the whole country of Germany. The spirit of working shoulder to shoulder to prepare for the raising of loved ones was catching on. No one could deny the changes taking place.

The latest innovation from Jerusalem was technology that efficiently separated water into two parts of hydrogen and one part of oxygen, which resulted in an environmentally clean supply of energy needed in areas where sun energy was not always available. Weather patterns had been moderated by divine intervention so that the seasons were mellow and rain or snow fell generously over all the earth, making water a plentiful commodity for all.

Between solar energy and hydro-oxy power, the energy problems of the world were a matter of history. The ability to duplicate production of the hydro-oxy fuel cell was quickly shared and implemented throughout Germany, as were the other advances that made preparation for regeneration of future generations simple and effective. Eden trees were thriving in the new hothouses throughout Germany. Lev felt overwhelmed with excitement and gratitude to realize that similar strides were being made in all the nations of the world, for all had now come under the authority of Christ, his Anointed, and the Ancients.

Fritz Rammel was one of the three who volunteered to work on Fred Gruber's home and Lev had to smile every time he thought of him. The skittish and shy man was growing more confident and full of love for life each day. He was becoming more and more optimistic about the future and less apprehensive about the raising of his own family as he prepared for the raising of Fred Gruber. Sometimes he talked non-stop as they worked. It was his way of thinking through issues he was uncomfortable with.

"Christ converted most of the Jews overnight when he fought for Israel that pivotal day of the invasion. He overcame the traditions and preconceived ideas of men so quickly. And he did it in my life also, though it took a little longer."

Fritz had been digging in the hothouse soil to plant the remaining dwarf fruit trees. He placed the last tree into its new home and smoothed the earth around it by quick pats with cupped hands. He worked with abandon just as he talked, and when he scratched his nose a smear of dark earth rubbed off which made Lev's smile even wider.

"And look at how my people look at you, Lev. You speak German without a trace of an accent, and people don't care that you're a Jew. In fact, they respect you for your heritage. The old ways of thinking are unpopular, and they don't seem to have a foothold now, at least not an obvious foothold." He stopped patting the earth for a moment, sat with his hands around his knees and spoke more softly.

"Perhaps there is latent prejudice, and we have yet to see it. There certainly will be a stir when my great great Grandfather is resurrected along with the others of his generation."

Fred Gruber Returns

The day of Fred Gruber's return had come and Lev faced a very angry man.

"Come on; don't fool with me, mister. I must say I'm very confused. My last memories were definitely of the battlefield. That's very clear in my mind. Then all goes blank. I don't know what I'm doing in your house, but thanks for putting me up. I'll clear out of here as soon as I get in touch with my commanding officer."

Lev tried again to explain the unbelievable truth to the young man before him. "You don't have a commanding officer, Fred. You're not in the army anymore. There aren't any more armies in the whole world."

"The army was my *life*." Fred Gruber became visibly agitated as he paced the floor of the living room. "What are you, some peace freak? Where am I anyway? Let me use your phone, sir, if I may. I must call headquarters. They will think I deserted."

"There's the phone. Make all the calls you want."

Fred stomped toward the phone and called the number familiar to him only to be told that the number was no longer in service. He dialed the operator and demanded the number of the German army headquarters. His faced turned red and he tried unsuccessfully to avoid swearing at the one who spoke to him. Then he slammed the phone down and glared at the stranger in front of him.

"Why are you playing with me? You know a lot more than you're telling me, and if you weren't valuable to me for information, I would punch you in the mouth."

Lev noticed Fred's hand had tightened into a fist.

"I'm a German patriot, a veteran of war, and I deserve to be treated better than I'm being treated. Nothing makes any sense. Can't you stop your games and level with me?"

"Fred, I remember feeling confused, and nothing made sense to me when I was first raised. I remembered my death, and the next thing I knew I was alive and well. You have been raised by the power of Christ, just as I was."

Fred shook his head vigorously and continued to pace the floor.

"Where are your glasses, Fred? Did you notice how keen your vision has become? And where are your tattoos? I checked your dental records and found you had a missing molar. Have you checked the mirror lately?"

Fred abruptly stopped pacing, his back toward Lev. He rolled up his short sleeve and examined his forearm. He looked around the room, and walked toward a mirror and opened his mouth.

"Impossible," he muttered. He turned to face Lev with a dazed look in his eyes.

"Come on, Fred; sit with me at the table." Fred obeyed without saying a word.

Lev poured hot tea and offered him some Eden fruit.

He took advantage of Fred's brief period of stunned silence.

"Fred, I told you what happened earlier, but you dismissed it outright, because it wasn't reasonable to you. What other explanation could there be for your perfect health, your eyes, your teeth…"

"My tattoos—I liked my tattoos—and they are gone…" He sounded lost and disappointed.

Lev smiled. "There are so many changes, it's a shock. It was for me too. My son was a boy when I died. He called me 'Dad' when he saw me alive again, yet he was a grown man. I could see the resemblance and I knew he was my son, but it was frustrating to find myself in two time frames without a bridge between."

Fred drank his serving of resurrection tea, and then proceeded to stuff his mouth with Eden fruit and Eden pastries.

"Good food." His words were muffled because his mouth was full.

"You are here by nothing less than a miracle."

Fred swallowed. He appeared calm and relaxed as he slumped back in his chair, and he spoke in a casual tone.

"You said you were on the battlefield that day, Lev. I remember trying my best to silence a stubborn pocket of resistance. I guess they got me. Somehow it wasn't supposed to be that way. The Jews kept fighting. They returned our fire no matter how much lead we poured into them. We called for air power to silence the resistance. Before the chopper arrived those stinkin' Jews hit our position. All I remember is the sting of hot lead in the top of my head. I knew I was fatally wounded. Somehow it wasn't supposed to be that way. I really wanted to live and keep killing those Jews."

Fred felt his neck and chest and found no wounds and could find no signs of scarring. He shook his head and squinted in perplexity.

"At least I'm not in that stinking land of Israel anymore. I hated that place. It's good to be back in the fatherland. How long did it take before those crazy Jews surrendered?"

Lev hesitated.

"You won't like to hear this, Fred, but the forces that descended on Israel that day were victorious only on the first day. The next morning there was a strange turn of events."

Lev described the electricity that seemed to fill the air, the failure of communications, and the resulting destruction of the enemies of Israel.

Fred's eyes were wide with horror.

"If I hadn't died that day, I would've died the next day—is that what you're telling me?"

"I'm afraid so, Fred. The world you knew then has changed. Years have passed since then, and now there are no armies or weapons. For the first time in the history of nations there is peace everywhere. And the home you are in is yours," Lev purposely diverted the subject. "It belongs to you, Fred."

Fred stared at Lev and slowly his somber expression melted into an uncertain smile.

"Lev, you're not kidding me, are you? You mean I own this beautiful house and all the land it's on? Who would be so generous to me? I never felt at home in any house I ever lived in. I never owned anything. I was raised an orphan. Why would anyone care enough to give me anything?"

"Christ cared enough for you to die for you and to raise you to a new life, Fred. He has given you an opportunity to start over again." Lev saw a tear well up in Fred's eye, and he took it as a sign that he could continue to speak hard truth.

"Fred, I don't know how to tell you this, but I must. I was the 'stinkin' Jew who killed you back on the plain of Megiddo. I died shortly after, from a chopper that rained death out of the sky. Its heavy firing tore off my left hand. I was also hit in the chest and knew it was the end for me. I didn't want to die either, you see. I asked to have the honor of being here for your awakening."

Fred pushed himself away from the table and a few inches farther away from Lev and stared at the floor, but Lev continued to speak.

"I volunteered to help build your house with three others. We worked really hard to make it comfortable for you, a place that you could feel at home."

"Then you're a Jew, aren't you, Lev?"

Fred's agitation returned, and he became fidgety and restless as he repetitively repositioned his cup and plate. He avoided looking at Lev.

"I can't believe this. Of all the German people in the world, why is it that a Jew is here with me today?"

"Because I am probably the one who killed you, and I wanted to make it right. Because Christ has blessed my people, and the blessing was to be shared with you, the German people, and all the people of all nations."

Orphaned

Fred drank the second serving of resurrection tea that Lev had poured for him.

"And there are others who want to make things right, Fred. Your mother, she really wishes to see you." Lev hesitated. "And then there's your father…"

"I'd rather be with *you*," Fred's words sounded hoarse, as if his throat was closing up. He closed his eyes tightly and began to sob. "I hate them. I hate them for leaving me. And I hate you—your people— for the trouble you've caused and the humiliation—for your successes. You people refuse to die off. You hold on, and you never give up— and then you succeed. But my own parents—they gave up—they left me—a child—I hate them—I hate…" his voice trailed off, overcome by the torrent of his emotions.

Lev sat by Fred as he slumped over the table, his whole body shaking as he wept. Lev sensed the heaviness of the burden that this man carried, and this realization made his own burden of anxiety suddenly lift.

Fred's Education Begins

Later in the day Lev gave Fred a tour around the house and the neighborhood. Fred followed him like a little boy, quiet and pensive yet intensely curious about all that he saw and intensely interested in all of Lev's explanations as they toured the features of his new home and hothouse. Lev described the education that was available to him through the instruction of the Ancients via his computer.

Lev continued to talk to Fred about the changes of the New Earth as they walked around the quaint newly constructed cottages in his neighborhood. He showed Fred the place where chapel services were to be held for his area and offered to accompany him to his first worship service.

On their return home, Fred was shocked as he viewed the footage from the final invasion and the sudden turn of events that marked divine intervention on behalf of Israel. He watched his own army disintegrate. He saw planes falling out of the sky and warships with lifeless crews drifting in the sea. He watched as the Lord took on the whole invading force on land, sea and in the air. There was no hand to deliver them from the anger of the Lord. First the forces assembled against Israel were annihilated. Then as news quickly spread of the utter defeat of their forces, it unleashed the anarchistic forces upon the nations. Mobs rioted and attacked their own governments with the police assisting them. The churches faced the wrath of the crowds and anarchy spread far and wide. Law and order were replaced with angry crowds who could not be placated.

"You've been telling me the truth," Fred said in a whisper, "and you are the only person I have ever known to show me love and kindness. And yet you are a Jew."

Fred slumped back in his chair and closed his eyes.

"I'm being cared for by a Jew…"

"Goodnight, Fred." Lev placed his hand of Fred's shoulder and then walked toward the door. "I'll see you in the morning."

Lev left the cottage with a light heart. There were many obstacles before Fred. He would face his mother who had abandoned him out of desperation. He would face an impossible self-centered father who cared nothing for him. He would face his old skinhead friends. The outcome was not in Lev's hands. Everything depended upon Fred's ability to change his mindset.

"When thy judgments are in the earth,
The inhabitants of the world will learn righteousness"
(Isaiah 26:9).

Chapter Twenty-Three

Lev saw Fred's rapt attention during the morning service. Fred was impressed with the text, "Repent ye therefore, and be converted, that your sins may be blotted out, when the times of refreshing shall come from the presence of the Lord."

The study leader's comments prompted Fred to whisper, "The only thing that will block my being blessed is if I'm unwilling to change." Lev nodded, and Fred continued. "Who is this man, anyway? He's great—makes a person think! He seems to know what he is talking about."

"He's from a small Bible study group that strongly opposed the invasion of Israel. According to what I've been told, many of their group suffered for their convictions in regard to Israel as well as other beliefs."

After the service Lev noticed two young men pushing their way through the crowd to meet Fred. Fred immediately greeted them.

"John, Ludwig, you both look fantastic! Isn't this New Earth amazing? I'm still trying to get my bearings."

"When can we get together, friend? We've got a lot of catching up to do."

Fred glanced at Lev, and then at his former friends.

"I'll have to see. My friend Lev, here, is helping me begin some courses of study on the Internet. He's going to give me a tour of the Science Institute this week."

"You were never the studying type, man—since when do you like to hit the books?" Ludwig replied in a glib tone.

"Since education has been taken over by the Ancients. It's awesome—even history, which I used to despise. I have a lot to re-learn, though. Somebody sure did a job on us. I can see now we were fed a lot of misinformation."

Both John and Ludwig seemed agitated and stared at him.

"Don't let this Jew lead you around by the nose," Ludwig whispered in Fred's ear as the two-shook hands with their old friend. They stared at Lev coldly for a brief moment and left.

"They were really rude," Fred stated to Lev as they walked toward Fred's home.

Lev let the subject drop. He knew that Fred was preoccupied with the possibility that soon he would be meeting his mother. Lev also knew that Fred was upset with his old skinhead friends who were raised a short time ago and had the apparent intent of spending some time with him.

Fred Visits the Science Center

After a quick brunch, Lev drove Fred to the Science Institute. Fred was excited about meeting some of the men who had devoted time each day to build his home.

The Science Institute had no security guards. Lev pointed this out to Fred as they drove up to park. Fred noticed that Lev was parking in the "Chief Executive" spot.

He finally said, "Lev, aren't you worried that the CEO might return from lunch and want his parking place? Usually, they don't take kindly to anyone taking their spot."

Lev answered, "I actually borrowed his car, so he won't mind. It will be there for him when he wants it. He's a pretty generous guy."

"Well, all right. I just didn't want you to get in any trouble. I know if we did something like that in the army, we'd be doing time in the guard house."

Lev smiled, "Thanks for being concerned, Fred. We don't have any guardhouses anymore. People behave themselves because that's the only option. We have a spiritual police force like you've never known before. If you try to do something wrong, you'll be punished on the spot—like having your arm paralyzed."

Lev introduced Fred to Herman, Hans and Fritz, and asked Fritz to take Fred on a tour of the facility while he answered the technician's questions who had lined up to see him.

Fritz Rammel was especially excited to meet Fred. His handshake was vigorous.

"Fred Gruber! You don't know what your raising means to me. I was afraid of this whole resurrection process. In fact, I even tried to sabotage Lev's computer, hoping to delay things." He spoke as they walked down a long corridor to the main manufacturing area.

"I was afraid of what it would be like to have those in that generation of my family raised. They did their part in Hitler's final solution...and I couldn't bear the thought of their humiliation and my own. But Lev helped me, and I have been undergoing some changes in my thinking. Then I heard about you, the skinhead killed by my friend, Lev, and I volunteered to help in the building of your home. And the more I heard about you, and Lev's desire to make amends to you, the more I got excited to see you raised up. I can hardly understand it, but as I started to look forward to your regeneration, I started to not be so afraid of the raising of my own relatives."

"Thanks for your help, Fritz! I appreciate all you and the others have done for me."

The afternoon flew by. Before they knew it Lev and Fred were driving back to Fred's home.

"There's an air of excitement at the Science Institute, Lev! The nuts and bolts of getting homes, computers and Eden fruit for generations to come—I want to be part of it!"

"You could work in a place like this in a year's time if you take all the courses that I point out to you."

"And that fellow, Fritz, he's quite a neat guy. He has a positive way of facing his challenges."

Lev nodded and then was silent for a moment. He sensed that it was time to bring up the difficulty that Fred needed to face.

"So, Fred, how about the challenge of meeting your mother?"

Fred was suddenly silent. He didn't say a word until Lev pulled into his driveway.

"You've done a lot for me, Lev. You owed me nothing, and you helped give me everything. Part of me wants to meet my mother, and the other part is so angry... I'll do it, but I won't make any promises."

Lev stopped the company car at Fred's home.

"That's all I ask, Fred. I'll arrange the meeting for the morning after next. Thanks."

Lev watched Fred leave the car, and shut the passenger door. Lev looked in his rear view mirror. He saw no one, but he had the distinct impression that he was being followed.

John and Ludwig Learn the Consequence of Wrong

The next morning Lev walked briskly toward his home after the morning's worship service had ended. John and Ludwig had wanted to talk with Fred and he didn't wish to interfere. Fred would have to make his own decisions. He wondered how Fred was faring when he heard a voice call to him from behind.

"Lev, wait up." It was Fred. "I told them they were both way out of line—and that they owe you an apology. They were very insulting in what they said about you. It was easy to hate Jews when I didn't know any of them personally. But now that I know you—I *can't* hate you. And if they knew you, I don't think they could either."

"Thanks, Fred, that took courage."

John and Ludwig were leaning against the entrance of the house when Lev and Fred arrived.

"Maybe they've come to apologize," suggested Fred in a whisper.

"Would you care to come in for some Eden bread and fruit?" Lev offered as he stepped in front of the two.

"Why don't you go home, Jew? We don't like you around here."

"Speak for yourself, John. Lev is my friend," said Fred.

"Well, speaking for myself, he's no friend of mine," John retorted, grabbing Lev's coat and holding him around the neck at the same moment that Ludwig stepped back preparing to give Lev a swift kick.

"What the..." John muttered, when both of his hands suddenly hung limply at his sides.

Ludwig lost his balance and fell to the ground.

"My leg—I can't feel my leg," he moaned.

Lev helped Ludwig stand and let him lean on him for balance.

"I'll take you both to your homes, and I'll tell you what you need to do to reverse your paralysis."

Lev awkwardly led Ludwig toward his car, while Fred and John looked on in shock until Fred finally realized that Ludwig could use his support on his other side. John and Ludwig said nothing as they were helped into the vehicle and remained silent for the duration of the short journey. Lev drove up to John's house, opened his door for him, and disappeared into the small house for a short time. Lev returned to the car by himself.

"So, how's he doing?" Fred asked.

"He's got mixed emotions and he's still sorting things out, but he was able to talk to one of the Ancients. I have to admit that he was honest about what happened. I believe the use of his hands will return to him within the hour. He's learning what life under strict righteousness is like. It's surprising how fast people learn. He could get away with everything before, but not now."

Lev recalled the words of a shaken John just before he left his home—"You aren't the lame idiot I expected in a Jew, but I can't shake the feeling I have—its like I still want to hate you and your people, even though it doesn't make sense anymore."

"The real issue at hand," Ludwig said sarcastically, "is being subjected to the influence and people we bloody well hate."

"The real issue," Lev responded in an even tone, "is that resentment and hatred are corrosive to the heart. The physical consequence of paralysis is a good reminder that one must change his attitude and learn to deal with his own honesty of heart."

Fred helped Lev lead Ludwig into his house and on to his living room sofa. Then Fred left to wait in the car. Lev returned in a short time with a tired expression on his face.

"So, how did it go with Ludwig?" Fred asked.

"I'm afraid he shot himself in the foot. He couldn't bring himself to be honest with Sarah. He'll have to bear his paralysis for the next two weeks. I suggested he call around for some crutches. I made sure that both he and John have enough fruit for the day, and I brewed up some resurrection tea. It'll be interesting to see what choices they make. I'll check on them tomorrow."

"It's like the parable in the worship service this morning. The King forgave his servant a huge debt, but the servant demanded full payment from another person, one who owed him so little. The servant ended up in prison, 'tormented by the jailer' until they found out how he could pay up. God set it up this way so we would learn righteousness. It's like you said, resentment and hatred only end up hurting the one with the attitude."

Fred was suddenly quiet. He understood that these words were a perfect fit for the choices before him in his own life.

*"When my father and my mother forsake me,
Then the LORD will take me up"
(Psalms 27:10).*

Chapter Twenty-Four

Lev arranged for Hans to drive Fred's mother to Fred's house. The first encounter between Gretchen Gruber and her son was awkward. She stood in the doorway with tears running down her cheeks. She paused in front of her son not knowing whether to embrace him or just say hello. Fred extended his hand and his eyes gazed directly into his mother's eyes. Then he looked toward the floor, still holding her hand.

"Come in, Gretchen," Lev interjected, trying to get her into the house and out of the cold drizzle.

"Hello, Lev, and thank you," Gretchen said.

Lev directed them to the table in the kitchen. She poured out her heart to Fred, between sips of Resurrection tea, though there were moments of overwhelming emotion when she was unable to speak.

"I've caused you a lot of hurt and pain, Fred, I know that. The only decision I am not sorry for is that I gave birth to you instead of having an abortion."

She described her struggles to survive once Fred's father left her and her determination to keep the child despite the threat of divorce. Against the advice of her mother and father, Gretchen left college, got a job as a barmaid, and barely made enough to make ends meet. Once the baby was born she could not hold down a job and was evicted from her apartment.

"I found myself in the street with no one to help and nowhere to turn. I left you on the doorstep of the orphanage with a letter that described my situation and that I would come back for you when I could. I asked them to promise me that they would give the letter to you if something happened and I wasn't able to come for you. But I never managed to get back to you."

"I never got any letter," Fred said softly, as he stared at his hands clasped before him on the table. "I was put into different homes, never for very long. I was a troublemaker, I guess, and most of the families treated me like an outsider. I used to have the scars to prove it."

Fred felt his shoulder and his forearms as the memory of his abuse returned to his mind.

"Finally, when I had enough I ran away and ended up on the streets. I became a member of the National Democratic Party, and they treated me like I belonged. I joined the army and couldn't wait to massacre as many Jews as I could in the final invasion. Then Lev, here, ended my life before I could end his. Now I find myself befriended by this Jew, in a world where there is no war. My scars are healed and even my tattoos are gone.... And for the first time I have a home that is mine, a friend who really cares about me, and then I meet you, my mother." Fred began to weep as he struggled to continue.

"I thought you had thrown me away—and I wondered who you were and why you left me…"

"And I never stopped looking for you, Fred. And finally—thank God…"

Gretchen could not continue. Fred moved his chair from the head of the table closer to the corner of his mother's place and leaned into her for a long and tearful embrace.

Gretchen and Fred Learn About Lev

Gretchen was pleased to learn that this was Fred's house.

"My, how beautiful, Fred! I have my own assigned portion of land, and the hothouse containing my trees of life has been built, but my house isn't completed yet. Perhaps it's a month away from completion."

Fred said, "I'll help you finish it, Mom. You're welcome to live here with me until it's finished. Lev and some of his fellow workers built this for me."

Gretchen was curious, and she asked Lev, "Why would you want to give your time and labor to someone who tried to kill your people?"

Lev explained, "Fred and I were on opposite sides in the war to take Jerusalem. I learned, after I returned to life, that he was in the unit across from me. It was my shot that hit Fred before I was hit by a helicopter that came on the horizon like a fortress in the sky. I learned we died about a minute apart, so when I was stationed here in Germany in your Science Institute, I inquired if I could help build Fred's house. I got permission to do this, and some of the boys from work helped me out. Germans are good workers."

Then Fred added, "Lev thinks if I study hard for a year, I'll be qualified to join in the work at the Science Institute, too."

Gretchen said, "If Lev told you that, you'd better get started studying, because Hans told me Lev's the chief of operations there and the most gifted man for the job they've ever had."

"Aw, gee!" Fred said. "Lev took me there and never let me know that he was in charge of that whole operation. I thought it was strange that everyone was waiting for answers from him. He parked in the main parking place and then I found him in the main office! But he made it look like he was just using the boss' place for a few minutes. That shows you what kind of person Lev is, Mom! He's really great!"

The morning passed, and Lev excused himself to make some phone calls. He then took a walk to let Fred and his mother talk more privately. Lev decided to visit Ludwig to see how he was doing.

When Lev arrived, he found Ludwig quite depressed. Lev asked if he had called around to get crutches. He hadn't, so Lev picked up the phone and found a place that had a pair they would gladly give to Ludwig. Lev picked them up and brought them back to show Ludwig how to use them. That brightened Ludwig's day. Lev checked to see if he had any food, and Ludwig hadn't picked any.

Lev took a basket and went into the orchard hothouse and filled it up so Ludwig would have some Eden fruit. Lev also told him that John was well now and to call him for any help since he was nearby.

Ludwig asked, "How come he's better now, and I'll be this way for two weeks?"

"Didn't I tell you to tell Sarah the whole truth without coloring it in any way?"

"Well, yes, but how could she know what actually transpired?"

"Easy! The same angel that paralyzed your leg saw everything and heard everything you did. Christ knew it, too. When Sarah checked with them, she knew you didn't tell the whole truth, Ludwig. John told the truth, but you thought you could get away with fudging the truth.

"I know firsthand how difficult it is to be paralyzed. You could have been made whole within the hour, but you thought you could do the wrong thing and lie about it. That doesn't work anymore, Ludwig. It's not Israel, but Christ who governs now. And Christ judges nothing by the seeing of the eye or the hearing of the ear, but he judges righteously."

"How long were you paralyzed?" he asked.

"Only about an hour, because I told the whole truth and because there was severe provocation by my old enemy, Reuben. By the way, we are now the best of friends, Reuben and I. Things change. The best way to get rid of an enemy is to make a friend of him."

Lev continued, "You know, it was me that killed Fred. We faced each other in battle and I killed him about one minute before I died. You probably died the next day, didn't you? What was it like?"

"I really can't describe it, Lev. I knew as well as everyone else that it wasn't going to be a good day—it was so dark and gloomy. What made it especially bad was that we were successful the day before. It looked like we'd just steamroll over the Jews the next morning. Our commanders were confident the night before. But in the morning, no sooner were we commanded to move out, when all radio communication stopped. Our commanders wanted to change the orders, but couldn't make radio contact. We wanted to turn back, but we were under orders. It was crazy. We were all trembling out of fear. Death was in the air. Suddenly, the sky lit up, and that's all I remember."

"Everybody confirms what you just told me. The only difference is that not one Jew died that day. I died earlier trying to keep you guy's back. Doesn't this mean anything to you, Ludwig? Can't you see that God fought against you that day? Can't you see that you can't fight God and win? Why are you still trying to fight him?"

"I guess I don't know when I'm licked," Ludwig said. "Lev, can you understand that I was taught to hate Jews since I was a child. My parents drilled this into me. Even the churches told us we had to take Jerusalem from the Jews for the glory of God. I'm just sitting here thinking how stupid I am! I have no personal reason in the world to hate Jews. It was just drummed into me—hate, hate, hate. I'm like those Palestinians who were taught to hate the Jews. They were taught they would go to heaven if they died killing the Jews. All of this is nothing but lies. Why didn't God stop these lies?"

"He has," Lev answered. "The day God fought for Israel was the day that God ended all lies and deception. God waited until those he was calling and selecting from among men were joined with Christ. Now that the 'mystery of God' is complete, a new age has dawned upon the world. Don't you see if God wanted to, he could have stopped men from doing evil all along? See what he did to you? He could have done that all along, but he allowed men and devils to show what was in their hearts. He allowed pride and prejudice along with injustice and deception, to run rampant in the earth. That day is past now, Ludwig. Before you are two pathways, one upward toward God and one that leads down to death. You must decide in your heart what you will choose. As for me, I am determined to serve the King and righteousness."

Lev was afraid he'd come on too strong. He paused and a long silence followed.

Finally, Ludwig said, "Lev, I apologize. I had no reason to want to hurt you except that the old master of sin still held sway over my mind. I've been a perfect idiot. You helped Fred out. You didn't have to do that. He told me that you were a super guy, but I hated you anyway, because I was dumb enough to think that hatred and prejudice had some value. Hatred got me killed once, and here I was still in the same ugly groove. I apologize sincerely, Lev. I'll take my lumps—I deserve them. I can tell you one thing though, I'm not going to march to the music of hatred and prejudice any more. Thanks for stopping by and getting me crutches and some food. I still have hands that work—can we shake to friendship, Lev?"

"Ludwig, this is a red letter day for me. Fred and his mother are at last in each other's arms and now you have turned from an enemy into a friend. God bless you, and don't turn back from the right way. Voices will call you to meanness and hatred, but the King has shown you the way of love."

Fred still needed to be reconciled to his father.

Lev needed to call Fred's father, Arnold Gruber, to confirm his appointment to see his son tomorrow. Arnold had his own transportation, so it was arranged to be at Fred's home at 10 o'clock in the morning.

Ludwig's Confession

The following morning Lev could see that chapel attendance had grown significantly. Most of all, Lev was pleased to see John and Ludwig present. It seemed to him that the services would have added meaning for Fred because love that had been lost was found again.

When time for testimony was opened, Ludwig stood up, supported by his crutches, and apologized for his behavior. He admitted he had compounded his punishment by not being forthright with the truth.

"I was a member of the National Democratic Party and I died in the invasion of Israel. Our commanders were so confident the night before, but the next morning all radio communication stopped. And suddenly everything looked grim. We wanted to turn back, but we couldn't—we were under orders. Death was in the air. We could feel it. Suddenly, the sky lit up, and that's all I remember."

Ludwig paused, and wiped a tear from his eye. "I have since learned that not one Jew died that day. God fought for Israel, and since my raising *I* have been fighting God. I took the role of commander in my own war. I have been miserable in my new life just as I was in the old. I tried to beat up Lev Aron, and my leg was immediately paralyzed. It will take two weeks for me to recover physically, and I am still recovering from the real problem in my thinking.

"It has finally occurred to me," Ludwig scanned the crowd and when he found Lev he looked at him directly, "that I have no personal reason in the world to hate Jews. Hate was drummed into me. The hate in my heart was like a poison. I drank of it, expecting others to die, but it was slowly killing my ability to love. And now that I am being freed from my toxic hatred, I can feel it."

Ludwig's voice became shaky and it took a great effort on his part to continue. "And I thank Messiah for showing me his love through Lev and Fred, and I thank God for this new beginning."

Ludwig's testimony was well received by everyone. He had been a rebellious person, trying to live with the old indoctrination in a new age. He set the tone for the meeting.

Some had never seen the instant punishment for evil before. It put the fear of God in many hearts.

When the services ended both John and Ludwig came and shook Lev's hand warmly. It was a very moving experience—just the other day they wanted to beat Lev up. What a difference the Lord made in their hearts in this short time.

Fred and Lev offered Ludwig and John a ride, but Ludwig said he could manage quite well with his crutches. So they returned home to catch a quick bite before Fred's dad, Arnold Gruber, arrived.

Arnold Gruber Meets His Son

Fred was not really eager to meet him.

"Do you know what it feels like to be abandoned by your own father? Do you know what it's like to know that you considered me an inconvenience that you wanted to be rid of? Do you have any idea of the pain this caused me?"

Fred's voice rose and cracked as he spoke to the man who sat across from him. Arnold listened intently to the young man's words, tears forming in his own eyes. He listened as his son described his difficult life with various families, and then his life on the streets and his life as a neo-Nazi.

Lev left the house for a walk to give Fred and Arnold some privacy. When he returned he went directly to the kitchen to prepare tea and a snack and heard bits of the conversation as Fred's voice turned from tones of anger to those of hurt and sadness. Arnold listened in silence most of the time. His occasional responses were short and spoken in an even voice.

When Lev brought in two mugs of Resurrection tea, he saw Arnold nod his head in agreement. With great emotion he said in a shaken voice, "You're right, Fred, I really failed you. You needed me, and I chose not to be there for you. I was entirely self-centered. I was a self-absorbed 'lady's man.'

"I was simply going on with my life. I was willing to stick it out with Gretchen if she would only rid herself of the problem—I wanted to go on with my life minus the inconvenience of a child. Fred, I'm so terribly, terribly sorry…"

Arnold related the fact that his alcoholic womanizing lifestyle had finally driven him to stand on a bridge as he contemplated suicide.

"I had no job, no lovers, I had lost everything. I was about to jump when a car stopped, and a man I didn't recognize began to talk to me."

Arnold recounted, "I finally placed who he was. Lutz Schmidt—one of the men that I had fired. Lutz actually thanked me for firing him, something I did out of fear that he would replace me. Lutz told me that firing him led to greater things in his life. He told me he would get me a job if I kicked my alcohol habit. He put me up in a motel, gave me enough money to put some respectable clothes on my back and one week's worth of food on my table. And that, Fred, was the beginning of my more respectable phase of life."

Arnold closed his eyes tightly and shook as he wept. Lev saw Fred's jaw tighten and his arm twitched. He could not bring himself to embrace his father. Not this time.

"Excuse me, but I think I need to go home, Fred. We—we will talk again."

Arnold stood up and wiped his eyes with the back of his hand.

Fred hesitantly extended his hand, held his father's hand tightly in an awkward handshake, and then turned away from him.

"Thanks, Dad," Fred said as Arnold approached the door.

Arnold walked around the room because of a need to compose his emotions. He was overcome at hearing his son call him 'Dad.' When he came to the mirror on the wall, he looked at his reflection and resisted an urge to run his fingers through his thick hair. Instead he watched his son open the door for him to leave.

"I love you, son. And I admire the man you've become."

Recap

Lev and Rebekah walked together in the moderate spring weather that had settled all across Germany. The sun shone brightly and the sky was a striking deep blue. Their warm brisk pace made the cool evening enjoyably invigorating. They had arranged to attend the same chapel so Rebekah could meet John and Ludwig, and Lev wanted to bring her up to speed on the day's events as Fred and Arnold finally met for the first time.

"Ludwig has had the most difficult time. It's taken a lot of courage for him to get to the point we saw today at the service," said Lev.

They both recalled the tall and lanky Ludwig as he stood and made his way to the front of the chapel.

Lev and Rebekah were passing by a park with iron wrought benches.

"Let's sit here a while, Lev," Rebekah said as she led the way to the bench. They sat down side by side. Lev put his arm around Rebekah, and she leaned into him, grateful for his friendship.

Lev wondered what other challenges would come to them in their final month in Berlin and beyond, wherever Christ and his Anointed would direct. He was to fly directly from Germany to France for his next assignment. Rebekah, on the other hand, was to fly back to Israel to for a brief visit and to receive her next assignment after meeting with the Ancients.

"Enoch, the seventh from Adam, prophesied of these, saying,
Behold, the Lord cometh with ten thousands
Of his saints, to execute judgment upon all,
And to convince all that are ungodly among them
Of all their ungodly deeds"
(Jude 14).

Chapter Twenty-Five

Franz Schleicher was adamant about using the planes that were already in process of production.

"Don't you see," he had spoken directly to Lev with his arms flailing up and down for emphasis, "if spiritual forces can protect these planes, why not finish what we have on the production floor? A few more in the air will not hurt. Be reasonable."

Lev looked at Franz's red face and realized how attached he was to the old ways.

He had come to France to modify the air industry, as well as the heavy equipment and automotive industries. The newest breakthrough provided the ability to convert water into hydrogen and oxygen, and this would be the new fuel to propel jets and high-powered engines at present. The internal combustion engine would be replaced with all electric power since the hydrogen could be easily used in fuel cells to produce electricity. But the company he was dealing with had expended great amounts of money invested in developing their old technology and they were still locked into profit making mentality. The new science would insure safety as well as quality, and the presentation was well accepted among the work force. There was great resistance by the management.

"You know about the environmental factors—the old planes just don't meet the new world standards—not in regard to the environment or in regard to safety."

Lev recalled Franz's expression as he gave his first presentation a week ago. The plant members and Franz, as well, had listened to the plans for the new system with rapt attention. When Lev described how the small tank of hydrogen could be vented if there was even a remote danger of explosion during a landing, he saw Franz's face brighten in a moment of understanding. Lev knew that intellectually he was convinced of the superiority of the new way. But the cloud of agitation quickly returned, and Franz nervously began to tap his pen on his open notebook, as he shook his head slightly back and forth. He was not ready to surrender to good sense when his own position, power and hope of profit were at stake.

Lev tried to soften the blow for Franz. He was careful not to take him or his belongings out of his office. He settled into an adjoining room and placed a sign on his door that read "Operations."

Time to Remove the Old

When steady streams of people came to Lev's office and then left with excitement in response to instructions and answers they received, Franz watched with annoyance, rapidly pressing the retraction button of his pen, creating a continuous clicking sound that seemed to soothe his nerves. Lev had entered his office just the other day, serenaded by the incessant clicking of Franz Schleicher's pen, and asked, "How long will it take to clear the floor of all old operations?"

"Let me see," Franz muttered to himself, still clicking his pen as he flipped through the pages of his notebook. "It's quite a task; you know...I'll need some time to go over these figures."

Lev had approached his desk, placed both hands on it and leaned over the desk so that most of his weight was on his hands.

"Franz, we have shipments of various components arriving for the new planes in two days. Initial assembly could begin, but we still have the old planes that are partially assembled sitting there. Do you have any idea how to solve this problem?"

"Impossible," Franz hurled out the word with a half whisper in staccato fashion, emphasizing the 's' sound with his impeccable French accent. He suggested that they wait until midsummer for a little more time and optimum weather conditions. "That way we may be able to salvage more parts." He paused. "There are millions of euros invested here, you know," he added lamely.

Lev sighed. All their hours of discussion regarding the advantages of the new system and the New Earth way of recycling of old materials and even Enoch's short discussion on the necessity of letting go of the old ways had not precipitated any change in his perspective.

"You have two days, Franz, two days."

Lev had turned to leave the office and noticed that the pen clicking had suddenly stopped.

"Confounded thing jammed. I suppose old world pens aren't acceptable either anymore," Franz mumbled in disgust. He grabbed the pen in his fist and struck it like a dagger into the pages of his notebook. When Lev turned back to Franz he saw that the pen had leaked and splattered little spots of black ink on the man's white newly starched shirt as well as on his notebook.

After a call to Mr. Werner Golten, the operating head of state, Lev had wondered if Franz had begun a new and sincere attempt to cooperate. Franz had visited his office an hour later with a decisive plan of action.

"I'll have all these partially assembled planes out in a day or two. I have trucks coming to take them away, so I'll have the decks cleared for the new operations."

"Good work," Lev smiled at Franz with sincere gratitude. "Good work."

Lev looked intently into Franz Schleicher's eyes, trying to read their mood. When his gaze fell on the small splatters of black ink on his white shirt, a feeling of uneasiness swept over him and he turned away.

The inkblots had proven to be a foreboding symbol, Lev thought to himself as he walked with a rapid gait fueled with frustration toward his apartment cottage. His mind was burdened with the events of the week as he pulled out his Direct Line Unit from his back pocket.

"Impossible," he said under his breath as he fingered the compact cell phone. "You can't put new wine in an old wineskin. It's impossible." He pushed the direct call button and immediately had an audience with Enoch.

Enoch's Encouragement

"Shalom, Lev." Enoch's warm voice greeted Lev and he felt an immediate spark of courage enter his heart.

"Shalom, Enoch. Things seem a bit rocky here." Lev paused for a brief moment and then poured out his story in a torrent of words. "A man by the name of Gerhard Bruning left the office today, claiming to be sick. We, of course, know that with Eden fruit in his diet, sickness is not an option. When I asked Franz what happened to him, he claimed that he had just developed a sudden pain in his arm and had to leave. I asked him outright if Mr. Bruning had tried to change specifications in the computer. 'His arm became paralyzed, didn't it?' I said, and then I asked him if he had any knowledge of what Mr. Bruning was doing. 'I know nothing about that,' he told me, and then he lost his voice. People are so stubborn. I just don't see how this is going to work."

Lev paused again for breath, and gave himself a moment to think. "And now I feel entirely silly because, of course, you know all of this. I arranged for both men to communicate with the Ancients earlier this afternoon." Lev bit his lower lip and stopped his pacing for a moment, waiting for Enoch's response.

"You are having a difficult time. Yes, Lev, I am aware. And more importantly, Christ and His Anointed are aware. One of His Anointed is working on the timing of events in this case and has been for quite some time. You are being cared for in a way that is beyond your imagination and awareness. There is a world of spiritual activity that is invisible to the eye, Lev."

Lev took a few slow steps and then resumed his walk again at a more leisurely pace, but his heart rate did not follow suit.

"I know what you say is true, but Franz called you a stubborn Jew and you know what Gerhard said to me when I explained what he needed to do to regain the use of his arm? He said 'You Jews think you know everything. Why don't you just leave a sick man alone?'"

Lev paused again, and his heart still racing with irritation. When Enoch made no response he hesitated to speak further, and the brief silence soon became an embarrassing silence.

"Enoch, I apologize. I am overwhelmed with human nature. Our habits are so engrained. And look at me. I have seen the Red Sea part in my experience as an ambassador for Christ, and here I am complaining about the same old manna."

"You are in a strange place, with new challenges, and you have been working very hard. You must take care of yourself, Lev, so that you will be ready to meet these challenges. And remember that there are others who are isolated in their service. Keep up your connection with them. You need each other."

Lev felt a wave of relief as he realized for the first time since his busy arrival just how alone he felt. He suddenly realized the impact of the fact that he and Rebekah were separated on different missions for the first time since his raising. And he realized that he had been too busy to pray and meditate, as had been his habit.

"Thanks, Enoch. I think I see what I need to do to meet my challenges."

"Shalom, Lev."

"Shalom, Enoch," Lev said softly as he quickened his step, eager to rekindle his connections with God and men.

A Lost Child

"You look like you could use some help. I can take you home if you like," Lev offered the little girl with large frightened eyes. He did not quite know what to say.

The girl shook her head vigorously.

"Not supposed to talk to strangers," she announced with tears that caught the glisten of the streetlight on her face.

"Yes, that is generally true, but little girls like you are not supposed to be out alone at night. Why aren't you at home with your mommy and daddy?"

"Mister, I'm lost, and I don't know my way home."

The child reached out her little hand to Lev, and Lev bent toward her and pulled her up. She stretched her neck back as far as it would go so she could look up at him.

"You are big."

"Yes, I am tall," Lev chuckled and immediately knelt down so that they could talk eye to eye. "Nothing can harm you in this world because Christ and his Anointed are watching over you. Did you know that? My name is Lev."

"My name is Ruthie and I like baby kittens."

After a short discussion the girl agreed to have Lev phone her parents from his cottage apartment. He served her some Eden fruit and Eden tea while he phoned the Toulouse Service Center to report a missing child had been found and that he was available to chauffeur her to her home. Minutes later he received a call that her frantic parents were very relieved that she was safe, and the service representative gave Lev permission to bring the child to her home along with directions, knowing who he was and his connection with the Ancients.

"Okay, Ruthie, let's get you home."

Lev found Ruthie on the sofa, half asleep.

"I like that fruit," she announced drowsily.

"You never tasted it before?" Lev asked, surprised that the plan for distribution of Eden fruit had not yet reached her family.

"I heard the fruit is magic. It makes people get better if they're sick. My sister needs it because she's sick, but there's just not enough to go around. It's because the Jewish people aren't fair."

Lev furrowed his brow as he helped Ruthie put her coat on and scooped her up to bring her to the car. They drove in a constant playful barrage of Ruthie's comments and questions.

"Mister Lev, what is Jewish?"

Lev smiled and shook his head in amusement at her twentieth question.

"A Jew is a person whose Great Great Great Great Grandfathers are Abraham, Isaac and Jacob."

"Jacob slept on a rock."

"Yes, he did."

"And he saw angels on a ladder."

"Yes, he did. You know a lot about Jacob."

"My Daddy says the Jewish people aren't fair. He says the Ancient people aren't doing it right."

Lev looked over at Ruthie after he had parked his vehicle in front of her house.

"Sometimes people don't understand each other. I would like to talk to your Mommy and Daddy and find out what's going on and why you don't have Eden fruit."

"You are fair, Mister Lev," Ruthie said as she reached for his hand while they walked the stone walkway to her house. They weren't halfway across the walkway when the door to the house flung open and two very anxious parents rushed out to meet their daughter.

Ruthie Is Returned to Her Home

Lev was cordially invited in and warmly greeted by Alex and Catherine Shuman. The name startled Lev, and he was sure he had heard it before. Catherine explained that she and her husband had been quarreling when Ruthie must have gone out the front door beyond their notice.

"Thank you so much for bringing Ruthie back to us."

"It was a pleasure to bring her; Ruthie's a breath of fresh air. And she knows quite a lot about Jacob."

"Esau was mad at Jacob, but then they made friends," Ruthie announced randomly as she played on the floor with a black and white spotted kitten.

"Ruthie tells me that you have no Eden fruit, and that you have a sick daughter. I don't understand why your family has not received your quota of Eden fruit. Even with the changes in the airplane factory, the place I am reorganizing, everyone is accounted for and provided for."

"Yes, Carmalina, our eldest. She's a teenager with a heart condition and all she does is sleep—I am so worried about her."

Alex's angry voice cut Catherine off.

"This is exactly why we were arguing. We heard about all the wonderful things the new arrangement was supposed to bring, but we have barely enough money for food. They let me go at that airplane factory of yours. I always thought we would be treated fairly under the Ancients, but it appears to be otherwise.

Lev excused himself, ran back to his car, and then ran back to the house with an armful of provisions.

"Eden fruit and Eden tea. Give Carmalina as much of the tea as she will drink, and one of each of these fruits daily. You will see improvement in her condition very, very soon. I will see that you are supplied hereafter."

Catherine rushed off to the kitchen to prepare the tea. Alex looked at Lev with amazement.

"Who *are* you?" he asked in an almost reverent tone.

"I'm Lev Aron, a Jew from Israel, sent here by the Ancients to help the quirks get worked out of the New Earth system because of old world greed. You should have received six months severance pay until your self-sufficient housing is built. And by now there is enough Eden fruit that you should have been receiving a quota, a priority quota, in fact, in view of Carmalina's condition. This was the agreement between the Ancients and all the European nations."

"I owe you an apology, Lev, and your people. I know the promises of God, but I thought that some hard-hearted Jews had somehow infiltrated the ranks of the ruling powers, and I got angry at the Jewish people."

"Mister Lev's great-great-great-grandfather is Abraham, Isaac and Jacob," was Ruthie's unbidden response. "And Mister Lev is nice."

Alex knelt down by his daughter and lifted her head in his two hands so that they directly looked at one another.

"Daddy has said some wrong things. The Jewish people are treating us fairly, and so are the Ancients. But some people haven't learned their lessons yet, and that's why we don't have Eden fruit to help Carmalina get better. But now we do, and things will get better now that Lev is here."

"I like Mister Lev."

Tears came to Lev's eyes as he saw how open the heart of this child was to love and truth.

"I like you, too, Ruthie. You've brightened a very frustrating day."

At that moment Catherine walked into the room with a look of relief on her face.

"Alex, her color is improving," she whispered.

Ruthie ran up to her mother and tapped her on her arm.

"Carmalina will be able to play with me tomorrow, right Mom?"

Catherine laughed through her tears.

"Well, if not tomorrow, then soon."

Lev arranged for Alex to meet him at the plant the next day so that the whole matter could be straightened out. He felt his anger rise, as he thought of innocent people being unfairly treated. On top of that, the Ancients were being blamed for someone else's greed. Lev wondered if he was partly to blame for not checking out the company's finances as soon as he arrived. And what did this mean in regard to the character condition of Franz Schleicher? Lev consciously pushed these thoughts from his mind.

Lev looked from Alex to Catherine and then to Ruthie who had fallen asleep at her Mother's feet.

"I don't know what to say, Alex."

Catherine opened her mouth as if to say something and then knelt down to lift her sleeping daughter into her arms. She held Ruthie close to her and remained silent, lost in thought.

Setting the Records Straight

Revived by a good night's sleep, time to study and meditate, and an inspiring worship service, Lev felt far more prepared to face the problems he knew would come his way. Lev pulled out his cell phone from his desk at the plant and tried to contact Rebekah again but was unable to reach her. There was so much to tell her about. He did not have time to be too disappointed, as the events of the day began to brew into an emotional storm.

Alex came to his office, and then Lev proceeded to call in the bookkeeper, Marianne Gestalt, to account for the disbursement of money in the past few months. An uncomfortable conversation ensued as Alex described the plight of his family and Lev questioned Marianne in regard to the company policy.

"Marianne, you must be absolutely truthful with me. The days of playing games with finances are over. The terms of agreement were that these good people who were laid off would be given six months' pay until they could become self-sufficient. Did you understand this matter clearly?"

At first Marianne tried to avoid the question and claimed that she did what she was told to do. Finally, she burst into tears and admitted that Franz and Gerhard were working closely together and had ordered the change in agreement. They planned to pocket the extra money and to give her a share.

Lev had Marianne make out a check to Alex for the money that his family was promised. Lev arranged the building of their new home with the Surveyors' Office and was told that the hothouse was ready for assembly. Lev confirmed that the Shumans would receive their quota of Eden fruit until their own trees could provide, and then had lunch with Alex.

Alex was very appreciative for all that Lev had done and expressed a desire to help in the work of restoration.

"Why don't you call around to your friends and see if you can get several building teams together. There are many hothouses waiting for assembly, and there are hothouse Eden tree specialists who can help you with any problems. After you receive instruction on building techniques you can help one another finish your new homes. You should be self-sufficient as soon as your trees start producing fruit."

"I will be sure to correct anyone's false impressions as to the just decisions of the Ancients," Alex assured Lev as he rose to leave, "and I hope I have learned to trust Messiah more completely, even when something doesn't make sense to me. Thank you again, Lev. I can't thank you enough."

Lev phoned Werner Gotten to have Franz and Gerhard removed from their positions. He spoke briefly to both men in regard to their need to phone the Ancients once again.

Gerhard spat out his pent up anger saying:

"I liked the world better before. You Jews think you can take over everything."

"Woe to the rebellious children,
Saith the LORD, that take counsel, but not of me..."
(Isaiah 30:1).

Chapter Twenty-Six

After the storm had subsided, Lev was ready to initiate the second phase of his work in France. He gave an automotive update to a selection of employees as he prepared to choose an automotive staff. He presented the necessity of reducing speed and the installation of anti-contact sensors that automatically braked before the human reflex could. The ideas regarding the new safety and environmental standards were not well received. An argument developed over speed limits on the autobahn highways.

"Excuse me," a tall blonde young man interrupted Lev's presentation, "but I like to get where I'm going and I like to get there fast."

The whole room burst into laughter and then applause. Lev laughed with them.

"Yes, I can see your hurry, especially when you have eternity to get where you want to go."

Again there was laughter and another round of applause.

"Safety is not negotiable," Lev stated and continued with his presentation. "Are there any questions?" he asked when he had completed his outline.

The same young man raised his hand again.

"I, for one, am not sure that I want to continue working here once my own home is built. At that point my salary will end, and I will be volunteering to help manufacture cars that don't even meet my own personal standards for quality. I'll be racking my brain and expending my energies when I'm not getting anything out of it."

The room was filled with the background sounds of each one talking to the other, in agreement and disagreement.

"After all," the young man raised his voice to gain back the attention of his colleagues, "There are places to see, beaches to relax on, and mountains to climb—why I should be carrying this workload?"

"Because you will miss out on the greatest adventure of all," Lev also raised his voice and the room grew suddenly quiet. "You will miss out on what it means to love. I have never felt as alive as when I assisted in the building of other people's homes, and when I helped prepare families for the raising of their loved ones. There is a mountain to climb that is far more challenging than any mountain you may have scaled. It is more exciting and requires more courage and fortitude than any Everest anyone could climb. It is the mountain obstacle of sin and death, fear, hatred, weakness and self-centeredness. You will have eternity to bask on your beaches, but you will have less than a thousand years to climb *this* mountain."

Again the room filled with applause. Lev could see that there were many impressionable people, torn between the prospect of giving back in gratitude, being on the cutting edge of technology, and a second option of living a life of ease and leisure. The vocal young man continued to be divisive and disruptive with his comments.

"I think it would take me eternity to tire of the beaches," he spoke out again.

Lev took a step toward the young man and again a quiet fell over the assembled body of workers.

"I have an announcement to make," Lev spoke in a serious tone. He looked directly at the outspoken man and then his eyes searched the full scope of the assembly.

"I am asking anyone who does not wish to make a commitment to this work to leave. Once everyone is self-sufficient a two or three hour workday will be adequate, and there will be plenty of time for vacations and travel. But in this transition time, we need everyone's extra effort. If you are not interested in committing to this work and you are still dependent on weekly salaries, you will be paid severance pay in full. If you are self-sufficient you will receive no further remuneration. I would rather have people leave now than to remain unsatisfied because they are not being compensated for their extra efforts. Everyone is welcome to stay only if you are prepared to do what is necessary to get this project up and into production. Stop in my office if you would like your severance pay."

The young outspoken man rose to leave and two others followed.

"I wish you the best," Lev said as he extended his hand for a farewell handshake. The outspoken man ignored Lev's extended hand.

"We're better off without the workload and responsibility while you get the credit. We're better off on the beaches."

The Rebels Resign

When Lev returned to his office after another one of many presentations for the automotive staff, he found the three men that chose to leave the staff arguing with the receptionist about the amount of money they had received. They had returned with the severance checks they were already issued, and they demanded to see Lev Aron.

"And what is the name of the one who has such avid interest in swimming?" Lev whispered in the ear of the woman that sat at the desk.

"Pierre Gasgon. He's quite the conniver."

Lev nodded in agreement, and then approached Pierre.

"I am puzzled about a comment you made at the meeting you walked out on. You said that I was getting the credit for your work. Will you explain that to me?"

Pierre avoided the question entirely.

"Your cars may be better, but we would have gotten there in a few more years. All we really needed were the trees of life, and we could have solved all our problems ourselves. But you Jews use the trees as a pretext for bringing us under a ruling hierarchy that centers in Jerusalem. We don't need your superior management."

Pierre's voice was biting with sarcasm.

"Do you know who the real ruler of this world is?"

"I know your answer. You are going to say Christ, and that's what you want me to say, isn't it? How do we know this? Have we seen him? Has he spoken to us? Sure these Ancients are intelligent men, but why should Christ speak to them? Why can't he speak to us?"

"You have seen the evidence: the blind receive their sight and the deaf their hearing and the dead are raised to life. You must be careful, Pierre, for you are in grave danger of speaking words that deny the very power of Christ."

"Just mail us our checks. We don't need to put up with this Jewish conspiracy, and we don't need to accept the sham of 'resurrection power.' I'm sick and tired of—" Pierre's voice suddenly quieted. He held onto his throat in panic, quickly reached for the nearest chair and sat down, as sweat beads appeared on his forehead.

"Pierre, what's wrong? Are you alright?" One of Pierre's friends asked with great concern.

"He can't speak," Lev explained as he handed Pierre a cup of water. "The Christ he refuses to acknowledge is letting him experience his power. He lost his voice for his insubordination."

Lev wrote down the phone number of the Ancients and handed it to Pierre's friend who had expressed concern. He instructed them to have Pierre write out exactly what happened, and then to read the message to the Ancient that would receive the call. The consequence and the remedy would be explained.

"Pierre will need your help," Lev spoke to the two friends who stood there nervously watching their friend. Please take him to his home and phone the Ancients immediately." Lev handed the three men their checks and watched them leave the office.

The Raccoon

As the weeks and months passed, Lev was pleased with the progress made on the first hand-tooled automobiles. They were powered by hydrogen fuel cells that activated electric motors, and they were ready for testing. But he wondered about Pierre and others who had shown resistance. Pierre had given Lev an apology over the phone through one of his friends.

"Dear Mr. Lev Aron, I wish to apologize for my behavior. I was insulting to you and to powers that I do not yet understand. I am trying to understand, and I will have the next three weeks to listen to others. I still think a little speed would be entertaining, and perhaps I can find a way to make speed safe if I promise not to do it for profit. Again, I apologize, Pierre Gasgon."

Speed for entertainment was certainly not an appropriate priority given the greatness of the needs for restoration and regeneration. Pierre had not volunteered to work on any projects to this point in time, and Lev heard that he had joined a group that called themselves 'the Edgers.'

The Edgers were absorbed with living on the edge in surfing, skiing, mountain climbing and sports in general, which was fine in itself, but a selfish endeavor in view of the amount of need in these early stages of the restitution process. They needed to learn about 'losing life to find it.' Human nature is often like the raccoon who grabs the apple in the neck of the bottle, but whose very grasp on the apple makes it impossible for him to possess it because there is not enough room for the paw and the apple to come out together. The only way to get the apple was to let go of it. There were some people, even on this

New Earth, who wanted happiness and enjoyment of life so badly they would not let go of their grasp.

Lev wondered if Pierre, Franz and Gerhard would kindle a passion beyond their own interests for the common good of all. The goats at the end of the Millennium were not condemned for what they did wrong. They were condemned for what they did not do out of love for others. The gift of eternal life would be neither appreciated nor enjoyed by any who did not wholly abandon to the higher lifestyle of love for others. Without that vital reform of the heart, the self-centered would not succeed in meeting the Divine standard of loving "thy neighbor as thyself."

Lev wondered again. What would happen to Pierre, Franz and Gerhard? They were starting out rather headstrong, but perhaps they would find the course they had chosen a rather empty one. There was plenty of time to learn the lessons needful if they would adjust their attitude.

"Neither do men pour new wine into old wineskins.
If they do, the skins will burst,
The wine will run out and the wineskins will be ruined.
No, they pour new wine into new wineskins,
And both are preserved"
(NIV, Matthew 9:17).

Chapter Twenty-Seven

"I did not request this nomination, so I am wounded by the charges leveled against me. While I would be happy to serve, I'm afraid I'm being wounded in the house of my friends."

Louis Vignette spoke in his mellowest voice to those who sat in the small Toulouse church, his arms gracefully punctuating his words, as if he were creating an invisible painting before the room filled with worshippers. Lev was surprised that he was so fascinated by this man, and, though he could not take his eyes away from him, he realized that the best word to describe Louis Vignette was 'hollow.'

Lev had been uncomfortable with him upon their first meeting. He had felt waterlogged by his overflowing commendation and praise. Louis Vignette had glided his way across the floor to stand beside Lev.

Louis had put his hand on Lev's back in a gesture of close friendship.

"Mr. Lev Aron, the man in charge at the large aircraft industrial complex here in Toulouse—what a load of responsibility is on your shoulders. And you come to us from Israel, the Holy Land, at the direction of the Ancients." Louis patted him on the back cordially. "It is such an honor to stand beside you now, as your friend."

Louis had been a prelate of one of the large Old World Churches in the area. He had made it clear that his services had been much in demand in his day, and that he had been well known for his ability to shepherd, to hear confession with compassion, and to hold confessors accountable.

As the days had passed by, Lev had seen the pieces of the puzzle being crafted, shaped and oiled by Louis Vignette as Louis had sought out individuals in order to learn something of their lives and their struggles, to praise them, and then to launch into a litany of his own former accomplishments. Lev had watched Louis as he waited for the moment when he would silently and without strain make the pieces come together in a perfect fusion of opinion so that he would be granted a position of leadership.

His moment has come, Lev thought, as he closed his eyes and sighed. The chapel members had called an impromptu business meeting.

One of the women stood up with a genuine request.

"Some of us were wondering if our very gifted and talented Louis Vignette might share in the leadership of the worship services?"

There were things about himself that the prelate had kept hidden— how to bring them up and when, Lev did not know.

Lev listened to the discussion, and then made his own comments known.

"Louis Vignette is a talented man, but I do not see the reason for dismissing John Reinhart from his position as leader of our services. I happen to know that Louis Vignette pushed very hard to send your forces into the battle to take Jerusalem. I have never heard him speak of this, or take responsibility for his grave mistake in this matter."

Lev could see that Louis was struggling to maintain his composure. His anger showed in the redness of his neck, a slight quiver in his voice and a slight tremble of his delicate hands.

Louis Vignette responded.

"Has Lev forgotten about the background of his ancestors, how they killed our Lord Jesus, the Lord of life and love? Of course that was a mistake and we have freely forgiven them for this. Why is my mistake being held before you? 'To err is human, to forgive is divine.'"

Lev again stated his opinion.

"I believe this decision would be a serious mistake. This is not a trial for or against Louis Vignette. Each of us stands or falls before his Maker. It is a matter of guarding our need to be spiritually uplifted. None of us know this man. He has been among us for two weeks. He left the former chapel he was associated with when he was asked not to serve there as study leader. There are things we do not know, and I think it best that the decision be tabled so that we have more time to investigate."

"May I address the question that Lev has brought to our attention? I left that congregation because I found a very harsh and uncharitable spirit there. And now I am being persecuted without a just reason or cause." Louis paused, and then continued in a smaller and mournfully sincere voice. "I will gladly withdraw my name from this nomination, if it pleases you."

A vote was called for and Louis Vignette more than won the majority.

John Reinhart, the current study leader walked from his place at the podium up to Louis and extended his hand.

"I believe that it would be best for me to temporarily surrender my position as study leader. May God bless you and each of us, in the ways we need it most."

Louis Vignette took John's hands in both of his and addressed him directly.

"We deeply regret your decision to step down. We thank you for your faithful service." He raised his hands and then lifted his eyes to scan the congregation. "I thank those who voted for me, and those who voted against me," he announced graciously.

The service continued under Louis Vignette's leadership, and Lev's heart sank as he listened to their new spiritual leader. Louis called for hymns of thanksgiving, spoke in brief platitudes after each song, and then called for testimonies.

The woman who first suggested that Louis be given a share in the leadership walked to the front of the congregation.

"I am so grateful that we are giving this wonderful teacher a chance. We have all made our mistakes. I know I've made mine. I thank God that this is a life of new beginnings."

"Thank you, dear sister," Louis smiled broadly. "We are all of one family, God is our Father and we are his offspring. Truly, He has given us all a new beginning."

Danzig Challenges Vignette

A second person arose, a man unfamiliar to Lev. He stood from where he was, in the back of the crowded room. Louis Vignette nodded his head to acknowledge the man's desire to testify.

"My name is Tom Danzig."

Louis coughed nervously and the color immediately drained from his face.

"I also was a prelate, perhaps Bishop Vignette remembers me?"

Tom Danzig looked directly toward Louis, but Louis coughed again so that his gaze went naturally to the floor.

"I wish to take responsibility for my hypocrisy. I had a large and prosperous congregation. I told them what they wanted to hear, and they rewarded me handsomely. I am ashamed to admit that I was a 'politician' in my church responsibilities. I was locked into a system that was supposed to represent Christ, but I am most ashamed to admit that I did not even have a personal relationship with Christ. I claimed to be a Christian, but I had no time to spend with Christ.

"I did not believe everything I preached. It always gnawed at my conscience that a loving Father would send all unbelievers to hell. I knew somewhere in my heart that God must have a bigger plan of salvation than that. Furthermore, I did not have the courage to stand up against the invasion of Israel because I saw a political advantage to the church in gaining possession of the Holy Land. I used my influence to send thousands and thousands of men to their death, and I did it to protect my position and the interests of the Church."

Louis was clearly restless and uneasy as Tom Danzig continued his testimony. The delicate fingers that had gracefully gestured to embellish his well chosen words now gave way to a nervous scratching of his neck and the back of his head.

Tom continued, "After the fate of the invasion was publicized, a general panic seized our people. Law and order were swallowed up by rage. I was attacked by the angry mobs, beaten and left for dead. I was taken to the home of an older man who had compassion on me and nurtured me back to health through many months. When I was able to be about again I grew a beard so most people wouldn't recognize me and that is how I escaped the fate that overtook most of my fellow ministers. My wounds have healed and now that I am on Eden fruit I am fully recovered. My scars of my wounds have all but disappeared. This new life is more than I could ever have asked for. I am so grateful for this new beginning." Tom's voice began to crack with emotion. "And I don't even miss my old popularity and power, because now I feel forgiven. I am truly alive for the first time in all my years, alive in being devoted to Christ."

Lev smiled and restrained himself from giving Tom a standing ovation. The contrast between Tom and Louis was overwhelming.

When Tom sat down there was the hum of conversation throughout the room.

"We will sing the Doxology, in closing," Louis announced, still scratching his neck, "and this will be our final prayer and parting thoughts for this service."

The flute and piano began to play the well-known hymn and soon many voices joined in. Louis took the seat behind the pulpit and for once, thought Lev, he was relieved to be out of the limelight.

When the hymn ended, Lev rushed to the back of the hall.

"Tom!" Lev called out to get his attention among the others who surrounded him. Standing before this sturdy looking man with large deep-set brown eyes, Lev held out his hand. "God bless you, Tom. Your testimony was an answer to my prayer."

Lev's handshake turned into a heartfelt embrace. Lev introduced himself and gave him a brief synopsis of his background and the two men began to talk as if they had known each other a long time.

"Were you surprised to find yourself on earth and not in heaven?" Lev asked, surprised at his own directness and candor.

"Not really. 'Not everyone who says to me, Lord, Lord, will enter the kingdom of heaven.' That verse actually used to trouble me in the old world. All I know is that I have come to know Christ in a way I never imagined possible, and I feel as if my greatest dreams have been made a reality. But I fear," Tom looked away from Lev across the room to the place where Louis greeted those who came to him, "that there are some who are still living in a dream world. I must try to speak with him," he added as he and Lev made their way through the lingering worshippers.

"Brother Louis," Tom spoke his name quietly, and then extended his hand. Louis looked surprise, then confused, then afraid. He studied Tom Danzig's face and then fixed his gaze on Tom's outstretched hand with his own hands still clasped behind his back. Tom placed his hand on Louis' shoulder briefly.

"Do you remember me, Brother Louis? I know that I look very much better than when you last saw me. We spoke of our fear of another French Revolution, and there it was happening before our very eyes…"

"Brother Tom," Louis whispered, his eyes wide, and then as if he suddenly felt he could capture the moment of drama for himself he reverted back to his embellishing hand movements. "Of course,

I remember you." His voice became calm and assured. "You were a great spiritual leader, and one of my heroes."

"As a man of the cloth I betrayed my congregation." Tom's words were spoken with conviction and drew the attention of those who were still in the room.

"You did what was necessary. We both did what we were called upon to do. We worked together, you and I, against extravagant odds, and we did what needed to be done," Louis asserted.

"We played the game of world politics. We lied to ourselves and to the people under our authority, and we encouraged anti-Semitic sentiment. If I had served my God as well as I did my church organization perhaps I wouldn't have been attacked."

"What are you implying, Brother Tom?" Louis asked as his hand scratched behind his ear. "You are being most uncharitable. You seem to feel that the savage crowds should have dragged me out of my place of refuge and attacked me viciously, as viciously as they bludgeoned you."

"You were there," Lev stated simply.

"What of that? Many people were there."

"You watched them beat your Brother and leave him for dead, and you did nothing."

"What was I to do? Would you expect me to stand by his side, waiting for the same fate to befall me?"

Lev spoke again as he reflected on matters.

"Instead, you ran away, and hid. You changed your name, and you put on civilian clothing. You stole the money that was hidden, not found by the mobs, and you bought food in the black market."

"All of these things are past. You bring up mud from the past, and you rub my face in it. It is most ungodly, and certainly not Christ-like," said Louis.

Tom responded with firmness and concern.

"The real issue is the present condition of the heart, Brother Louis. Until I opened my heart to Messiah the dirt from my past clung to me whether anyone spoke of it or not. I do not harbor anger now, though I did at first. I only know that I needed to live Christianity before I tried to preach it. I think that the same principle applies to any who want to preach."

The weeks continued to pass by quickly. Lev and Tom became fast friends, and Lev offered him a supervisory role at the automobile plant, assured of his grasp of technology as well as his grasp of higher principles in human relationships. People loved Tom and his forthright friendliness. All three plants were becoming more efficient and Lev could see that his services were in less demand.

Louis Vignette continued to preach as a spiritual leader to a small group in another area of Toulouse having lost the office he had just gained. There was no word on any change in Gerhard or Pierre. Marianne, the bookkeeper that had worked with Franz, eagerly joined in whatever work she could find to do. Lev learned from her that Franz had spent a miserable few months brooding over his loss of position and being reduced to a common worker. But when he heard of the date that his sister was to be raised, a sister that had died when he was an adolescent, he began to prepare for her resurrection.

"I believe I actually saw him smile the other day," Marianne added. "I think he's starting to experience the excitement of love."

Franz finally contacted Lev and related his heartfelt apology. Lev could sense his great excitement over the raising of his sister as well as to other building projects he had volunteered to do.

Lev felt a wave of sadness overwhelm him. He knew that his time in France was drawing to a close and realized that these people had become another family to him. He remembered his hesitancy to take on the assignment and now he did not wish to leave.

It was with great joy and sadness that Lev stood before the three work forces assembled together.

"I enjoyed working with each of you. We labored together to get things organized, and then struggled together to start the production process. Even in the heat of this difficult assignment, you have worked tirelessly without regard to the clock or to our own weariness. Eden fruit gave you the energy, but love for Christ and your human family channeled your energy into making our world environmentally clean and much safer. And now you are preparing for the raising of your families, and you are helping others prepare for the raising of loved ones. I have seen you seek out and reach out to the needs in front of you and I have seen you respond in love. It is this spirit of sacrifice and dedication that Christ will use to turn this world into paradise once again."

Lev looked over the sea of faces, their smiles and their tears, and he felt a wave of love and joy wash over him.

"Ointment and perfume rejoice the heart:
So doth the sweetness of a man's friend by hearty counsel"
(Proverbs 27:9).

Chapter Twenty-Eight

Lev's heart burned within him as he left for home. His family was a sacred treasure. As he landed in Israel, Lev rejoiced to be in the Holy Land again—the place where his ancestors had lived and died for thousands of years—and where they would live again. The place where Jesus walked—the greatest treasure that God gave to mankind. Lev knew why his heart was burning within him. No other land was touched by God's hand like the Holy Land.

Lev expected to see his family as he disembarked from the plane, but no one was there. Perhaps they were too busy, he thought. As he picked up his baggage he couldn't believe his eyes—there was Enoch! He embodied the true beauty of holiness. Enoch opened his arms and embraced Lev.

"Well done, Lev, well done. I told your family not to meet you. You'll come with me to our offices in the Holy City. You are to meet with our committee first. Not that you are going to be debriefed. We know everything about your work and all we have are good reports. You've served the King very well!"

Enoch continued, "We are especially gratified for your work in Europe. We knew there was a residual dislike for the Jews. This dislike was not a common prejudice that most people carry about in their hearts, but dislike that was taught very carefully in their homes, in the streets, the schools and the churches. It isn't normal for anyone to undertake the destruction of a whole race of people. Yet, anti-Semitism was carried out systematically with a frenzied blood lust. The Ancients were shocked to see what happened in the death camps of Europe."

"We sent you as our ambassador, not just for your technical skills," Enoch went on. "There were others who knew as much or more than you. We sent you, Lev, because you have shown a unique ability to deal with confrontation and prejudices. We needed a man to get the technical changes underway—that was important. But more important to us was your ability to work effectively in a hostile environment. You were able to gain the respect of people who had learned hatred toward the Jews. More than this, Lev, you persevered until you turned enemies into friends. That is what we wanted—and you did better at this than we could have hoped for. Well done, Lev, well done!"

"You will have one week at home with your family," Enoch instructed. "You'll spend that week in an intense learning project being directed by your brother, Jake. That's why I picked you up—so we could use the time getting you oriented on your new assignment. Jake thinks you can learn what you need to know in about a week. There'll be constant schooling needed on this project, and it will be available as it evolves."

A Love Feast

Enoch led Lev into an office where the lights were turned off. After entering the room he turned on the switch. To Lev's surprise and joy, there was his whole family. Rebekah, who had returned to Israel earlier, ran into his arms, followed by Jake, Rachel, Anya, Ariel and Hannah. And, to his unexpected joy there was Allon and Annie. What could be sweeter? Lev thought.

Enoch said, "God is the God of families and we're all of the family of Abraham. You'll have two hours for your love feast. Then Jake and Lev must meet with our committee. Because you are all family and we know you are trustworthy, you may be there as guests. Now, there's fruit on the table, various fruit juices, and Eden cakes. You all deserve this honor."

Allon said, "Let's talk as we enjoy the feast the King has provided."

"Good idea, Allon," Lev said.

Ariel Aron asked the blessing on the food and fellowship. It was an unspeakable blessing to have his parents there Lev thought.

Lev wanted to hear from everyone present.

"Annie, you must quickly tell us how you made out with the Indian tribes in Brazil."

Angel of the Amazon

"Well, Uncle Lev, I left home an immature woman and returned a matured human being. The people appreciate the blessings afforded them more than most who are used to a higher standard of living. Having sufficient food and a comfortable dwelling place was beyond their dreams. Theirs was a society that struggled for food and shelter all their lives.

"To have the trees of life and a beautiful air-conditioned home is heaven to them. They had been exploited by the western world as well as demon religions and were ruled by ignorance and superstition. The truths they have learned were like having someone turn on the light in a dark place."

She continued, "Their political circumstances were untenable. They hung between two worlds—the new and the old. They could not compete in the information age and the old way of life had become increasingly difficult and unacceptable. Living in the jungles is not easy even under ideal conditions. There was disease, polluted water, lack of sanitary conditions and practically none of the blessings of modern standards.

"I arrived after the trees of life had been planted. When everyone was given his own plot of ground and the Eden trees, life changed for them. As soon as they began eating Eden fruit their health, strength and vitality blossomed. The most incredible change came as their minds improved exponentially. You would not believe how smart they are now. They sit enthralled watching the learning programs sponsored by the Ancients.

"They have grown in physical stature. Many of them were quite short, but now they equal in stature to other people. With their deformities disappearing, they are becoming a handsome people. It's amazing to see them take quantum leaps from their primitive lifestyle. They are into the computer age and technology poses no fear to them now."

Lev felt goose bumps. Annie had just been a young lady. Now she was telling tales of being the angel of the Amazon. He had heard the Indian tribes loved Annie. She was a giving and loving human being. If people couldn't be reached with love, they wouldn't be reached.

Ariel and Hannah Arons' Report

Ariel cleared his throat. "Well son, it took me about a week to get adjusted to being raised to life. It is such a seemingly fairy-tale experience, which even as you're experiencing it, you are afraid to close your eyes for fear this wonderful dream will suddenly disappear. Of course, having all of you present at my return made it easier. I believed you when I couldn't believe my senses. I knew you were real and that helped me accept the reality of life in the new world.

"I did what you did, Lev, when you came back. I knuckled down to catch up in this information world. I found the instructional programs so absorbing, that I was pulled into the new world of information. Never has learning been so easy. I was amazed how much I could retain. In a few short months I was able to fit into this high tech world. One other thing, Lev, I have renewed my study of the Bible with the new understanding that I have. For the first time in my life, I know what God's plan is for the world and for me. The confusion of religion is gone. I always loved God, but his heart and plan had been hidden from me."

Dad continued, "Recently I was told I could begin preparing for my parents return. Your mother, Rachel, Jake and I have been working on preparations for their return. It is only a few weeks away, and we have everything ready. My great Grandfather and Grandmother were among the lucky ones to get out of Europe to Israel before the Nazis started incinerating the Jews. They worked hard to build this land. My great Grandfather fought in the 1948 war when the odds were one hundred to one against Israel. Yet Israel won the war and became an independent nation. My parents and grandparents both know what it was like to be hated and persecuted. The Jews escaped Europe only to find the Arab world waiting to drive them into the sea. They were hated because they were Jews. Their joy will know no bounds when they find Abraham is in power in Jerusalem and the whole world is seeking the promised blessing from the seed of Abraham."

"Mom, it's your turn to fill me in."

Hannah added, "Well, Lev, if anyone had told me that such a day as this was coming, I would never have believed it. The world I came from was dying. You couldn't die fast enough—people wanted to kill you to speed up the process. Since returning to life, I have never been so fulfilled. As we eat the Eden fruit, life is pulsing in our veins, and the ravages of sin and death are slowly leaving us. I was never too well in my former life. I never dreamed I could live in a world without sickness of any kind, without pain. Suddenly, we have been delivered from death and dying.

"My children and grandchildren are sane and beautiful. Now Dad's parents are returning and soon mine will be back. We've already planted the trees for their homes. The joy of my life is that Abraham, our great forefather, is back serving as a prince in this world. We shall not rest until Adam and Eve are finally back again. What a triumph of God's grace that will be!"

She continued, "I work at a clothing center, where cloth is woven and made into clothing. It is so high tech that computers and machines do most of the work automatically. Supplying those coming from the dead with clothing is a massive project. The materials we have now are wrinkle free. Between providing for those who are living, and those who are coming back to life, we turn out clothing by the truckload everyday. Our task is easier because we do not have so many different sizes as they did before—no short or tall and no obese or skinny. Every day is filled with joy. My prayers at last have been answered."

Anya

Lev looked at Anya. "What's been going on with your project, Anya?"

"I did a lot of investigating to find if I could in any way help the man who had murdered me, Lev. I discussed it with Rachel and Rebekah. They thought it was a good idea, too. So we called the Ancients' hotline for counsel."

"Leah answered the phone and told us that one of the Hamas terrorists responsible for my death had no living relatives, so I could build his house and be responsible for his return. I have no anger or fear of them, only pity and a desire to see them turn their hate into love. My discussion with her was helpful in broadening my love especially for my enemies.

"Leah gave me good counsel and I traveled to Palestine to locate Abu Mohammad's plot. It was a fascinating experience to research his roots. I found his mother had raised him in a camp like so many other young Palestinians. He had been schooled to memorize the Koran and hate the Jews and Western nations. He was involved in my murderous attack at age eighteen. He had been promised paradise and virgins for his faithfulness in killing Jews."

Anya continued, "Then Abu attempted to board a bus in Israel with a suicide bomb. The bus driver suspected that he was a terrorist and he was able to prevent him from boarding the bus. The bomb detonated killing only Abu. We wonder what Abu will think when he finds me greeting him instead of the seventy-two virgins in paradise."

Lev said, "I'd like to be there when he returns. Do you have a date yet?"

Anya said, "It depends how fast we can build his house. Rachel and your folks are helping me, but because it is a distance away, it's taking more time. I hope in a few months from now. We'll let you know, Lev. It would be great to have you with me."

Rachel

Lev then asked Rachel to tell her story. She said, "When Annie left home it was time to have my own home. Jake thought it best that I have the newest home, because they are improved over our older dwellings. So Jake and your parents helped build my own home. Now I have my own lovely house not far from Jake.

"I, too, have been studying in the evening hours. I've taken Lev's formula. I try to divide my studies between spiritual and physical things. Trying to know the mind of God is man's noblest quest and the most rewarding. I've also gone with Anya to Arabia to help with Abu's plans. I hope to assist them as they work on his house."

Lev said, "I am going to be sitting on Jake's doorstep for the week. So I'm not going to ask him what he's been doing. From what I hear, he's at the center of breathtaking research. I'm to learn about it this week and then I'll be shipped off somewhere. However, in the service of the King one never asks how, why, when, or where."

Rebekah

Lev then asked Rebekah to tell of her experiences. She said, "I had a wonderful time in Europe. I didn't meet with any of the difficulties that Lev did. Everyone seemed thankful for the sweeping changes taking place. I worked as a coordinator of some projects. This entailed a lot of travel and telephoning while trying to get a clear mental picture of how to integrate everything to avoid duplicating unnecessary work.

"I got cooperation from everyone, and only once or twice did prejudice against me as Jew surface. The prejudice that I ran into was isolated. How thankful I was to see righteousness prevail everywhere. I learned to love all those people and they showered me with so much warmth and love, that it was hard to leave."

Allon's Ghana Report

Lev left Allon to the last.

Allon said, "Well, Ghana had been a far off place on this earth that I had not given much thought to. However, now I'm so happy I was sent there. These people were eager to enter the new age. Life had been full of every kind of problem—especially poverty. Many people lived in hovels with no running water or sanitary conditions. Though the land was very productive and hunger was never much of a problem."

He continued, "I had none of the problems that Dad had. Everyone was eager to work and have this project completed. My only problem was to send people home to get some rest. They worked tirelessly and with unabated enthusiasm. My biggest concern was that these people were too backward to be handling our advanced technology. Was I ever wrong! These people had started eating from the trees of life very early, and they were brilliant. They were eager to learn and when they did not understand something they were frank about it. They didn't pretend to know anything they didn't.

"Some on-the-spot instructions enabled them to grasp matters readily. I soon found some of them with better ideas than my own. The factory is now in full production and only needs a little tweaking to increase its capacity. Of course, much of our success was due to the machinery we received from Israel. It only needed to be assembled and hooked up with electricity, and then it started to produce."

Time Running Out

Their time together was running out and the family began to clamor for Lev's story. It was a joy to share his experiences.

He had barely finished when Enoch walked in with Huldah, Sarah, Elijah and John the Baptist.

"We planned this little gathering as a way to thank you for your services to the King. You have served him well. We all thank you. However, our work is still in its infancy, and we will need you and others to continue in the service of the King. There will be time to relax and have leisure once everything falls into place. The first quarter century of the resurrection will be the most hectic. It is hard to transform people who made war and trouble into builders, planters and husbandmen. But this is well underway. Every nation is now on board. We're a long way from getting people to love each other, however, and that will be the hardest task."

Enoch announced that time had run out. Then he said, "We have one more question for you. Rebekah, will you accompany Lev to Seattle to work as a team?"

She answered with delight, "Yes, Enoch, I will surely go!"

Home, Sweet Home, Again

Lev learned he would be sharing his home with a visitor who needed a place to stay for a few months. Abdul Hasad was from Saudi

Arabia. He was being instructed at the institute where Jake worked to take back plans for computer production to his home country. Abdul was extremely intelligent. He had a different spirit toward the Jewish people than what was once common in his homeland.

The lights were on when Lev got home. Abdul was studying late into the night on the television education network. He greeted Lev warmly and apologized for occupying his home. Lev assured him it was a privilege to have him and he was welcome to stay as long as wished. Abdul told Lev that his bedroom was ready with fresh sheets. Lev excused himself, exhausted from the day's travels and prepared for a good night's sleep.

When he awakened, Lev notice Abdul was up, had picked fruit for the day and made some fresh juice. Lev dressed quickly and met Abdul in the kitchen, thanking him for his service.

Abdul responded, "Lev, it was my privilege. I knew that you were exhausted last night. I've heard of the great work you did in Europe. You have endeared yourself to those people. Only words praising you have reached us. At any rate, I'm glad you and I are now both bending our knees to the Lord Christ. I must confess, Lev that I grew up on a diet of hatred toward the Jews. It was blind hatred, with no truth or justice in it. When you finally learn the truth, how ugly that hatred now seems." Lifting his glass of juice, he said, "Let us drink to love and friendship as we both bow in service to the King."

Lev lifted his glass, "Yes, to love and friendship in service to the King."

Abdul joined Lev and they soon arrived at the chapel, early enough to greet old friends and meet new ones as well. The chaplain was an excellent student of God's Word, so it was a joy to listen to his short presentation.

Back to Work

After breakfast they embarked for Jake's institute. Abdul was learning some advanced science there to take back to Saudi Arabia. His country was no longer supported by oil exports, and had now become an eager member of the regeneration program emanating from Israel.

Lev spent some time reviewing the whole operation, and then went into the heavy science area that had found a breakthrough in gathering anti-matter and harnessing it as a powerful source of energy. This was far more technologically advanced than harnessing atomic energy. It was unique in its ability to produce an enormous amount of energy for sustained periods of time, making it ideal as a propellant to the aerospace industry. It was very safe if handled properly, but could be harmful if not properly used.

Jake was there to learn the industrial requirements to secure anti-matter and then to prepare it for air and spacecraft propulsion. It would need a large manufacturing facility and that would be the part that was his assignment. He was to learn how it was produced and the facilities needed to obtain anti-matter in sufficient quantities. They had a small plant in Israel that was operational in producing anti-matter, but it could only produce enough to use in experimental engines that could harness this newfound energy.

Allon explained the methods they had used to secure anti-matter. Anti-matter had remained out of reach until they had found a method to produce it efficiently. Now that they could produce it in sufficient quantities, it would revolutionize air transportation. Fortunately, Lev didn't need to know the science of anti-matter. He only needed to follow the guidelines to produce it. He had to learn, however, the dangers in handling it and how to proceed safely in producing it.

This was a rather intense learning experience. Fortunately, Jake had been working at this for quite awhile and had fathered some of the breakthroughs. Jake not only knew the answers to Lev's questions, but also was able to enlarge his comprehension by asking him questions to see if he understood correctly what he was being exposed to. Lev's mind was alert enough to understand the basic concepts and remember enormous amounts of information. He comprehended very well what Jake was teaching.

Eaglewing

The week slipped by quickly in this intense atmosphere. They had chosen the foremost manufacturer of aircraft, now called Eaglewing. Actually, this company had pioneered in anti-matter some years earlier, but failed to find a breakthrough in producing it, so it just languished. When they heard of the breakthrough in Israel's ability to produce anti-matter, they were eager to get on board.

Lev learned that he would be going to the city of Seattle to get the project underway. The Eaglewing industrial complex had been retained, though its corporate structure had changed into a world community service center. They had learned of Lev's success in Europe and had sent a message of welcome to come and guide their project. It was good to know that they were eager to take on the project and showed a warm attitude about it.

When the time came to say farewell, Lev felt a tug on his heartstrings. However, this time it was easier, knowing Rebekah would be at his side.

Allon drove his parents to the airport. Lev admired the eight hundred-seat plane that looked like the former stealth bombers. Rebekah appreciated that the Eden tea and juices for beverages and Eden fruit would enable passengers to arrive bright and ready to go. Life was so simple and natural.

"But they that wait upon the LORD shall renew their strength:
They shall mount up with wings as eagles;
They shall run, and not be weary;
And they shall walk, and not faint"
(Isaiah 40:31).

Chapter Twenty-Nine

Rebekah closed her eyes and felt soothed by the faint hum of the plane's engine, comforted as she reviewed the memories of their brief time in Israel. She was on her way with Lev to Seattle.

What a joy it had been to return to Israel even though the stay had been over before she knew it. She had spent a refreshing day with her parents helping them tend to Eden trees on the farms that had been entrusted to them, while Lev was with Jake learning about anti-matter. The time with her family left her feeling happy and at peace, for the hand of God was evident in their radiant faces and in all she heard of their lives and restitution work as it continued grandly on in Israel.

Rebekah remembered how startled she had felt when her secure phone had rung, interrupting their lively conversation and laughter as Hannah finished serving the last piece of resurrection cake to Ariel.

"Oh, my dears, its Enoch, calling our Rebekah while she eats in my home," Hannah had said, overwhelmed by the honor of having one of the Ancients call one of her family members in her presence.

"Oh, she's blushing." Rachel, had teased when she noticed the red that rose in Rebekah's face. "She always did have a problem with compliments."

Rebekah had smiled and swept her hand through the air as if to dismiss background sounds that distracted her.

"Rebekah, you know we have chosen Lev to supervise the anti-matter project in Seattle, Washington. You also have shown great ability to work with people and with their emotions while in Europe, and you have a talent for growing things and first hand knowledge of Eden tree cultivation. We requested that you accompany Lev to supervise the hothouse projects, to manage Eden fruit distribution and to oversee personnel." He paused. "Are you willing to take on the tasks?"

"Yes," Rebekah answered. "I'd be thrilled and honored, Enoch."

SeaTac

The United States had been among the first of the nations to come up to Jerusalem to comply with the new authority invested in the Ancients. It took a number of months with no rain for the nation to decide to cooperate with Israel. It was difficult for a nation that had formerly been known as a superpower to go to Israel, a nation that had been dependent on her for so many years. Many people had blamed Israel for the turn of events that led to the final invasion, and the United States had abandoned her. No longer a superpower, no longer the one in control, the United States was directed to come to a nation that had formerly been no bigger than New Jersey for help and direction. It was a hard pill to swallow.

Yet, there were many who were convinced that cooperation with Israel and the Ancients was the only possible way to survive, both physically and spiritually. Agnes Watts was one of these people. She and her husband Scott met Rebekah and Lev at SeaTac Airport and drove them to a motel near Eaglewing.

"As soon as the armies that descended upon Israel were destroyed, it was obvious that the victory of Israel was a miracle, and I was ready to bow my knee to the new King. There are pockets of those who seek Christ, but there are many who are apathetic, fed up with religion in general. I'm not sure how your message will affect them. I am curious to see how Eaglewing people will respond," Agnes observed.

"And she's curious to see how I'll respond, also," her husband Scott said dryly. "Guess I'm one of those 'fed up' apathetic ones," he said, with a biting sarcastic edge to his voice.

"Fed up with religion and maybe fed up with apathy, too." Rebekah said looking at Scott from her vantage point in the back seat and wondered what made him so closed and bitter.

Assignment—Eden Fruit

"I have a treat for all of you," Rebekah announced at a very early morning meeting to the large assembly of the men and woman of Eaglewing. Many in the audience looked at her without expression, as if they were bored and as if they were resigned to their boredom with no change on the horizon. They reminded Rebekah of a room full of wilting plants, their paper-thin leaves drooping and limp.

"How many of you have tasted Eden fruit?" A few hands went up. "How many," Rebekah tested her audience, "have never tasted Eden fruit?" A greater number of hands went up. "How many never really got out of bed this morning?"

"We want our coffee," one voice responded.

"They say there's no more coffee. Can Israel help us?" another voice called out, followed by a ripple of laughter.

Rebekah laughed also, encouraged at the momentary spark of interest.

"Yes, Israel can help. At the back of the room you will find hot tea and fruit. Your first assignment is to drink the tea, eat the fruit, and then we'll talk about it. You have twenty-five minutes."

Rebekah placed herself at the back of the room so she could serve the refreshments and greet people. When Rebekah called the meeting back to order everyone had returned to his or her seats. She saw great improvement in their faces, and she smiled.

"How do you feel now?" she asked.

"I think I'm awake!" one voice called out.

"I actually feel like getting to work," said another.

"What is it?" a third voice asked.

Rebekah smiled and explained the origins of Eden fruit, the tree farms her parents nurtured, and the shipments of trees, saplings and fruit that had now reached every nation on earth.

"Before now, Eden fruit was available only to the sick and dying, but soon this perfect nutrition will be available to all who seek it from Israel. Starting today, you will be provided with a daily supply of these fruits, and you will also receive the resurrection tea I described to you because the work you are doing here will demand your wholehearted precision and accuracy. The effects of Eden fruit on the human body are profound. The processes of death and deterioration will end as soon as you make a diet of this fruit. Your mind will reach what used to be considered a genius status in several months."

There was a round of applause.

"I will provide training and support as each of you completes the installation of your own hothouse. I will teach you all you need to know in regard to the care these trees need." Rebekah scanned her audience and felt gratified at the newer signs of life and interest that showed amongst the crowd."

Rebekah received a warm round of applause as she took her seat and Scott Watts walked from the audience to the podium.

"Perhaps Eden fruit will solve all our problems," he said tongue in cheek. "Thank you, Rebekah; we shall be very interested in the effects of this wonder fruit." He paused and went on.

"The project we are undertaking is a huge one, with a revolutionary impact on the aerospace industry for it will provide clean and safe air travel for mankind."

Rebekah could see that Scott was impressed and motivated by cold hard facts. This made him able to support the anti-matter project, but hesitant to believe in the powers of Eden fruit. His faith would take root by experience.

"This operation will require full time and effort, and if anyone does not wish to give full dedication to this project, please feel free to leave." He paused again, and when no one rose from his seat, he continued.

Introducing Lev

"And now I present to you your new supervisor sent by the Ancients, a native of Israel, Lev Aron. He will be head supervisor of the 'Eaglewing project.'"

There was another round of applause as Lev replaced Scott at the podium. Lev described the commitment necessary for this project, the dangers, and the need for to-the-letter accuracy.

"Everything that is done must receive my authorization. There must be a super discipline in this project. We dare make no mistakes and need no maverick helpers. Check and double-check all the way. We are dealing with new and unbelievably powerful energy. Though we are protected by the unseen forces of Christ, we are responsible to do all in our power to make their intervention unnecessary."

Rebekah watched Lev become intense and filled with excitement as he leaned over the podium and clutched onto its ledge on either side with each of his hands. It was as if he was on a wild ride at a carnival, and he *was* on a wild anti-matter ride of sorts. It was as if he would fall off if he didn't hold on with all his might. He masterfully described the general plan for building the plant where anti-matter will be produced, and the basic principles of anti-matter and its use. The audience seemed captivated by the immensity and the potential of this project, and Rebekah felt grateful that she had been asked to be part of this service. Lev announced a lunch break with Eden fruit available at the cafeteria, to be followed by another meeting of video presentations.

After lunching with a friendly group of workers and being introduced to many new faces, Rebekah made arrangements to meet with the hothouse outlet and arrange for the shipments for each of the Eaglewing people.

As she was leaving, Scott called out to her, part in jest, part in sarcasm, "I wonder if it's possible for anyone to get fed up with Eden fruit?"

Rebekah looked back at him over her shoulder, smiled and said as she walked on. "I guess you'll have to experience that for yourself."

Eden Fruit Brain Power

Lev was immediately immersed in plans and discussions with the plant supervisors at Eaglewing, while Rebekah made herself known and available as support to Lev and to these people who were still not fully living up their privileges because they had not yet adjusted their thinking to deal with Christ as the unquestioned authority of earth. Each day she stood by the serving table during break and greeted each individual by name and poured resurrection tea. At lunchtime she was in the cafeteria, helping to serve tea and fruit.

"Josh! How did the morning go? Still feeling that need for coffee?"

Josh looked slightly puzzled at the warmth of her friendliness and her ability to remember his name. He stood just outside of those waiting to be served, and listened to person after person being greeted hospitably by name and with some kernel of information important to their lives.

"Betty, how's your father doing?"

"John, did you notice the date of your daughter's return? It's coming up soon."

Josh ambled over to his usual table of the 'free spirits of the younger generation' as they had been dubbed by their fellow workers. They had been advocates of holistic medicine, animal rights, and greater diversity.

"She's got a photographic mind," he whispered, "unless she's some kind of robot. You wouldn't believe the names she remembers and the details of people's lives. It's incredible."

"I think it's kind of weird. I think something weird is going on here...a conspiracy or something," said Leonard.

"Oh, come on, Leonard, she's too sincere for that," Josh defended.

"Why don't we test her?" suggested a young woman with auburn hair and wide green eyes.

"Okay, Gwen. Go for it," Josh said, as he watched Gwen rise from the table and walk over to Rebekah and invite her to sit with them.

Leonard pantomimed a drum-roll while Rebekah and Gwen walked toward their table and announced in the mock voice of a MC, "Introducing the most capable Eden fruit eating woman you could ever want to meet, Rebekah Aron."

Rebekah sat by Gwen and smiled at Josh.

"I take it you're skeptical about the long-term effects of Eden fruit, Leonard. Why don't you ask Cynthia, over there? Her brother had severe asthma; about three months ago he contracted pneumonia. It was terrifying, but after being given the tea and the fruit, he's symptom free."

Leonard was visibly taken aback. She knew his name. She knew a lot of things.

"So what's *his* name?" Leonard challenged as he randomly picked someone at a far table.

"Gerald. And he has a sister named Gracie."

"And what about her?"

"Connie. She's really interested in geology."

"What's the square root of 676?" Josh asked as he pulled out a calculator from his back pocket.

"26."

"Of 7,777?

Rebekah paused.

"Gottcha!" Leonard pointed to the woman across from him. There was an edge of satisfaction in his voice.

"88.1873."

Josh leaned on his hand and scratched his head by his ear. "And you attribute this mental acumen to Eden fruit?"

"Absolutely. My expertise in the old world was the arts. It certainly wasn't math. In fact, I struggled for a C in trig."

"So, you never get sick?"

"No, I don't. In fact, since the invasion of Israel, no one has been killed or hurt in the Holy Land because Christ became the Sovereign of the nation."

Gwen nodded in agreement. "Actually, that's true of all the nations who have come under his control. I always used to read the obituary pages, and there aren't any names there since we came under the rule of the King. Some speculate that it's some kind of a change in the atmosphere, some temporary phenomenon."

"It's because of Eden fruit. Even though Eden fruit has not been distributed to every single person, as yet, Christ and the Anointed know who are in desperate need. They provide a way for the tea and fruit to reach a person, and literally they can be saved from the jaws of death," said Rebekah.

"That's hard to believe," Gwen queried.

Why Wasn't God There for My Daughter?

"So if God is all powerful, and He has all this ability, why has He permitted all the death and suffering in human history in the first place?" Josh countered.

"My daughter contracted the aids virus by a contaminated medical needle that had not been properly disposed of and accidentally fell in her bed and pierced her. It was a matter of years, but she wasted away." A familiar voice sharp with sarcasm and challenge joined in the conversation. He had been standing one table down, listening to the test of wits inflicted on Rebekah.

"The all powerful God doesn't look all that competent to me. Where are His mercies—and His power, for that matter?"

"I'm sorry, Scott, for the pain of that experience. She will be raised in four months, and she will be raised healthy. The final outcome of all the suffering in our history will be perfect life on a perfect earth and wonderful relationships with God, with Christ and with the whole human family."

"How did you know that—about my daughter? You never mentioned it before when we talked."

Josh redirected the conversation back to the original question.

"Why not cut out the suffering and go straight to the perfection?" he asked. Josh slumped back in his chair, arms folded and legs straight out, one crossed over the other.

Rebekah suddenly realized that her audience had grown. Most of the people in the lunchroom were very quiet, straining to hear their conversation. At that moment a bell rang that marked the end of the lunch break.

Josh rose and extended his hand.

"Thank you, Rebekah. You make me think. I like that. There's a lot for me to sort out, so maybe we can talk again."

"It would be my pleasure, Josh. Perhaps we can talk more when I check up on your hothouse installation."

A number of people came up to Rebekah with brief comments, questions and challenges in regard to the conversation they overheard and in regard to their hothouse projects. Rebekah pulled out her calendar and jotted down times when they could meet.

Scott had retreated to the far end of the room, very close to the exit door. He stared at Rebekah, and shook his head almost imperceptibly in disagreement with a pained look on his face, and then he left the room.

A Spiritual Desert

Rebekah and Lev had found their first worship service to be small, but inspiring. Rebekah's inquiries had brought to light the fact that many were studying and worshipping in the privacy of their own homes, still leery of any organized church services because of the previous Old World experience with church inconsistency. But of the ones who dared to attend, each had experiences, verses and questions to share in their informal meetings. Though little in number, they sang praises to God from their hearts. Rebekah and Lev had much to contribute, as they shared their experiences, their privileges of service, and their firsthand accounts of life in Israel. People were especially fascinated with the miracle of resurrection and the amazing healing properties of Eden fruit. Word began to spread, and each day the numbers of people increased slightly.

Rebekah's experience in dealing with people was reflected in her next brief presentation to the people of Eaglewing. She spoke to a room full of people who were alert and interested. Again she announced her desire to meet with each individual in regard to their hothouse projects and any questions or problems that might arise in regard to that and Eaglewing personnel issues.

"It has been exciting to spend time with so many of you, and I won't be happy until I have personally spent time with each one here."

There was a round of applause, for the audience was convinced of her sincere interest. They were genuinely appreciative.

"Now for a question. How many of you are enjoying your daily supply of Eden fruit and tea?" Rebekah spoke clearly and with enthusiasm.

"Eden fruit bodybuilders!" Josh called out.

Rebekah smiled at him, and then surveyed her audience.

"How many of you attend worship services each morning?"

Two hands in the back row shot up. The picture of wilted saplings again came to Rebekah's mind. Their physical lack of energy would be easily treated with Eden fruit, but their spiritual apathy would be more of a challenge.

"If you don't seek to worship God and learn His ways every day, you are living in a spiritual desert," she said, and in that split second her eyes locked with Scott's. His look was challenging as he stared at her briefly, and then looked away.

"The noblest science is the knowledge of God and His Son. To know God is life eternal. Eden fruit and its healing energizing properties come from the love and provision of God and Christ. But if you have only physical health—even perfect physical health, and you are missing a personal relationship with them, you are still only half alive."

Again Rebekah's eyes met Scott's. This time he did not look away.

"I encourage each of you to find a worship service near you and give it a try. Shalom."

There was a moment of silence, and then one person clapped, followed by another, and another until the room was filled with applause.

During the morning break Rebekah was at her usual place, serving resurrection tea, when she noticed an emotional young woman she immediately recognized as Ruth Ensel, a new office receptionist in the Eaglewing complex, speaking with Josh. Josh pointed toward Rebekah, and the woman quickly shook her head. Rebekah took a deep breath and excused herself, giving her large pot of tea to Leonard and walked over to them.

"Good morning, Josh."

"Shalom, Rebekah," Josh spoke quickly and left just as quickly.

Cancer Leaves a Bitter Heart

Ruth Ensel had never showed any interest in spiritual things. She was always proper, and always gentle, but she had fenced out devotion to God and Christ as some mystical bad habit. The few occasions Rebekah had spoken to her, she had been as cold as ice.

Rebekah asked, "Ruth, do you know what it's like coming back to life again after being dead for many years?"

Ruth answered, "How would I know? All I know is that my brother and I lost our father when we were children. That was the saddest day of my life, because I really adored my father. I've been bitter about losing him ever since. He made our little family so happy. He was always there for our little problems and needs. I lived in his eyes and when he came down with cancer it changed everything. He became very ill, often full of pain. It tore my heart out to see him waste away and finally die. I hated God for taking him away. They told me he was in heaven. Why would God take him to heaven when we needed him here so very much? God had everything—why would he need to take my Dad away?"

"My mother had to go to work to support the family," Ruth continued. "She had to take whatever work she could get, and it didn't pay much. We lost our home. My mother was saddled with medical bills and we had to move to a very shabby neighborhood because we were so poor. My mother was a hero, working long hours to put bread on the table. Eventually she got a better job, but not before we learned what it was like being poor, not even having enough some days to buy lunch in the school cafeteria. We would pretend that we weren't hungry, my brother and I, because we were too proud to ask for help."

"Do you think God can make it all up to you, Ruth?" Rebekah asked.

She seemed startled by Rebekah's question.

Rebekah proceeded, "By chance, are you making preparations to receive your Dad back to life? Wouldn't that begin to make up for losing your Dad in your childhood just a little?"

God Moves to Bless

"Yes, on both counts. I can hardly believe it will happen, Rebekah, but I've been assured that it will. So my brother and I and a few of my cousins are helping to build his house. We have already planted his trees and garden. Maybe God will make up what I lost. I never thought about it that way. It will be such an extraordinary thing though to have him back. However, I won't be his little girl anymore. I guess that won't matter too much."

"I think you'll always be his little girl. His absence will only make his return sweeter. You know, Ruth, God's ways are equal. It is man's ways that are not equal. God has promised to 'wipe away all tears from their eyes; and there shall be no more death, neither sorrow, nor crying, neither shall there be any more pain: for the former things are passed away.' God has never been unmindful of human tears. He has promised to 'wipe them all away' and leaves mankind richer for having savored evil. Best of all, nobody will be left behind.

"You know that God sometime in eternity decided to permit the reign of evil. God knew how costly it would be and what great suffering it would cause. He didn't order it but He permitted it. No one in heaven besides God knew how virulent sin would be once it became active. In the short six thousand years of human history and sin, rivers of blood have been spilled, and some thirty billion people have died. God would never have permitted this to happen if the end result would not bring greater blessings to mankind than the sum total of all their sufferings. Do you believe that, Ruth?" Rebekah asked.

Rebekah continued, "Do you know that dying is no longer a natural process. People who eat Eden fruit are returning to their youth and sickness and sorrow are already passing away. It is not as though we don't see this evidence all around.

"In Israel, which has been ahead of you in accepting Christ's rule, many parents and grandparents are already living again. I know what it is to have a loved one raised from the dead. Lev, my former husband, died in the battle to save Jerusalem and was resurrected. I must tell you Ruth, the biggest problem your Dad will have when he returns is to adjust to the time lapse since he died. Lev felt like Rip Van Winkle when he returned. Fortunately, he had his loving family around him to assure him it wasn't a dream. It takes about a week for the mind to adjust to the time gap."

"It's so encouraging to hear of your experiences and the wonderful promises of God, Rebekah, I always thought you were a religious fanatic. I know both you and Lev have a wonderful way of dealing with people; you are always kind and understanding. I've never heard you say a harsh word or use a superior tone of voice. I admired that about you. However, many of us here have kept our distance from you in religious matters.

"Thank you for taking the time to speak to me, Rebekah. Everything you said makes sense. Not only so, you gave me a reality check. I've been closing my eyes to the great drama unfolding right before my eyes. Now I see that even our work here is all a part of producing a new energy source for safer air travel. Thank you, Rebekah. For the first time in my life those little roots of bitterness in my heart have left me."

"You know, Ruth, if you and I are obedient, we will not have just a few years to enjoy our loved ones, but an eternity of serene and noble fellowship. Ruth, if you have any question on building a house for your father, just give me a call. I've built several of them already. While you will have slightly newer designs and also different material because wood is abundant here and it wasn't in Israel, much is still the same. We may be able to save you time and grief. We love building homes for people. That is what we might be doing if we weren't on assignment here."

Rebekah was glad for this conversation because it was proving her hunch that when people began to experience the powers of Christ bringing to life their loved ones, it would in itself be a religious experience. She found a great deal of comfort in this exchange with Ruth. Rebekah asked if Ruth lived close to the chapel that she and Lev went to.

"Yes, and I have heard good reports about it, but I have been living apart from God all my life. I think I should change that. It doesn't take faith any more to believe in the power of God. Who else but God and Christ could bring back people from the dead?"

"Certainly no human power is capable of that. I also have seen the power of the trees of Eden. Since I have been living on Eden fruit I have never felt healthier nor has my mind ever been as bright. I know this is all being done by the higher power of Christ. I have had a stubborn streak in me. I have steadfastly locked God and Christ out of my life. It was not because I couldn't see what was happening. I was among those stubborn ones who didn't want to go to Israel for help. It wasn't until the drought almost devastated us that I voted to come under the authority of the Ancients. We had no other choice. We were on our knees. However, I thought we could get the blessings of Christ, without serving him. I have been strong-minded in my resistance, Rebekah. However, I received good for evil and I am ashamed of myself."

"I'll look forward to seeing you tomorrow at the chapel services, Ruth. We started out very small, but are now gathering numbers as more and more people want to thank God and Christ for all that has been done and all that is now being done as well. You know unless Christ died for us to provide the ransom price, we would all still be in our sins."

"I'll be there tomorrow, Rebekah. Thank you for taking time out of your very busy schedule to talk to a stubborn person such as me. It's been the knowledge that my father is returning that has electrified me. I have to stop fighting God and start worshiping him and Christ. Yes, I will be there. If I can smoke out anyone else, I will bring them as well. I have been a long time fighting God, but now I'm happy to come under his wings."

Rebekah went to her work with a lighter heart. She was convinced that people would find themselves drawn into a closer relationship with Christ as they received more of his mercies and saw more of his power.

*"He bowed the heavens...
And darkness was under his feet...
"He made darkness his secret place;
His pavilion round about him were dark waters...
"He sent from above, he took me,
He drew me out of many waters..."
(Psalms 18:9, 11, 16).*

Chapter Thirty

"Scott," Rebekah made a point of sitting next to the fair-haired man at lunch. "What is keeping you from joining us at worship service?"

The services were now packed with worshippers, including many of the workers at Eaglewing. Her question was direct, eager and caring, and Scott had to respect her genuineness. He considered reseating himself, but could not bring himself to be that rude.

"I guess it's that I don't really feel the need. I have Eden fruit, after all."

"Tell me, Scott, are you happy?"

Scott drew a sharp breath inward.

"Rebekah," he sighed with the fingers of one hand moving slowly over his temples, "do you never tire of asking me questions?"

"You have Eden fruit and that will bring you health and vitality. 'Man shall not live by bread alone, but by every word that proceedeth out of the mouth of God.' Eating the Eden fruit will not compensate you for your failure to live by the 'Word.' I just want you to be all that you are meant to be."

Scott doodled with his forefinger on the rim and side of his cup.

"So tell me, Rebekah, why did this wise and competent God wait so long to give us these blessings? Why didn't he just start the New

Earth arrangement right after Christ's death?" The old edge of sarcasm in his voice surfaced again.

"What if God had created Lucifer with immortality?"

"He would have had an indestructible evil in his universe. But what's that got to do with waiting all this time?"

Rebekah smiled. "Give me a minute, Scott. That's exactly why God chose not to create any being, not even his Son, with immortality. Indestructibility is a condition only given to one who is proven to be incorruptible in character. Then the powers of immortality are safe."

"So?"

"God wanted to create a divine family out of human beings that would be thoroughly tested during the time of active sin in the world. They would absolutely surrender their lives to Christ. And he wanted to give them the gift of immortality after they were tested and proven. They are in heaven. It took all that time to test 'the Anointed Ones,' this 'little flock' of people."

"The Little Flock" Was Given Priority

"But what does that mean to me? I lost my daughter so that some people could go to heaven?"

"You lost your daughter because the love and wisdom of God permitted freedom of choice, and Adam chose to disobey. God chose to make it possible for her to live again, forever, at great expense to himself. He gave His Son, and Christ died a criminal's death of crucifixion, for her and for you."

Rebekah paused and took a deep breath. "If He hadn't waited so long, you never would have been born, and neither would she. He waited until the earth was 'full.' So now you both have the opportunity to know Christ with eternal life on earth along with billions of others."

"They're in heaven and I'm here on earth. What kind of support is that?"

"Already they have made decisions and overrulings on your behalf. Their power is invisible, but you will experience the results of their wisdom and love over and over in your life. Their life stories are available on the Internet, under Archives of the Anointed."

Scott was silent for a moment. "You don't know what it was like for me." Big tears welled up in Scott's eyes. "I watched her die, Rebekah, and there was nothing I could do. Some of my Christian friends told me that if I only had enough faith, she could be healed. My faith failed her."

"Well-meaning people failed you by telling you something that wasn't true. God's choice to heal has always been *His* choice. Most often He chose not to interfere for a greater good. Tell me how you will feel when you have your daughter in your arms again, Scott."

The bell rang and Scott rose to his feet. They walked together to his office in silence.

Love of Technology More than Love for God

Lev was in rare form as he supervised the anti-matter project in Seattle. He was in awe of the powerful energy they were working with. Lev felt that checking and double-checking the work was not a burden. It was necessary very much a part of his job.

The only thing that dampened Lev's spirit was the fact that some of his workforce was motivated more by love of technology than love for God and providing service for their fellow man. More than once in the first months of the project Lev had confided this to Rebekah.

"They love the challenge of the task, but they miss the reality of God's power that they are working with. It's all technical knowledge with no spiritual insight. If they would only realize the reality of God in their work, they would experience the intensity of this adventure. They would begin to see the reality of God in every aspect of their lives. And then they would know what it is to be truly alive."

Rebekah watched Lev with affection as his quiet exuberance grew and intensified when with the passing of time he saw a gradual change in the attitude of those he worked with.

"They're getting it, Rebekah, they are actually getting it," he said as he paced back and forth in his office his arms waving in the air for emphasis. "They are beginning to see the whole picture—the power of God, His love for them, and their privilege to pass on His love in their work and in their personal lives. The rays of the Sun of Righteousness are shining everywhere. Look at the light in their eyes. Did you notice Josh? He's so happy now. And Lenoard the cynic is now Lenoard the compassionate. And Ruth? And Scott?"

The factory building had been completed quickly and the assembly of all the mechanisms took place smoothly. The second stage of the project began when there was enough volume of residuals and it was monitored carefully to be sure that no buildup of heat occurred. Actual containment of 1-gram units of anti-matter for deployment would take place in the third stage.

Lev himself tested and rechecked numbers and specifications side by side with each section of his work force. He did all he could to insure that the process would not get out of control. In the final days of the project Lev went over emergency procedures, grilling everyone in operations should a sensor send out a danger signal.

Finally the day came for the actual production of anti-matter. All personnel not needed in operations were sent out, and the whole area was cleared for several miles around the plant. A call was made to Enoch, and Lev explained that they were ready to proceed. He broadcasted Enoch's response over the audio system so that everyone in the large plant could hear.

"Shalom, Lev, and to all at Eaglewing. May God be with you. Our spiritual forces have been watching the operation and they will be there with you also. We are confident that if there has been any human failure, our spirit forces will not allow any harm to come to anyone. You may proceed."

Soon a phone rang, and there was an announcement that the first particles of anti-matter had been stored. Lev's excitement, however, could not be contained, and he ran up to every one of his workforce he came across and embraced them with gusto."

After an exuberant and brief call to Enoch, Lev found Rebekah in his office. He held her by the shoulders and stared into her eyes.

"You've been such an important part of this project, providing Eden fruit for the body and encouraging the spirit of these people. We now have the technology to meet the physical and temporal needs of humanity without delays or shortages; it will allow the Ancients to concentrate on the really big challenge of rehabilitating people who are raised with lots of baggage of sin. Thank you, Rebekah. Thank you, Lord."

Leaving Eaglewing

Lev and Rebekah had made arrangements to leave Seattle. Lev, Rebekah and Scott Watts stood on a small stage of the large Eaglewing auditorium before a room full of Eaglewing people. Rebekah and Lev each spoke to the Eaglewing audience that had become part of their family, to express their deep gratitude for the leadings of Christ and his Anointed in bringing their lives together.

As Lev spoke into the microphone, Rebekah reviewed the events of the past year. Slowly Scott had become more open to new truths. He had looked forward to the raising of his daughter and the anticipation brought him joy. He had begun to attend worship service, but was quite reserved at first and always sat in the back. He and Agnes had worked eagerly and tirelessly on their daughter's house. Rebekah smiled to herself anytime she remembered the change in Scott since the day that his daughter had been raised. It was a spiritual milestone to be with a loved one when they were raised and it was most often a life-changing event.

There was now a steady flow of people raised to life. Many people were strongly appreciative of the powers of Christ as they experienced more of his mercies and the depth of his power and love. Those who had seriously harmed others were not as happy about the resurrection process. There was nowhere to hide, no way to escape from a complete disclosure of every sinful act. But the mercy of Christ was there for them, also, and Rebekah marveled at the persistence of many to reach out to those who had caused them such pain in the old life.

Money and political prestige and the misuse of physical and emotional power were no longer an influence on the New Earth as the great social equalizer of resurrection continued to level the hills and lift up the valleys. The Bible had also received a 'resurrection' of sorts, as the book that so many considered 'dead' and 'antiquated' was now alive with promises and insights that people could see and experience in their own lives.

Lev wound up his comments. "I would like you, Scott, to replace me in my position when I leave."

Scott put his arm around Lev and spoke into the microphone. "I would be honored, Lev. I would be honored. We cannot thank you enough, Lev, for your technological brilliance and your intensity for God. And Rebekah, we cannot thank you enough for your spirit of love and perseverance." Scott turned toward Rebekah. "You never gave up on me, even when I had given up on myself." He turned his head toward Lev, and then toward the audience. "You have both helped us experience what it means to be truly alive." The audience applauded.

Rebekah spoke into the microphone. "I remember the first day I stood before you. You looked tired, you reminded me of a grove of withering saplings, and you missed your coffee. Now I see your radiant faces..." Rebekah's voice faltered with emotion, "and most of you have started partaking of every Word that proceeds from the mouth of God—and you have received new life, motivation, and healing of heart from Christ and his Anointed.... I love each of you... And it has been an honor to be a part of your life."

"Eden fruit!" Lev called out, as he came up to the microphone, clapping. Tears welled over Rebekah's eyes, and Lev wiped away the tears that blurred his vision of their Eaglewing family into an indistinct mass of moving colors and shapes. Ruth Engel stood, and Leonard, and then Gwen, and Agnes and soon the whole room stood as they applauded in heartfelt gratitude to Christ for these ambassadors from the Holy land of Israel.

"Well Done"

Their elation began from the moment their plane landed in Ben Gurion Airport, and increased when they saw Jake and Rachel waiting for them. The tears that ran down their faces turned into laughter that could not be suppressed.

Both were surprised when Enoch also joined them and escorted them from the airport to the Headquarters of the Ancients. When they were led to an office down a long corridor and entered a darkened room, the three were shocked and surprised when the lights were turned on and they saw almost all of their living family members in the same room at the same time, eager to greet them. They were all seated at a long wooden table and served Eden fruit, Eden bread and grape juice by John the Baptist and Sarah.

"Well done, Rebekah, in reviving the wilted saplings. Well done, Lev, in launching the successful anti-matter project." Enoch spoke as he poured juice into each cup.

"We assembled you all here because we wanted to formally thank each of you for your willing service. Each of you knows your next assignments, except for Lev and Rebekah. We will call them back to our office in about a week for their new opportunities of service. Until then, Shalom. Christ is well pleased."

The three Ancients left the room, and Ariel stood and raised his hands toward the heavens.

"We thank You, Lord, for this time together. We thank You for life, and for the blessing of this new beginning that goes on and on to each generation. We thank You for each one here—for the mercies and joys of service that have been given to each of us. In the name of Christ our Messiah, Amen."

There was a moment of stunned silence, as they were each overwhelmed with gratitude. They stared into each other's faces and tried to drink in the reality that they were all together in the same room.

"I propose a toast," Annie announced in an overly formal voice as she held up her glass of juice. "To life!"

As the glasses clinked, each voice repeated the toast. The chatter began and never stopped. Two or three would ask a question at once, followed by laughter, and then they would give the others permission to speak first, followed by laughter, so that no one knew who should speak first. Finally it was decided that they would share their experience one by one, around the room.

Anticipation for the Next Assignment on the Horizon

Lev sat by Rebekah in Enoch's office, tapping his fingers on the arm of his chair while both Enoch and John the Baptist sat on the desk engaged in quiet conference with each other. Their week had gone by before they knew it, filled with laughter, conversation and time to relax with family.

"You have both done very well," Enoch began. "We needed someone to get technical changes underway, Lev, and that was important. But more important to us was your ability to work effectively in a hostile environment. You were able to gain the respect of people who disregarded religion, and you persevered until enemies turned into friends. You showed great ability to deal with conflict and resistance. And you, Rebekah, you are sensitive and intuitive, and you have an affinity for helping living things grow. You also show remarkable ability to deal with conflict and to win over the hearts that resist with truth and love. Christ and His Anointed are pleased. And so are we."

Enoch stood and began to pace the floor slowly as he continued. "The first quarter century of the regeneration will be the most hectic. There was so much devastation from anarchy and war. It will continue to be a challenge to dissuade people from making trouble and war and instead encourage them to build and to plant. The technical factors in providing for the needs of the people have progressed well. Every nation is now on board. But the hardest task will be to encourage people to live outside of themselves and to honor Christ and love their fellowman, especially in some cases."

John walked over to the New Earth map that covered the far wall of the office and with a thick pen he circled an area on it.

"We would like you both to return to France. The hydrogen-fueled planes are working well, Lev, and will be in use until we get our fleet of anti-matter planes built. The man you left in charge at the Institute has done an excellent job, but there are some problems that need attention. And Rebekah, we would like you to touch base with all the operations you visited previously."

"However," John took a few steps toward the two that sat before him, "this is not the only reason we wish you to return to Europe. Before you hear our request, I feel compelled to remind you that we serve the Lord Christ. Anything he would ask of any one of us would be but a reasonable service in light of all he has done for us. He will accomplish his purpose, with or without our help. The blessing is in being willing to help, whatever the assignment."

John paused, and Enoch continued.

"Our task for you will be quite different, more difficult in some ways, than anything you have been asked to do."

Lev and Rebekah glanced at each other.

"We ask you, Lev, to receive Adolf Hitler, and we ask you, Rebekah, to receive Eva Braun, one of his lovers, respectfully back to life."

Lev grabbed tightly onto the arms of his chair. Unwanted images sprang to his mind: ghettos, overcrowded trains that led to Treblinka, Auschwitz and Dachau, rows of rude wooden bunk beds with four and five to each bed, terrified eyes, eyes full of despair, pits with layers upon layers of emaciated naked bodies, wheelbarrows of lifeless bodies being wheeled to the ovens, a man with a black moustache, right arm outstretched and heels clicking in salute before a frenzied audience of German soldiers, and the Nazi swastika blowing in the breeze.

Rebekah placed her elbow on the arm of her chair. Then she looked up at John and clasped both her hands together in her lap in a gesture to maintain calmness.

"We are Jews. He considers Jews as swine. He killed some five million of our people. Wouldn't we be a thorn in the flesh—to him and to Eva?" Lev queried.

"This is the choice of Christ and his Anointed, and we know it is well thought out," John replied.

Rebekah said nothing in response. Lev's knuckles were white from his rigid grip on the chair arms.

John continued. "He will be raised in town where he was born in Braunau, Austria. We do not want his toxic addiction to hatred to affect the more vulnerable German audience in Germany. He must be given a full and fair opportunity to change, so that his heart of stone will be softened to become a heart of flesh. He can make the choice to live and it is possible to turn his life around despite the colossal evil he has done. Although he has a heavily seared conscience, and it will be very difficult for him."

Enoch spoke. "If you choose to accept this assignment, nine months from now you will revisit the people and the operations you dealt with on your first trip. After two months you will travel to Braunau and build homes for Hitler and Braun. But no one will coerce you into accepting this request. It is an individual choice."

Rebekah sighed. "I feel inadequate to handle people who have so much blood on their hands. We are worlds apart in many ways, and I don't know how to deal with them."

John responded. "If they fail, it will not be because you were inadequate. You will only be responsible to provide them a fair opportunity to own up to their sins and to seek God's forgiveness, as well as the forgiveness of those whose lives they have destroyed. The depth of the love of Christ reaches down to them just as it does to us."

"You have one week to make your decision," Enoch said as he led the silent pair back down the long corridor. "Shalom."

"But he that is greatest among you shall be your servant"
(Matt. 23:11).

Chapter Thirty-One

A week later Lev and Rebekah met with Enoch. They announced, "We have decided to accept your offer."

Instructions and Briefing

"We have thought about this a long while," Enoch acknowledged. "In the first place, none of the German people are eager to assist in bringing Hitler back. While he still may have many secret admirers who clandestinely sympathize with him, few want to associate openly. Hitler is a fallen hero now that the truth is known that he caused untold suffering for the German people as well. Millions of people died as a result of his diabolical plot to rule the world. Here was a man who could not rule himself, but had fits of anger and contempt for others. He wasted the German youth in a hopeless war even when all his generals knew he had lost the war. Instead of surrender, Hitler was willing to expend the last German. In the light now shining, he is seen for being in reality a madman."

John the Baptist informed them, "We could request this service from others, and to please us some would volunteer. However, building houses is not the problem. This could have been done easily. But this Hitler lived in dread of facing up to his sins. He showed no pity to any who stood in his way. He killed or incarcerated his own people without a shred of mercy. Like many other dictators, he rose to power by cutting throats and stabbing backs."

"No other person in civil history so enchanted a nation as did Hitler," John continued. "Of course, in the religious world, this was normal conduct for some people—to imagine that a heavenly mantle was spread over their shoulders. Those who had illusions of grandeur are going to have serious problems on their return. Don't forget, they will return divested of all their power, all their prestige, all their influence, and their privileges and with the realization that they must admit to their sins. From being worshiped to being looked down upon and despised. Remember, God's ways are equal."

Lev questioned, "If these two learn that we're Jews, won't they demand that we leave their presence? They'll be coming back with the same hatred that characterized their lives. They haven't changed while sleeping in the grave."

"True," Enoch admitted, "they haven't changed in the grave. However, before they died, they saw everything that their scheming and clawing had gotten them disintegrating into ashes before their eyes. Hitler's generals were putting on civilian clothes in order to escape Germany. His kingdom was in ruins and many knew that his refusal to surrender was wreaking havoc on the people. The war was lost pure and simple, but he destroyed Germany in the vain hope that somehow his glorious Aryan race would prevail. Not only so, but he was a coward that did not want to own up to what he had done. Hitler and Eva both committed suicide. They had so many people that hated them; they knew that they'd be dragged through the streets by the Red army. They chose suicide instead."

"Well, sometimes, it is just a matter of choosing how you wish to die," Lev concluded. "When you see a person standing in the window of a burning building with flames starting to envelop it, we do not call it suicide if we see one jump to his death. He or she had a choice of dying in the flames or jumping to his death. It's what they did at Masada, wasn't it? Everybody chose sudden death over slow death by torture or crucifixion at the hands of the Romans. They also refused to surrender and maintained their honor. I guess Hitler took the easiest way out not knowing the resurrection would make him face his crimes. Is it possible that if the Americans had taken Berlin they might have surrendered to them? Not likely. In that Russia took it, Hitler knew he would not have civil treatment. The Russians were in no mood to show any kindness."

"That is a good analogy, Lev," John continued. "That's why we think you have a tempered reasoning mind that can deal with Hitler's outbursts and ravings. Once he learns he is no longer the Fuehrer, he might become more rational. He'll probably have suicidal tendencies. He doesn't want to face all the millions of people he killed. Jews were the cause of evil in the world according to his thinking. Consequently, when he finds a Jew in his living room taking care of him and not dragging him out before the public to face their hatred and scorn, he might calm down a bit. There are no longer SS men to act as his goons. He'll be declawed and defanged, so his growl will only be noise."

"Our wish is to give him the best chance at being rehabilitated," Enoch added. "He was full of hatred and was, therefore, a miserable person. He was domineering and possessive—very intimidating and abusive. We know that as he went into the grave, so he will return. Nothing changes while they slept in death."

John said, "We have chosen you both because you know how to deal with people in a kind but firm way. You have dealt with hundreds of people in difficult circumstances, but have won the respect and admiration of some who hated you and wished to harm you. You may have to be innovative at the outset when they return. You must not let either of them dictate anything to you. The sooner they learn they exist only in the covert of Christ's mercy, the better. The old ways of getting to power by abusing other people won't work.

"We think both of you know enough about human nature to take on this challenge successfully. We call it a challenge, because it will take all of your patience and skill in dealing with someone like Hitler to help him to come to terms with reality. He'll find it painful to have no power and be dependent upon you for guidance and help. He must know that millions of people loathe him with a passion and would gladly die to injure or kill him. He doesn't have to know that spiritual powers will protect him as they do all others. He'll learn that soon enough. At first he must be handled like a fierce dog on a short leash with a muzzle. He'll calm down and hopefully become civil in his relations with others."

What about Eva?

"Eva was under something like a spell with Hitler. She knew that she was not the love of his life, but she accepted her role as his paramour. Eva probably did like him, but it was also the glamour of being associated with the man who ruled the nation and who hoped to rule the world as well. She knew that a woman named Geli was the love of his life. However, Geli was young and although she enjoyed the favor of a powerful political figure, she often flirted with younger men. This caused Hitler a fit of jealousy, so he assigned SA Nazi chaperones to follow her at all times. Geli felt trapped. Finally, when Hitler forbade her to leave the apartment while he went away on a trip, she shot herself in the heart. This devastated Hitler and caused him to languish. So Eva had to live in Geli's shadow. She will not be nearly as much trouble as Hitler, but still she will need enormous growth and development to stand on her own two feet and grow into moral maturity."

Enoch added, "Lev, you must know Hitler was a very sick person. He will be returning in full health and vigor, but with little stability of character. Even more importantly, at some point in his life he was possessed by the devil. Now the devil seldom descended to such depths, but when it suited his grand agenda, he did. For instance, it is written of Judas after Jesus gave him the sop, 'Satan entered him' (John 13:27). So, yes, Satan has possessed some people."

John then said, "Hitler will return to the village where he was born in Braunau, Austria. He has a lot of sympathizers, but most of them are not in Austria. If left in Germany, he might still find misguided followers who loved their ill-gotten power to hate and persecute. While he would easily be prevented from any activity, yet his toxic addiction to hatred of other people is not a healthy environment for either him or others to feed on. He must be given a full and fair opportunity to change his heart of stone to one of flesh. He can do it, although he suffers from a seared conscience and that is the hardest to heal. Lev, you have shown a remarkable ability to deal with hostile and angry people. That's why we have chosen you for this task."

Lev inquired, "How should we proceed? The mere mention of Hitler's return is going to raise angry passions as well as some secret sympathizers. There are people who would gladly die for the privilege of strangling him with their bare hands. People who lost their entire families in such cruel and ruthless ways cannot believe that such a scoundrel should have a chance to gain eternal life. How can a man with so much blood on his hands, with such orchestrated and well-planned death camps, be allowed to walk this earth again? I have never dealt with anyone so evil. And on top of this, I'm a Jew! When he finds this out he'll probably burst a blood vessel in his anger."

Enoch said, "When Hitler learns that you have helped build his house, Lev, he will be somewhat beholden to you. While it is true that he could have had many volunteers to build his house if it was done secretly, few would want it to be known that he or she was associating with a man of such tarnished image. Likewise, Eva Braun likely will not suspect you are Jewish, at least not for a while. She knew what was happening and at what a low level the Nazis were operating. She knew that the first thing Hitler did when he came to power was to end the rule of law of the Weimar Republic. Hitler imagined he was above all laws forgetting that God is ruled by His own laws. How could such a wretched human being want all law subordinate to his whims? This is the stuff of ruthless emperors and kings. Who, with a shred of nobility left in his heart, could not see the evils of such a course? They were in a league with Satan and knew it. When it came to own up to their deeds, they all wanted to disappear into the woodwork. By the way, many are still hiding from confessing their evil deeds."

John said, "Not everybody is going to be able to make such a great transition from their past. If they fail, it will not be your fault. You will only be responsible for giving him a fair opportunity to own up to his sins and seek God's forgiveness, as well as the forgiveness of millions who died because of his evil designs. You know people like Hitler have strikes against them before they even begin. They were incessant liars, abusers of people, very proud and without a shred of sincerity or kindness for anyone who did not support their evil deeds—these border on total depravity. Hitler will come back with his father's original name, Schicklgruber. It will soon get out that he is Hitler, but this will give him a chance to get his bearings. As we all know, it takes a little adjustment when one returns to life. Everything is so new and strange. Even we, who are perfect, took a little getting used to this new world of high tech."

Lev and Rebekah were told to prepare to leave in a few days. They would be returning to their previous employment to assist in smoothing out difficulties that had arisen. Lev's task was to help get the technical agenda on course and assist the new manager in learning to work with people as a team, not as a boss. Rebekah was to restore good relationships between various operations that had become a little tangled. However, this was not their main mission. As soon as they accomplished these initial goals, they would begin building houses for Hitler and Eva. They would both be returning to life in the same locality. They were to put off as long as they could their meeting together.

Revisiting the Science Center

Lev and Rebekah flew out of Israel after saying their farewells. No one asked them where they were going, so they were relieved. Franz Schleicher picked them up at the airport and seemed genuinely glad to see them again. They were taken to the hotel where Lev stayed last time.

In the morning someone from the Science Center came to pick Rebekah up to catch her train. Lev went off to the chapel wondering if Louis Vignette was still the chaplain there. When he entered, many people recognized him and came over to greet him. It was a warm reception to say the least. As the services started Lev noticed that Louis Vignette was not serving as chaplain. He said nothing, joining in heartily with the hymns of praise. The chaplain was a very capable speaker and from what he heard, very well grounded in the Word. The services were beautiful and uplifting. At the end of the service Lev went up to thank him for such a beautiful service.

"Someone told me you are Lev Aron. Well, welcome back. I have never heard so many speak well of someone, as they do of you. My name is Andrew Ganz."

"Pleased to meet you, Andrew. Whatever happened to Louis Vignette? He was serving here when I left?"

"Well, he kept losing the support of those meeting here, so he claimed that someone had poisoned the waters for him and left. He has tried to take over several chapels since, but never very successfully. He does not come out to any services now and is quite upset that people don't appreciate his leadership."

"Well, he succeeded in replacing John Reinhart, who was a wonderful chaplain. I understand that John is now serving at another chapel. Do you know of him?"

"Yes, indeed. He is a man who knows God and is well studied in the Word. His chapel is one of the largest in this area, and growing. By the way, I did hear that Louis Vignette is having some home meetings with a group of former ministers. None of them succeeded in attaining chaplain status so they opted to have their own type of meeting. Part of the problem of some of these former ministers is that they have not owned up to the fact that they misled a lot of people. Even though they may have felt they were serving God, none of them taught of this wonderful time of restitution of all things. You'd think they would admit that they weren't clear on what God's plan was. Perhaps they'll come around."

After a grand season of renewed fellowship, Lev headed off to the science center. He walked to work that morning enjoying the beautiful scenery. Everything was bursting with life. Much of the old city had been removed and turned into private homes with gardens. The city smoke and grime were gone. Everything was pristinely clean with orchards and flowers filling the landscape. The new cars and trucks running on hydrogen were environmentally pure. Even in the making of steel or metal requiring high temperature hydro-oxy power was used. Gone were the old smokestacks and clouds of pollution. If only hearts could be made pure so easily, Lev thought.

Jesse Comer

Lev entered the center on time and was greeted with cheers as he walked to his office. Everyone came to him to shake his hand and express his or her affection. After about a half hour everything settled down and he called a general meeting. Franz Schleicher seemed glad to have him back.

Franz knew how to deal with people from what Lev had observed of him before. However, he had not kept up on his studies, so he did not have the technical grasp of the very complex operation. His assistant, Jesse Comer, was on top of the technical requirements, but wanted to be the boss, and he rode roughshod over people. The Ancients had it sized up correctly, so Lev knew the problem as soon as he walked in the door.

Lev began the meeting complimenting them on the remarkable work they had been doing.

"You know Martin Luther shook the religious world of his time when he preached 'the priesthood of all believers.' Well, I would like to shake you all up by saying 'every worker is a boss.' Within a few short years, when everyone learns all there is to know about this industry, you may take turns at directing operations. We don't have any competition, but neither do we need to grind out unnecessary planes. When we have enough planes, we will close operations periodically or reduce working hours. Boom and bust are a part of history. It used to be that not all people were gifted with bright enough minds to do every job. That's no longer true. In a year's time anybody and everybody will be able to do Mr. Schleicher or Mr. Comer's job if they sit down and study all the courses about this operation. Every factory in the world today serves to make what is needed for human comfort and the common good. Everyone is self-sufficient, no one is poor, no one is sick, no one is feeble and no one lacks anything needful."

Lev continued, "When God made man, he made him lord of earth as well as lord over all its lower creatures. He did not make him lord over his fellow men. Sinful conditions brought about the castle on the hill and the barefoot peasants in the valley—the rich and poor, the nobility and the peons. Now the hills have melted and the valleys have been raised. A great and proper leveling has occurred in society and will continue until all stand before God's throne as sons of God again.

"I will be here only for a month or two. I have come to see all of the advances you have made since I left and to see if there are any areas that can be improved. I hope you will all be open to any suggestions. I've worked with many of you in the past and you know that I never left anyone thinking they were working for me. You are all working voluntarily for your fellow men and the common good—we all are serving the Lord Christ. The principle that Jesus preached is still true, 'But he that is greatest among you shall be your servant.' So I would like to try an experiment for a day only."

They were all ears as Lev explained, "Mary Ann, you have been working for a long while and probably know most of this business as well as anyone. I should like you to be in operations today. Mr. Comer, I think you should take on Mary Ann's job, just for today. See if you can improve her operation in anyway. Mary Ann, Mr. Schleicher and I will be watching over your shoulder, to double check your decisions, because we cannot let anything happen to stress operations. You will be observed for not only how you manage the work assignments, Mary Ann, but also for the tone of your voice and for your ability to work with people to solve problems. Just for today. Are there any questions?"

Lev could see that Jesse Comer wasn't happy leaving his position for a less glamorous task. Jesse's face was a little red, thinking that he was being put down in the eyes of all the staff members. Lev wondered if Jesse was half tempted to quit. Jesse had just gotten to a position where he could give instructions and he didn't like this one-day demotion, as he considered it.

"See if you can improve Mary Ann's operation, Jesse," Lev said.

He grumbled under his breath and went out to her station. Mary Ann was a little at sea at first, because she didn't know all that needed to be done, but Franz Schleicher knew exactly what needed to be done so he kept her informed. Mary Ann didn't know all the technical data, but Lev filled in the details. Within a few hours things shaped up and Mary Ann had things running smoothly.

When they broke for lunch, Lev invited Jesse to eat with Franz and him. Jesse swallowed his frustration and grudgingly agreed. Lev could tell he was debating whether to give him a piece of his mind and walk off the job. The only thing that kept him on the job was that it was only for a day, and he really liked his new position.

Learning How to Serve with Love

At lunchtime Lev commended Jesse for his technical grasp of the operation.

He looked up and said, "Mr. Aron, you put me down big time today. Do you think you can win me over with a little praise? I must tell you I almost walked out of here today and was going to forget about coming back."

"Why? Don't you like to serve your fellowman? Why would you spend so much of your time learning every detail of this technical business and then walk away from the opportunity to use that ability and knowledge?" asked Lev.

"That's the whole point, Mr. Aron. You are minimizing my knowledge and expertise by trying to make it seem that knowledge is not necessary here."

"Well, I regret that's the conclusion you have reached. Nothing could be further from the truth. The only reason I came here was because I had absorbed all the information I needed to run this operation. No one else here was privileged to have that information. This was all leading technology and only a handful of people knew it. I was one of the privileged few. I left my comfortable home in Israel and came here without any pay or any reward. It was my privilege to serve my fellow man. Mr. Schleicher, was I unkind or unfair at any time with you or any of those in operations here?"

"Absolutely not, Lev. It was I, who had been unfair and unkind, but I have learned since from my mistake, and I must tell you I have not let a day go by without looking into my heart to see if I have been unkind or unfair. Eternity is too long to practice the old vices."

"Let me ask you, Jesse, if I may, did you find any way to improve on Mary Ann's operation?" said Lev.

"Not really. Actually I think I messed up some things, and I spent most of the morning trying to undo the mess. However, that was an unfair position to put me in. You knew I would have trouble trying to do the job, much less in finding ways to improve it. I don't know what joy you get out of putting me down this way."

"Jesse that is the last thing in the world I want to do. It would be a mean spirited thing to put anyone down. Why would I do something dreadful like that? I asked you to try to do Mary Ann's job knowing full well you couldn't do it as well or improve upon it. After all she has been doing this for a long time and is highly proficient in her work. However, let me ask you, did you learn to appreciate the work that she does?"

"Yes, I realize now a little better what she does and how well she does it."

"The only reason this whole operation gets things done is because everyone does his or her job. Everyone is important. Remember the story of the horseshoe nail — the loss of one nail set off a chain reaction resulting in disaster. You know, Jesse, ten very valuable people have left under your leadership. This caused a disruption in the work and created a heavy burden on those who remained to take up the slack. It takes time to find people who are skilled and bright enough to cover these jobs. While people are all becoming brighter every day, still we do not have instant knowledge and we do not develop instant skills in a day. Now, Jesse, do you have an explanation why ten people have left this plant?"

Owning Up to Responsibility

Jesse swallowed, "How would I know that? People are free to go. They are all volunteers. What can I say when they leave?"

"Well, what did they tell you when they resigned?" Lev asked.

"All right, I will level with you. Several did say they didn't need all the aggravation they were getting. Others said they didn't feel their suggestions and viewpoints were any longer respected. Others just left with lame reasons, like, 'I need a breather away from this place.' I guess I do bear some responsibility. I know I'm not a smooth operator and have been substandard in my ability to communicate and deal with people. I apologized to them if anything I said or did added to their burdens. It wasn't enough for them to stay. When the first person left it created a little ripple in our work here, but when one after the other left, I found myself losing control. I became tenser and frustrated trying to believe I could get along without them. I sensed all along they were leaving because of the way I was dealing with them."

"Why didn't you let Franz handle all the matters you were not gifted in personal dealings with the staff? You know he is an old pro at that—he could've smoothed out relations and scheduling without demeaning anyone."

Jesse said, "I should have done that, but I guess I was getting too heady. You know, this is the first time I had an opportunity to handle such a big operation. I thought because I was sharp on the technical details, that it qualified me to play boss."

"We don't have bosses anymore, Jesse. That went out with the old world. 'One is your Master, even Christ; and all ye are brethren" (Matthew 23:8). We are to serve one another in love. You know the simple reason all these people left? You didn't treat them in a loving way. It's one thing to be stern when people are doing something wrong, and quite another to treat them sternly when they are doing their best."

Franz joined in saying, "Lev is right. I must tell you, Lev was stern with me when I tried to cheat the workers here. He was right in doing that, because I was behaving badly. Lev turned out to be the best friend I have ever had, because he awakened me to my wrong course. When I corrected my way of dealing, it was because of Lev that I was invited back. When he left this plant there was hardly a dry eye. He was brilliant, but he cared about everyone and everyone's feelings. Did you notice all the cheers when he entered the door? They were genuine, Jesse. To have a friend you have to be a friend. Even when mistakes were made, Lev was never cranky or tried to fix blame on anyone. He shouldered all the blame and heaped all the praise on others. "

Jesse lost some of his self-centered air, and for the first time acknowledged that he had been behaving badly. He said, "Lev, I guess I wasn't prepared to deal with people as I should have been. How can I defend myself against the evidence stacked against me? I blew it—I know that. Even though I knew I was somewhat to blame for all these people leaving, I was too arrogant to change my way of dealing. I guess I wanted to be boss too badly and disqualified myself from being boss at all. If you want me to, Lev, I'll step down. I am to blame—what can I say in my defense?"

"Jesse," Lev said, "I would be making an even greater mistake than you made if I accepted your resignation. You have the technical knowledge that is badly needed now. Six months from now, maybe everyone in this plant will know as much or more than you, if they choose to study. We need your technical skill very much here now. We also need those workers who left. You have gotten a few replacements, but they have a lot of catching up to do. If I can get them to return, will you make an extra effort to learn management skills? Even more importantly, all you have to do is love these good people and show that you respect and appreciate them. When you are upset, make sure that you ask Franz to handle the situations. We don't want bosses here—we want all our workers to be friends to each other and to pull together."

Jesse said, "I asked them not to leave, but I guess they knew that all I was concerned with was myself. I wanted to look good. I knew it looked bad when so many volunteers left, but my real reason was to protect my image. I admit I cared nothing for these people. Lev, I came from a broken home, my parents divorced when I was six years old. My father not only divorced my mother, but I think he divorced me as well. He missed all the child support he could, and never called or paid any attention to me as I grew up. My mother was a good woman, but she lived a hard life trying to provide for me. She had no time for me. So I became a self-made man. I know I lack social graces."

The Best Book for Dealing with People

"May I suggest the best book to learn how to deal with people?"

"What? I promise I'll read it." Jesse said.

"The Bible," Lev answered.

Jesse looked a little startled.

"Yes," Lev said, "Particularly the New Testament. That's where I learned that I must love people if I want them to be my friends. Now, occasionally, you'll love people who will not love you in return. There's always a Judas here and there who looks at love as weakness, and generosity as stupidity. You'll find them occasionally. In this age their ranks are thinning. There is no devil around to confuse people. If you treat a person as a dog, don't be surprised if he or she bites you."

"I suppose the Bible wouldn't do me any harm," Jesse exclaimed. "I'll start reading and studying it today. I grew up with virtually no religious training at all. My whole idea was to learn all I could, because knowledge was power. It worked for me. I got good grades in school because that's what I knew I needed to distinguish myself. I still try to distinguish myself, I guess, in my own self-centered way. I guess I don't know how to love."

Lev said, "Read 1 Corinthians 13. I was brought up a Jew. I had never read that book in my life. I read the Old Testament, but Jews were not supposed to read the New Testament. When I read that chapter on love, it opened a window in my life that had been closed and shuttered. Light has been pouring in ever since."

They finished their lunch and frank discussion together a little past the hour. Lev said, "Jesse, starting this afternoon I shall call the people who left employment here if I can reach them. We really need them to get things running smoothly again."

During that week Lev managed to reach all ten former volunteer workers. They were very pleased to hear from Lev. Many wanted to come in to visit. Lev suggested that they come in to help the distressed organization. One by one they agreed to return as long as he managed affairs. The following week Lev personally greeted each as they returned. Cheers went up from all the employees, and the one who cheered the loudest was Jesse.

They had a little celebration with beverages and cake, taking off about an hour to welcome them back. As the celebration hour ended, Jesse stood up and said, "I have an apology to make to all of you, not only those who have returned, but all of you who have remained while enduring my unkindness. I confess my lack of sensitivity and am truly sorry. I hope you can forgive me."

Getting the professional help back on the job immediately began to take the wrinkles out of the operation. Within a month production returned to normal and the quality also returned. Lev took Jesse on all the work assignments and in every place that had unresolved problems. Jesse observed him talking to all of the concerned parties and engaging them in the problem solving. Jesse learned that no matter how much one knew there was wisdom in a multitude of counsel. He was surprised to learn how many people came up with brilliant insights and solutions.

Time for Braunau

As Lev's time drew to an end, Jesse thanked him for showing how to get things done. He realized the need for the input and help of each person. Jesse had stopped being a maverick and had become a team player. He also had learned to appreciate Franz who had endured his arrogance patiently.

Lev's task was now done and it was time to turn to the real reason he had come to Europe. Lev said farewell to the staff. It was a love feast and he found the warmth genuine. Even Jesse came up and gave him a hug. He thanked Lev repeatedly.

Franz had arranged for Lev to have his own automobile. It was a new vehicle that used hydrogen as a power source. It was a pleasure to drive and it felt good having a vehicle to get around in. Lev thought he would need it where he was going.

Lev slowly headed for Braunau, Austria. He was grateful not to be asked why he was going there. He drove slowly through the beautiful countryside with almost a sense of reticence for his new assignment.

"Where the tree falleth, there shall it be"
(Ecclesiastes 11:3).

Chapter Thirty-Two

Lev arrived in Braunau, and as he explored the town he thought to himself—one would never suspect that a person who caused such havoc in the world was born here. Perhaps seldom in history has a man been responsible for so many deaths and such unspeakable suffering. The mind cannot focus on the millions of deaths. We are not made to conceive of anything so large. It is just a big number. If we were to relive each life and how it met its tragic end, only then we would be able to even begin to conceive of such massive tragedy.

To think that God has total recall of every human being that ever lived, a complete record of every thought, word and experience for the entire life of each and also a record of their genetic code is hard to conceive of. However, whether we can conceive of it or not, does not matter, that is what the resurrection guarantees. There of necessity has to be the preservation of identity and total memory recalls, otherwise character identity would be lost or marred. God must give to each a new body (1 Corinthians 15:35).

Lev was to live in the home of Johanan Krook who had left to go to America to make preparations for his son to return to life who had died in an automobile accident. The house was among the newest designs and Lev could see many improvements over his own home. Lev enjoyed most having the beautiful paradise garden to pick his food for the day. There were a number of trees blossoming and each month another set of trees would produce ripe fruit. In these enclosed gardens the scent of blossoms was much greater.

No one knew Lev's mission. He just told the neighbors he would be building a house for a man no one else had volunteered for. Everyone thought that was noble of him. To his surprise, he found several people who volunteered to help him. They had already built homes for their returned parents and were in between other similar projects. Lev thanked them and told them he would indeed appreciate a hand. He informed them as soon as he got all the information together he would seek their assistance. They seemed eager to help.

Lev did not tell them whom he was building this house for yet, and if inquired of down the road, he was to tell them it was a man from the family of Schicklgruber. There had been many families that had that name so it would not raise immediate concern. Lev wanted this to be as low key as possible, at least until the proper time, when it would be necessarily known. He thought Hitler would not come back with his characteristic mustache and would be younger in appearance and a little taller in stature. Other than that, it would be the same domineering and brooding person.

Building Hitler's Home

Lev was soon told that he could begin to lay the foundation on Hitler's property. Also, the trees had already been planted and the glass enclosure for the trees from paradise would begin shortly. The next day Lev drove to the site and found it within walking distance from his temporary house. The factory confirmed that the Ancients had released the order for delivery of this housing material as soon as the foundation was laid.

Lev was amazed at how efficiently everything was run. There was no red tape, no foot dragging anywhere. Promptness characterized all operations and there was also a warm and friendly atmosphere, almost an eagerness to serve. When he called to inquire about the house for Adolf Schicklgruber, no one raised an eyebrow, so Lev knew the name was common in that area. The party on the phone said in a rejoicing tone, "Another of our brothers is returning. May the Lord be praised! We are here to help prepare his housing. Are you his relative?"

"No," Lev replied. "He was just an unfortunate person who no one offered to build for, so I just happened to be free and offered to do so."

"That is good of you. The Lord will bless you for your sacrifice. Tell us when you have the foundation laid, and you are ready for the materials and all its inner workings to be shipped. It will take several days after that to deliver it. We have the address here already. We were expecting your call, Lev."

That evening Lev gave Rebekah a call. She was expecting him and was eager to meet with him. Lev drove over to her place as soon as he had things underway. She had been working on Eva Braun's house, and was just a little ahead of him in building Eva's home. She had several people helping her and the work was progressing well. Lev found that she, too, was deeply concerned about Eva's return. While Eva was not the evil agitator that Hitler was, she was emotionally unstable. She once shot herself in the back of the neck to gain Hitler's attention and then made another attempt at suicide.

They spent the evening talking about strategies they might employ in the early hours of their return. They had been told that both Eva and Hitler would be returned on the same day.

Lev had some heavy equipment dig the hole for the foundation. They had prefabricated forms for the concrete, so all they had to do once the footing was laid, was to put the forms in place. With a couple of helpers to assist Lev, the forms were up in one day, and the next day the concrete was poured. It needed to set for several days. He then called to confirm the delivery date, and found it would be about a week's time. That was marvelous, because it would give the concrete time to set and season.

After his arrival and when things were underway, Lev sought out the local chapel. He arrived just in time for the hymns of praise to start, so Lev sat down near the back. The singing was superb and hymns were like prayers in song ascending heavenward.

The chaplain was a clear Bible expositor and spoke briefly as why the truth about restitution had been lost for so long.

He said, "In a world flooded with Bibles and learned people, the true concept of God's purpose for man was lost. Now we know what God is doing because we see it all around us. Back then, this present work was not foreseen, even though the Bible spoke freely of it. However, this was true only generally, for there were men and women who spoke freely of this feature of God's plan, but they were dismissed as visionary. Now we know who told us the truth and who didn't. The passing of time always will vindicate the truth, and show up the error."

His sermon was short and in closing he quoted the many scripture verses foretelling this blessed time of regeneration.

After the closing hymns and prayer Lev went up to the front to thank him for his inspiring presentation. He introduced himself, saying, "My name is Lev Aron, visiting in the area for a while. I must tell you, your service was a joy to hear. I always like to hear a focused presentation of God's Word. Have you been serving as chaplain very long?"

Alois Haider Tells His Story

He said, "My name is Alois Haider. I died in the battle to take Jerusalem. When I awakened and found out I had been misled, I decided not to allow myself to be misled again with regard to the truth of God's Word. I took into account the present reality and soon found that much of my religious training totally missed the purpose of Christ's return. I have learned through constant study under the Ancients what I had been blinded to before."

Lev said, "Alois, I too died in the battle for Jerusalem. I was on the other side in that battle. Since I have come back to life, I found that my religious training had blinded me to Christ. Like you I started studying the Bible and have reached the same conclusions. Here we are, coming from two different religious backgrounds, both from confused teachings. How clear it all is now. We have come from two different vantage points to the same understanding. May the Lord be praised."

This paved the way for a close relationship with Alois. He was very sincere and earnest. Lev enjoyed his honesty and humility. He also was knowledgeable in the Bible and his discourses were always well researched. Lev came to enjoy his fellowship each morning.

One day he asked what Lev was doing. Lev mentioned he was building a house for a man who had no volunteers to work for his return, and as he had a few months to spare he volunteered.

Alois was very pleased to hear that and said, "I will be glad to help you. Give me the address, Lev; I'll join you after the services tomorrow."

Lev returned home for breakfast that morning inspired and happy for the added help he would be receiving. That would make the task easier. It was a joy to contemplate working with one he had been at war with. That the war was evil was apparent now. It was all hype and propaganda. Yet he knew he was working to make provisions for a truly great deceiver of modern times. It was an eerie feeling. He really was not looking forward to his task. Lev had dealt with hate and prejudice in both his present and previous life.

Here was a man who willingly became the tool of the devil in orchestrating more violence and hatred than would be thought humanly possible. From all the information Lev could gather on him, he was not a totally insensitive man. When his generals treated him to a special session where he was to see Jews machine-gunned down, he became sick with a queasy stomach when he saw it actually happening. He thought this type of killing operation was brutalizing the German troops. He had no intention of stopping the killing; he only wanted it to be less sanguine in appearance.

With the aid of the psychologists he chose to use a gas chamber in conjunction with crematoriums. They even had soft and beautiful music played while people were forced into what was to be a shower but in fact was a lethal gas chamber. The devil could not have devised a better killing tool.

When the housing components arrived by truck, there were two of them to help unload everything and get everything lined up. Alois helped Lev that day, and it was welcome help indeed. He was very capable and knew a lot about building. He had helped build several homes already. He was a very reverent man, and Lev could hear him singing off and on during the day. He didn't look at the clock either. When they had put in a normal workday, he continued with Lev for several more hours as he tried to get everything lined up for the cranes that would lift various components onto the foundation. Actually, it only took a day to get most of the main structure of the house up. The roof would be put in place on the morrow. Things went much faster in building these houses, as much of it was prefabricated.

The next day they had the roof on and with that they could have a leisurely time of it. Putting in all the wiring and the heating systems and the septic systems all would take longer. The design was ingenious and Lev was amazed how easy it was to put a house up now. Occasionally, he got an extra hand, but Alois was there every day without fail. Alois knew the person who was returning to life was from the last century. Many were starting to return from the twentieth century, and they were amazed at how much the world had changed. Most of all, it was the simplicity of life, how secure it was and how peaceful. Everyone returned to financial security and a very high standard of living. They were all amazed that what men had sought through all the ages past: security, abundant supplies of food, energy self-sufficiency and their very own piece of paradise was now everyone's portion.

Building Completed

After about six weeks they had the building ready. They were two weeks ahead of schedule. Lev had selected clothing and supplies for the household. He laid in all the necessities for a comfortable home. Having a car made it easy to pick up the various necessities. Lev even had gotten a Bible and some very good books that were in line with the reality of today's world. He had thought he would leave them in the small home library for Hitler to see on a rainy day. Lev had reported to the Ancients and particularly to John the Baptist that he had everything in readiness and he could appoint the day of Hitler's return.

Lev learned that Rebekah and her helpers had completed all the necessary preparations for Eva Braun. She also had contacted those in Israel that the work was all done. She learned that on the first day of the following week Eva Braun would return to life. Rebekah made sure there were some Eden tea and little niceties to snack on. She even made two resurrection cakes, one for Eva and one for Hitler who was returning on the same day. Not that they would celebrate together. As a matter of fact, they would not be told of each other until they had stabilized themselves and had gotten over the shock of finding a huge hole in their existence.

Rebekah called Lev the evening before Hitler and Eva returned. She was very apprehensive as to how things would turn out. She felt she could manage the first initial hours of Eva's return, because she would be totally dependent on her for information and guidance. However, once she was oriented and began taking charge of her life, it might be a strain on Rebekah to remain with her. She called Lev and asked him to come over.

Lev drove over to Eva's new house to share the evening with Rebekah and also pick up a resurrection cake for Hitler. If anyone had suggested Lev would ever be doing something like this, he would have been fit to be tied. Hitler would be the last person in this world that Lev personally would have lifted a finger to help, much less assisting in his return. However, now Lev realized his old hatred was for the deeds of Hitler rather than for the man himself. Perhaps his person and his deeds were inseparable, but that was what the passing of time would reveal.

Lev also knew that Hitler's first love, Geli, had returned to life a little earlier. She, too, lived not far from Braunau, about 35 miles in the city of Salzburg. She had taken her life when Hitler secluded her in an apartment and had posted two SA officers to prevent her from going out to flirt with the young men of the area. Lev would provide this information to Adolf at the right moment; he would also tell him about Eva when the suitable moment came.

Rebekah and Lev shared each other's apprehensions that evening. They were both nervous and had a sense of revulsion at what they had been asked to do. No one but the Ancients could have prevailed upon them to undertake this task. However, when John the Baptist, of whom Jesus declared, "Among them that are born of women there hath not risen a greater than John the Baptist" (Matthew 11:11), made the request, they were constrained to comply.

Rebekah and Lev both held all the Ancients in awe and reverence, but John the Baptist commanded an even greater reverence from them. He was a man who knew God and Christ in a way that one could feel. There was warmth that radiated from his person that overwhelmed them. They knew that many people who had suffered at the hands of Hitler would tend to abhor him for doing what he did. However, they didn't worry about that. They were only returning good for evil and that is the way it should be in this time of regeneration.

Lev stayed at Rebekah's place longer than usual. They both felt they would have a troubled sleep, so there was no need to hurry to bed. It was no more than a half hour drive back to Lev's house. He stayed until close to midnight, and finally with a tender kiss and hug they parted for the night. Lev brought the resurrection cake that Rebekah had made and placed it in the refrigerator when he arrived at his residence.

Lev spent a lot of time in prayer that night and knew that Rebekah was doing the same. He had a fitful sleep that night. He would fall asleep and awaken in a cold sweat. Normally he was eager to jump out of bed in the morning, but this morning he wished he could hide under the covers. However, he took courage when the light came streaming in the window. Lev went out and collected the Eden fruit for the day's meals. He heard that Hitler might have been a vegetarian for a good part of his life, so he would take to this fruit readily.

"Let favor be shewed to the wicked,
Yet will he not learn righteousness;
In the land of uprightness will he deal unjustly,
And will not behold the majesty of the LORD"
(Isaiah 26:10).

Chapter Thirty-Three

Lev waited around quietly trying to read from the Word, but found he could not concentrate. He had never been so nervous since he had returned to life. When the appointed time for the awakening had arrived, Lev listened carefully for the first signs of life. He thought he heard some drawers opening. Lev guessed Hitler might be looking for some clothes. He purposely had kept them out of his hands so that he would not get dressed and leave via the window or go storming out of the house. He was a modest man and would try to find something to cover himself.

After a few minutes Lev heard the door open a crack and saw him look out. Lev called to him saying, "Good morning." Lev saw he was draped in a towel around his waist. He said, "Adolf, I have some clothing for you. I will leave the clothing outside your door." Lev saw the door open a crack again, and he grabbed the clothing and slammed the door. He never said a word.

Soon he came into the parlor and Lev greeted him. He did not say anything in return. He seemed confused and uncertain. Finally, he gruffly demanded, "Where am I?"

Lev looked at him long and steady, letting him know that he was no longer in charge.

He shouted along, with some profanity, "Where am I?"

Lev could tell he was a domineering person. Lev continued his steady gaze at him.

"So you are Adolf Hitler Schicklgruber?"

That startled him.

Again, he demanded to know, "How do you know my name? I do not know you. If you will let me use the phone, I shall call headquarters and be removed from your residence."

Lev said, "Here is the phone," as he handed him his hand-held cell phone.

Hitler became angry. "What is this some joke, young man? This phone has no cord."

Lev answered, "It doesn't need any. Just dial your number, and see what you get. To make you more comfortable, here is a regular phone."

Hitler quickly dialed a familiar number. He heard it ringing, and that assuaged his anger a bit. Finally, an operator told him that number was no longer active. He started swearing again and threw the phone on the floor.

It was good for Hitler that Lev knew the angels would prevent him from flattening him right then and there. Lev restrained himself.

Lev told him beforehand, there would be no operator, and to pick up the phone and try another number and wait for the answer.

Hitler bent over angrily and picked up the phone, and dialed a second number. He had the same results. Suddenly he realized there was no help anywhere to be found. He stared for a few seconds in disbelief; it was beginning to sink in that he was just an ordinary person in this great big world. His demeanor changed when he realized he was isolated from his sources of power. Hitler sensed Lev could not be intimidated or maneuvered into doing what he wanted. Gradually, he calmed down and began to speak in a civil tone.

Lev felt sorry for him. Here was a man that had millions bowing before him, whom they worshiped and idolized, whose very word meant life or death to millions, now suddenly without a single person to boss around. That must have been humiliating to be bereft of all power and prestige in a moment. That was all over, but could he accept this truth?

Hitler Changes His Attitude

Lev was satisfied that he had won the first round in this bout with Hitler. Once Hitler knew he had to survive by his own wit and cunning, he changed his attitude slightly. He knew Lev was not one to be kicked and bossed around, so he changed his tactics. He decided to be civil and softer spoken. Lev welcomed that, because once he knew he was not in charge of anyone any more, he became more like a human being.

Hitler complimented Lev on his lovely home and the beautiful surroundings. Lev thanked him kindly, but did not choose to tell him that it was his home at that time. If he had done so, Lev was afraid he would have ordered him out.

Having gotten through this first round with Hitler, Lev tried winning him over with a little kindness. Lev asked him to come with him into the kitchen area. Lev asked what he would like to drink. He said, "Normally, I do not drink coffee, but I will have some this morning, if you don't mind. I am quite frustrated. I do not know where this place is, nor even who you are, and why I find myself in totally different surroundings. Please bear with me, for I am absolutely frustrated. And by the way, who shaved off my mustache?"

Lev answered, "You do have a lot of questions. I'm sorry I do not have coffee, but we all drink a new kind of tea that is more healthful and stimulating."

Lev poured him a tantalizing cup of tea and set it before him. Hitler thanked Lev in his second attempt to be civil. Lev knew the frustrating feeling of coming to life after being dead for several years, but it must have been more so for one to return nearly a century later. Lev offered him some fruit from paradise and encouraged him to take some. To assure him it was good to eat, Lev bit into the luscious fruit. Hitler then nervously took a bite. His eyes opened wide, and he exclaimed, "This is excellent. I love fruit and vegetables, but this is fruit I never tasted before, but it is good. Is this from some tropical island?"

"No, it's right from the orchard in the rear of this home. It's mainly all that is eaten. When you eat this fruit, it will return your body and mind slowly to perfection. That's what I have been eating for a long time now."

"That sounds ridiculous, but it is so good I wouldn't mind eating it forever. I have been a vegetarian. May I have another piece of fruit? Anyway, I must know where this is, and how I got here. You have been insolent young man and have ignored my questions. I expect an answer when I ask a question. Is that understood? I have SS men who can make people talk. Do you know whom you are talking to?"

Threatened With the Gustapo

"I certainly do know who you were and how you managed to kill millions of people. As for your SS troopers, they are all gone. You are all alone in this world with only me to help you out—so enough of your arrogant threats. I must tell you that there are millions of people who would strangle you with their bare hands if they could, and many of them would be Germans. You are very fortunate to have me around. If you walked out of here with your mustache, you might immediately be recognized. Even the way it is, I have had a hard time keeping people from suspecting who you are. You are probably the most despised and hated man in the world today. I have been trying to hide you from being recognized. That would create a violent reaction in the hearts of millions of people."

Hitler became very sullen and quiet. He was not a man of courage.

Lev said, "How about another cup of tea? It is so good. I have had a special cake made for you, and I am sure you have never tasted anything as good as this before."

Not waiting for any response, Lev cut him a nice piece of cake and filled his cup with tea.

Hitler ended all his threats very suddenly. He realized Lev was not one to be bullied into submission in the first place, and certainly not by someone like him in the second place. He was deep in thought sitting there staring into space. As he sized up the situation, Hitler figured he had better be nice to Lev.

After a long pause, he finally turned to the cake and using his fork, he tasted it. He soon voiced his delight saying, "This is the best cake I have ever had."

After Hitler had eaten, Lev suggested they settle into the living room. Lev told him to have a comfortable seat because they needed a long and frank talk.

First Lev asked him, "Adolf, does your head feel different today then it has been for many years?"

"Now that you ask, yes it does. For the first time in many long years my head does not feel like it has cotton in it along with a dull headache. Why do you ask?"

"I shall be very frank with you," Lev said. "I happen to know that you were possessed by the devil for many years. Now for the first time, you are free from the devil's hold upon you. The devil is now totally restrained just as the Bible says he would be, chained in an abyss (Revelation 20:2, 3). You are free at last from his control over you, but not free from the guilt and shame you accumulated in serving your master, Satan. Now, Adolf, tell me about your last days in the bunker before you took your life."

"I did not take my life. Here I sit as living proof. You are not looking at a dead man for I am indeed alive and I might add very well, indeed. I have never felt better."

Lev said, "You knew the Germans had lost the war, yet you let millions of Germans fight on knowing fully that your Third Reich was in process of destruction. The Allied forces had one thousand bombers reigning death needlessly on your people nearly every day. Why didn't you surrender and end this needless carnage?"

Hitler jumped to his feet in anger.

"Who are you to question me? My people were Germans—we were the superior race. We could not lay down our arms and surrender. I believed that we would win the war and that we would conquer the world. If you are telling me we lost the war, I do not believe it. I believed that somewhere the glorious German army would appear to crush the Russian forces as well as the western powers. Anyway, the extra two years enabled the Germans to rid the world of several more million Jews. If we surrendered, these swine would have escaped."

Which Nation Now Leads the World?

"Do you know which the most powerful nation in the world is today?" Lev asked.

"Probably the United States," Hitler answered. "They had Germans in that country that is why."

Lev said, "I don't know how to tell you this, but you are very wrong. The most powerful nation on earth today is the Jewish nation."

Hitler's face turned red with anger, and he said, "Lies, lies, lies! Why are you tormenting me with lies? There is no Jewish nation. The glorious German army eliminated these swine. The added two years of suffering the German nation endured in the war was the pain we bore in order to continue our annihilation of these swine. Don't you see these Jewish swine are the enemies of the world, the scourge that we needed to get rid of?"

"Adolf, will you please sit down, and stop ranting and raving? You do not know many things. You are not listening, you cannot bear to hear the truth, and you are behaving like a fool. Now sit down and listen to me. For the moment, I serve as the only friend you have in this whole wide world. You have forgotten what I told you. There are millions of people in the world today who would gladly die for the privilege of strangling you with their bare hands. Do you understand this?"

Lev could see Hitler found what he was telling him extremely distasteful. His face turned red as he tried to control another outburst.

Finally Hitler shouted, "Where are all my soldiers, where is the glorious German army? Where are all my generals and aides? Where am I? Tell me, you idiot. I don't want to hear orders coming from you. I demand to know!"

Lev could see the rage in Hitler's face. He suspected the truth that he was completely isolated from his power base, but he could not accept that. He used to let his outbursts of anger send people scurrying and trembling before him, but Lev sat as impassively as Buddha. He was determined to browbeat Lev into submission to his authority. Of course, that was the last thing that Lev would allow.

Lev was determined to dominate Hitler to give him a taste of his own medicine. He was absolutely powerless, totally ignorant of his true position and Lev alone provided his window to the world. He needed Lev desperately, but Lev did not need him. Lev could see he was a difficult man to like or to even put up with. He was sorely exasperating Lev's patience. Lev knew his trouble though. He knew Hitler was desperately trying to find some link to his glorious past, some power point he could contact to secure some base of his former power.

Lev could not help him find a new base of operation because the whole Nazi nightmare was gone. He had to learn to live a humble life without ever again using and abusing people. His days of operating and maneuvering were over. He was just plain Adolf, with a host of people who hated him, and with no one to help him, not even the devil. If he was to make it in this new arrangement of regeneration he had to live down his sins, replace hatred in his heart with love, and seek to serve the needs of others.

Every outburst on his part only delayed Lev's telling him the information he was trying to get out of him. Part of Hitler's insecurity was in the fact that he had a century gap between the world that was and the present one. They say it is lonely at the top, but from what Lev was witnessing it was even lonelier being at the bottom—out of power, out of support, out of office, out of everything he clawed his way to secure—was all gone. The realization was maddening to Hitler. Even worse, when Lev reminded him that millions of people would gladly die for the privilege of strangling him with their bare hands, it frightened him.

Adolf Realizes His Helpless Condition

Finally, Lev said, "Adolf, are you finished ranting and raving? You know, I don't have to listen to you, and I won't. Another outburst and I will leave you. You will be alone, and totally ignorant of what has transpired since your death. Totally unaware of how you have been made alive and what conditions you must meet to continue your existence. You are absolutely without any power base. The Third Reich is no more, and will never be again, thank God. The devil used you as a pawn to do almost as much evil as any man on the face of the earth. You exist only through the mercy of Christ and Israel under the Ancients. You have sorely tried my patience."

Lev stared directly into Hitler's eyes that then averted his gaze. It finally began to sink in ever so slowly that his days of being the big boss were over.

"You are just a little fish in a big pond now," Lev reminded him. "All your glory days are past, and now the specter of those millions of people you killed and tortured are coming back to haunt you. Every human being that ever lived is coming back to life again. No one is left behind. That means you must face every person you killed and tortured. It means that all the Germans you condemned to freeze and die, because you refused to allow your own troops to retreat, will be looking for you. All the Germans needlessly killed because you would not surrender until there was nothing left to surrender will be looking for you. All the Jews you hated with such a passion and killed and tortured who are now your greatest benefactors will be looking for the man named Adolf Hitler. Is that you Adolf?"

Hitler turned pale as Lev spoke. Finally, he said, "Is this some kind of nightmare? My last experience was a nightmare. Our German army was torn to shreds. My generals were deserting, trying to become civilians. We were down in a bunker while the Russian army was closing in on us. I knew if they caught me alive they would torture me to death. I had no other choice but to take my life. Eva wanted to die with me. I gave instructions to burn my body so they could not desecrate it by dragging me through the streets or hang me in the public square like Mussolini.

"Do you know that only a hair's-breadth stood between victory and us? If I had not paused when I had all our landing craft ready to invade England, we would have succeeded. I waited for the German Luftwaff to clear the skies over Britain. They could not clear those Spitfires from the sky. While we paused, the Allied planes destroyed our barges and landing craft. England became the main base for the

United States to pour armaments into. There, Lev is where the tide of battle turned on us. Had we taken Britain, we could then have finished off the Russians and the glorious Third Reich would have spread its flag over Europe and Russia. Waiting for the Luftwaff to clear the air over Britain was my Waterloo."

Finally, Hitler was opening up about his past. He was at last confiding in Lev some of the torment of his past. Lev then said, "Do you think you would be better off today if you had won the war? Would you have continued to abuse and kill people as you pleased? You would now have countless thousands and millions more who you would have to face and apologize to!"

Hitler Begins to Realize His Situation

The concept of people coming to life again strained Hitler's thinking process. He repeatedly tried to dismiss it. He had no idea of how he got here or where he was. He was faced with the fear that this was all a dream and that he would awaken in the bunker again while the Russians were closing in on him. However, he lost his belligerent attitude as he spoke of how he lost the war. He turned pale.

Even though he was surrounded with a beautiful home and the fragrant smell of blossoms in the garden with the trees of life, Hitler had the albatross of all his former sins hanging around his neck, and he could not rid himself of it. He had no trouble believing that millions of people would gladly die for the privilege of strangling him with their bare hands. Of course, Lev didn't tell him yet that he was protected from any physical assault by spiritual powers. Lev allowed him to sweat a bit. Lev knew he was still suicidal and would just as soon be dead, as alive and having to take responsibility for his heinous crimes against humanity.

Finally, Lev said, "Adolf, you have been telling me about yourself. How about if we forget about you and all your crimes against humanity for a moment? Let me tell you my story. My name is Lev Aron. I died trying to defend Jerusalem from great and overwhelming armies sent down by the so-called Christian world. Germany was well represented in that great invading host. That was the last battle on earth against the Jews. We Jews fought bravely the first day. I died among the first casualties of that war. The next day was dark and gloomy. Electricity was in the air, people's hair was standing on edge, and a foreboding fell over the invading army. They moved out trembling in their tanks and airplanes. They had their orders. Central command tried to stop their forces from making an attack that day. It was too late. They lost all radio contact. They waited helplessly and soon the whole sky lighted up with fire. Millions were destroyed that day. The whole invading army was destroyed by God's power.

"That ended the war and then religious leaders responsible for sending all these millions to their death were violently assaulted. Priests and ministers who blessed that invasion fared as poorly as those in the French revolution. After that the nations were torn apart by anarchy. Now, the only nation that survived intact was Israel. It has become the leading nation of earth. Men such as Abraham, Isaac and Jacob have all returned to life and are leading Israel and the world. It was John the Baptist who asked me to come here and make provisions for your return to life. Would I have done it otherwise? Not on your life. They wanted you to have a fair opportunity at making full recovery and they made a special plea to make provisions for your return."

"Are you a Jew, then?" Hitler asked.

"That is right, and I have to remind you that you may have Jewish blood in you. Your grandfather was Jewish."

He jumped up, yelling, "That is not true, those are lies, lies, all lies."

"Well, Adolf, in a few years you will meet your grandfather, you can tell him that." Lev continued, "You see in this time we are living in, only the truth is spoken. Your whole Third Reich was built on lies. You used hatred to come to power. Anything built on hatred cannot stand. Eventually the truth will be known. You were a master of deception, but no longer. Deception is over. God's ways are equal. You must now live down all the pain and suffering that you caused to countless millions. You sowed hatred and now you want mercy. You killed people wantonly and now you want life for yourself. You were cruel and ruthless and now you would like to be treated kindly. How are you going to face all the people you killed, maimed, abused and mistreated? I wouldn't want to be in your shoes. You didn't think that everyone you killed and abused was coming back, did you?

"Now that Satan is bound and in the abyss, your mind is clear, your brain doesn't feel like cotton is pressing on it. How do all your evil deeds look to you now?"

"What can I say?" Hitler said, "I must be having a bad dream is all I can say. What you are telling me sounds like a fairy tale. How can I believe you? I don't know who you are, much less do I know about these Ancients you speak of. I cannot explain being here. My last recollection was being in a besieged bunker in Berlin. I took cyanide and then shot myself. I should be dead and now I find myself alive.

The pounding artillery is gone and I hear birds singing in the trees. At first I thought this was a hospital, but it is nothing more than a very nice house. I looked at myself in the mirror and I look much healthier than before. I was a sick man, but I do not have an ache or pain or even a scar anywhere. I used to feel, as you suggested, that I had cotton in my head all the time. People said I had an aura about me, and I did. It was a depressing feeling all the time. Can you explain where I am and how I arrived here?"

A Civil Hitler

At least Lev observed he was starting to talk in a civil tone and was anxious for some logical explanation. Lev then said, "What I must tell you will be hard for you to believe, but every word is true. You were very dead indeed. And so was Eva Braun."

The mention of her name caused Hitler's face to light up.

"They then poured gasoline over you and charred your bodies beyond recognition. This was at the end of April in 1945. Many thought that you had escaped to South America along with hundreds of Nazi criminals through the offices of the Vatican. However, the Russians found your remains and more or less secreted this information. Germany was in ruins. The Russians brought trucks in and emptied all the factories of every bit of machinery. If they could have taken the buildings, they would have done that. They hated the Germans with a passion for their brutal treatment of the Russians—for leaving countless thousands of Russian men, women and children to die in the open fields without food or shelter in the dead of winter. Every rule of decency in the treatment of prisoners was violated. You were fortunate to be dead before they found you. They will be looking for you now that you are back among the living.

"We have purposely played down the name of Hitler and have gone to your original family name of Schicklgruber to keep people from trying to hurt you. Soon enough, the truth will be known, but this will give you a chance to think about how you are going to face the millions you killed and tortured. You have one valid excuse, and that is that the devil possessed your mind. Satan also possessed Judas, so you are in bad company.

"How dare you link me in with Judas? I was loyal to the German people; I labored and sacrificed for them. I saved my people from bankruptcy and brought prosperity to Germany. I was good to the Germans."

"That is what you like to think. If you were your own judge, you obviously would not condemn yourself. Yes, you did bring about a wartime industry of prosperity. You then plunged your people into pain and suffering on a massive scale. Could you count all the Germans who died because of your madness? Did you see all the cities and towns of Germany in ruins? Did you feel the hunger of starving Germans who could not get food at the close of the war and after the war? You were no savior to the German people. You lied to them, making them believe they were a superior race and only victory would follow them. It did not. Germany was a basket case after the war. If it had not been for the kindness of the United States that provided generous financing under the Marshall plan, Germany would have taken a half-century to recover.

Germans Would Be Looking for Their Leader

Also, you were ruthless with any German who reproved your madness. You surrounded yourself with 'yes' men because that is the only kind you could stand having around you. No, Adolf, with friends like you, the Germans didn't need enemies. You promised them everything, delivered nothing. Instead of a glorious thousand-year Reich you gave them a nation of ashes. Many Germans will be looking for you also. Many would like to strangle you with their bare hands. How are you going to face them? Sooner or later, you are going to own up to your past, all your lies and deceit, all your double dealing and treachery. I wouldn't want to be in your shoes, Adolf."

Lev knew that Hitler was not used to such frank talk. Here a Jew was putting him down and there was not a thing he could do about it. Lev knew Hitler longed to have some of his SS men take care of him in their own inimitable way. Yet Lev was the only window Hitler had to the world. He was frightened that perhaps what Lev was relating to him was true. How awful it was to learn the truth too late. If he had only known these things before, he could have changed his ways. How could he have known that every person killed would be back and every evil deed would be known? There was nowhere to hide. No lies to tell to justify him before the world, much less before Christ.

Lev decided to give Adolf a breather. He said, "Let me show you how we build houses today and the wonderful fruit of life."

Hitler seemed eager to have a respite from Lev's relentless reminders of his past. So as Lev arose, Hitler did also and followed him through his house.

Lev took Hitler through all the rooms showing him features he had not dreamed of before. Lev showed him how the house was energy self-sufficient.

"This house will never need a drop of oil or gas. A hydro-oxy fuel cell provides all the energy you will ever need."

Then Lev took him out to what looked like a huge hothouse, but it was the enclosed Garden of Eden trees that would provide perfect food in endless supply. Lev explained that this is all the food anyone ever needs.

"Sick people get well quickly by eating this fruit and well people who eat this fruit will gradually gain human perfection."

It smelled like paradise with blooming trees and a generous array of flowers and vegetables. Everything was just beautiful. Lev said to him, "Isn't it wonderful to be alive again?"

Hitler muttered something under his breath that Lev could not quite hear. Lev knew Hitler had tried being an artist, so he did have an eye for beauty. Actually, he may have had a sensitive nature for he was not happy to hear of his vile actions. He could only wish that some magic wand could take away his past and leave him alone to enjoy the present without all the baggage of sin he was carrying.

When they strolled outside, Hitler saw the new Mercedes and was pleased to see it.

"Ah," he said, "That is good German engineering."

"No, not really. It is good Jewish engineering. This automobile runs on fuel cells that turn hydrogen into electricity. Hop in and I'll give you a drive about the community."

The car ran quietly since it was powered by an electric motor. As they drove around the community seemed to have a little nostalgia of the past. Finally, Hitler said, "This reminds me of my hometown of Braunau, Austria. It is beautiful country, but the place has a haunting resemblance to that town I knew as a child. Am I dreaming this or is this really that beautiful little town of my birth? I left at two years old but have revisited it many times. This is all so beautiful but I have never been so frustrated before. It is so peaceful yet I have no peace."

"You are indeed in Braunau. This is where you will live. I am glad you like it. It is very beautiful and peaceful. How could a young man who started out in such a lovely place become the angry Adolf Hitler?"

Lev decided he had been a little hard on Adolf, so he changed the subject temporarily to see if he would recognize any of the various features of this territory. Amazingly, Hitler was able to point out the scenery that he remembered from his visits there. This changed his demeanor. He wanted to forget his former political exploits, and turn for a moment to the stern days of his youth. Perhaps he was thinking how good it would have been if he had followed in his father's footsteps and had become a civil servant. How different things might be for him now. All the pomp and glory he had enjoyed had lasted only a moment, and now he was a defeated and broken man.

Where was the adoring crowd shouting, "Seig Heil!" This world's glory was so fleeting and how soon it all passed away. The pomp and pageantry he had enjoyed in the hour of his power did not equal the pain and distress he was facing now and had faced as his saw his dreams for the Third Reich go down in flames. If he only had known the outcome, perhaps it would have tempered his poisonous hatred. The price he was going to pay for his reckless and mean binge of destruction was far greater than the grand feeling of power he had had for a moment. What a poor paymaster the devil was. No one yet has ever had a happy experience in dealing with the devil.

After the Day in the Sun

After driving through the now lovely neighborhood, Lev thought he would try driving through the village of Braunau to an address at 15 Salzburger Vorstadt. They had transformed this apartment building where Hitler was born into a "House of Responsibility." The citizens of the area wanted to mark Hitler's birthplace so that they could tell the world this should never happen again. He was only two years old when he moved from there, so he did not remember it from his childhood. However, he had visited it several times in his lifetime and it brought back a flood of memories.

Perhaps he now wished he had not forgotten those precious moments when life was for living and loving. What had turned him into a monster that was driven by hatred to kill and destroy with such reckless abandon? Was there no inner voice to tell him that this was wrong? Was there no spark of human compassion that could stop this madness as he looked into the eyes of hopeless victims going to their death? Had the devil destroyed the last vestige of human kindness in his heart? How could he be convinced and have convinced so many others into thinking that by killing Jews and Gypsies that all the evil of this world could be corrected? How could so many brilliant and educated people be so deceived for so long? Could he have stopped the ascent of the Star of David that was backed by God's irresistible power? Could he have annulled the Bible prophecies that forecast of

Israel, "Though I make an end of all nations whither I have scattered thee, yet will I not make a full end of thee" (Jeremiah 30:11)?

Hitler was very quiet on the drive back home. Lev could see he was a frustrated man. Having been at the height of power, with the powers of life and death in his hands, he had developed a twisted personality. It is one thing to have people under your thumb, and it is quite another to have people who really love you and care for you as a person. When Herod the Great died, the one who ordered all male children under two put to death in the hope of destroying Jesus, he told his trusted general to kill all of the officers under him when he died so there would be genuine sorrow at his passing. Unfortunately, the sorrow and mourning that took place was not for him.

They returned home to enjoy their usual delicious meal of fruit and topped it off with his resurrection cake. Hitler spoke to the fact of how good he felt. He said, "I do not remember ever feeling as well as now. I had a lot of problems with eating before for some years and this present diet of fruit pleases me to no end. I cannot get over how fulfilling this food is and how stimulated my mind feels.

Lev explained that the Ancients had returned with seeds from the Garden of Eden. This was the food, which if Adam and Eve had continued to eat they could have lived forever. However, because of sin they were driven from the Garden of Eden and an angel with a "flaming sword" had kept anyone from entering that garden. Seeds had been preserved and now have been planted worldwide.

Lev said, "Those who return to life, such as you and I, will find the mind increases dramatically over the months as they eat of this vitality renewing fruit. Those old and infirm that eat this fruit have their infirmities removed and they start to return to the vitality of youth."

Hitler said, "It sounds like a fairy tale, but I cannot deny how good it makes you feel. You know, I was a very sick man in my last years. My doctors could do nothing for me. So you cannot imagine how exciting it is to feel so good — without an ache or pain. Tell me, if you will, what happened since I left this world in 1945?"

A Lesson in Germany's History

This is what Lev had been waiting for. Here was an inquiry not given as a command or even as a demand. Hitler really wanted to know what transpired since his last day of life. Lev said, "If you are sincere in that question, I will tell you."

"Of course, I really wish to know. If you claim to have come back to life like me you must know how frustrating it is to find a big hole in your life, during that time when you were dead. Even though it feels good to be alive, there is a feeling of frustration at the huge gap there is in your life. You cannot lose nearly a century without experiencing frustration when you come back. You must know what a struggle this is for me."

Lev said, "I do indeed know. I felt exactly as you now feel. It will take you about a week to adjust to the fact that you are alive, that this is not a dream from which you will awaken and find yourself in that awful bunker again. You are indeed alive again. You would have very happy prospects of perfect health and life if you did not have an albatross of evil deeds tied around your neck. At any rate let me tell you what happened after the war.

"Germany surrendered unconditionally after your death. The Russians stole all the machinery in your factories; they just took truck after truckloads of machinery, picking your factories bare. Your cities were in ruin and starvation was rampant throughout Europe. The United States sent food provisions to Europe as fast as they could, but there was no way hunger could be averted in Germany as well as in all of Europe. This meant that Germans suffered greatly. All of this was unnecessary suffering, for everyone knew you had lost the war two years earlier. If you had surrendered then you would have ended the carnage of war and the bombing of your cities and factories. It must have been more important to the devil to continue killing the Jews than to save Germany from the pain they were experiencing.

"At any rate, food finally did arrive in Germany. The United States initiated the Marshall Plan by which huge sums of money and food supplies were provided to get Germany and all of Western Europe back on their feet. Soon Germany and Western Europe became prosperous again. Only East Germany, which had been taken by the Russians, remained backward. Then in 1989 the iron curtain around Russia was broken and the wall of partition was broken down. East Germany was brought back into the German nation. This required enormous sacrifices on the part of West Germany to spend billions of marks for the reconstruction of this dreary bit of real estate. However, this was done. Soon Germany led all of Europe into an alliance, creating a common currency and finally an agreement for all the nations in this union into a socialist form of government.

"To make it short I must tell you that after World War II, in 1948, the nation of Israel was born. After several wars it continued to grow, becoming a leader in world technology. Finally, the nations encouraged by the Christian communities, made what you would call, Adolf, the final solution of the Jewish nation. A great and overwhelming army came against the Jewish state to take Jerusalem away from them, and God only knows what they would have done if they had been victorious. I was in the leading edge of Israel's defense. I was killed the first day of that battle. The invaders killed many people and many were taken captive in Jerusalem. The next day God intervened. They said you could feel death in the air. The forces gathered against Jerusalem were all miraculously killed that day. Millions of dead soldiers were strewn over the land of Israel. The nations who had sent their forces against Israel were invited to come down and look at the carnage. When they returned home and the people learned that God had destroyed all their forces, they dragged their civil and religious leaders, who had sanctioned this effort, through the streets. Following this, general anarchy broke out and the nations in their former types of governments fell."

The New Rulers of Earth

"Following this, the Ancients returned to life in Israel, bringing with them seeds from the Garden in Eden. Israel received their Messiah and then became the sole surviving nation of earth to remain intact. Since that time Israel was the first nation to receive their dead back to life again. They are several years ahead of most other nations in this process. People from the twentieth century are now coming back to life. The Ancients asked me if I would volunteer to build a home for you, Adolf. I really did not want to do this, I must tell you. You were the last person on earth I wanted to work for in building a home and making all the preparations necessary for your return to life. However, finally they convinced me that I could deal with you better than most people because I have had a series of successes in dealing with people who were reticent to accept the leadership of Israel. Because our technology is so far ahead of the other nations, in the end they could not refuse it. At any rate, I had the task of being your mentor in your return. That is a very quick review, Adolf. Does that help you at all?"

"Yes, thank you, it does. I find it difficult to believe everything you have told me, but at least that is a better understanding than I had before. I was completely at sea and hopelessly confused. Even if what you have related to me is only half true, at least I have a vague idea of the gap in my life. Did I hear you correctly say you built this home for me?"

"Yes, that is correct," I said. "You have received this house without any work on your part. However, you will be expected to build similar homes for both your parents. And if you have a shred of good will in your heart, you may also help build homes for others as well."

Hitler Dismisses Building for His Parents

Hitler mused over that a while, finally saying, "I am not used to manual labor, but perhaps I can engage some help to do this. I must confess I have reserves of money and gold in the banks of Switzerland. I can easily have these homes built for them. I would not leave my parents without provision for them."

"I must tell you, Adolf, there are no banks in Switzerland or anywhere in the world. Neither does the world run on money of any kind. If you are not willing to work for your parents, other people will have the privilege of doing that."

"That would be good of them; I should certainly appreciate that kind of generosity."

This was a sore disappointment to Lev. Hitler seemed unable to make any sacrifice on behalf of anyone. Here he had received a new self-sufficient home built by a Jew, after having pillaged the homes of Jews, after having stolen their homes and property as well as their lives, yet he was without any sense of indebtedness or willingness to return the favor given him. He was refusing to help build his parents' home and would be less likely to lift a finger for a Jew. Lev could see he needed an attitude adjustment.

When night arrived, Lev showed him the marvels of television in conjunction with all of the educational programs. Entertainment in the old sense, where people sat stupefied for hours being entertained with trashy programs, was not to be found anymore. All programming had to have some redeeming value. Most information came in the form of educational programs where one could learn everything one chose to. Hitler had to admit, after watching the first program on modern history for about an hour, how much one could learn in that type of program. Lev chose this type of program because he knew he was interested in history. Then Lev showed him scenes from the battle against Jerusalem that he had told him about. Hitler was astounded to see carnage of that battle. He had never seen total annihilation, with millions of corpses scattered over the land, with wrecked tanks, weapons of war and planes falling out of the sky.

This reinforced everything that Lev had told him. Lev could see that this distressed him greatly. He still held hatred toward the Jews, and for him to realize that God miraculously destroyed the invading army, made him realize how out of harmony he was with this present arrangement. He was amazed with the technology of programmed television where you could select any kind of information you wish. The color and detail was so much more superior to the old movies he had seen. The fidelity of the sound was just astonishing to him. Lev played some Beethoven for him much to his delight.

Finally he said, "Do you mean that this house and property is all mine?"

"Yes, that is true. I built this house for you with a few people assisting me from time to time. Other people planted the garden of paradise for you."

He then said, "Do I understand this house needs no outside energy?"

"That is correct. The Jewish people have made it possible to efficiently turn water into hydrogen and oxygen. We then use fuel cells to turn hydrogen into electricity or we burn hydrogen for heating purposes in the winter. Therefore, each house today is totally self-sufficient. There is no need for generating plants for electricity or any electric poles marring the beauty of earth. Do you see any electric poles anywhere today?"

"No, now that you mention it. And the trees bear fruit in succession all twelve months of the year?"

"Yes, indeed. You will not see trucks and trains rushing over the earth delivering food, coal, oil or gasoline anymore. Everyone has his own food supply, and it is life-sustaining food. All other things that are needed are made in local factories. Everybody must work a little bit; usually three hours a day in various factories is enough to keep everyone supplied. Because there is a steady return of people to life, it requires a lot of extra work to make provisions for all returning."

Work Seems Demeaning

He inquired, "You mean I will be required to work for three hours a day?"

"No, all work is voluntary. If anyone chooses not to help, he is free to spend his time however he wishes. Usually, though, people are glad to join in the work that is being done. It is a great learning experience to see all the automated factories. They need skilled and intelligent people to maintain and direct these operations. However, anyone may learn to do any task usually in a week or two of courses offered on television. This is really the first true brain age. People eating the fruit of life increase their learning power exponentially month by month. Soon anybody will be able to do what only a few professionals could do before. Knowledge and information are pouring in as never before. Now, though, with an hour or two devoted to study everyday, one can keep up with all the changes.

"There are still some people spending long hours in creating breakthroughs in technology. However, once we develop the critical advances that we need to have a tight control on all the requirements for bringing back the whole human race to life, everything will ease off. Leisure to learn will be the richest experience for all mankind. The days when men and women worked from dawn to dark to feed and to clothe themselves are all past. Now men and women may spend their time reaching their full mental capabilities. We do not have sick or infirm people to care for, and only a limited number of children to provide care for. Our world now is about twenty times more efficient than it was before. None of our resources are wasted on war, policing, jails, gambling or drunkenness. Everyone builds and plants—nobody tears down or destroys the work of other people. No energy is wasted."

Finally, Lev said, "Would you like to retire for the night? You have had a full day, and, I think, quite frustrating as well. Tomorrow should be better for you and each day thereafter. You will cease thinking that this is all a dream and that you will wake up in the awful bunker where you were trapped. You know God has no pleasure in the death of him that dies. He invites all to chose life and live. However, this is a world where love reigns. Those who cannot learn to love will not last through this century."

Hitler decided that he should turn in. Without saying a word he headed to his bedroom. He did not thank Lev for any of his efforts during the day. Lev knew he was a moody person, and dismissed his rudeness, but he certainly hoped he would learn to be more civil. When he was the ruling dictator, he could do no wrong. He was surrounded with "yes" men all the time. He could scream at them, abuse them, dismiss them or have them executed. He had had the power to be cruel and no one could reprove him. He chaffed under Lev's refusal to be browbeaten or intimidated by his outbursts.

Lev retired to his room exhausted from having to deal with him that day. He had brought along a diary to record all the events of the day. Lev had a good memory now, and little would escape him, but he thought a diary would help establish every detail of the events that transpired. So before Lev turned to his Bible studies that night, he wrote a short record of his first day's experiences with Hitler.

The next morning Lev awakened at the usual hour and Hitler was
still sleeping. Lev tended to his morning rituals for everyday living,
and then picked fruit for the day. He also had made fresh juice for the
morning. Lev then left a note that he had gone to the chapel services
and would be back within an hour or so. Hitler could have his own
breakfast if he chose to.

Hitler Left Alone

Lev drove to the chapel, not wishing to leave the car there for
fear Hitler would drive off. It was a joy to meet normal people again.
Few people can handle absolute power, because as they say, "Power
corrupts, and absolute power corrupts absolutely." What seemed to
him as the greatest achievement in his former life—obtaining supreme
power, was in fact, the most damaging experience to his possibilities
of attaining eternal life?

The services were very refreshing to Lev, almost a tonic to his
heart. Lev sang earnestly the hymns of the morning and enjoyed the
study in God's Word. Everyone was very friendly, and it was a joy to
deal with loving, sensitive people. While they were a long way off
from perfection, still they were earnestly striving to reach that goal.
When one sees someone with painstaking effort trying to overcome
human weakness and attain to the fullness of the love of God, it was so
encouraging. No one, of course, knew Lev's purpose here. He was just
engaged in a run of the mill activity. He only wished it was. He knew
he was facing a very challenging personality to deal with. Lev really
prayed for wisdom to know how to proceed.

Lev returned home to find Hitler was up and eagerly having his
breakfast. Lev greeted him with a warm good morning, only to have
him grunt something that Lev could not make out. He apparently was
in one of his dark moods, so Lev just let him be. He could be civil
when he wanted to be and that was usually when he wanted some
information. Lev thought that Hitler did not ask him to leave because
he found himself dependent on Lev and fearful of being identified
as Adolf Hitler. He apparently took seriously that millions of people
would gladly die for the privilege of slowly strangling him. He still did
not know that he was protected from such an experience by spiritual
forces and Lev was not going to tell him this yet.

Hitler Inquires About Eva

When his tone of voice sweetened Lev knew he was going to seek
more information. Finally, he said, "Lev, when is Eva Braun returning
to life?"

"Why do you want to know?" Lev asked. "What makes you think she would want to associate with you now?"

That statement upset him and his face darkened.

"Eva loved me! She did, and I think she always will! I need at least one person who loves me in this world. I gave myself to the Germans and what are my thanks? I have a Jew prepare for my return to life. Where are all those people who worshiped me and chanted my name in ecstasy? Ungrateful swine, that's what they are."

Lev had dropped Eva's name earlier precisely to see if it would awaken his curiosity. It certainly did. The heart always returns to those places touched by love.

"What about Geli, aren't you interested in her?" Lev asked.

Lev knew she had been the love of his life, and he wanted to see how Hitler would respond to her name.

He said, "You only mentioned Eva to me earlier. Why didn't you mention Geli before? Tell me if Geli is alive. You seem to know everything. I need to know if Geli is alive."

Lev purposely paused for a long time before answering him. This annoyed Hitler greatly. He was used to demanding answers and getting them immediately. Was he not the great Adolf Hitler? Lev was determined not to let him think he was in charge for one minute.

Lev finally said, "You know, Adolf, there is no obligation on my part to provide you with that information. I have no knowledge as to your intentions toward either Eva or Geli. You seemed responsible for both of their deaths. Why would I provide information to you about people you hurt before?"

Hitler turned red, and seemed about to explode. Finally, in a burst of profanity, he rose up and walked out the door.

As he left, Lev reminded him, "Don't let anybody see you, because someone is liable to recognize you and a riot will occur."

Lev watched through the window to see where he would go, and sure enough, he stormed over the property of his home. Obviously, he was controlled by fear, and he was truly afraid that someone would recognize him. Lev noticed that morning that he shaved his upper lip so as to keep his mustache from growing back. There was nothing for Lev to do but to wait for his return. Lev had been through this with him yesterday. He tried to browbeat Lev into submission again today. He lost this round as well.

About twenty minutes later Hitler returned. He had left his breakfast dishes on the table. When he returned, Lev told him to clean up his mess, because he was not about to do that for him today. Hitler was outraged again about having to be asked to do, what to him, was demeaning work. Lev could see he was going to be a handful today. So Lev went off to his studies in the Bible, and left Hitler stewing in the kitchen.

Lev left his door open. Soon Lev heard him rattling some of the dishes. Hitler realized his endeavors to be boss were not going to work today even as they did not work yesterday. He was learning, but very slowly. He really liked things neat, but he felt like he was being treated as a servant. It did not take much to get him in a mean mood.

Pruning Trees a New Experience

After a few hours, Lev noticed him pacing up and down the living room seemingly muttering under his breath. Lev entered the room as cheerfully as he could and asked if Hitler would like to learn how to trim the trees in his orchard. He was dumbfounded at the thought, but this time he got control of himself and agreed to see how it was done. The orchard was such a beautiful and peaceful place with the smell of blossoms in the air. With a pair of pruning shears Lev showed him what branches might turn into suckers and needed to be cut away. Hitler had an eye for detail and learned the lesson very quickly.

Lev gave the shears to him and let him attend to another tree. He actually enjoyed this work; even though he still felt it demeaning to have to do such manual labor, at least while anyone was watching. Lev told him to then pick up the clippings and they would strip off the leaves and dry them to make tea. That nettled him, but he decided to do as he was told, because he really wanted to know about Geli and Eva.

At lunchtime they sat down to eat. Lev bowed his head in prayer. He did not wait for Lev to finish praying but started eating. Lev could hear him munching on the fruit. This food pleased him immensely because not only was it absolutely delicious but so very fulfilling. You did not have to stuff yourself, but one or two pieces of fruit constituted a complete meal. They still had some resurrection cake, and he showed great interest in that. Never did he ask who was so kind as to bake a cake for his return. As they ate, Lev knew he was dying to know about Geli and Eva. Lev did not say a word about them until finally, in a very pleasant voice, Hitler asked, "Lev, could you please satisfy my deep desire to know about these two women?"

"Yes, I can do that," Lev answered. "You must learn that you are now just a little fish in a big pond. You have no influence, no power, and no nothing. You are nobody. Even worse than that, you have a terrible history of meanness and evil. You must learn that you must always be civil and then maybe I will be glad to provide you with the information you seek."

Hitler did not like Lev's lecturing him, but gritting his teeth he endured it today, because he knew he had to in order to secure the information he desperately wanted.

After he finished eating, Lev noticed he even cleaned up after his meal, cleaning the table and dishes. He even took Lev's plate and washed it. Finally, Lev said, "Adolf, both Eva and Geli are alive. Should I invite both of them to your home together?" Lev knew he did not want Eva to meet Geli, but Lev just played along asking an innocent question.

"No, no, no," he said. "I do not want to meet them together."

"Whom do you wish to meet first?"

"I want to meet Geli first. I must meet Geli," he said.

"Well, I can call her today, and see if she is willing to see you today or tomorrow. She probably is back from her voluntary working hours. Shall I call her or do you want to call her?"

"Will you call her please, but do not tell her about me, not yet. I should like to surprise her," he exclaimed.

"Very well," Lev said. Picking up the phone, Lev called her number that he had memorized. He heard a sweet voice answer the phone, saying, "Good afternoon, this is Geli."

"I am very pleased to hear your voice. You do not know me, but my name is Lev. I have some very important matters to talk to you about, but I must do so in private. These are matters of great interest to you. If you are free today or tomorrow, I have an automobile and could be at your home in about a half hour."

"Why, yes, of course, my afternoon is free, so why don't you come over. I hope it is good news you will be bringing. Do you know where I live?"

"Yes, I have your address and know that area, so I will be there in a short while. I will be looking forward to meeting you. Thank you for making yourself available on such short notice."

Hitler stood by taking in every word that he could. He seemed aglow at the prospect of meeting Geli, the love of his life. They got into the car and drove to her home. The scenery was all so lovely. This was beautiful country. Adolf was very pensive. Lev could tell he was in deep thought. He knew it was because he had deprived her of freedom that she had committed suicide and that bothered him greatly. Oddly, the millions of people he deliberately killed did not weigh on his mind. They were just statistics, all nameless and faceless, just creatures that needed to be disposed of because they seemingly stood in the way of the grand designs for the Third Reich. Well did Jeremiah say, "The heart is deceitful above all things, and desperately wicked: who can know it?" (Jeremiah 17:9).

"For God shall bring every work into judgment,
With every secret thing"
(Ecclesiastes 12:14).

Chapter Thirty-Four

They arrived at the address, and they both proceeded up the sidewalk to Geli's home. It was very beautiful and in a lovely setting. Lev rang the bell and soon Geli appeared with a bright smile. She was a very gregarious person. Lev introduced himself and then asked if she recognized the person with him. She studied his face for a moment and then said, "Yes, of course. I did not recognize you without your mustache. You must have come to remind me of my folly in taking my life."

"No, no, my dear. The blame for what happened rests upon me and I have never forgiven myself. Your death left a void in my life that has troubled me continuously."

Geli then said, "I was very young and foolish at the time. I should have been more forthright with you, and told you I did not love you. I foolishly flirted with a lot of men and at first I was flattered to have the attention of a budding politician. Since I have returned and learned what a tyrant you turned out to be I could never have been a partner to such evil."

Poor Adolf, those words caused him to whither. He surely thought she would fall into his arms and they would renew the old relationship as though nothing had happened. He looked like he was going to cry. He gained his composure quickly and said, "Geli, you are still angry with me, but give me a chance to make it all up to you. At the moment, I am newly returned to life, and just trying to find my way. Soon, however, I shall come to prominence again. Meanwhile, let me just be an old friend."

"I could never return to my flirtatious days. I am more mature now and I chose more carefully the company I keep. How could I enjoy keeping company with such a notorious murderer of our time? You had to be insane or sold yourself to the devil, or both. When I learned that millions of people died in your failed effort to create a glorious Third Reich, I was glad that I died before anyone could have associated me with you in that unparalleled evil. No, Adolf, I did not love you then, and certainly any vestige of sympathy for you in your crimes is all gone. I am sorry to be so brutally frank, but you have no special place in my heart. I wish you well, and I hope you have the courage to live down your crimes against humanity."

He stood there stunned, thinking, "Say it isn't so."

Meanwhile, Geli turned to Lev. She asked, "Are you Lev Aron, the man our people are so fond of? You have been a true friend to our people here. You have served us tirelessly and have been such a noble example to us all. Thank you. How did you happen to be associated with Adolf? You come from different worlds—one of light and the other of darkness."

Geli Turns Hitler Away

Hitler could not believe that Geli, the love of his heart looked upon him as a murderer from the kingdom of darkness. He was crushed. How could life change from one extreme to the other? He had been the darling of the German people, and now he was among the world's greatest murderers. Men died gladly in support of Hitler and now nobody wanted to be seen with him, and even worse many would like to strangle him.

He turned away devastated, saying, "Geli, how can you be so cruel to me, I always loved you!"

This brought tears to her eyes. She said, "Adolf, it pains me to hurt you, and grieves me that I cannot return love to you. I must be truthful to myself and to you. I loathe all the evil that you are responsible for. I do not loathe you personally, but I realize that you were in a sense victim of the corrupting influence of power. It takes a man of great stature to handle power in a proper way. From what I can see you used power in a self-serving way. Your friends now loathe you, as do your enemies. Somewhere out there may be some secret sympathizers with your evil deeds, but they are sick people who are misfits in a world of righteousness."

Geli's words were very sincere and she refused to coddle him with sympathy. The sooner he accepted responsibility for his evil deeds the sooner healing could start. As long as he minimized his systematic murder of innocent people, he was only hardening his heart. Confession of sin is the first requirement of repentance. As long as sin is not admitted, it will be rationalized, justified and dismissed. So far he seemed to demonstrate no willingness to admit culpability of any kind.

Hitler Reacts to Rejection

Suddenly Hitler's face filled with anger. He just turned away and went to the car and slammed the door shut upon entering. He did not like her sermonizing and speaking down to him as though he were some monster. His dream of Geli embracing him and smothering him with affection was dashed to pieces. He still had not shown a shred of remorse for the carnage he was responsible for. He was giving evidence of a person with a seared conscience that is very difficult to heal.

Geli said to Lev before he turned away, "I suppose he wanted to surprise me, and, in fact, I was surprised to see him again. Forgive me for being so brutally frank, but when I learned what kind of a man he turned out to be since I have returned to life, I feel I was blessed in ending my life, and not being pulled into his evil world. Had I lived in any relationship with him he would have surely tainted my heart with his mad hatred of people. I fear riches and power may have caused me to close my eyes to his unspeakable madness that is now a part of history. It pleases me that I was spared such unsavory association. One cannot keep company with evil agents without suffering some contamination. I don't know how you are able to try to be a mentor to him. He seems to be a direct opposite of you in every way."

Lev smiled, and said, "Geli, you are very kind to me. I admire your courage. Coming from you, it may bear some fruit down the road. He was taken back by your strong denunciation of what he did and will be unfit to drive home with. He is in the car filled with anger and I can see him brooding from here. Please understand that Hitler was possessed by the devil and, in fact, he served the devil very well indeed. Now the devil is in the abyss but evil influences still are lodged in his heart. Only Christ can heal that condition, but I don't know if he is willing to be purged from his sins. Thank you for the privilege of getting to know you, and Shalom."

Lev returned to the car and waved to Geli before they drove away. She stood there waving bravely, and Lev found her wishing to close an unhappy chapter of her life. He knew Adolf was in an ugly mood. His almost pleasant demeanor as they drove to meet Geli was now suddenly turned to ice. What made the matter worse was the fact that she had complimented him while she renounced his evil deeds. He sat silently brooding all the way home. Lev did not know what his next plan of action was, but there seemed little evidence that he accepted an acknowledgment of his guilt.

As they arrived home he stormed out of the car and slammed the door as he left. He did not come out of his room for most of the afternoon, but remained there brooding. Lev decided to leave him be with his thoughts. Maybe something she said would sink in. Hitler would remember his words to Geli forever—"I always loved you." His long and secret love for Geli had been totally rejected. He had dreamed that had he not tried to control her she might have lived and loved him in return. Today that dream was shattered and Lev felt his pain. It is not new that love has not always been a two-way street. Countless millions loved and did not have love returned. This has been pain shared by both men and women. Some love has had to be hidden, for it never had a chance to flourish.

Lev spent the afternoon studying both holy and technical matters. At the supper hour Hitler came out of his room, his anger abated, but still unusually quiet. He seemed eager to eat but kept his feelings to himself. He did enjoy the Eden fruit and some other vegetables that Lev had made to embellish their supper meal. Lev had also made several juices that he relished and they ate the last piece of his resurrection cake. This seemed to revive his spirit.

Soon he broke his silence and he began to inquire about Eva Braun. He asked, "Do you think you could arrange for me to meet her?"

Eva Now Sought

"Do you wish the meeting to be a surprise or would you rather call her and make arrangements to meet her when it is convenient?"

Hitler's surprise visit to Geli had been a disaster, so this is why he suggested they call her first. After supper Lev picked up the phone and called Rebekah. He wanted to call her anyway. It was always such a joy to talk to her. Lev spoke Hebrew so no one but Rebekah and he knew what their conversation was about. Lev learned that Eva was not nearly the problem to deal with as was Hitler, but she had not had a really happy life. She was a little cast down and she was somewhat troubled by her complicity in the evils of the Third Reich. After a brief exchange, Lev asked Rebekah to put Eva on the phone. When she answered, Lev said, "I have a surprise for you. Hang on and I will put someone on the phone you have not heard from for a while."

Lev motioned to Hitler to take the phone. Lev whispered, "She does not know it is you."

Hitler spoke, saying, "Eva, my darling, it is I. Do you remember me?" She immediately recognized his voice.

"Oh, Adolf, it is you. How good to hear from you. Are you all right? I think about you so often. I still remember those last hours together. The world was so dark and gloomy. I awakened to a bright and beautiful world. It is like a dream."

"Yes, yes," Adolf said. "Can we arrange a meeting my dear when it is convenient for you?"

"Of course, my dear Adolf. Let me ask Rebekah who has been helping me adjust to all these new arrangements when it would be convenient for her to receive visitors." After a brief interruption she returned, saying, "Tomorrow or the following day would be fine in the afternoon."

Turning to Lev, he asked, "Would tomorrow afternoon be possible for you to take me to Eva?"

"Yes, certainly, I would happy to take you there," Lev said. Of course, Hitler didn't know the source of Lev's joy would be to meet Rebekah.

"Good," he said, "Tomorrow we shall be there in the afternoon." They conversed for a bit and then said their farewells before hanging up.

Lev saw his mood change immediately. He had something to look forward to tomorrow and here was a person who would not rebuff him or put him down. He really longed for his old world where he was enthroned and everyone yielded to his sovereignty. The taste of power was so sweet to him. It didn't matter whether people loved him; he liked mostly being in control of other people. He was a bundle of contradictions, and very difficult to fully understand. He had a soft side as most people do, but could lock out compassion with unbelievable ease. Nothing that stood in his way or his goals could be tolerated. He had been so unbelievably successful while practicing his vices that virtue seemed to have little appeal. He got to the top of the world without virtue, but then that is true also of the devil.

Lev thought he might be interested in some educational programs. He seemed mostly interested in modern history and current affairs. He was quite impressed with the teachers on television, who were mostly the Ancients. Fortunately, the programs could be translated into any language. He realized their superior knowledge and their great gift as teachers. No matter what the subject, they made it incredibly interesting. He was amazed at what transpired after Germany surrendered.

He was heartened to see it rebuilt from the ruins of the war. However, his joy ended when they saw some additional scenes of the siege of Jerusalem defended this time by God. When he saw the great number of people, who died and the chaos among the nations that followed God's destruction of the invading forces he became very uncomfortable. Quickly, he decided he needed to retire for the night.

Geli's Meeting Recorded in Lev's Diary

Lev continued his studies for a while and decided also to turn in for the night. Lev addressed his diary again. He wanted to record Adolf's meeting with Geli. Fortunately, Lev remembered every word spoken between her and Hitler. He double-checked it to make sure it was accurate. Only then did Lev go to sleep. Lev loved character studies and Hitler had a most unusual personality. At times he could be sensitive and human, but he could change in an instant and turn into a brooding time bomb.

Lev awakened the usual time the next day. After attending to his personal care in the morning, Lev strolled out into the garden to collect fruit for the day. He gathered some supper vegetables and fruit for juices as well. Some figs were ready to eat and Lev collected this into a splendid array of food. He prepared the juice and had a little before he hurried off to the chapel.

Lev knew Adolf was up, but he stayed in his room until after Lev had left. He liked being master of his estate while Lev was away. He still needed Lev, so he did not ask him to leave yet. Lev's Jewishness did not seem to bother him. If only the officers of the Third Reich could see him with his Jewish butler or chauffeur or whatever Lev was.

Lev came to the chapel to get a breath of fresh air. It was so wonderful to hear people praising God and thanking him for their blessings. It was beautiful to see people who loved other people and who were not using them to get where they wanted to go.

Lev returned later than usual from the chapel meeting because he had the time to get in a little extra fellowship. There were so many new ones who had returned to life and it was beautiful to see them eager to live and love and be happy. The darkness of the past while still remembered was quickly replaced with joy and love.

When Lev arrived home, to his surprise, Hitler was nowhere to be found. Lev figured he must have gotten his courage up to take a long walk. Lev figured he would not be gregarious, and would not stop to talk to people he might see. He really seemed to enjoy the fact that people did not recognize him as the notorious Adolf Hitler. He suspected the day would come when his identity would be known, but until then he would enjoy being anonymous.

About noontime he came walking briskly in. Lev could see he was looking forward to meeting Eva and was hoping she would be happier to see him than Geli was. He was very agreeable and even tried to be helpful pouring juice and setting the table for the simple but delicious meal. He relished the fruit and the new way of eating. He remarked that he used to suffer from indigestion occasionally no matter how carefully he selected his food. Now, he could not believe how peaceful his stomach was.

Lev remarked, "Well, Adolf, are you thankful for what God has done for you? Perhaps you should come to worship with me on the morrow?"

Lev thought Hitler was sorry he had expressed his wellness. He was not exactly ready to praise God for his blessings yet. After they had lunch, he helped clean up the table and acted like a regular person for a change. Lev told him as soon as he was ready they would be off to see Eva. He went to his room to groom himself with a little extra care and appeared ready to go.

They drove off through the beautiful countryside. Adolf did have an eye for natural beauty. As a matter of fact, he asked if he might secure some painting brushes and supplies.

Lev said, "Yes, there is a place not too far from here where we can get you everything you need to practice your artwork. Perhaps tomorrow we will drive there. You will enjoy the countryside even more as we pass some mountains along the way."

He was delighted at the thought of getting back to his art. That is what he really wanted to be. How much richer a life he would have enjoyed had he been able to live as an artist. Hitler wondered if he would have avoided the stigma of history if his life had remained in art.

If environment alone was responsible for his crimes against humanity, then a good and holy environment will undo the warp created by an unfavorable one. Is it not written, "Every man's work shall be made manifest: for the day shall declare it, because it shall be revealed by fire; and the fire shall try every man's work of what sort it is" (1 Corinthians 3:13). Lev began to appreciate that God's ways are equal. Environment alone will never determine anyone's eternal destiny. All evil precipitated by environment may be repaired by wholesome conditions if there is first a willing mind and heart.

Hitler Meets Eva

They arrived at Eva Braun's residence that afternoon. It was quite similar to Hitler's home with some different designs that made them look dissimilar on the outside. However, Rebekah's feminine touch had turned it into a warm and beautiful home. Rebekah met them at the door. Hitler was on his best behavior today. He had actually picked a beautiful bouquet of flowers to give to Eva. They were invited into the living room, where they were seated waiting for Eva to emerge from her room.

When she emerged, she seemed happy to meet Hitler. He rose and greeted her with a kiss and hug, saying, "My dear Eva, it is wonderful to see your beautiful face." Her face was radiant as was Hitler's. He seemed happier at this moment than at any other time. He could be very civil and actually warm at moments. That was good to see, because buried within him was a decent person trying to surface.

Lev suggested that Rebekah and he take a walk and leave Eva and Adolf alone to renew their relationship. She agreed.

Lev was eager to be alone with Rebekah. They had not told them that they were formerly husband and wife. Lev wanted to know how she had faired in dealing with Eva. As they left Eva and Adolf were holding hands and they obviously were glad to be alone with each other.

Rebekah said, "Eva hasn't been too much of a problem. She lives in a little world. Her life revolved around Adolf. Because he had such a stormy disposition, she had to endure his up and down moods, but he always managed to treat her reasonably well. As the German hopes began to sink, he actually was drawn closer to her. She shared his nightmare and tried to comfort him. I learned that he encouraged her to leave to save her life. She chose to stay with him to the bitter end. Eva told me that 'as they were together in life, she wanted to be together with him in death.'

"I tried to get her to enlarge her world beyond just one man whose evil deeds will surely haunt him day and night. Staying with Adolf is not an option, I reminded her, and even if it was, it would mean she, too, would have to live down his odious past. Eva had, and still has, the ability to close out reality. The millions murdered by Hitler's lust for Jewish blood didn't seem real to her. She just blocked it out of her mind. It was that simple. How could she block out the millions of men, women and children sent to the gas chambers, I asked her?

"She answered, 'I had heard these whispers, but I felt Adolf divorced himself from the ugly part of carrying this out. He had subordinates who eagerly carried out the unending genocide. Hitler orcestrated all of this, but always kept his hands personally unspotted with blood. He did all this with white gloves on, as it were.'

"She continued, 'As a matter of fact, on one occasion in the early days when Jews were machine-gunned down while falling into big pits, he was shown how this was carried out. He was visibly shaken and almost lost his lunch watching this. He returned home and told me this type of killing must stop. He thought it dehumanizing for the soldiers to do things that way. He then consorted with the scientific community of Germany to find a way to do this without blood and body bits flying in the air. Soon they gladly provided him with poison gas chambers and gas incinerators as a less sanguine way to carry out the same program of genocide with companies bidding to make the poison gas.'

"I tried to reason with her, saying, 'Eva, did you ever plead with him to stop this madness?'

"She said, 'It would not have changed his mind. This whole genocide scheme was a part of the whole Nazi package to purify the Aryan race. It was all orchestrated on a higher plane than any one man. It was as though Satan himself authored this deadly scheme but it was locked as a stranglehold on the minds of the whole German leadership. This was like some sacred calling of the Nazi party and not even Hitler could have changed it.'

"Eva said that she knew this whole genocide scheme was wrong and mad, but that she loved Adolf and he needed her, especially at the end, his trusted officers were all taking off their uniforms and trying to act as plain ordinary citizens. They did not want to take the blame for evil deeds of the Third Reich. It was a sinking ship and it was every man for himself. Hitler felt betrayed and deserted. He could not believe his glorious German army had been broken and defeated. He imagined that they would appear out of thin air to drive the Russians far away. His gloom increased as the Russian's closed in on the bunker. He had nightmares of the Russians dragging him through the streets. He was determined not to let them have that pleasure. He provided her with a cyanide pill to take once he knew it was too late for them to escape. He did not want her being dragged through the streets with his corpse.

"She knew there was no escape. She had decided to share his fate early on, and she wanted it to end like Romeo and Juliet. The last day, when the Russians were shelling that neighborhood, the hour had come and Hitler was very solicitous. He offered her some water to take with the pill. He kissed her tenderly and embraced her. They were to take the cyanide pills and then instantly be shot in the head but she just took the poison. He had given his last order to have their bodies burned. They said they did not have enough fuel to do the job thoroughly."

The Reaction to Being Alive Again

Lev asked, "What was her reaction at being alive again? I know what a shock it is to be alive again in strange surroundings."

"I was unsure as to what she might do, so I did as you suggested. I did not leave clothes for her for fear she might leave through the window. I heard faint sounds as she moved about in her room, but finally she opened the door wrapped in a towel. That is when I greeted her and gave her clothing. She seemed pleased to see I was not some kind of army officer. When she finally appeared all dressed she seemed frightened and very insecure. I tried to allay her fears and assured her that she was in friendly territory and that all danger was passed. That calmed her down, because I knew she was terrified at being apprehended. Even though her surroundings were peaceful, her mind awakened with the same turmoil it was in when she died.

"It took awhile for her to trust me. She believed I was some kind of agent posted here to make sure she did not escape. She soon found the doors were never locked and obviously this was not some kind of pleasant prison. Little by little she confided in me. When she learned I was Jewish she could not believe that I had helped build this dwelling for her and that I was here to help her to make the transition from her former life to the present conditions."

She then asked about Adolf. "Did he go to see his first love, Geli?"

"Yes indeed. I gave him a choice as to which he might wish to see first. At first I asked him if he wanted to see both of them together just to see what his reaction would be. This startled him and he immediately made it clear that he wanted to see them separately and that he wanted to see Geli first. He was really excited about seeing her. He seemed to have no conscience about the millions of people who died at his orders, but he took Geli's death deeply to heart. He was terribly disappointed when she told him she never loved him and now when she knew how many people he had murdered she was glad she killed herself, so that none of that guilt was on her hands. He was absolutely devastated by her very frank abhorrence of his actions. He was almost in tears when he said, 'I always loved you.'

"It would have been wonderful if he had saved a little love for mankind. It is a mystery how his affections could be so narrow and limited. It was a self-serving love centered in his love of self. He did have an unhappy childhood, so maybe he never developed a wholesome love for other people. He became obsessed with dominating people. He made his deal with the devil and now has to suffer the shame for his unforgivable cruelty."

They had walked for about an hour before returning. When they returned, both were happy and in a jovial mood. Lev had never seen Hitler in better spirits. Eva was also smiling and laughing. They had been a tonic for each other. Rebekah invited them to stay for the evening meal. She said she had made a special cake to celebrate this special meeting.

Hitler Learns Who Made His Resurrection Cake

Adolf said, "Oh, it was you who made that resurrection cake, was it?"

"I knew you would need a little cheering up, so I tried to help in that way. Did you enjoy it?" asked Rebekah.

He replied, "Rebekah, that was the most delicious cake I have ever eaten. Thank you, it was very kind of you. It is heartening to know that not everyone in this world hates me."

Lev said, "Adolf, we all hate what you did, but only Christ is capable of judging you because he reads the heart. We will know you are on the road to recovery when you learn to hate what you did as well. As long as you are in denial, or refuse to own up to your responsibility for the war crimes, no healing will take place. You know King David sinned. He showed true greatness in living down his sins, and he became a man after God's own heart."

Hitler said, "No one will ever forgive me for what I have done, much less will Christ."

Lev said, "Christ will look closely at the present condition of your heart. Everyone knows that what you did was evil. You have to acknowledge that your actions were very wrong and then throw yourself on the mercy of Christ. No healing will take place as long as you are in denial of what you did."

He remained silent after that for a while. Eva quickly changed the subject by asking them how they enjoyed their walk. Rebekah replied, "We were deeply in love before Lev died in the war to save Jerusalem, and our love keeps growing now that he is back. Lev has been such a noble person. He loves righteousness and hates iniquity. Adolf, you could not have had a nicer person to help you get adjusted to this new arrangement."

Hitler did not know what to say. He was not one to compliment anyone except if he had some ulterior motive in doing so. Eva, answered for him, saying, "Yes, he has been treated fair enough by Lev, he told me so himself."

That was the nearest thing to a compliment that Lev had ever received from him. Soon Rebekah invited them to her lovely table for their evening meal. Lev offered grace before they ate and Hitler behaved by remaining quiet during the prayer. Eva joined in the Amen. Lev asked her, "Eva, have you been to the chapel services with Rebekah yet?"

Eva Attends Chapel Meetings

To Lev's surprise she said, "Yes. And I must tell you, Lev, that I enjoyed it. I have learned more than my whole lifetime about God's plan. I did not know how ignorant I was of the Bible. The chaplain makes the Bible come alive and everything he says is so simple and logical. The people there are so nice. Of course, I have not told them my last name yet. Maybe, they will shun me when at last they know."

"Don't worry about that. Rebekah and I know who you both are. Have we hurt you in any way or even been unkind to you?"

"No," Eva replied. "As a Jew you had every reason to hate us. Yet it is the Jewish nation that has provided us with a self-sufficient home and everything we have, even our life that comes from Christ. We have been treated better than we deserve."

Adolf froze up during this conversation. He was not willing to admit publicly anything. He hoped the conversation would move in another direction.

The meal consisted of their usual delicious fruit with some added vegetables that Rebekah knew Hitler liked. Then Rebekah brought out her baking delight. Hitler smiled with pleasure. He had a sensitive stomach formerly, and now everything that he ate left him only fulfilled, without a pain or discomfort of any kind. Rebekah served him a big piece. He smiled broadly, and said, "Thank you. This is absolutely delicious; I have never tasted anything better in my life."

Eva joined in also, saying, "Yes, Rebekah, you must show me how to make this. Perhaps I can make Adolf a cake like this soon."

Lev asked Adolf, "You have never inquired about any of your top officers. Have you ever wondered how they fared after the war?"

What Happened to Eichmann?

"Why should I?" he answered, "They served not because they liked me. If any of them thought they could replace me they would have done it in a moment. The only reason they served so well was because they liked the power I gave them and they were fearful of me. Eichmann enjoyed his job of being the exterminator. He was cold and ruthless, and he loved having the power of life and death over people. He carried out the extermination of Jews with an unbelievable passion. Other men might pause or faint in such work, but not Eichmann. By the way, whatever came of him?"

Lev explained, "Through church ratlines he was able to escape to South America where he lived peacefully for several years. However, the Jews learned where he was and kidnapped him and brought him to Israel. There he was tried for his crimes against humanity and sentenced to death. He once said, 'I will go to my grave laughing.' He was not laughing when they executed him."

That ended Adolf's inquiry about his generals. It made him uncomfortable to learn how Eichmann had been apprehended and executed. How could a man responsible for the death of millions of people be so squeamish about the death of one man?

They spent time talking again after supper. Both Eva and Hitler seemed to enjoy talking to them and all their prejudices against Jews were momentarily forgotten. When finally it came time to go, both expressed appreciation for being together again, and thanked both of them for making the reunion possible. Hitler took Eva's phone number and promised to keep in touch with her. Lev kissed Rebekah as they left and Hitler likewise kissed Eva very tenderly.

Lev never found Hitler happier than this day. But just as he was getting used to his new life and beginning to really enjoy the simple life he led, he became worried that as soon as his identity became known a lynching party would surround the house. Lev had not told him that no physical harm would come to him yet. So Lev decided to tell him that spiritual powers were now employed to immediately punish any attempt at violence. He said, "Adolf, I must tell you that your life is secure. Spiritual forces immediately intervene and will punish any act of violence, no matter who it may be directed against."

Why Didn't You Tell Me that I Was Protected?

"Oh, why did you wait so long to tell me? You know I have been worried that a mob would surround our house or car when they learned my identity. I dreaded thinking of what would happen if a violent mob identified me and started to assail me."

"I did not want you wandering off and having your identity become known. If you could live peacefully in this neighborhood for at least several weeks before you are identified, it will lower the concern of the local people. They will not perceive your presence as a threat to the well being of this community. Were you to start being abusive of other people in public your tongue might be stopped, and they might seek to identify you. The Ancients would be obligated then to reveal your true identity. They usually publish lists of people who have returned to life, but they have delayed this purposely in your case to let the community see that you can behave yourself. These Ancients have taken full responsibility to see to it that you have a full and fair opportunity for repentance and reform."

Lev continued, "As it is, one person did notice you today as we drove up to Eva's house. Rebekah was fearful that some are suspicious of Eva, but out of respect for Rebekah they have not pressed her for the truth. Sooner or later your cover will be blown, and there will be angry crowds outside your house or my car. I must tell you in advance that they cannot harm you. If some try to do so they will be punished on the spot by having a hand or a leg paralyzed. In the event this should happen, just remain quiet and let me handle the crowd. I have been well respected, and out of courtesy to me they will hopefully listen to reason. However, you have no reason to fear physical violence. Some will probably try to harm you, but spiritual powers will prevent that."

Hitler seemed relieved by this assurance, even though he doubted any spiritual force would intervene on his behalf. He would prefer to tiptoe through society unrecognized. However, he had to own up to what he did and confess before the world that he was being guided by the devil in all the evil that he brought upon the world. How else would it have been so successful if it did not have the "prince of the power of the air" behind it? At any rate, he was not about to make any confession at the present time. He actually became a little smugger knowing that he was protected by spiritual powers. Of course, he did not like the idea of the angry crowds confronting him. He used to have the Gestapo take care of them, but if such protection was no longer available he was grateful for the spiritual powers that he hoped would take his side.

Lev was disappointed that his sole concern was that his little head would not be touched. He still had his own doctrine of hatred in his heart, and was still in sympathy with his dreams of the Third Reich.

As Lev turned in for the day, he addressed his diary. In it Lev noted Hitler's happiness at being united with Eva, and his intense interest in spiritual protection.

Lev arose at the usual time the following morning to go through his usual routine of tending to his personal hygiene and then of collecting fruit and some vegetables. He squeezed some juice and Hitler appeared in time to start eating his breakfast. Lev gave him his usual greeting and to his surprise he returned it. Lev was about to leave to go to the chapel when he noticed a large crowd of people coming up to their door.

An Angry Crowds Seeks Hitler

"Please stay calm, Adolf; I think this crowd is angry. Do not do anything to antagonize them. Perhaps I can quiet their concerns."

Lev saw Hitler's face turn pale as he heard the shouting outside. Lev opened the door and the angry crowd demanded to know if he was sheltering the monster Adolf Hitler.

Lev spoke calmly to them, saying, "I have been assigned by Christ through the Ancients to provide guidance to this man. Yes, he is Adolf Hitler. I did not choose this assignment, but when asked to take it by John the Baptist, I could not refuse. I know your feelings, and it is proper that you have righteous indignation about having such a man in your neighborhood. However, there is no neighborhood that will welcome him, and the Ancients thought that this area would respect their decision that this is the best place for him to return. They felt that he must be given a favorable opportunity to repent and reform. If he does, Christ will forgive his sins—if not he will be destroyed within this century. Please do not take justice into your own hands. Christ is the righteous Judge, and you may be sure that Adolf Hitler will either change for the better or failing that, he will be destroyed. His own personal character attainments will determine his destiny."

One of the crowd shouted, "We do not want that man here. He is a disgrace to humanity. If the Ancients want him, let them have him. We don't want this scum of the earth here."

A great shout went up, and Lev tried to be heard, but it was useless trying to get their attention. Two men raced up to the door and shoved Lev aside. He offered no resistance and decided to let the spiritual powers take care of the matter. Hitler who had been sitting at the table bolted toward his bedroom, but he was too late. One of the men grabbed him, and the other wanted to punch him. Immediately his right arm was paralyzed. The fellow who had caught Hitler decided to release him with a swift kick, only to have his leg paralyzed. The others had gathered around inside and they paused momentarily when they saw both men suffering from paralysis.

Lev managed to catch their attention.

"Listen to me. You will all be paralyzed if you continue this assault. No one can hurt or destroy in Christ's Kingdom. I know what it is like to be paralyzed because I tried to do what you are doing today and I had my arm paralyzed. If you feel so deeply about this matter, here is my telephone. I shall call the office of the Ancients and you may choose one of your numbers to be your spokesperson. They will listen to you, but you must also listen to them. They are perfect, much wiser than you, and within a few minutes you will hear from the top. Remember, they are not bosses they serve Christ. Be very careful, be very reverent knowing that these are Christ's agents."

The crowd became calm. Someone said, "Let Frederick Mittler be our spokesperson."

The Ancients Called

"Good," Lev said. "Frederick will please step up to this phone. It is a speakerphone so you can hear what the Ancients are saying. Please all remain quiet. Because they serve Christ, they will not tolerate any foolishness. Be very direct in addressing your concerns, and above all show respect for Christ or you might all be paralyzed."

With that Lev dialed the personal number that John the Baptist had given him in the event something like this should happen. When he answered the phone, Lev said, "This is Lev. There is an angry crowd here concerned about Hitler being in their community. Frederick here has agreed to be the spokesperson for the crowd. Will you please speak to him?"

Everyone heard John the Baptist's voice, saying, "Yes."

Lev handed the phone to Frederick. He could see his anger had left him, and he was shaking now, as he was about to address one of the greatest men that ever lived. He said, "Your Honor, we are a group of angry people who just learned that Hitler is in our midst, being afforded every convenience and being cared for by Lev Aron, whom we know to be a good person. We feel this man is a disgrace to humanity and we request that he be removed from here. We are sorry that we have been so vocal, but we have people in our midst who suffered at this man's hands unjustly and very cruelly. Would it not be better to send him to Siberia or some such forsaken place? This man is a monster and we feel justified in remonstrating in having such an undesirable person around."

John the Baptist listened very graciously. Finally, he said, "Frederick and all those assembled, you are justified in feeling righteous indignation about all the mass murders and abuses heaped upon countless millions of people. Do you not know that Christ has not forgotten one of Hitler's victims and will bring each and everyone back into a wonderful world for them to enjoy? Christ cannot let Hitler be treated as he treated others. He must be treated in a way that will fulfill all righteousness. There was a man named Saul who persecuted Christians, putting both men and women to death. Later he was converted to Christ. Later his name was changed to Paul and all through his life he bore continual sorrow for having persecuted the saints. If Hitler lives, he will be made to face the millions whose death he caused. He will have an awesome load of guilt if he should repent and become converted. Please do not concern yourself with his punishment. Christ is the righteous Judge. Do not sin by taking judgment into your own hands. Do you have any further comment, Frederick?"

Frederick was thoroughly chastened and the crowd was in hushed silence. Even Hitler standing by heard this truly great man speaking. His face was ashen and he was trembling. Frederick said, "Thank you, your honor. Accept our apology. We will bow to the King."

Lev said, "Do not hang up." He asked for the phone, saying, "This is Lev. We have one man with a paralyzed arm and another with a paralyzed leg. Will you speak to them or have someone else do so?"

"Put them on one at a time, and turn the speaker phone off."

Lev handed the phone to the man with the paralyzed arm first. He heard him explain his predicament. His anger was all gone as he meekly spoke with John the Baptist. Lev listened and knew that he was telling exactly what had happened as truthfully as he could. Soon, he was relieved to learn he would be healed within the hour. The man with the paralyzed leg was placed on the phone and he too was soon told he would be healed within the hour. As usual, Lev knew that both were told not to repeat this kind of conduct, because next time their punishment would last much longer.

Soon the crowd dispersed. Lev invited the man with the paralyzed leg to sit down in the parlor until his leg was restored. He thanked Lev and seated himself feeling a little embarrassed.

Lev offered him some juice and he gladly accepted. He was a little faint and badly shaken by this experience. For some in the crowd this

was their first experience in seeing someone paralyzed. Some had heard
of this happening but had not witnessed it. Hitler observed these events
today very carefully. However, he decided to retreat to his bedroom.
He really wanted to be out of sight. Unfortunately, he was pleased
by this spiritual protection; it was more effective than the Gestapo
in many ways. He knew it was a hundred per cent efficient with no
possibility that anyone could succeed in hurting him physically. Lev
was afraid that this would cause him to be intransigent and at ease in
his old ways.

Shortly, the man with the paralyzed leg found himself healed and
was ready to go to his home. Lev insisted on driving him home because
he was afraid that he might still be in a little shock.

He said, "I appreciate this kindness, but it has not changed my
mind. How can you cover for this evil man, one of the worst criminals
of all time?"

Lev Explains Why He Is There With Hitler

"Well, I do not want to defend my actions personally, because
I did not personally choose to do this. As you heard, the Ancients,
representing Christ, wished me to take this assignment. It was at first
offensive to me. They noticed my reticence to accept and would have
released me from this task. However, I could not refuse to honor their
good judgment. They are going out of their way to give a crazed
murderer a full opportunity to change his life around. No one will be
able to say when this is all over, that he was never given a fair chance
to recover. He is being given the full opportunity to repent and reform.
Failing in this, we are told, all 'which will not hear that prophet, shall
be destroyed from among the people' (Acts 3:23).

"So far he is not responding in a normal way. I have dealt with
many people, but so far he is the most unresponsive person I have had
to deal with. He does have a good side, and he knows how to turn it on
when he wants something. However, he must be given considerable
time to change his thinking process. Remember, he got to the top of
the world in power and glory, by being a scoundrel. Before he learns
the way of righteousness, he has a mountain of unrighteousness to
remove. He can do it, but to be successful he really has to put his heart
and soul into the effort. He has millions of victims to face and make
peace with. Can he do it? Yes. Will he do it? I do not know. He will
need to turn into a saint to actually accomplish this."

As Lev dropped the man off, he thanked him, saying, "Lev, I came
to your place very angry this morning, but I am returning at peace. I

must learn to trust Christ and the Ancients as you do. You were very brave to prevent our actions. You knew what was going to happen if we were going to act like a lynching party. I realize that Christ is in charge and I should not take matters into my own hands. How are you going to prevent this from happening over and over again? People have every reason to hate that man. Few men in history have been more ruthless. Many would die for the privilege of killing him. I fear if there was no intervention we might have beaten that man to death. Anyway, the Lord Christ will judge him."

"Now you've got the right idea. If we were in the old world and we apprehended him, there would have been nothing wrong in punishing that man. However, now Christ is in charge and we must leave matters to his absolute righteousness. Be sure to pass the word along."

"God resisteth the proud" (James 4:6).

Chapter Thirty-Five

The following day Lev found Adolf rather pleased that matters turned out so well for him. He seemed a little bolder in his demeanor. Lev asked him if he still wanted to secure painting supplies.

"Yes," he answered. "If I had remained an artist, I might have been a happier man. People are not grateful for all that I did for them. As soon as the going becomes difficult, they lost their enthusiasm for the glorious Third Reich. Ungrateful swine they proved to be."

Lev was taken aback by his hostility to his own people. He could only assume that Hitler felt if they had made greater sacrifices they could have succeeded in the quest for world dominion. Lev said, "Adolf, you are still out of touch with reality. It was your meanness and brutality that made the Russians fight with a fervent passion. When they saw how you made no provisions of food or shelter for captured people, leaving countless thousands to die of exposure and starvation, they knew they could not submit to German rule. The Battle of Stalingrad is where the tide of battle turned against you. The Russians fought bravely. They were unwilling to surrender. Many thought it was better to die than to suffer from German abuse. Had you been humane, perhaps they might have surrendered."

"We could not be humane; we did not have enough food or provisions for our own soldiers, so why should we worry about the enemies? Anyway, the Russians were swine, unworthy of any help from the Germans."

"I fear you have an attitude problem," Lev retorted. "Wherever did you get the idea that you are superior to other people? You behaved as a savage, and yet somehow think you are superior to others. Where did you learn to hate people so much? Do you not know that without love, you are nothing in God's eyes? You must adjust that attitude or you will be a candidate for the second death."

"Just what I need, a Jew lecturing me," he snarled.

To Lev it seems that mercy of the Lord in preventing harm to come to him had strengthened his resolve to keep his idea of his own supremacy. This was a great disappointment to Lev. He obviously was not responding to the favor being shown to him.

He was not used to dealing with people as equals and the thought of him being less than equal brought out his savage outburst.

Hitler Must Walk for His Art Supplies

"Look," Lev said, "You can walk to get your art supplies. I see no reason to help you. You do not appreciate a single thing that I have done for you. Until you learn to appreciate the kindness of other people, you will never be a kind person yourself. You just do not know what a nasty person you are. If my kindness to you is only going to strengthen your weakness, then there is no point in showing you kindness."

Hitler said, "Then give me the keys to the car and I shall drive myself. It is a Mercedes, a good German car, and I know how to drive it."

Lev said, "I have news for you. The only thing German about that car is the name Mercedes. All the engineering was done in Israel. It was first built in France and then later in Germany. I brought all the technology to the plants from Israel, and I personally supervised the construction of this model car. Furthermore, you need an attitude adjustment before any more favors are granted. I have had it with your arrogance and insolence. I must tell you; I remain here only out of courtesy to John the Baptist. Had he not requested me to look after you, I would certainly not be here."

Hitler suddenly realized he had pushed too far. It was not like the old days, when he could badger other people and get away with it. He did not say he was sorry, but he began to brood.

Lev sensed his irate voice had made him back off. He was not retreating out of kindness, but he knew he was not going to get anywhere pushing Lev or anyone else around anymore. Lev did not have to put up with his insolence, and he had made this very clear to him.

As much as he hated to admit it, he realized that Lev was in charge here. The great Adolf Hitler was no longer in charge of anyone or anything. Lev then told him, "Adolf, you will never be in charge of another person again. You are unfit to lead people until you learn to rule your own self."

"If you want to walk to get your art supplies, it will take about an hour and a half to get there and the same to get back. I will give you a map. I hope no one recognizes you now, because it is now known that you have come back to life, and many people are looking for you. I will not be around the next time a crowd of people descends upon you. Too bad they are not allowed to beat you up, because perhaps that is the only language you seem to know."

He asked Lev for directions, and then he stormed out the door. Lev thought that perhaps a good long walk would clear his mind. He was gone for a good part of the day, and in late afternoon the phone rang. Lev found out that Hitler had been recognized. An angry crowd had surrounded him but apparently someone knew that they could not strike him, for they just formed a circle around him and would not let him pass in any direction. Hitler apparently had forgotten and tried shoving the person standing in his way. Immediately, his two arms were paralyzed. He soon pleaded for someone to call Lev's number and someone did and told Lev what happened and where this crowd was.

Lev Summoned to Aid Hitler

Lev took his sweet time getting there. As he drove up, he thought the crowd would immediately disperse and let Hitler be free. But they still kept him walled in. Lev was in no hurry to plead on his behalf. He just sat in the car waiting for the crowd to tire of walling him in. After about twenty minutes, someone said, "Let's leave this monster to go home. We can catch him some other time. Maybe someday, the Ancients will permit us to hang him." With that they left him, and a poor shaky Hitler, with two arms paralyzed, came over to the car, begging Lev to take him home.

Lev opened the car door to let him in. He was terrified, not only from the angry crowd, but also of having his two arms paralyzed. He knew the only way they could be healed was by the Ancients. This vexed him because he was so helpless now. The fact that he had to plead with the Ancients for mercy was very demeaning to him. He was learning that the spiritual powers acted on both sides of the street. They protected him earlier but now he was being punished. He also felt the disciplines of righteousness. He was learning he was not in charge of this world that was controlled by righteousness.

Lev realized that Hitler was paying a high price for his surly attitude. He learned the wrong lesson when spiritual powers intervened to protect him earlier. He thought he could employ spiritual powers to keep people from remembering his evil deeds. They did not do that. He was only kept from being abused physically. Mentally, he would have to live down the evil that he did. Sooner or later he would have to face every man, woman and child he had killed. How do you explain this vile conduct in a righteous world? There are no rationalizations to justify such evil. Now all these crimes against humanity seemed so ugly and depraved. There are no soft euphemisms that anyone can employ to make those heinous actions sound anything less than diabolical. It was this that was tormenting him now. He could not sweep this under the rug. It would not go away. It was like an albatross about his neck that he could not unfasten.

Hitler knew that he was too proud to seek mercy, too guilty to fain innocence, too vile to overlook and there were too many millions to face with a sincere apology.

Lev drove him home in utter silence. He said nothing to him nor did Lev sympathize with his plight. This was a shadow of things to come for him and he had better seek the advice of the Ancients as to how he could live his sins down. How could he repay society and humanity for his crimes against them?

When they arrived at their home, Lev said nothing. He merely opened the door and helped Hitler out. Hitler did not thank Lev for picking him up or say one word to him. He knew that he had been insulting and offensive to Lev. Lev was repaying him good for evil. He did not like it, but he really needed Lev's help now. He could not even dial the Ancients.

Lev was determined to let him stew in his own juice until he sincerely sought his help.

When they sat down for supper, Lev placed the fruit before him, but he could not use his hands to eat. He was helpless and embarrassed. Lev had his prayer and then started eating. Hitler looked longingly at the fruit, but he just sat there. Lev was not going to offer to feed him until he apologized. Lev was not going to dial the Ancients either. He knew what he had to do to be healed, but he was too proud to ask Lev to make the call. He sat there looking like he was going to cry any minute. Lev ignored him and after he had finished eating Lev cleaned the table and went into the study. The great Fuehrer was now a basket case and all by his own doing. Lev was hoping this would start his mind working in the right direction, but he was still too proud to ask for help. Soon he left the table and Lev saw him trying to get off his shoes without success. Lev still said nothing.

Hitler Forced to Apologize

Hitler could not take off his coat nor tend to his personal needs. Finally, he blurted out, "Lev, for God sake, help me. I apologize for being so abusive. For all the favors you have done for me I have treated you very badly. I deserve what you have done to me by leaving me in my own mess. Will you please call the Ancients and hold the phone for me?"

"Yes, now that you are acting like a civilized human being. You know I will not take any of your belligerent behavior. If you can't be civil, you will not get help. Is that clear? The sooner you learn this, the sooner you will make progress in this new arrangement. You are no longer the boss of anyone. Is that clear?"

He meekly said, "Okay, I get the picture. Please call the Ancients."

Lev then said, "You must be totally honest, because they will check with the spiritual forces that paralyzed you. If you distort the truth and try to color your actions to make yourself appear favorable, then you will be punished for much longer, as much as two weeks. Think carefully now about what happened and then tell it as accurately as you can. I know you have difficulty telling the truth, but you must do so, or it will not go well with you. Tell me when you are ready to tell the true story to the Ancients."

He sat pensively for a few minutes, and then said, "All right, please dial them up."

Lev dialed the number that he was so familiar with. Someone at the office answered. Lev told the party he needed to talk to an Ancient to see what may be done for a man with both arms paralyzed. Soon a bright voice came through, saying, "This is Sarah, how may I help you?"

This is Lev Aron and this call is for Adolf Hitler who suffers now from two paralyzed arms. I shall hold the phone to his ear while you speak to him."

Lev could hear faintly most of her messages to him. It was very much as Lev told him. Soon it came time to explain his conduct that day. He said, "I was walking down the street to go to a place to get some painting supplies. Someone recognized me and began shouting, 'Here is Adolf Hitler the greatest murderer of all time.' I tried to walk past him but he followed me shouting the same words over and over. Soon a crowd gathered around me because there were many people in the area. One person got right in my face shouting at me, and I tried to push him out of the way. My two arms became paralyzed. I did not strike him but I did shove him. Finally, someone must have called Lev, and he came and picked me up and rescued me from the crowd. I do not know why I was paralyzed, but no one in the crowd that taunted me was affected in anyway by spiritual forces."

"The crowd did not hurt you in any way, did they?" She asked.

"No, not with physical harm but only with words did they assail me."

"I shall check this out. Please hold on." After several minutes Sarah came back on. She said, "You will have your arms healed within the hour. You don't deserve this, really, but I fear I would be punishing Lev to have him take care of you. You must understand you will not be protected from your past. As long as no one injures you physically, you will have to endure the shame and contempt of your past. We cannot blame the crowds for remembering your evil deeds. See to it that you do not lay a hand on anyone, or your punishment will be much worse next time, is that clear?"

"Yes, yes, I understand."

"You must understand you were punished today for using violence. This was not punishment for all the evil of your former life. You must live that down by pleading for forgiveness to the countless millions whose lives you destroyed. Not only so, but you must work tirelessly in doing good to others in some small way to demonstrate you have repented and have good will in your heart. Many people are justified in hating you. You have been an absolute monster, and I regret saying, I do not hear true repentance in your heart, only a desire to make yourself comfortable. If you do not stop thinking only of yourself I do not know how you will make it. For Lev's sake you are going to be healed within the hour. Shalom."

The Promise of Healing

He perked right up hearing that he would shortly be healed. And true to her promise, in about twenty minutes his arms started to tingle and came to life again. He then returned to the table and ate his supper meal. He cleaned up after himself, and then returned and said, "Thank you, Lev."

He then went into his room to brood. He had a sullen disposition at times. Lev could see that he must have been extremely difficult to deal with when in power. Lev remained in his room ignoring him for the most part. Lev was used to his hourly mood swings. He could be quite pleasant when he wanted something otherwise he was quite surly.

He went to bed very early, or at least the light was not shining under his door. Lev found himself rather weary with putting up with him. However, Lev determined to do the best he could to help him turn around. He must try to join the human family if he was going to hope to make a complete recovery from his past. Lev, too, turned in earlier than usual, but not before he recorded in his diary the events of that day.

The next morning Lev had breakfast alone and then went to the chapel meeting. When he arrived, Lev knew the news that Adolf Hitler was alive and that he was assigned to help him find his way was known. Most people were very friendly to Lev, even some that had surrounded his home. It was amazing that once they knew that Christ was in charge of everything how they took a different attitude about matters. Most people wanted to know how Lev managed to live with him.

Lev said, "He is not all that bad to live with. He is a moody person and used to abusing people. He does not know how to treat anyone as an equal, and never does he recognize anyone as having superior abilities. Of course, he has only been alive for a short while, perhaps in a few years he will become a full–fledged human being."

One person said, "Yes, but how can you stand to be around a man who murdered and tortured so many people. Doesn't that trouble you? Don't you just loathe him and wish you could wring his neck?"

Lev said, "Christ is in charge of administering justice, not me. My task and my assignment have been to do everything to help this man turn his life around. He needs to grow morally and mentally and I have to try to create an environment to give him some hope that he can reform and make good in spite of his criminal record. He is not the kind of person that anyone might seek out for friendship. He does not know how to be a friend. He has alienated himself from the human race for most of his life. He has no spiritual qualities. He does not know how to pray nor does he see the necessity for this kind of conduct. I must tell you one thing about him that everyone should know. He was possessed by the devil himself, and actually much of what he did was due to Satan's long battle to destroy God's natural people and also God's spiritual people."

The Chapel Meeting Refreshes Lev

The hymn singing started and everyone joined in heartily. It was like being in a sane and holy world again. Here people were seeking God and trying to live on a higher plane. Hitler did not have a clue about how to do this, nor did he yet have such a desire. He lived in his own world resenting that he had lost his power and position, and still not knowing that he would never regain it. Lev sometimes was led to believe that he was scheming on how he might maneuver things to create part of his old world again.

The services were a breath of fresh air and Lev enjoyed every part. The chaplain came over after the service to say, "If I can help in anyway, Lev, let me know. I will come any hour of the day or night if he gets to be too much for you. I know that this must be your most difficult assignment yet. You have had one success after another, and here you are up against impossible odds. Nothing you do is successful in making a saint of him. And so far you apparently haven't been able to turn him into a human being."

Lev said, "You certainly have this figured out correctly, chaplain. In every other assignment, even though I had opposition and faced some angry people, this is the first time that I am totally at a loss to know what I can do to get him started down the right path. He can be pleasant when he wants something. When he does not get his way, he sulks. When he becomes angry, he can be belligerent."

When Lev arrived home, he found Hitler had his breakfast and was pacing up and down the living room. He said nothing so Lev just went about his own affairs. Lev knew he wanted something, but Lev was not going to volunteer any service until he asked properly for it. Soon Hitler said in a very civil tone, "Could you arrange to take me to the supply place today and then on the way back stop off to see Eva? I would appreciate that favor, Lev."

A Favor Requested

Lev said, "I can do that. Why not? Let us first call Eva and see if it is convenient to visit her today. There is the phone." Lev also gave him the number should he want to call on his own.

Hitler dialed and said, "Good morning. This is Adolf, and Lev and I were wondering if it would be convenient to drop in on you so that I could see Eva, and, of course, I know Lev will be glad to see you."

Rebekah must have then placed Eva on the phone and soon they were talking. Soon Lev heard him say, "Good, we will see you later this morning. Good day, my Eva."

He asked if he might drive the car. Lev thought that was a bold request so he said, "No, I think not. This is a different type of car than you are used to. You would need driving lessons. This car runs on fuel cells that make the electricity necessary to turn its electric motors.

You could learn it easily, but you must earn that privilege. They do not provide cars for everyone you will notice. Someday, you might have the use of a community car, as they become more readily available."

They drove to the place to secure his art supplies. He asked, "What do I do for money. I have no money and how will I secure these things I need?"

"They are free. Everything is free in this world. Your house has been provided for you free of charge. Your clothing is also provided the same way. We serve one another. Next week, you will be expected to put time in at a local factory. Your first week of orientation will be over and you should render community service of some kind. You will be able to build a house for your father and mother when it becomes time. You will notice nobody sits on his or her hands all day. We study in the evenings to learn how we can become productive in this technical age. Everyone who eats Eden fruit learns very quickly. You should be studying every night to learn how to serve."

Lev knew right away that he did not like him telling him that he should be studying. He liked to be scheming of what he might do to regain some of his former glory. Unfortunately, he was not having much success at it, and this made him sad. Anyway, when they went into the supply store he picked out what he needed to pursue his artist's life. He thanked the man who was the manager. With that, they returned to the car and drove off to see Eva and Rebekah.

This put Hitler in a good mood again. When they arrived, he hurried out of the car and knocked on the door. Eva opened it and they greeted each other with a kiss. Eva seemed radiant and eager to see Hitler. She seemed the only one in this world who loved him, or at least so it seemed.

Eva's Presence Protested

Rebekah soon appeared to greet Lev, and he kissed her. It was always such a pleasure to see her. She was becoming increasingly beautiful and was more gracious and charming than ever. Lev asked, "How have you been managing? Have you had any flares–ups in the community over Eva's return to life?"

"Yes, yesterday after it became known that Hitler was back, someone found Eva's name on the resurrection list. When they learned that you were assisting Hitler, they soon correctly surmised that I was harboring Eva.

"A crowd gathered outside our door. Apparently, they had heard that violence of any kind would be punished summarily, so they tried to behave themselves. No one used violence; however, they were protesting her presence here. They felt she was unfit to be in this noble community. Eva was quite frightened by it all. Somehow she felt she could dodge all responsibility for the evil that was done. The crowd felt she was guilty by association with one of the greatest murderers of all time."

Lev, too, had wondered why these two merited such a lovely place to return to. However, now every place had its beauty and all places were under Christ's rule so they must have chosen the right place for Hitler and Eva. Here, while the people were properly mindful of Hitler's sins against humanity, the people were at least amenable to leaving them both to Christ's wise way of dealing with them. One had to remember; they did pay with their own lives for their sins. That did not mean that mountains of sins committed were wiped clean.

Hitler and Eva seemed very happy to see each other although they were troubled by the social rejection. Just as the Nazi officers removed their uniforms and donned civilian garb hoping to blend in with society and not be noticed, so Hitler and Eva had hoped their notoriety would be forgotten, but "The evil that men do long lives after them."

Hitler and Eva in the day of their pride and glory never imagined the shame and disgrace they would carry in their return to life. One wonders, if they had only known the truth of the resurrection and that their sins would follow after, if it might have altered their course. Now, if they had a choice, they may have preferred to remain in the sleep of death forever. But "as in Adam all die, so in Christ shall all be made alive."

Lev and Rebekah Leave for a Walk

Rebekah and Lev decided to take another walk and leave Adolf and Eva to have private time together. The community was beautiful and walking along the roadway was invigorating. Lev asked Rebekah, "Has Eva become less of a problem to you since we last met?"

"I think she still has her former bunker mentality. There is a whole world of life, people being regenerated, and the great challenge of mankind being reconciled first with one another and at last being reconciled with God. However, Eva, is still hunkering down in the past, trying to create some of her own personal fulfillment in a life with Adolf. The present has significance to her only in endeavoring to create some happiness from her troubled past."

Rebekah continued, saying, "When you think of the millions, he caused to be stuffed in cattle cars for days on end. For the dehumanizing concentration camps, abounding with lice, starvation, cold, heat, and being treated worse than cattle. Then those human experiments under his direction that were cruel beyond description. All these memories are irrevocably linked to this man. This has to be a cold calculated and systematic murder unparalleled in human history."

Lev said, "Even when the war was lost, they kept these death camps going until they were liberated, not wishing to let one day pass without more Jews being killed and cremated.

"One factor, and one factor alone, made my time spent here tolerable. That was that Hitler was indeed possessed of the devil. This does not mean Satan overpowered his will, but rather that he prostrated before his master and sold himself freely to the devil. However, once under the devil's control, perhaps he had to pursue such an evil agenda even when his own humanity might have dictated another course," Lev explained.

After Lev and Rebekah returned Lev saw a group of people coming down the road leading to this house. He quickly managed to whisk Adolf away before they arrived. Looking in the mirror Lev noticed that they did stop at Eva's house, but only to let them know they were being watched and that her presence here and the visits of Hitler were not welcome.

He couldn't say that he blamed them. Many a time in Lev's former life, he dreamed of returning some of Hitler's evil upon his head. However, Lev knew now that Christ would do all things well. Even without protests and shouts against him, he bore an odium that clung to him. While other men and women were rejoicing in life, he was not free from his guilt–ridden past. Millions of people would look upon him, knowing that this was the man who killed their children, destroyed their families and ended their lives in the most cruel and devious way. Those who gladly served in his killing operations would want to distance themselves from it and most of all from Hitler. Lev wondered how he would manage to live all his sins down. It was very possible for him to do so, but so far Lev saw no inclination toward repentance.

They arrived home shortly. Lev called Rebekah to see if the crowds had dissipated and was grateful that they had done so. While they left without any violence, they did make known their loathing of Hitler's deeds and Eva's association with him. This left Eva shaken and upset. This was just her first week, and already the load of guilt she carried was heavy indeed. While there might be some sympathizers in this area with the Nazis no one wanted to advertise it. Hitler would have to search long and hard to find friends in this new society. However, Lev believed that was his game plan. He knew how to bide his time until he could get some secret sympathizers with his cause. This is what distressed Lev about Hitler; it was his constant desire to use people to get to the place he wanted to go. Lev saw no change whatever in his game plans.

The following week, Hitler was to volunteer at a nearby plant that produced clothing. He had not studied the required courses despite Lev's urging. Lev thought he wanted to fail so he would be excused from any labor. He seemed to feel that it was beneath his dignity.

Lev thought he would drive him to work the first few times, just to be sure no mischief occurred. They arrived at the plant where everyone had been forewarned that Hitler would be working. He was very nervous as he looked into a lot of angry faces. The person in charge decided to give him a job driving a forklift, removing the finished fabric to another part of the plant where garments were made. This kept him out of contact with most people, and hopefully after awhile, they would forget who really was working here.

Hitler on Work Assignment

Once Hitler was assigned a job, Lev sought to talk to the manager. She said John the Baptist had contacted her with specific instructions on how he was to be treated. Lev was told that she had advised everyone in the plant that any assault on Hitler would result in the assailants being paralyzed in some of their limbs. He must be given a full fair opportunity to do his work and that his judgment was not in anyone's hands, but Christ's. That saved the day here Lev thought. Without that message surely a riot would have occurred as soon as he stepped into this building.

Lev realized that as Hitler was now in a routine of life that his time with him would be very short. Lev had walked him through his first week of life. It was a privilege to serve the King even in this capacity. Lev had tried his hardest to do his best, even though many times his patience had been tested to the breaking point.

When Hitler arrived home that afternoon, he wasted no time in the garden but hurried in shutting the door behind him. Later, Lev asked him, "How did your first day at work go?"

"Positively awful. I do believe everybody hates me. Where are all those people that madly cheered me? I have fallen from being the darling of millions to the vilest man on earth. How can this be? What has happened between my last life and this present one? I wish I could go back to the former days."

Lev said, "Do you think that if you could go back now, with knowledge of everything you have learned recently, that it would make you live like a normal human being? Would you stop your evil against the Jews?"

This question caught him off guard. He stammered and said, "How can I know what effect it would have upon me?"

"Well," Lev said, "If you are learning nothing in these days of mercy and grace being shown you, that is very sad indeed. What you are saying is that you are still in sympathy with your evil deeds. You knew they were evil, your generals knew they were evil; the whole German nation knew they were evil, and yet you would not change your past deeds even if you could. How sad, Adolf. Satan is in the abyss, but I think he left his heart with you. Have you no mercy or kindness in your heart? What would you think if someone took your children and your family or Eva away in a cattle car to be killed? Can't you understand the enormity of the crimes for which you have been guilty?"

"Why are you concerned with my guilt? What about all the evil the Jews did to our nation?"

"What evil did they do? There may have been a few Jews that may not have done the right thing along the way. That does not make them all guilty—men, women and children. Does it?"

"Ah, they are all Jews when they grow up. Will you stop lecturing me? And when will you be leaving?"

"Well, now that you asked," Lev said, "I'm waiting for a call from John the Baptist at anytime. I think I have helped you as much as I could. You have had the most generous treatment imaginable. But for the spiritual protection afforded by the Ancients, I fear the crowds would have killed you. Many have loved ones that you murdered, and also some whom you murdered have returned to life. They all will be looking for you. If you don't change your attitude, I fear you will not last the century."

"Well, remember, one thing. I did not ask to be brought back to life. I never wanted to return. I have been brought back against my will. I would be better off sleeping. Then those people could hate me all they wanted to. I didn't care then when I was dead.

"Lev, you don't know how it feels to be hated. Everyone loves you. What do you know about how I feel?"

"People don't hate you, Adolf. That is a myth you have to unlearn. They hate the dark deeds you are guilty of. You should hate them too. Once you learn to love righteousness and hate iniquity, the people will learn to love you, too. You have to love to be loved and you have to renounce your evil deeds as a snake sheds its skin. As long as you justify your past you will be unhappy here."

After supper, the phone rang. Lev answered and to his delight John the Baptist was on the phone. He said, "Good evening, Lev. You have done your job well. Thank you on behalf of all the Ancients here. Please do not take responsibility for Hitler's failure to respond. He will have a long time to resist righteousness if he so chooses. You will pick up Rebekah tomorrow and return the car. You will then take a plane back to Israel for a week's vacation. If you are both willing to continue serving the King, you will then have another assignment. Shalom."

THE END

Alive Again is followed by *From Ashes to Beauty, Fingers Stained with Evil, Adam and Eve Live Again* and *When the Thousand Years Expire.*

"And of Zion it shall be said,
This and that man was born in her:
And the highest himself shall establish her.
The LORD shall count, when he writeth up the people,
That this man was born there"
(Psalms 87:5-6).

Chapter Thirty-Six

Epilogue

"Born in Zion"

It did not take long for people to notice that certain members of their generation were missing. Some had been friends; others were those they had considered to be their enemies. Some were spouses, some children, brothers, sisters, fathers, or mothers. It was gradually becoming known that the "missing" people had, in fact, been "born in Zion." By following the "Lamb" faithfully unto death, they had been raised to immortality as part of the Bride of Christ, the Anointed.

Those "born in Zion" were only a "little flock"—a very small number among earth's billions. Yet the people being raised on earth were very aware that these individuals weren't anywhere to be found.

Questions kept flowing into the offices of the Ancients, and one by one, stories appeared on the Internet. Surprising testimonies revealed that although some of these faithful saints had been among the physicians, lawyers, teachers, and noble men of earth, most of them had been esteemed foolish, uneducated, poor and despised. In fact, many priests and church members who had expected to be raised to heavenly glory, found themselves back on the earth. To their surprise and chagrin, some whom they had mocked, even persecuted and killed, were nowhere to be found.

But there was no mistake. God, Himself had done the careful selection of each member of the Bride of Christ, according to His highest standards of perfect love and righteousness. God could read their hearts and those honored, indeed, had been found more than victorious conquerors through many severe tests.

It was said that each member of the Anointed Bride of Christ had passed through similar experiences to each member of the human family being returned to life on earth. By this design, the Anointed was able to understand and sympathize with every struggle facing those who were raised to life again. Testimonies of people who had known those "born in Zion" in their former life bore this out.

John A. Meggison
Galena, Kansas

John was known in his community as a Bible scholar and lecturer. His in–depth knowledge of the Scriptures made him a favorite speaker at various churches. Often when the ministers could not serve due to illness or due to out–of–town appointments, they would engage him to serve in their place. In his younger years John had been a colporteur placing *Studies in the Scriptures* in countless homes in New England.

He then decided to go to the Massachusetts Institute of Technology for three years in electrical engineering. He also learned Greek in his studies there and enjoyed reading the New Testament in its purest form. He became a national lecturer and wrote a commentary on the Bible that had proved invaluable to those who used it for Bible study help.

He was a Bible Student, and as part of their discipline would not accept a paid ministry. So he worked a regular job to earn his living while his evenings and weekends were engaged in his first love— teaching the Word.

When the CEO of the electric generating station where he worked had died, they offered him the post. He felt the job would take too much of his time and, therefore, recommended another employee of the company be given the job. They followed his advice. His vision of Bible truths kept him in constant demand in giving Bible discourses or leading in–depth studies. His gentle mannerisms combined with his profound knowledge of the Scriptures made him a treasured speaker. Most of all, he knew God in a personal way and was eager to share that knowledge with anyone with "hearing ears."

Many who inquired about him and his equally devoted wife, Gladys, were at first disappointed to know he had not been found among those regenerated on earth. Then to their joy they found that both John and Gladys had been "born in Zion."

Sarah Ferrie, Glasgow, Scotland
By her Fiancé, Peter Morgan

She had broken our engagement—and my heart—because she would not be "unequally yoked." But I had always loved Sarah Ferrie, and always will. Sarah Ferrie, better known as "Aunt Sarah" due to a multitude of nieces and nephews, was the warmest, outgoing lady you'd ever meet.

I searched the streets of Glasgow for a glimpse of her smiling eyes in vain. Even her bedding shop, where weekly Bible classes had been held for years, no longer existed. I asked everyone I met if they remembered her, and learned many did. Aunt Sarah had been a zealous Christian, cheerfully witnessing to everyone she met.

After her Christian conversion, some of Sarah's friends were convinced she had become mentally unsound and sent her to Dr. John Edgar. Dr. Edgar not only proclaimed Sarah in full possession of her mental faculties, but in due course of time, I was told, he also became convinced of Sarah's religious beliefs.

It was said that Sarah always carried a bright silk bag with sweets and Bible tracts that she passed out to everyone that crossed her path— including passengers on the trains. In her fifty-fourth year, Sarah sold her bedding shop so she could devote her full time to missionary work. They called it "colporteur work." She traveled from town to town, living in small rooms with all her life's belongings in a trunk. She even sold her jewelry to help finance her work. Someone said one of her nieces sold a five-diamond ring and had given Sarah part of the funds for her Bible work. Sarah had converted five Christians with the proceeds of the five diamonds.

I learned that when Sarah was in her sixty-sixth year, she had kept her missionary appointments through sleet and storm, resulting in a serious cold that developed into pneumonia. Her earthly pilgrimage ended a short time later. After an extensive search, I realized I wouldn't find Sarah Ferrie on earth. Sarah was with her Heavenly Bridegroom.

Dr. John Edgar, Glasgow, Scotland
By his Brother, James Edgar

When I returned to life, I found five members of my family were missing—my father, John Edgar, my brothers, Dr. John Edgar and Morton Edgar, and my sisters, Eva and Minna.

I was the fourth member to become seriously ill and die in the short space of two and a half years, bringing a heavy load of sorrow and grief to our family. Before I died, my sister Minna was frantic, as I had no desire to convert to Christianity. Being a sincere Presbyterian, Minna was convinced I would be tormented eternally and tried in every way to bring me around, to no avail.

But I couldn't find Minna or the other four anywhere when I returned. Family members informed me that Miss Sarah Ferrie had met Father and converted him to her religion. The other four also had followed.

My brother, Dr. John Edgar, had been a famous surgeon. I found his obituary in the *"Glasgow Herald,"* Friday, June 10, 1910.

"We regret to announce the death of Dr. John Edgar, of Clairmont Gardens, Glasgow, which took place yesterday evening in a nursing home. Dr. Edgar became suddenly ill toward the end of last week, and on Monday it was found necessary to perform an operation, which unfortunately proved unavailing. Dr. Edgar, who was the son of the late Mr. John Edgar of Mansewood, Pollokshaws, was well known in professional circles as an outstanding specialist in the departments of obstetrics and gynecology. He was born in Glasgow 48 years ago, and was educated in the University of Glasgow in arts, science, and medicine, taking degrees in all three faculties. After qualifying in medicine, he took special post-graduate courses abroad, and on his return to Glasgow at once commenced special studies in the hospitals in the departments in which he has since distinguished himself.

In 1896 he was appointed one of the surgeons to the Royal Samaritan Hospital for Women, a position which, till the time of his death, he occupied with much acceptance. He was also, on the retirement of Dr. W. L. Reid from Anderson's College Medical School, appointed to succeed him as a teacher of midwifery and gynecology, where his teaching was highly appreciated by the students.

Dr. Edgar took much interest in the work of the Glasgow medical societies, at which he was a frequent attendee, and in two of which he reached the position of vice-president. He was author of many important contributions to the proceedings of these societies and to the medical periodicals. For many years he has had a large consulting practice in Glasgow and neighborhood. He was a great favorite with his professional brethren, who regarded him as a man of considerable talent, and his untimely death, at an early age, is a matter for very deep regret.

In his recent years, Dr. Edgar had gained considerable popularity as a speaker on religious subjects, having traveled in connection with this work over nearly all the populous centers in Great Britain and many parts of the continent. His lecture, "Where are the Dead?" has reached a circulation of 40,000. Last year, accompanied by his brother Morton, he visited Palestine, delivering lectures in Jerusalem. They also visited the Great Pyramid in Egypt, spending some time in exploring and measuring its internal passages. A volume is at present in the press detailing their scientific symbolism and pointing out many significant parallels in Scripture chronology and time prophecy."

They told me that after his conversion, John had become fully consumed with his new faith until his death eleven years later. I learned that some of the lecture halls in which John had spoken had rooms that held over 4,500 and hundreds had been turned away for lack of room. John and Morton were scholars, giving many lectures and writing several books about the Bible and the Great Pyramid.

From everything I read and heard, I realized my five missing family members were diamonds in the Lord's crown and had been "born in Zion" as members of the Bride of Christ.

This selection of "the bride of Christ" has been going on since Jesus' First Advent. "Many are called, but few are chosen." So for nearly two thousand years a small number of "overcomers" have met the hidden requirements of those that loved the Master to be rewarded with a share in his throne. "They shall live and reign with him the thousand years."

Printed in the United States
35836LVS00003B/43-336

9 781593 302818